For Gretchen
May Fortuna be with you always!
JP xoxo

DOMINVS

DOMINUS BOOK 1

JP KENWOOD

JPK PUBLISHING
jpkenwood.com

Cover art and design by **Fiona Fu**
Lion cub publishing logo by **Catherine Dair**

ISBN: 978-0-9981548-6-2

Published by JPK Publishing

jpkenwood.com

DEDICATION

For my wonderful editors, **Molly Beakers** and **June E. Rigby**. Thank you both for all of your feedback, patience and humor, and for helping to make this a better story.

And for the amazing **Fiona Fu**.

Thanks also to Fouzhan P. for proofreading.

AUTHOR'S NOTES

This is Book 1 of my 4-book, erotic m/m historical fantasy series, ***Dominus***. While many details are historically accurate and the overall plot is tied to major events and prevailing cultural attitudes during the reign of the Emperor Trajan (AD 98-117), the twisted tale and the main characters are entirely fictional.

Book 2 in the ***Dominus*** series, ***Games of Rome (Dominus Book 2)***, and Book 3 in the ***Dominus*** series, ***Blood Before Wine (Dominus Book 3)*** are also available in eBook and paperback. Check your favorite retailer.

Please note that some historical facts have been changed to suit the alternate history plot. For example, according to the relatively scant ancient sources, Publius Aelius Hadrianus (Hadrian) did not return to Rome after the Second Dacian War. Moreover, the ancient language of the Dacians has been lost. In this story, modern Romanian is used to represent the ancient Dacian language. Many thanks to M. Obretin for help with the Romanian phrases. All mistakes are my own. Latin is, in general, avoided for the Roman characters. These are BBC Romans; readers will notice modern British English slang and dialogue patterns. Other details, especially those regarding the ages of the sexually active characters, have been altered from ancient norms to comply with modern sensibilities. All major characters in this story are 17 years old or older.

General notes on Roman nomenclature

The names of the characters, especially the Roman characters, in this story can be challenging at first, so here's a quick summary of how Roman names worked. In the Imperial period, Roman male citizens most often had three names (*tria nomina*). Our protagonist, Gaius Fabius Rufus, is a perfect example of typical Roman male nomenclature.

The **first name** (*praenomen*) was used only by those most intimate with the man—his family, his lovers, and his very close friends and most trusted clients. There were a limited number of Roman male first names, and many first names were very common. Gaius was an extremely popular first name, as were Lucius, Marcus and Publius.

The **second name** (*nomen*) indicated the man's family or *gens*. It denoted either the family into which he was biologically born or the family that adopted him. Gaius Fabius Rufus hails from the Fabii family or the Fabian clan, one of the oldest and most esteemed patrician families of Rome.

The **third name** (*cognomen*) is akin to the modern notion of a nickname and was either given to the male child by his family or chosen by the man himself. In public life, most men were referred to by either their first and family names (Gaius Fabius) or their family name and nickname (Fabius Rufus). Many famous historical figures are familiar to us today by their nickname, such as Cicero (Marcus Tullius Cicero). Gaius Fabius Rufus's nickname, given to him at birth, means 'red-haired.'

Roman women did not have a first name (*praenomen*) nor did women take their husbands' family name when they married. Instead, women received the feminine form of their father's family name (*nomen*). Thus, Gaius Fabius Rufus's wife, Marcia, hails from the Marcii clan, another old and distinguished founding family of Rome. Lucius Petronius Celsus's daughter was named Petronia after her father's clan. Some women were also referred to by their nicknames (*cognomina*).

Advisory: This work contains sexually explicit scenes as well as graphic language, dubious consent, mild torture and violence and may be considered offensive to some readers. Intended for adult audiences only. **Not intended for anyone under the age of 18.** Please store your files where they are inaccessible to under-aged readers.

PROLOGUE

AD 2010

Piazza della Rotonda, Rome

I PAUSED AND LET THE PEN DANGLE BACK AND FORTH LIKE A PENDULUM between my fingers. Of all the possible careers I could have picked, why the fuck had I decided to become an archaeologist?

And what exactly did I remember from that day three long years ago?

I glanced down at the scribbling in my notebook.

14 July 2007: The day started out like any other scorching summer afternoon on the outskirts of Rome. I was sweat-drenched, sleep-deprived, and hung over. Again.

A SURLY WAITER INTERRUPTED MY WRITING WHEN HE DROPPED A BOWL OF store-bought snack mix, a cold bottle of Italian beer, and a dirty glass on my wobbly metal bistro table, dented from years of use. I shoved my hand in the back pocket of my jeans and pulled out my wallet to check I had enough euros for this overpriced tourist trap.

But the view was worth the outrageous cost. How many lovers had sat right here in this very spot, holding hands as they kissed beneath the majestic facade of the Pantheon bathed in raking afternoon light?

Stick to the task at hand, Hughes. Write down everything you can remember.

Standing next to the drawing tables under a shade tree at our excavation site, I swallowed another swig of lukewarm swill from my water bottle to wash away the artificial taste lingering in the back of my throat.

SHIT, WHAT A NIGHT THAT HAD BEEN. THE GUY I'D HOOKED UP WITH HAD worn a disgusting flavored condom. Sure, I had a couple of normal rubbers stashed in the pocket of my leather jacket, but he insisted on using his peppermint-flavored cock wrapper. What the hell was the name of that guy with the skinny minty pecker?

Marcello?

No, that wasn't it.

Mario?

I'd met him at a trendy gay bar four blocks off the main piazza of Santa Maria in the quaint neighborhood of Rome known as Trastevere. I'd gone out alone that night, as usual. There he'd stood in the center of the dance floor, swaying his perfect tight butt to the music, his smooth olive skin set off by a white tank shirt and a pair of faded cut-offs. After some flirting and a couple of dances, we left together on the feeble excuse to check out this new place Peppermint Prick swore served the best Limoncello in Rome. Turned out that Mario—or Matteo—spent most of the night bitching about everything under the sun. He was definitely not worth the three drinks I'd bought for the whiny little shit. So why did I blow whatever-the-fuck-his-name-was in that dirty bathroom stall of that wine bar in Trastevere?

Focus on writing this down!

Shit, what was it Stefano used to say to me five or six times every damn day for the entire excavation season?

My former colleague, Dr. Stefano Struzzo, was and is a very straight, married middle-aged man with five kids and an ex-wife. He had, and still has, excellent connections within the Italian archaeological ministries. And —bless his homophobic heart—Struzzo always preferred to pretend I wasn't gay. Struzzo and I never talked about my romantic life, or lack thereof, for the first four years we'd worked together. Not once. He never asked what I did on our free weekends or if I went out. Although I didn't go to the clubs or bars often, I hooked up more in Rome than I ever could have imagined back in that conservative, God-fearing backwater college town.

Well, I used to.

All right, back to the damn journal.

"CARLO, I MUST SPEAK WITH YOU," STEFANO SAID.

"Did you find an inscription explaining the meaning of all this shit, Stefano?" I asked.

Struzzo frowned and pointed towards trench twenty-one. "Sara's been digging the fill in our medieval well and she's discovered the rough edges of an unusual cut. It's something *molto bizzarro*."

"Shit, we don't have much money left in the accounts for this season. How many euros is this gonna cost us?"

He shrugged before we strolled over to the well. I crouched down until my knees cracked. The medieval well was a meter and a half wide shaft we'd been excavating for days. Fantastic stuff had been recovered so far: architectural fragments, some decent diagnostic pottery shards, and a Roman bronze coin. Well, it was badly corroded and barely legible useless disc of metal, but it had once been a fucking coin.

I hollered down into the well opening, "Hey, Sara. What did you find there, kiddo?"

After a few moments, Sara's head popped up, her bright yellow construction hard hat slanted to one side over her short, spiky hair. Her face peppered with dirt, she pulled down her paper dust mask and grinned. "Holy crap, it's stuffy in there. Oh, I found a cut in the well wall, Dr. Hughes."

Sara opened her arms as wide as her short body could stretch. "It's a big section of the well shaft with a different surface. Rougher, less well built. A repair or something, I think."

For five years, our second century Roman villa site on the Via Tiburtina, located three miles outside of the modern city, had been totally predictable. Sure, we'd discovered layers of complicated late Roman occupation beneath the expected, time-consuming thick phase of medieval bullshit. But there had been nothing unusual or expensive, nothing that would have drained our then paltry research budget.

And then that afternoon, with less than two weeks left in the season, we'd stumbled upon a large and probably deliberate opening in the well wall.

Stefano squatted down beside me with a grunt.

"All right," I said. "Define the edges of the cut with your trowel, Sara, and we'll shoot survey points. When the measurements are recorded, we'll clean it off and see what we've got going on."

"What are you thinking, *caro*?" Stefano lit up a cigarette and took a deep drag. His chain smoking had wrought havoc on my lame attempt to quit that year. With a smirk, my partner held out his open pack of smokes. After I'd wiped the sweat from my brow with my forearm, I pulled a cigarette out. Stefano lit it with his pink plastic lighter.

"I'm thinking our nice and simple well has a big fucking hole in it that shouldn't be there."

It took us well over an hour to measure, record, photograph and clean the edge of the opening in the well wall. Not surprisingly, the situation turned out to be more complicated than we'd originally thought. At some point in the past, someone had constructed a crappy patch of small rocks and low quality mortar in an attempt to close off the strange opening. When we brushed the crumbly mix, it collapsed without warning. We wasted more time cleaning that mess up. To pass the time, Stefano and I sat cross-legged on the ground near the well opening and chatted.

"So here's what I think, Charlie." Stefano started to scratch lines with the edge of his lighter in the dirt as he speculated out loud. "Our medieval well diggers had dug down about three meters, hoping to tap a water source, when they ran into a problem. They hit something unexpected, and that caused damage to the well shaft. They slapped together a plug of rocks to try to seal up the hole and save the well."

Stefano ground his cigarette butt into the dirt and immediately lit another one. "After our peasant diggers built the flimsy seal, they realized the futility of their efforts and gave up. But before they left, they dumped dirt down the shaft to fill the hole up, using the same dirt they had on hand from digging out the well in the first place. Does that sound plausible, Charlie?"

"It's as good a hypothesis as any at this point. It explains the jumbled nature of the finds in the well. And given the dates of the ceramics, all this medieval digging and refilling happened before or during the eighth century."

"*Esatto*," Stefano replied with a grin.

Forty-five minutes later, the time-consuming cleaning was finally finished. Stefano climbed down into the well with our research assistant, Maria, an Italian graduate student from the local university, to examine the now exposed rough opening. A small group of students from my American college hung around nearby, chatting and sharing jokes as they hauled buckets of sieved dirt over to the refuse pile.

And that was when, as the saying goes, the budget-busting shit hit the archaeological fan.

"Holy Madonna!"

"What did you find?"

"This hole in the well shaft opens to a large and well-preserved underground corridor. Our medieval well diggers broke through a Roman wall. There's a substantial debris pile I can use to climb down to the floor of the passageway. This is—this is *magnifico*."

As a gaggle of my college kids watched, trading the occasional joke or snide remark, Stefano's voice echoed up from the bottom of the well. "Would you get my *telefonino* and toss it down to Maria, Charlie? We have *un problema molto grande*."

Urgent phone calls from the bottoms of ancient wells are never a good sign. And the cell signal usually sucks.

After I gently dropped the cell phone into Maria's cupped palms, I asked, "What's going on down there?"

"Dr. Struzzo is ringing the ministry," Maria answered. "We need a forensic specialist, pronto. Giovanni might be in town, if we're lucky."

"There's a burial?"

"We have skeletal remains of two adults."

No more than ten minutes later, covered in dust, Stefano and Maria climbed out of the well on our homemade excuse for a ladder.

"No cell signal?" I asked sarcastically.

Struzzo pushed back his thick, graying hair with his fingers, lit another cigarette, and furiously pressed buttons on his archaic mobile flip phone. As he waited for someone at the ministry to answer, he looked at me with a frustrated scowl and said, "It's not a burial, Charlie."

"What do you mean, 'not a burial'?"

"It's not a grave. The skeletons are resting on the floor of the corridor, probably in the same spot they died. Go see for yourself."

After I climbed down the rickety wooden ladder into the well and crawled through the meter-wide opening, I clicked on my flashlight and pointed its bright beam into the blackness of the arched passageway.

Struzzo was right. The medieval well diggers had stumbled upon a Roman structure. There was nothing unusual about that since ancient Roman ruins are hidden everywhere below the streets, buildings, and surrounding fields of modern Rome.

After I scooted down the loose hill of debris about another three meters, I was standing on the corridor floor. But it wasn't a corridor. Stefano was wrong. It was more like an alcove.

A dead end.

The space was empty and relatively unremarkable, except for the significant sections of colorful painted frescos preserved on the brick walls.

I shouted up to my colleague, "I don't see anything unusual, although these frescos are going to cost a small fortune to consolidate and restore. And the walls aren't second century. They're much earlier—Late Republican, I'd estimate. Where are the skeletons?"

"You have to go farther in to see them, Charlie," Maria shouted down.

I walked about two meters into the dark vaulted space when I first saw it.

Them.

Two human skeletons resting on the herringbone brick floor. Covered with a layer of whitish dust, they appeared to be intact and undisturbed. The beam from my flashlight reflected off something metallic, so I moved closer and squatted down for a better look. The metal object turned out to be a dagger, resting on the ground by the ribs of the larger of the two skeletons. The knife's carved handle looked to be made of ivory and was shaped like a cat's paw. It was likely Roman in date, probably second century given the fine craftsmanship, but I was no ancient weapons expert. We'd hire a specialist to analyze it for us.

I took a deep breath of stale but cool air before scampering back up the steep slope of the debris pile and through the opening. Over the edge of the well, Maria looked down at me with a worried look on her face.

"Did you see the dagger?" I asked.

"*Si*, Charlie. It's a spectacular find but concerning, no? Dr. Struzzo is contacting the ministry. We might have evidence of a crime."

I wiped my brow and sighed as I checked my watch. With less than two hours of field time remaining, we wouldn't get much more done that day.

"Maria, please tell the students to start cleaning up and packing away the tools."

"*Si*."

"No, wait!"

"What is it, Charlie?"

"Please tell me you have an extra cigarette."

Maria tossed down a smoke and her lighter. I lit the cigarette and inhaled before squatting down to look back into the pitch-blackness of the mysterious, long forgotten space.

"Welcome to 2007, you poor Roman bastards."

Nitimur in vetitum semper, cupimusque negata.

"We are ever striving after what is forbidden, and coveting what is denied us."

Ovid, *Amores*, III, iv, 17.

1

AD 107
The Quirinal Hill, Rome

MAXIMUS BENT OVER, PRESSING HIS PALMS AGAINST HIS THIGHS, AS HE TRIED TO catch his breath at the bottom of another set of steep stone steps. Streams of perspiration poured down the hollow of his broad back.

"Dominus, where are we going?" he sputtered to himself.

Max and his patron, Gaius Fabius Rufus, had spent the better part of the early afternoon jogging up and down the steep slopes of Rome in the blazing heat. During the hasty journey from Gaius Fabius's mansion to wherever they were headed, Max had tried to keep up, but the general scaled every damn staircase two steps at a time. Commander Fabius knew every district and back alley of this city better than he knew the curves and ridges of his own stiff cock. And today, his master was clearly on a mission.

Former master.

Max was no longer Gaius Fabius's property. Not since that night soon after the general had returned home from war. One moment Max had been Dominus's coddled pleasure slave—in the next moment, he was his freedman. A 'client' of Gaius Fabius Rufus. His new title sounded important, but what were the benefits of Dominus's unexpected gift of conditional freedom? Not all that much had changed, Max realized, except that he'd been booted out of Dominus's bed.

Stop calling him Dominus, he reminded himself. Again.

After wiping the sweat from his forehead, Max shielded his eyes and looked up the stairs into the glare of the midday sun. Rome was a labyrinth of narrow streets, stone colonnades, and steep stairways. And in the summer, the humid air always carried the overpowering stench of sickly-sweet oleander mixed with baked rat carcasses and shit.

Max licked his dry lips and shouted, "Commander, wait for me!"

His silhouette hollered down, "By the gods, can't you move any faster, Maximus? We're already fucking late!"

Before Max could answer, Commander Fabius disappeared into the blinding light. Max labored to the top of the stairs. There was no sign of his crimson-haired patron, only crowds of poor men and a few hags dragging their squawking brats through the noisy, filthy streets.

Max ran his fingers over the solid handle of the dagger strapped to his torso beneath the folds of his tunic. The emperor had ordered more frequent police patrols to curb street violence, but senseless attacks in broad daylight still occurred in parts of the city. This seedy neighborhood, packed with run-down apartment buildings and shiftless delinquents, was ripe for crime.

Best to get out of this shithole, and fast.

Max spotted a narrow staircase at the end of the block and ran towards it. Just before he reached the bottom step, a group of inebriated soldiers loitering in front of a shabby tavern stepped out of the shadows and into his path.

"What do we have here? A runaway?" the shortest of the gang squawked, wads of white spit bubbling up at the corners of his pudgy mouth. "Where's your owner, slave?"

"Answer the centurion's question, Ethiopian," a taller soldier with a shaved head slurred.

Max slipped his right hand under his tunic to grasp the handle of his concealed dagger. Although they weren't dressed in full battle gear, the brutes were armed with short swords. Max counted five soldiers as they surrounded him.

Another soldier belched. "I'd wager it's a convict that's escaped from prison or the arena cages."

One brute shoved Max. Another elbowed him from behind.

They pushed him towards a dark recess between two dilapidated buildings. In his peripheral vision, Max saw stairs just a few feet away. He drew his dagger and backed out of the suffocating circle of thugs.

"I'm not a slave!"

The drunk and armed louts laughed, slapped each other on the shoulders, and tossed back more rancid drink. They crowded around again, forcing Max towards the open door of the tavern.

"That's your weapon, savage? A little bitty knife?" The shaved soldier slapped the back of Max's head, while another snatched the dagger out of his grip.

"Now be fair, Macro. He's got a plump, delicious brown rump begging for some proper attention. Haul him off the street. We'll school this heathen not to point a knife at a soldier."

Two of the men grabbed Max.

"I'm a freedman and a client!"

"Sure you are, Ethiopian."

"Get off me! I'm a client of Gaius—"

The wiry-haired centurion punched him in the face and ordered his men to take Max to a cell in the rear of the tavern. As they dragged him through the smelly establishment, gamblers and prostitutes cheered at the unexpected entertainment. After barging into one of the back rooms and ousting a whore and her client, they bent Max over and pinned him down, pressing his face against the hard surface of the stone couch.

So the Fates had decided he would die on this scorching day? He would draw his final breath draped over a filthy brothel bed?

Max shut his eyes and whispered a farewell prayer to his gods.

After ordering two of his minions to stand guard at the threshold, the centurion strolled to the back of the small dank cell. He lifted Max's tunic and grunted perversely. Max heard him spit into his palm, followed by the sound of slime being rubbed over flesh.

"Officers first!" the centurion cackled with lust.

"If you insist."

A honed blade sliced through the centurion's gut, exiting above his navel. He gurgled and groaned while his body jerked in spasms against the rigid metal, before he collapsed onto the floor in a puddle of piss and blood.

Expressionless, Gaius Fabius stepped back and raised a second sword.

"Who's next? I'm late for an appointment, so let's be quick about this."

The two soldiers inside the cell froze with their mouths agape. Neither man could utter much more than high-pitched whimper; they quickly loosened their hold on Max and stepped back.

"Commander Fabius," one of the soldiers mumbled.

"Neither of you imbeciles has served under my direct command. How do you know me?"

"I recognize you from your portrait statues in the Forum, sir."

"I was witness to your rousing campaign muster before the siege of the Dacian capital, Commander."

After he dropped the borrowed sword to the floor, the general stared directly into the bald soldier's wet, piggy eyes.

"This man, the one you dragged in here to rape, is my fucking client."

"We didn't know, sir."

"But how unfortunate it is for you, soldier, that I know each and every one of you bastards: your name, your rank, and your eagle. You're imperially fucked, Macro."

The Commander unsheathed his personal dagger, adorned with an ivory handle carved in the shape of a lion's paw, and cut a scrap of unspoiled cloth from the dead centurion's tunic.

"Here, use this to wipe off that blood, Maximus. We can't have you showing up to an exclusive function covered in filth, can we?"

"Yes, Dom—I mean, Commander," Max corrected himself.

As Max cleaned off the blood, his patron barked more instructions at the hapless soldiers. "Strip his corpse and throw it into the common rubbish dump. When you're finished, wait at your homes for my fucking orders. Do not leave the city. Do you understand?"

"Yes, Commander Fabius," they murmured in unison.

They lifted the centurion's bloodied body and shuffled out, heads lowered in deference, making sure not to look the general in the eye. After they'd left, Gaius Fabius cupped Max's jaw and turned his former slave's face to the left and the right. Finally he smiled with relief as he rubbed his thumb over Max's cheek. "No serious wounds. You're fine. Let's go. And stay close this time, pet."

His pulse pounding in his ears, Max chuckled nervously. "Thank you for rescuing me, sir. But—but I'm no longer your pet, Commander."

"Nonsense! You'll always be mine, slave or not. Your new status doesn't change that, Maximus. You'll always need my protection."

Max looked down at the dark pool of blood and piss on the floor. He closed his eyes and swallowed, nodding as he said, "Yes, sir."

"Let's hurry. It's not much farther. And don't get fucking lost this time." The general darted up the staircase just outside the entrance to the tavern, with Max close on his heels.

With his fierce amber eyes focused straight ahead, Commander

Fabius weaved through the crowded streets like a lion charging through the winding corridors beneath the arena. Max had never witnessed the games, but he'd heard about the incredible web of tunnels designed to maneuver exotic wild animals up to the stage for slaughter. During an exclusive dinner party before the last war, the Emperor's architect, Apollodorus, described the complicated underground network hidden beneath the wooden floor of the great amphitheater. A fascinating story.

Of course, most times Max only overheard trivial nonsense when he attended one of Commander Fabius's dinner parties. But he paid close attention to every word of the guests' conversations, convinced even frivolous tidbits of information might prove useful to his master.

Shit, former master.

Max sped up and trotted alongside his patron. "May I ask a question, sir?"

"As long as you don't slow us down."

"Where are we going, sir?" Max asked as he looked around. The houses and public buildings were much more opulent than those shabby apartment blocks located on the lower levels of the Quirinal Hill. This more exclusive neighborhood was colorful, with lush foliage, vibrant flowers and tended gardens. And it didn't smell like stale piss.

The general stopped in his tracks and pulled Max out of the traffic. Locals of all shapes and ages, many dressed in costly fabrics, strolled by them as they stood on the curb.

"Didn't I tell you, Maximus?"

"No, Commander. You said we had an errand to run. And here we are, running. But to where, sir?" Max tilted his head and smiled.

"For how many olive harvests have you been alive, Max?"

"Near thirty, sir."

"Thirty years already?" Commander Fabius reached up and gently brushed the raw swollen flesh of Max's bruised eye with his fingertip. "You are still bloody gorgeous. Perhaps I should be selfish and rescind your freedom."

The general winked and threw his arm over Max's brawny shoulder, veering them both back into the stream of pedestrians.

"We're visiting Gnaeus Decius's estate," the Commander said. "There's a private auction at his garden pavilion today. The event has already started, but I'll arrive in time for my purposes."

He moved closer and lowered his voice. "Decius instructed the dealer to set aside the choicest offerings until my arrival. He's a smart businessman and a loyal client of Lucius Petronius. Now let's move, freedman."

"Yes, sir."

During their recent visits to the slave markets in the capital, Commander Fabius walked away empty-handed, completely unimpressed with every creature he saw.

But today was different.

The general had certainly never sprinted up the hills and through the neighborhoods of Rome to attend a slave auction.

As Max trailed his patron through the bustling streets, people stepped aside and stared. Commander Fabius's auburn spiral curls bounced up and down with each deliberate stride. Certainly Max's patron wasn't dressed to make a show of his supreme rank; he wore an unadorned, ordinary tunic with a wide belt slouched to one side. It was a nondescript costume that contrasted in an amusing way with his expensive red shoes. Gaius Fabius Rufus wouldn't forego his dear patrician footwear under any circumstances save the battlefield.

Shit, even if Commander Fabius hadn't been a prominent member of the imperial court, he would still have attracted attention. It was the confident, fuck-it-all way he carried himself—his natural dominance.

Of course, people might have also noticed those dark splotches of blood all over the front of his light-colored tunic.

As they marched through the streets, Max readjusted the leather travel sack slung over his shoulder and tried to imagine what creature could be worth all this effort. The general's close friend, Lucius Petronius, must have discovered an exceptional young nymph for the commander's consideration. That had to be it. Commander Fabius already owned two beautiful boys, but he had only one nubile girl—that quiet blonde, Zoe, whom Max rarely saw during daylight hours.

Zoe wasn't his responsibility.

And, lest he forget, there was Callidora, although Max was fairly certain the commander didn't fuck her any more. Shit, that woman's arrogance grated on his nerves. And she'd grown even more brazen ever since Commander Fabius promoted her emerald-eyed spawn, Simon, to serve as his favorite villa whore.

Yes, it was obvious.

The general would replace Callidora with a younger, more submissive slut. Two boys and two girls; it made sense.

Max fantasized about Callidora's departure, her arms flailing and her long brown hair flying about as she was dragged away, begging the commander to reconsider his decision to get rid of her. His smug smirk vanished when another long flight of stone steps came into view.

"Decius's grounds are up here," Commander Fabius hollered between huffs as he scaled the first four steps. "His estate is behind Salus's temple precinct."

After he took a deep breath, Max started his ascent but stopped when he reached the third riser. "Commander, wait!"

"By Priapus's prick! What is it now, Maximus?"

"You told me before we left to remind you to change into more appropriate attire, sir." Max glanced sideways at the travel bag slung over his shoulder. "And a quick wash perhaps? I mean, for the blood and all, sir."

Gaius looked down at his stained tunic, rolled his eyes and nodded. "Right."

Pulling the damp fabric away from his skin, the general descended to the bottom of the staircase. He closed his almond-shaped eyes and tightened his jaw before speaking low and smooth, "My client, Manlius, owns a small bathing establishment in this neighborhood. Follow me."

After turning a corner down a side street, they found the entrance to Manlius's modest bath facilities. The large wooden door was closed and bolted shut, with 'FOR LET' painted in crisp white letters on a board nailed to the doorjamb.

"Why didn't the halfwit inform me he'd shut down these baths? It's his fucking obligation as my client to notify me about all his transactions."

"Perhaps it's a recent development, sir?" Max thought for a moment and then asked, "Commander, doesn't Theodorus run a business for you in Rome?"

"Yes, he does. And it's not far from here. Shall we pay our dear Theodorus a surprise visit then?"

Max grinned. "Yes, sir."

~

A SHORT WALK FROM MANLIUS'S BOARDED UP BATHS, THE WORKSPACE Commander Fabius had purchased for Theodorus was neither large nor elaborate, but the location was profitable. No doubt a constant stream of steady customers had kept his old friend occupied.

Max had always wondered how Theodorus was getting on with his new life in the capital. In his younger years, Theo had enjoyed a comfortable existence as a pleasure slave down at the Commander's seaside villa; as a freedman, he now dealt with the hardships of surviving the hustle and bustle of Rome. The drastic change must have been difficult.

When they arrived at the shop, Theodorus was busy attaching a strap to an expensive piece of footwear. After their bodies blocked the daylight streaming in from the doorway, Theo glanced up from his work desk, pushing his long, grey-streaked bangs away from his eyes.

"I'll be right with you, gentlemen."

At first, Max hardly recognized his dear friend. He looked thin and tired, with dark hollows under his once bright, beautiful green-blue eyes. Theo couldn't have been more than forty years old, but with his slouched posture and gaunt frame, he appeared a decade older. Or more.

"Greetings, Theodorus," the Commander said softly in his distinct velvety voice.

"Dominus?" Acting on instinct, Theo dropped to his knees on the hard floor next to the bench and bowed his head. Commander Fabius walked over to him and carded his fingers through Theo's thick locks. Gently, he lifted his former slave's head and stared down into his astonished eyes.

"How are you, pet?"

"I — I — I'm well, Dominus. Business is brisk and the profits this month should be substantial. Are you in need of shoes or..." Theo couldn't control his tongue. The Commander touched his index finger to Theodorus' full lips to hush him.

Theo had been so confident and handsome once.

"I'm no longer your master, Theodorus. But I am pleased to learn my profits are up. I knew you'd succeed. Now stand up. You remember Maximus?"

As Theo scrambled to his feet, Max fought the urge to run over and embrace his former slave mate.

"Hello, Max." Theo's voice swelled with affection.

"Greetings, Theo."

Commander Fabius unbuckled his plain belt and tossed it to Max. "Theodorus, I need to change out of this soiled garb and wash up for an important affair."

"Yes, Dom... I mean, Commander. Please, make yourself at home. Well, it's your property. What I mean is, um—I'll fetch some fresh water for you, sir." Dangerously close to hyperventilating, Theo grabbed a large pot filled with dirty water and rushed outside into the street.

"Pass me the satchel, Maximus." With his wardrobe change in hand, Commander Fabius strolled to the shadows at the back of the shop and lifted his tunic over his head. Light beams coming in through the doorway illuminated the curves of his broad back muscles and his toned arse. He turned around, his cock dangling between his thick, hairless thighs. A lump of desire clogged Max's throat. It had been so fucking long since he'd wrapped his lips around...

"Go see if Theodorus needs assistance. You haven't had a chance to speak with him since he left the villa, have you?"

With a shake of his head, Max snapped out of his cock sucking fantasy.

"No I haven't, Commander. Thank you, sir." He bowed his head and darted out into the street, easily catching up with Theo near the gushing water of a public fountain on the corner. Without a word, he gathered the shorter man into a lingering embrace.

"Theo! It's great to see you. Are you all right, really?" He cupped his friend's face with both palms until Theodorus gently pushed him off.

"Yes, Max. I'm fine. It's not a bad life. At least I have a profitable trade that pleases Dominus. Dom did look pleased, didn't he?" Theo flashed a strained smile as he placed the emptied basin on the ground under the fountain stream.

"Yes, he did. Quite pleased."

"How's life down at the villa?" Theo asked.

"Filled with pampered young cock suckers, as usual. Most days I'm nothing more than an old nursemaid. It was more fun when you and I shared the playroom bed with Dom. Now those were good times, eh?"

Theo turned away, laughing softly, and then looked back into Max's eyes.

"How is—how's my son?"

"Simon's well. He's the reigning favorite now, the lucky little sprite. Simon's taller than you and he has your eyes, only greener."

"Does he ever…" Theo choked on his question. "Does Simon ever ask about me?"

"Not often." Max carefully wiped a piece of dirt off of Theo's freckled cheek. "You look well, my friend."

They stood there quietly, speaking only with their eyes, as people elbowed past them to get to the fountain. Theo finally broke the bittersweet silence.

"We better get this water back to the shop now."

As the two retraced their steps towards the store, Theo said, "I didn't know Dominus was in Rome. Where are you headed, if I might ask?"

"Gnaeus Decius's estate. Have you heard of it?"

"Yes. It's a nice place, not that I've ever been inside the walls, mind you. But it looks quite grand from the outside."

"I'm sure it's magnificent. There's an auction today. A private one." Max raised one brow.

Theo snorted, shaking his head. "Shit. So, will it be a boy or girl, do you think?"

"I don't know. Girl, I hope. I've got my hands full already with Nicomedes and Simon. I don't want to imagine the mischief those two rascals have been up to during my absence."

When they re-entered the workshop, Theo gasped. Their bronzed god of a former master was parading around the room, stark naked, as he examined Theo's handicraft. The Commander must have heard them return, but he didn't bother to look up.

"A customer came calling, Theodorus. I told her you would return before long," the general mumbled, picking up a particularly posh pair of braided sandals. "These are very well-made, Theo. Perhaps I should order some new shoes."

"Yes, sir." Theo carried over the bowl of water. He spilled some on the floor, trying not to stare at his former master's supremely nude, muscular body. "Can I be of any other service? Is there anything else you need, Commander?"

"You'll help me wash, Theodorus."

Theo smiled as a flush of pink erupted over his neck. "It would be my pleasure, sir."

"Wait outside on the street, Max, but don't stray too far. If my memories are reliable, this won't take long."

A short while later, Gaius emerged from the shop into the bright sunshine, dressed in a crisp and very clean striped formal tunic cinched with a broad black belt decorated with silver studs.

Proper attire for a posh private auction.

"Theodorus' mouth is as skilled as I remembered. See to it our young Simon's cock sucking skills soon outshine his father's mastery, Maximus."

"I'll make it a priority when we return to the villa, Commander." Max's lips curled up at the corners. Gaius smirked, adjusted his emptied balls and tightened his belt. He cleared his throat before he barked, "All right then, let's go!"

~

WHEN MAX AND HIS PATRON REACHED THE TOP OF THE LAST STAIRCASE AND skirted around the high marble precinct walls, the grand entrance gate to

Decius's secluded estate appeared. A pair of well-armed guards stood at the portal.

"Greetings, Commander Fabius. Gnaeus Decius has been waiting for your arrival. Vedius, escort our most esteemed guest and his slave to the pavilion."

Max made a pained face at the guard's faulty assumption but remained silent.

"What is your name, guard?" the general inquired.

"Marcus Bulbus, sir."

"Bulbus?" Commander Fabius stifled a laugh, no doubt tickled at the guard's unfortunate and yet strangely apt name, given the exceptionally round shape of the man's large head. "Are you a veteran?"

"Yes, sir. I fought with the Fifth Macedonica."

"A fine group of virtuous and loyal soldiers. What was your rank?

"I carried the eagle, Commander."

"That is a high honor indeed, Bulbus. Tell me, have Lucius Petronius Celsus or Publius Aelius Hadrianus arrived yet?"

"Counselor Petronius arrived before the sale began, Commander. You should find him at the pavilion in the company of your host. And our most esteemed Aelius Hadrianus sent word of his intentions to attend. He hasn't arrived, I'm afraid, and the event is nearly over, sir."

The general flashed a bright but blank grin before pressing three silver coins into Bulbus's palm.

"Be sure that I learn of Aelius Hadrianus's arrival before he gets close to the auction pavilion."

"Understood, Commander." Bulbus nodded. "I'll handle it personally."

Without any further formalities, Commander Fabius and Max turned to follow their guide who was waiting for them a few steps ahead on the paved garden path.

As the three made their way down the gravel-covered walkway, the guard Vedius glanced over his shoulder every so often to keep an eye on them. Although their twitchy escort was out of earshot, the Commander lowered his voice.

"Of course our furry princess is bloody late. Publius Aelius Hadrianus always prefers to make a splashy entrance," Max's patron jested with a twinkle in his eye. "And I'd wager good coin my dear little brother, Publius, sent word in advance to secure pre-sale rights to whatever he's in the market for these days. I want to acquire something exceptional before he shows up and inflates the prices."

"Yes, Commander."

Well, there it was.

Another pleasure slave would soon be crowding the playroom down at the general's seaside estate. Fortunately, a new bird wouldn't directly affect Max's workload. His primary duty now was to manage, discipline, and train Commander Fabius's pleasure boys. Handling those scoundrels kept him busy enough.

As they followed Vedius under a vine-covered trellis and down the verdant garden footpath, Max wiped his sweaty brow again. Perhaps, now that he was a freedman—a client of Commander Fabius, the Lion of the Lucky Fourth—their host might offer Max a cup of chilled wine.

2

Gnaeus Decius's estate on the Quirinal Hill, Rome

"EVER SEEN ANYTHING AS BLOODY TASTELESS AS THAT?" GAIUS FABIUS TIPPED his chin at the extravagant structure as he poked Max in the side with his elbow.

As they walked closer towards Gnaeus Decius's garish auction pavilion, Max's eyes widened. In front of the round building, a circle of naked cupids holding their tiny stone dicks urinated streams of pink-colored water into a basin beneath a large statue of Pan fucking a she-goat. From the roof, strings of bronze and silver breast-shaped shields twirled in the breeze and, up above, gilded roof tiles shimmered bright in the sunlight. Gossamer peacock blue curtains suspended from gigantic erect phallus hooks gently billowed between slender green and purple marble columns.

"It's quite—well, colorful, sir."

"Unfortunately, it seems our nitwit Decius spared no expense on his monstrosity."

A boisterous uproar of laughing and shouting erupted from behind the fluttering translucent curtains.

Clang!

The unmistakable clash of bronze cymbals. The signal that another wretched soul had been sold to the highest bidder.

When they approached the main entrance, an armed guard with short grey hair saluted them. "Welcome, Commander Fabius. Your host will be most pleased you've arrived. Surrender your weapons, if you would."

"My weapons? This is a new development."

"I'm afraid so, Commander." The guard gulped. "After that regrettable incident at Hostilius's auction last month, Decius feels the need to—well, to take precautions, sir."

With an annoyed shrug, Gaius slipped his hand through the loose armhole of his tunic and drew out his dagger. He'd heard some old fart had been stuck like a pig over an auction dispute. The bastard probably deserved it. Decius was prudent to ensure that sort of mayhem never happened at one of his exclusive events. Carefully, he handed over his ornate ivory-handle knife.

"Don't misplace my property. I've carried this blade for many years. It has sentimental value. Right, Maximus?"

Max lowered his eyes and smiled sheepishly. "Yes it does, sir."

"Thank you for your cooperation, Commander. Please, this way." The guard held back the indigo entrance curtain and motioned them inside.

Despite the early afternoon breezes blowing in through the sheer fabrics, the interior of the circular auction hall was oppressively humid. As Max pulled at the collar of his tunic, Gaius scanned the crowd of aristocrats from a discreet spot just inside the entrance. They weren't alone for long.

"Gaius Fabius! Welcome to my humble hovel, Commander!"

"Greetings, Gnaeus Decius."

"The esteemed members of our Emperor's court are most welcome at my private events." Decius wiped away the sweat drops soaking his fleshy upper lip. "Today's merchandise is particularly choice, if I may say so. I do hope, Commander, that you won't go home empty handed."

Gaius looked over the portly man's shoulder. "Excuse me, Decius, but I'm seeking out an associate of mine."

"Of course, but do enjoy yourself, sir. And please give my most warm greetings to our most revered Emperor." Decius bowed and wandered off, no doubt to ingratiate himself with another visitor.

Gaius grumbled out of the side of his mouth to Max, "That man is a fucking pompous bore, but his slave auctions are often worth the effort."

The stifling space was filled to capacity with aristocrats of all shapes and sizes and their servants. All of the men appeared relaxed and jovial. The anticipation of taking home fresh flesh to fuck, enhanced by Decius's generous supply of fine Falernian wine, had put all the guests in jolly good moods.

"Over there!" As he pointed, Gaius's pressed lips melted into a sly smile and his eyes narrowed with delight. He'd found who he was looking for. Despite the crowds, it wasn't too difficult to spot the distinctive profile of Lucius Petronius Celsus. Towering over a group of men, the tall brunet appeared to be entertaining his companions with one of his absurd vulgar jokes.

"Come, Maximus!"

Gaius forged a path through the sweaty, exuberant mob. Although they were frequently slowed by a pat on the shoulder from this or that fellow, he ensured they never lost momentum. He'd seen Lucius Petronius just a few days earlier, but he'd barely had an opportunity to touch his handsome lover, let alone fuck him.

From the elevated auction stage, an olive-skinned auctioneer hollered above the clamor. Aristocrats paused their conversations and turned to assess a naked blond boy standing on the platform with his eyes cast to the floor and his thin arms folded neatly behind his back. A wooden placard touting his attributes dangled from a cord tied around his slender neck. Gaius stopped to scrutinize the scrawny thing.

Max asked, "Should I retrieve more information about that one, sir?"

"Don't be daft, Maximus. It's too skinny and too young. And besides, I already own a blond boy. Nicomedes might be an impetuous imp, but he's my blond imp," Gaius scoffed with a smirk. "Lucius Petronius has something particular in mind for my consideration. Not that I expect to purchase a damn thing here, but what's the harm in humoring our dear solicitor?"

"Gaius! Over here!" Lucius Petronius frantically waved his burly arm like an overeager schoolboy. Sharply dressed in his formal senatorial garb, his muscular frame cut a path through the pack. His light blue eyes sparkled with desire as he hurried forward and wrapped his long arms around Gaius's torso, hugging him a bit longer than was wise in such a public venue. Clearly Lucius had imbibed a tad too much of Decius's wine.

"Let go of me, you colossal twit." Gaius chuckled, as he pushed Lucius back a step. They had to be careful. People were watching.

"You made it here in time," Luc cooed.

"I promised you I'd be here, and here I am."

Lucius curled his large hand around Gaius's bicep and pulled him towards a spot to the left of the auction dais. "I arrived early to claim a prime couch for us. We'll have a clear view of the sale, and a sneak peek at the naked lovelies waiting by the side of the stage. You are here just in bloody time!" he slurred, far too loud.

"In time for what?"

"For the scrumptious delight I mentioned. You haven't forgotten, have you? You'll be interested. I'm quite sure of it."

Gaius leaned in and whispered seductively, "I'm interested in fucking you, Luc."

"You're coming to dinner tonight," Lucius answered brusquely. He moved closer and spoke very softly into Gaius's right ear, "Listen, gorgeous. Aurelia and Petronia are leaving today to visit Aurelia's cousin. I swear we'll have the house to ourselves this time. I've told Euphronia to prepare something decadent, with ladles of creamy sauce I intend to lick off of your—everything." Luc stuck out the pink tip of his tongue and wiggled it. "Now lie down and let's enjoy the festivities. It shouldn't be long before the fetching thing is offered up."

Both men stretched out along the adjacent cushions, face-to-face and raised on their elbows, as Decius's scantily clad servants brought over drinks and tasty tidbits. Max took his position behind the couch, ready to attend to Gaius's every whim.

The clang of the cymbals announced the blond boy's bum had a new home.

Scooting closer to each other, Gaius and Lucius watched the stage being cleared while the dealer's assistants prepared the next slave for auction.

"So, Counselor Petronius. Tell me more about this exceptional opportunity."

"A dark-haired provincial delicacy. Or so I'm told. I ran into Decius on my way to the courts and he raved about this new acquisition for his auction. He drooled, actually, the disgusting pig."

"Dark-haired? As dark as yours?"

"Darker. Pitch-black locks, Gaius. You don't have one of those, do you? Decius, the dolt, thought I'd be interested. He even offered early purchase rights to me. Me, of all bloody people! The foolish prat doesn't know his own greased paw from a harlot's stained lips." Lucius collapsed into cackles. His strong, sculpted features still managed to look spectacularly handsome.

"Then it's a girl?"

Luc slapped his friend's shoulder. "Of course it's a girl! You, my dear Gaius, have enough fuck boys for both of us. Well, that's debatable, I suppose. Anyway, your exquisite bitch, Callidora, is getting long in the tooth. You need a fresh serving of twat, my dear."

"So now you're deciding where I'll dine and what I'll fuck? How highly considerate of you." Gaius clenched his jaw. Lucius Petronius could be such a bossy bastard—sexy, but pushy. Always the lawyer.

Sipping his wine, Lucius flashed a coy smile. As he opened his mouth to respond to Gaius's quip, the auctioneer's voice bellowed through the space.

"Gentlemen, may I direct your eyes to this nubile nymph!"

"Ah, that must be her! You have to confess she's fucking splendid, right?" Lucius crowed before tossing back another gulp of wine.

Peeling his eyes off his lover's face, Gaius appraised the naked thing now on the auction block: a slender young girl of no more than fifteen years. She sported shiny waves of black tresses that flowed down her back to her waist, and full breasts that were firm and pouty. Her skin was as creamy as milk and her features impossibly delicate. Deliberately, as if instructed, she lifted her wide blue eyes and smiled in the direction of their couch.

And that was when another creature standing off to the side of the auctioneer's platform caught Gaius's eye. Entranced, he only half-listened to Lucius drone on.

"Decius says she's from hardy mountain stock. Good bones, sound, and quick-witted. Look at that lovely smile. You'll enjoy her for years."

Gaius stared at the stage, his lips parted with desire. Lucius smirked when he noticed Gaius's cock stiffen and tent the folds of his tunic.

"Send Maximus down to the dealer's table," Luc urged. "Gather her details and demand a private inspection."

Gaius gnawed on his bottom lip but said nothing.

"Gaius?"

Finally, he muttered, "I've never seen anything that magnificent."

"Ha! I knew you'd be pleased. Max, go speak with the auctioneer's assistants about her attributes and report back to us—the attributes Commander Fabius can't already see, that is."

"Commander?" Max asked.

"Hmm?"

"Should I get more details, sir?"

Gaius snapped out of his trance and turned. "What?"

"That slave girl, sir? Should I inquire with the dealer?"

"For fuck's sake, no! Max, come closer. Do you see that ebony-haired Adonis standing just off the stage?"

Max squinted, while Lucius furrowed his brow as he studied the silhouettes standing in the dimly lit corridor on the side of the auction dais.

"The, um—the *bearded* one, sir?" Max responded, scratching his head.

"Yes, that one." Gaius leaned forward and pointed. "Shit, look at it. What a fucking exotic specimen. Not some damn run-of-the-mill Greek whore, that's for sure. Go learn everything you can about him, Maximus. Quickly!"

As Max trotted off towards the stage, squirming his way through the crowd, Lucius began laughing, tears welling up in his eyes.

"You are joking, right?"

"Why?" Gaius snapped.

"A bloody bearded barbarian? Oh, Gaius—sometimes you are so predictable. I should have known, love."

"He's stunning, Luc. Look at those long, sinewy limbs and that exquisite voluptuous bum. It's hard to say for sure from this distance, but his dark hair looks excessively coiffed, don't you think? These crass dealers so often err on the fussy side in terms of presentation. But no matter, that can be easily fixed."

Lucius rolled his eyes. "It's drugged, Gaius. Look at the way it's bobbing and swaying back and forth. There's no way to know its true nature when it's stupefied on whatever concoction they forced down its throat."

"The sedatives will wear off."

"Yes, they will. And when they do, you, my friend, will have a wild savage on your hands."

Gaius smiled, glancing sideways at his companion. "That boy will require a firm hand."

"I hadn't realized you were looking for a project, darling," Lucius groaned.

"Neither had I. It must be the will of the gods."

"Now you're a philosopher as well? Horseshit! Do not bring the gods into this. It's the will of your insatiable cock, darling. A powerful force of the cosmos in its own right."

Max reappeared, panting.

"What's the report?" Gaius asked.

"It's a Dacian, sir, recently captured by scouts during a reconnaissance mission along the mountain border." Max paused momentarily to catch his breath. "No known diseases or physical faults. The beast is heavily drugged, Commander."

"Anything else, Maximus?"

"They claim — well, the dealer alleges it's a virgin, sir."

Smirking, Gaius turned to his companion. "Inflating the value, you think?"

"An unsullied bum often costs extra coin." Luc winked.

"Does he have an estimated price, Maximus?" Gaius asked.

"Six—six hundred silver pieces, Commander."

"Six fucking hundred denarii for an untrained Dacian? That's bloody robbery." Gaius turned to his friend. "Perhaps, as my loyal and devoted associate, you could negotiate a cheaper price for me, Lucius Petronius?"

"You really want that shaggy barbarian, don't you?"

Turning to look towards the stage, Gaius leered at the alluring Dacian captive listing back and forth on his feet in the shadows.

"He's already mine."

While Gaius and Lucius discussed the most effective strategy to lower the slave's price, the gate guard, Bulbus, came rushing up behind Max. He whispered something into Max's ear before disappearing out the back exit of the pavilion to return to his post.

"Is there a problem, Maximus?" Gaius inquired.

"Excuse me, sir, but there's important news."

"Get on with it."

"Aelius Hadrianus is headed towards the auction pavilion with his entourage."

"Of course he fucking is!" Gaius sighed with a snarl.

"Publius is here? I had wondered where our princess was hiding on this most glorious of afternoons. How marvelous he's decided to grace us all with his noble presence!" Lucius mocked with an effete swirl of his hand, before softening his baritone voice. "You'd better watch out, my friend. Your dear fellow ward appreciates a luscious apricot as much as we do. If your barbarian catches Publius's fancy, he'll outbid you. You may be the emperor's second in command, but our spoiled twit usually gets what he wants. He is, after all, our Emperor's presumptive choice for heir to the imperial throne."

"That's nothing more than a baseless rumor! Marcus has never once made his intentions for the succession clear. No one knows yet who he'll designate as his heir."

"Gaius—love, you're fooling yourself. Our Emperor surrenders to every demand of our enchanting and formidable empress. And Empress Plotina wants Publius as heir designate, not you. She's pressing hard for him to succeed to the throne. We both know that."

Gaius sat up, nostrils flaring and fists clenched. "Stay here and bid for the Dacian on my behalf, Lucius. And make damn sure I get him. Don't overpay, mind you—but get him! I'll attend to Publius."

"Good luck, soldier." Luc grinned, as Gaius rose to his feet and smoothed out his tunic.

"Fortune has nothing to do with it. Victory hinges on judicious strategy and careful execution." Gaius bent down and growled in his amused lover's face, "Don't disappoint me, darling."

The clash of the auction cymbals sounded and the raven-haired girl was now the property of a cruel, crippled old codger. Gaius shook his head in disgust as he made his way to the exit.

OUTSIDE OF THE PAVILION, GAIUS SHOUTED ACROSS THE LUSH GARDENS, "Publius Aelius! I didn't know you were coming!" His voice dripped with forced affection.

Stretching his arms wide open, he marched towards the younger man standing in front of his group of attendants. The closest person Gaius had to a real sibling, Publius was a flamboyant, immature little prat who both annoyed and charmed him. They'd spent years growing up under the same roof back when they were both Emperor Trajan's young wards. Like most brothers, they shared many adventures, many laughs, and far too many secrets. Many unsavory matters were hidden behind the massive gilded doors of the imperial palace.

After spotting Gaius, Publius Aelius gasped and hastened his pace, practically skipping into Gaius's embrace. They hugged and patted until Gaius shoved Publius back, holding him firm by the shoulders as he stared into Publius's pale blue eyes. The insecure twit cowered under his palms like a skittish slave girl. Publius Aelius Hadrianus was unfit to lead a horse, let alone the legions. And certainly not the fucking empire.

"Gaius Fabius! How—how have you been?" Publius stuttered with a slight lisp, as streams of sweat poured down his forehead. "Shit, it's unbearably hot today, isn't it? I feel like a wax doll in the blazing forge of Hephaestus. I'm positively melting." Publius huffed, dabbing his soaked brow with a piece of expensive scarlet cloth before handing the vile rag to his attendant. "What are you doing here, Gaius? Are you in the market for another plaything?"

"I had hoped to find something tempting, but the selection was entirely unimpressive. And the auction festivities are nearly over."

"Over? But I thought…"

"It was a tedious parade of uninteresting stock. Nothing special, and nothing remotely novel. Not a single item would have interested you, Publius, not with your impeccable taste in bed warmers. What a waste of time. But at least now I can enjoy the immeasurable pleasure of your company."

Gaius seized Publius's head and kissed him hard on both of his slimy cheeks, just above the wiry fur of his strawberry blond beard barely covering his blemished skin. He caught strong whiffs of oriental spices—his brother's typical overpowering perfumes.

Publius squirmed a bit, and his voice shot up two octaves as his arms fluttered about. "What a complete tragedy! I traveled all the way across Rome in this inferno for nothing? Damn, I was so looking forward to perusing some lovely bums. But, by the grace of Fortuna, it is an unexpected pleasure to see you, my dear Gaius."

"A fortunate occurrence, indeed. Let's sit over there by that fountain. We must catch up, Greekling."

"Stop calling me that, Gaius!" Publius playfully swatted Gaius's forearm. "You know how much I hate it."

Gaius wrapped his right arm around Publius's shoulders and dragged his brother towards the far corner of the garden, away from his entourage.

"Rubbish! You love that pet name—you always have. Sit with me for a while. It'll be cooler in the shade. We wouldn't want your fair skin to burn in this sun. Empress Plotina would be furious if her little Greekling returned to the palace all pink and blistered."

~

Back inside the pavilion, the dealer's assistants were on the stage, busy with the final preparations for the sale of the drugged Dacian. It was suffocating inside the pavilion. The dazed captive could barely stand; the assistants were bickering about who would hold him upright for inspection. Meanwhile, in the audience, men were mulling about, some too drunk to walk, others falling asleep, while still others were distracted, deep in conversation.

Over by the side of the stage, stretched out along the couch, Luc squashed his face with his palms and sighed. "Max, I'm bored. Come here and sit next to me," he purred as he patted the woven fabric of the couch cushion.

It was an unusual request, likely encouraged by too much drink, but an invitation Lucius knew Maximus could not refuse. Lucius Petronius was a powerful man—only a step or so below Gaius Fabius on the political ladder of Roman aristocracy. Of course, his position had made his long-standing, clandestine affair with the auburn-haired general all the more dangerous. Lucius had realized the perilous risks long ago, back in Athens when he'd seduced the gorgeous, brilliant young patrician. By the gods, he missed those carefree college days! Now, as the chief legal counselor to the emperor, Lucius was playing with fire. If the weasels of the imperial court discovered he and Gaius were lovers, both of their reputations would be destroyed. Roman men didn't screw each other senseless. They had slaves and wives for that.

"As you wish, sir." Max sat down on the edge of the couch.

Lucius handed the freedman a cup of wine, and Max pretended to take a sip. "It is very good wine. Thank you, sir."

"Tell me, Maximus. How do you like your new freedman status?" Luc smiled and moved closer.

"Very well, sir. Commander Fabius is a generous man."

"To you, perhaps. With me, he's a selfish prick! I've been trying to convince him for ages to sell me your divine body. And now it's too late." Lucius's exaggerated look of disappointment quickly turned preposterously pathetic. "Do you think the cruel bastard freed you only to deny me my one true desire?"

Max shrugged at the odd question. Lucius was kidding, of course. Yes, he'd fucked Gaius's stunning Ethiopian slave several times over the years. Maximus was an eye-catching and tasty delicacy he and Gaius enjoyed sharing, but Luc felt nothing special for him. Lucius smiled as he pictured his own statuesque pet, Bryaxis. He adored his precocious rascal more than he cared for anyone. Well, almost anyone. He sighed and watched the freedman lift his cup again and swallow a hearty gulp of wine.

"What is this, Max? Dried blood?"

Luc rubbed a spot on the back of Max's neck, sending shivers down the Ethiopian's spine.

"Um, I'm not sure, sir. I suppose it could be blood."

"Why is that?"

"I encountered a bit of trouble on the way here—a drunken centurion and his henchmen attacked me. Commander Fabius remedied the situation, sir."

Lucius laughed. "I bet he did. A street brawl, I take it? Knowing Gaius, I'd wager that's one officer who sorely regrets his daft mistake."

"The centurion is dead."

Luc shook his head as he chuckled. "Well, that's about as regrettable as it gets, isn't it?"

Max flashed him a bright, handsome smile. Luc could never fault Gaius for his excellent taste in enthusiastic, attractive boys. Slave girls, especially untrustworthy wenches like Callidora, on the other hand? Lucius couldn't comprehend why Gaius had kept the old whore for so many years, or why for that matter his friend needed another lad. Gaius had his talented blond slut, Nicomedes, and now another ravishing boy named Simon. And, freedom or no freedom, the general still had Maximus by the balls.

"Tell me, Max. Why do you think your patron is interested in purchasing this untamed hairy beast?"

"Perhaps he craves more war booty," Max suggested, as they turned to watch two monstrous brutes drag the good-looking, dark-haired young savage up the rickety wooden steps. The naked, disoriented creature was pale and shivering; his chalk-covered toes scraped along the wooden boards of the platform while an auction sign swung to and fro from the cord around his neck. The Dacian's large eyes were nearly closed and unfocused.

Lucius leaned over and waggled his dark brows. "Show time!"

ON THEIR WAY OVER TO THE BENCH BY THE FOUNTAIN ON THE OTHER SIDE OF the garden, Gaius casually plucked a pink rose off a bush. When they reached the marble seat, he gingerly threaded the thorny stem through the thick reddish-golden curls above Publius's left ear. "For you, Greekling. Sit."

Publius slowly sat down and folded his arms over his stomach. "Gaius, I've missed you. The palace isn't the same without you," he pouted, looking down at the grass.

Gaius rested his hand on his brother's shoulder. "How is our dear Emperor?"

Gods, it had been too long since Gaius had paid his respects to the emperor—far too long. He would have to rectify that, and soon. He sat down next to his brother, hip brushing up against hip.

"He's restless and ornery. Peace doesn't agree with Emperor Trajan, as you well know. But he's keeping himself busy lately with his grandiose public projects. He's entrusted that arrogant Greek trickster from Syria to oversee the construction of the new forum. What a farce! Have you seen what that incompetent fool has proposed? I could have come up with a design much more worthy of our Emperor's glorious triumphs." Publius sighed in dramatic defeat, as he unfurled his arms and rested his furry chin on his fists.

"Apollodorus is here? In Rome?"

Gaius had spent much time on campaign in the company of the emperor's Greek architect and military engineer. He'd be the first to admit Apollodorus could be an arrogant nit, but he was bloody brilliant as well. And the man was a most entertaining dinner companion.

"Sadly, yes. He's staying at the palace, marching about and barking orders like he owns the fucking place! He has no bloody respect for me, Gaius!" Publius's cheeks and neck were slowly reddening as he worked himself up into a full-blown hissy fit.

"Don't get your tunic in a twist, Greekling. Appy is just one of those flighty creative types, that's all. I have no doubt he admires you."

Publius dismissed Gaius's reassurances with a flick of his wrist and then raised his eyes. "You respect me, don't you, Gaius?"

"How could you ask that? Of course I do. Your skills on the battlefield are near legendary." Gaius clenched his teeth and staved off a smirk at the ludicrousness of his own horseshit compliment.

"Do you—do you think that gorgeous lawyer friend of yours, Lucius Petronius, respects me? I mean..." Publius swallowed. "I'd hoped he would be here."

"Publius Aelius!" Gaius snorted so hard he had to stop to catch his breath. "Do you still have a crush on Lucius?"

"No, not really." Publius slumped his shoulders. "Well, yes—I suppose I still do. It's silly, isn't it? He is barely aware I fucking exist, Gaius."

"I highly doubt that, my brave little soldier. You are quite noticeable." Gaius ruffled Publius's locks, mussing his carefully arranged fussy hairstyle.

"Really? Do you think I...?"

Suddenly a massive load of greenish-white bird droppings splattered all over Publius's shoulder. He jumped up and shrilled, "By the gods, I've been shat upon! It's a good omen, isn't it, brother?"

"I can't think of a more favorable sign, my dear Publius." Twisting to the side, Gaius covered his mouth with the back of his hand as his whole body shook with repressed snorts.

~

"AND LAST ON THE BLOCK THIS AFTERNOON, AN ESPECIALLY UNUSUAL AND particularly rare offer for your consideration, gentlemen!" The auctioneer's call trumpeted through the hot air trapped inside the pavilion, causing the guests to rouse from their naps or hush the buzz of their conversations. One of the assistants gripped the drugged Dacian by the jaw; his fingers pressed cruelly into the young man's flesh as he positioned his face for a better view.

"I present a lovely Dacian lad, a delightful thrill for those of you who prefer ticklish whiskers and some feisty spark in your playthings. Estimated to be around twenty-one years of age. Good health, solid bones. Not trained, obviously."

The crowd snickered, as one idiot shouted, "Is that shaggy pup at least house broken?"

The bidding began.

"I offer two hundred pieces of silver!"

The auctioneer laughed and then hollered, "Did I forget to mention it's a virgin, ripe for defiling?"

"Four hundred!"

The auctioneer motioned for his men to turn the naked boy around.

"Surely you noticed this perfectly shaped, delectable and, let me repeat, unsullied bum, gentlemen? You won't find a more round, tighter rump at any auction this year."

"Four-fifty!"

Lucius eyed the Dacian's attractive, shapely backside for a few moments before turning to Gaius's freedman. "So, Maximus. Commander Fabius tells me you're now the handler for his pets down at the villa."

"Sir, are you going to bid? The price is climbing quickly and Commander Fabius was adamant about not wanting to pay too much for it, sir."

Lucius grumbled, sat up straight, and shouted in his deep, rich voice, "Five hundred denarii!" Then he relaxed, returning his attention to Max. "And, as the handler, you are the official fellatio trainer for his boys, correct?"

Max grinned. "It's an exhausting job, sir."

"Seven hundred!" Shouted another bidder.

"Oh, for the love of Diana." Lucius glanced at the stage and yelled in an annoyed tone, "Eight hundred!"

The steep boost in the bidding caused many in the audience to laugh and hoot and holler. Soon the whole building rumbled with noise—men screaming at each other, curses flying about the space.

~

Out in the garden, Publius gazed in the direction of the growing ruckus coming from the pavilion. He squinted and asked, "What is going on in there? I thought you'd said the auction was over? You must have been mistaken, dear brother."

Fuck.

Gaius raised his eyebrows and shrugged nonchalantly.

Publius jumped to his feet, bouncing up and down on his sandal-clad toes. "Let's go investigate this commotion. It must be something special to cause such a loud fuss."

"Yes, it must be," Gaius answered with a blank expression while his mind screamed a stream of obscenities.

"Hurry, Gaius!" Publius yelled impatiently over his shoulder as he began half-walking, half-running towards the pavilion. Gaius easily caught up with him, and they both approached the entrance.

"Welcome, Aelius Hadrianus! Please surrender your weapons."

"I have no weapons, guard. I have robust personal escorts to protect me, thank you. Now be so kind as to step the fuck aside!"

Publius Aelius could be one rude little cunt.

They walked past the curtains, but couldn't get close to the stage. Men were standing on their couches, waving their arms, downing cups of wine and pointing at bidders who were screaming out numbers.

Frozen in his tracks, Publius slobbered when he caught sight of the bearded boy up on the auction block. Swaying on his feet, the captive's wrists were held firmly by two brutish auction assistants. One grabbed the barbarian by his long, black locks and jerked his head up so his sublime face was easier for the crowd to admire.

"Gaius, do you see that utterly fabulous creature?"

Gaius narrowed eyes and mumbled, "Yes, I see him."

"Nine hundred and fifty denarii!" An aristocrat shouted from across the room. Gaius winced.

"What is it?"

"It appears to be a northern barbarian, brother. It'll be difficult—illiterate, dull-witted, and violent. Not your type, to put it mildly," he responded, clenching his teeth again.

"Really? But it's so pretty. The lad just needs a good hot bath, and some time with my barber."

"And two sets of fucking sturdy iron shackles."

"Gaius, you're exaggerating. I'm going to bid on it."

"It's your coin, Publius. Waste it however you see fit. Be mindful that our esteemed Emperor would not approve of such a reckless purchase."

"Fuck him!" Publius went rigid, and then lowered his voice. "I did not just say that. But I am bidding." He cleared his throat and shrieked, "Twelve hundred pieces of silver!"

"SHIT!" MAX BLURTED OUT, AND LUCIUS LAUGHED. HAVING CAUGHT SIGHT OF his patron and Publius Aelius Hadrianus over by the portal, Max's eyes were so wide they nearly glowed against his rich brown skin.

Lucius slapped Max on the back. "Ah, I see our dear Publius has entered the fray. Let the games begin."

"The price stands at twelve hundred denarii, gentlemen," the auctioneer yelled. "Do we have another bid for this intact barbarian kitten?"

The room quieted, as men muttered to each other in hushed voices. No one was so bold or daft to dare counter a bid by Publius Aelius Hadrianus, rumored heir designate to the imperial throne and vindictive twat extraordinaire. Enemies of Hadrianus never lived very long.

Slowly, Lucius stood up on his couch—an impressive and breathtaking sight given that he was well over six foot tall and broad as a bull. He looked straight at Publius and donned his most charming, seductive smile.

Everyone in the pavilion fell silent, all eyes glancing back and forth between the two men.

Luc nodded a coquettish greeting to Publius, batted his eyelashes, and then roared, "Two thousand denarii!"

STANDING BEHIND PUBLIUS'S LEFT SHOULDER, GAIUS'S GRIMACE MORPHED INTO a thunderstruck smile.

"That gorgeous, audacious son of a bitch!"

Lucius winked at his lover.

Publius gulped, awkwardly tossed an exaggerated wink back at Lucius, and then staggered a bit as if the wind had been knocked out of him.

The auctioneer inquired, "Aelius Hadrianus, do you wish to place another bid?"

Catching his breath, Publius raised a finger to demand a moment's pause. "Did you see that? Your insolent and extremely attractive friend just challenged my bid. And, by the gods, I do believe he's flirting with me. Tell me brother, what should I do?"

Gaius snarled softly into his brother's ear, "Let Lucius Petronius have the beast, Publius. That's a fucking insane price for an untrained barbarian. And besides, if you allow our impudent lawyer to purchase the animal and save face in front of this crowd, Lucius will certainly owe you a favor or two, won't he? You never know when Counselor Petronius's famed talents in the courts might be useful to you."

Publius closed his eyes for a moment and then nodded, giggling. He cleared his throat again and yelped, "I'm no longer interested!"

"Any other bids?" The auctioneer hesitated, and declared the sale final. With a thunderous crash, the bronze cymbals severed the thick tension in the hall. Some men cheered while others shook their heads in disbelief.

~

LUCIUS CLAPPED HIS HANDS TOGETHER ONE TIME AND SAT DOWN, WHEN MAX said, "Sir, you just outbid Aelius Hadrianus. And you paid two thousand denarii for a Dacian mongrel."

Max's mouth hung open in disbelief.

Lucius pinched Max's cheek and chuckled. "No, I didn't. Your gorgeous patron did. My dear Gaius is the only man I know who could get away with stealing a shiny new pet right out from underneath princess Publius's sniveling nose."

Grinning as he licked his bottom lip, Lucius gently lifted Max's face with one finger. "So, Maximus the Fellatio Trainer—how does your prick feel about scratchy Dacian beards?

3

Gnaeus Decius's estate on the Quirinal Hill, Rome

"Two fucking thousand denarii, Luc?" Gaius screamed at Lucius Petronius. Well, not screamed. More like whispered, in a completely fucking pissed off way, trying to keep his voice low so as to not draw too much unwarranted attention from the other distinguished guests. Around the hall, men were gathering up their things, bidding their farewells and slowly meandering out of the pavilion. The sun was low in the sky, but the stifling heat hadn't relaxed its stranglehold one iota.

With a wry smirk, Lucius tossed both of his hands up. "Listen, Gaius. You told me to get the hairy thing, and I did, darling."

Gaius stepped closer, fists pressed against his thighs to temper his anger. Luc's breath hitched; his thickening arousal pushed against his striped tunic. He pressed his left palm against the fabric covering his groin to try and settle his zealous cock.

"Publicly humiliating Princess Prat was not a bright move, counselor. Fortunately, he's easily distracted and should eventually forget your transgression." Gaius backed off, but stepped forward again, pointing his thumb at his own chest. "And, for the record, Luc, I won the barbarian, not you."

Lucius chuckled as he crossed his strapping forearms. "How do you figure that one?"

"I was the one who convinced him not to challenge your outrageous bid, not you and your flirtatious charms."

Gaius's anger melted to concern.

Yes, he was pleased Publius hadn't taken the Dacian home, but he also feared the unknown repercussions of Lucius's foolhardy antics. There would be retribution, not to mention the price Gaius would now be forced to pay was a small fortune for an unbroken captive. As they bickered, he caught a glimpse of Max swallowing a gulp of wine before scooping up the leather satchel.

"Gaius, listen. We both know that Publius—" A pudgy finger tapped Lucius lightly on the shoulder.

"Lucius Petronius, excuse me, sir. I apologize for interrupting, but the dealer has informed me your remarkable purchase is ready for private inspection."

Lucius exhaled and relaxed his shoulders. Fortuna had offered him a simple way out of this pissing contest. Soon the lawyer would return home to prepare for dinner and a night of hard shagging. Sex after a spat was always tantalizingly rough, always satisfying. Where had Luc hidden those braided leather bindings after the last time Gaius had tied him to the bed and pummeled him into delirium?

The lawyer wrapped his arm around Decius's small sunken shoulders. "Gnaeus Decius, my good man! We haven't had a moment to chat, have we?" He glanced back at Gaius, before pulling his fawning client in close. "You know this lovely Dacian thing I've just purchased? I'm transferring ownership of the property to my dear friend, Gaius Fabius. Apparently, some of us can never have enough distractions. And not to worry, our esteemed Commander has agreed to cover the bid and all incidental fees. Haven't you, Commander Fabius?"

Gaius rolled his eyes. "How incredibly generous of you, counselor. Now I owe you a favor in return, don't I? I'll settle that debt tonight, Lucius Petronius. Count on it."

With a knotted brow, Decius glanced back and forth at the two of them. "Oh, my. This is most—most unusual. But, of course, as you wish, sir."

"Decius, where is this inspection room?"

"I'll escort you there personally, Commander Fabius." Decius extended his upturned palm towards the exit. "This way, please."

"Maximus!"

"Coming, sir."

Gaius moved close to his friend's satisfied grin, and spoke low and soft, "You, my dear Lucius, need not be present for the inspection. I'll see you later for dinner. Have everything ready, yes? I suspect we'll both be starving by then."

Lucius pressed his hand against his groin again, rubbing his palm up and down his shaft. He smiled and silently mouthed, "You're fucking welcome, darling."

~

THE INSPECTION ROOM WAS LITTLE MORE THAN A STORAGE SPACE LOCATED AT the far end of a set of slave barracks behind a large aviary building. Inside the vacant cell, one small window allowed a beam of orange-infused afternoon sunlight to stream into the middle of the room. And at the center, standing in the waning golden spotlight, stood a naked and disoriented Dacian captive named Allerix.

Allerix, second son of King Thiamarkos.

With his limbs numb from the paralyzing drugs forced down his throat, Allerix could barely stand. The same two goons who earlier had dragged him across the auction stage were holding him upright for the purchaser's personal hands-on appraisal. Allerix could hear muffled banter, but he couldn't see. His eyes wouldn't focus, and his lids were so heavy he could hardly force them open more than a crack.

"That was a mad price for a savage, if you ask me," grunted one of the brutes.

"Those rich twits have more coin than they know what to do with. Causes the prices for bloody everything to go up!" griped the other.

Pacing back and forth behind him, the crabby dealer grumbled, "Enough, both of you! Greed fuels my profits, you idiots. And my profits fill your stomachs. Where is this Roman purchaser? Come and get your new furry stray, and let's be done with this!"

With a bang, the door to the inspection room slammed opened. Allerix's spine stiffened as he tried to swallow. It was time to perform. His last scraps of honor, not to mention his life, depended on it.

~

"COMMANDER FABIUS!" THE FABRIC OF THE DEALER'S TUNIC SHUFFLED AS HE practically touched his chin to his knees. "It is a most welcome surprise to be visited by your glorious and most distinguished greatness."

"This is the Dacian?" Gaius asked as he slowly walked around to the side of the group standing at the center of the sunbeam circle in the middle of the brick floor. He remained a few feet back in the shadows, waiting for his eyes to adjust to the dimmer light of the toasty storage space.

"Yes, sir. This is the slave that Counselor Petronius purchased, ready for final inspection. Is Lucius Petronius on his way, sir?" the dealer stammered. He'd clearly never personally met someone of such high rank. He was so utterly dazzled he didn't notice when Decius stepped into the room with Maximus behind him.

"Septus, there's been a change of plans," Decius calmly interjected. "Counselor Petronius has transferred ownership of this slave to our most esteemed Commander Fabius."

"How wonderful indeed! I've never before had the incredible honor, Commander, of providing my goods and services to the imperial court." Septus bowed again, his voice cracking with giddy enthusiasm. "And never to the emperor's most victorious general, conqueror of the Dacian enemy!"

"Shut up, filth, and move aside."

~

Even though he couldn't move a muscle, Allerix's pulse raced. Gaius Fabius Rufus—the bastard who'd ordered his legions to destroy their capital city and ruthlessly massacre Allerix's cousins and countrymen during the wars? He'd never seen the notorious monster himself, but he'd heard his father discuss the bloodthirsty fucker's dogged lust for victory, no matter what the odds or consequences. As reality sunk in, Allerix shivered uncontrollably and broke into a cold sweat.

The Roman looked him up and down for a few moments, before nodding with satisfaction. "Payment in full will arrive at your offices tomorrow morning. I trust my word will be sufficient collateral for this evening. Now, give me your cloak."

"Yes, Commander. Anything you wish," Septus replied.

"Maximus, take hold of the slave. The rest of you leave. Do not go far, Decius. I want to speak with you again before I leave for dinner."

"Yes, Commander Fabius. I'll be enjoying my aviary just outside the dormitory. It's been too long since I visited my feathered friends."

Septus bowed once again and groveled. "Farewell, most esteemed Commander. It has been my greatest pleasure doing business with you, sir."

"Get out, pig." The Roman pointed to the door, but then shouted, "Wait, stop! What poison did you give the captive?"

"Poison, sir?"

"The drugs, you dolt. What are they?"

"Just a simple potion that temporarily disarms the more agitated ones, Commander. The recipe is a trade secret, but it's not harmful. I assure you the effects will wear off completely by morning, sir."

"For the sake of your worthless hide, that had better be true. Leave us."

Septus and his minions shuffled out of the room, with Decius following after them. Gaius walked over, closed the wooden door, and returned to stand in front of the Dacian.

"What an awe inspiring creature."

Gripping the lad by his biceps, Max spoke over the Dacian's shoulder with genuine worry in his voice, "Sir, he's shivering terribly. Perhaps he's ill, Commander?"

Gaius pressed the back of his hand against the slave's forehead. "Yes, I can see he's shaking, but it's not from fever. His skin is cool to the touch. It's those fucking drugs, Maximus. This is the last time I will purchase anything from an auction."

He cupped the lad's jaw and lifted his face. "He is strangely beautiful, isn't he?" Gaius traced a finger pad down the gentle slope of his small, slender nose and across the boy's impossibly full lips. "Such a unique face —delicate and graceful, but masculine as well. The whiskers will have to go, eventually, but even with the beard he's..."

Gaius swallowed. "He's breathtaking."

As he lightly brushed his fingertips over the swell of the captive's cheek and then over the curves of his arched eyebrow, Gaius sighed. "Thanks to that swine's vile potion, he's in a sorry state. His eyes won't focus, but his lashes are long and dark and thick."

He let go of the slave's face and stepped back. "Max, lift up his arms."

Starting with the lad's wrists, Gaius inspected the Dacian's arms and upper bodybefore squatting down to scrutinize his hairy legs.

"Are you pleased with him, sir?"

"His body is exceptionally fuckable, but I'm not assessing his beauty. Recently, younger Dacian royals have adopted the foolish habit of immortalizing their high rank through permanent tattoos. Those markings have become extremely valuable on the battlefield for identifying them. According to our emperor's orders, royal Dacian princes are condemned to death by the beasts in the arena without possibility of ransom. Few know about the royal markings, however. For obvious strategic reasons, we don't want the idiots to stop tattooing their bodies. All right, he's clean."

Gaius took hold of Allerix's uplifted wrists. "Check to see if there are any markings on the backs of his thighs and calves, Max."

"Yes, Commander." Max bent down. "There are no tattoos I can see, sir."

After handing his new investment back to his freedman, Gaius took each of the Dacian's hands into his palms and ran his experienced touch over the slave's long fingers. They were strong but smooth and unscarred. They bore no calluses or other damage caused by hard labor in the fields.

Gaius coughed to clear the lump of desire in his throat. "The magistrates have kept careful lists in our archives of every known royal who either died, was captured, or escaped to the mountains during the wars. Possession of a Dacian princeling is a treasonable offense. Make sure to find out his name, Maximus."

Gaius lifted one of the boy's limp hands and pressed it tenderly against his lips. Max shifted his feet. "Will you be keeping him then, sir? Here in Rome, perhaps?"

Without warning, the Dacian pulled away from Gaius's tender touch and thrashed against Max's firm grip. He lifted his droopy eyelids and glared blindly. Calm and in control, Gaius stared back, savoring the fierce look in the lad's eyes—hazel eyes that betrayed an angry, beautiful young man filled with desperation and defiance and raw resilience. He seized the slave by his long, damp black hair. "Do not bloody fight me, boy."

With one last feeble bit of resistance, the lad jerked his head away. Suddenly, his eyes rolled back in his head as he lost consciousness and fell limp into Max's arms. Even though the Dacian was young and fit, the drugs and oppressive heat and manhandling had taken their toll.

After he exhaled a breath, Gaius shook his head and laughed. "Well, he'll be a handful, won't he? I'm definitely keeping this beautiful feral cub, Max, but not here in Rome. My lovely wife would throw a fit if she discovered a Dacian mongrel wandering about the mansion. We'll transport him down to my Campanian villa to be properly trained."

"Yes, sir."

"I'll inform Decius I'm leaving the boy here in his slave quarters for the night. You will stay with him, Maximus. Make sure he remains untouched. And fucking figure out his blasted name while I'm gone."

"May I ask where you will be, sir? In case there is, um, an emergency?"

Gaius whispered, "I will be pounding Counselor Petronius's impossibly tight arse. Do not disturb me over some trifle. Handle it. I trust your judgment, Max. I'll have Decius assign one of his attractive lads to you for anything you might need."

Gaius lifted the cloak and carefully wrapped the woven fabric around the Dacian's bare shoulders, bundling him in the cloth like a parent comforting a chilled child. He took one more lingering look at the slave's placid, ashen face and kissed him softly on the lips, before pulling back, his fingers tangled in the lad's wet mane of ebony hair. He leaned in and hummed against his neck, "I'm going to relish breaking you, cub."

After he stepped away and readjusted his tunic, Gaius smiled. "Sleep well, Maximus. First thing tomorrow, we'll leave this suffocating oven of a city and head south for the refreshing breezes of the Campanian coast."

Lucius Petronius's house on the Quirinal Hill, Rome

On either side of the portal to Lucius Petronius's grand house, two torches sat in ornate metal brackets fixed high on the wall. The torch on the left was unlit while the one to the right burned brightly. Gaius grinned at the familiar sight of his lover's simple signal. It was getting dark and his stomach grumbled for food. Since the quiet street was deserted, not a spy in sight, he rapped his knuckles three times against the large wooden door.

After a few moments, the iron bolt pulled back with a loud thud and the heavy entrance door slowly opened. And there he stood, on full display like a prized bronze statue, dressed in a ridiculously short Greek-style tunic baring his right arm and barely covering his groin. The tall, striking man leaned his shoulder against the marble doorjamb, his long legs crossed at the ankles in a casual way, his arms folded across his chest. A stranger would have thought he owned the fucking place.

"Greetings, Commander Fabius. Why, we haven't had the pleasure of a visit since—five days ago, wasn't it?" The twenty-eight year old flashed his broad, lop-sided smile and arched one of his dark eyebrows.

"I see your ever indulgent master has finally promoted you to door-keeper." Gaius pushed past the slave, undressing him with a leer as he strolled by.

"Among other duties, sir." The brunet pushed his cheek out with his tongue and winked with a mixture of confidence and contempt.

With his strong features and defined muscles, Bryaxis was still powerfully alluring after all these years. Even now as a grown man, not much younger than Max, Luc's favorite remained a savory feast for the eyes. Gaius unfastened the clasp of his cloak and threw it at his lover's pet. It had been a long day; he was tired and hungry and horny.

"Where is your master, Bryaxis?"

After shaking out the wrinkles, folding the cloth, and carefully draping the cloak over a stool, Bryaxis cocked his head. "Last time I saw him, Dominus was pacing back and forth in his office. He seems anxious over something."

Gaius rushed forward and backhanded Bryaxis across his face. His signet ring left an impression on his cheek. Gaius grabbed him by his jaw, digging his fingers into his flesh. He jerked the tall slave's face down.

"Why you disrespectful piece of shit. It is not your place to judge Counselor Petronius's mood! You answer my question and no more. Do you understand me?"

Bryaxis swallowed and nodded with a slow blink of his wide but still obstinate eyes. "Yes, sir."

"Lucius may allow you to strut about as you wish and mouth off freely, but I'll be damned if I'll tolerate your fucking flagrant arrogance!"

After Gaius released his harsh grip, Bryaxis elegantly collapsed to his knees, clasping his hands behind his back and bowing his head towards the vestibule floor. He kept his eyes fixed on the abstract patterns of the geometric mosaic and bit the inside of his cheek.

"Gaius! You've arrived at last!"

The throbbing of Gaius's temples subsided and his entire body relaxed as he anticipated Luc's bear-hug embrace. After two thick arms wrapped around his waist from behind, he felt strong fingers rub lightly across his tunic-covered abdomen. Lucius nibbled his left ear and whispered, "Greetings, my gorgeous soldier. I hope you've come with full balls and an empty stomach."

"You'll tend to both afflictions, I trust." He leaned back and placed his hands on Lucius's thick forearms.

"What are best mates for? Pardon me, darling, but why is Bry down on his knees? Are you two starting the fun and games without me?"

"Hardly. Your whore needs discipline. But I've already told you that for years now, haven't I?"

Lucius kissed his cheek and murmured, "Hush, Gaius. We both appreciate a bit of pluck in our pets. Bryaxis is a brilliant legal assistant and, as you well know, an even more brilliant lay. A sprinkle of sass only adds to his appeal, no?"

"He's bloody soaked in sass."

"Perhaps then you'll be so generous to help out a dear friend and demonstrate some of that famous Fabian discipline for us this evening." Luc reached down and ruffled Bryaxis' golden-streaked brown hair with his long fingers, and was rewarded with a grateful moan. He took hold of a fistful of locks and gently forced his pet's head back to gaze into Bry's large, expressive gold-green eyes. "What is that mark on your face, pet?"

Gaius coughed before he confessed, "He was insolent, so I struck him."

"Did you, then? Bry, be a good lad and go inform Euphronia to finalize dinner. Commander Fabius and I will be dining in the garden."

Bryaxis rose gracefully on his impossibly long legs and nodded silently before strutting off to the kitchen. As the patter of his bare feet across the colorful floor tiles faded away, Luc draped his muscular arm around his companion's shoulders and led him to the wide colonnaded corridor that opened out onto a lavish, lamp-lit garden oasis at the back of the estate.

"Don't ever strike my pet without my permission, Gaius."

"I'll admit I acted rashly, Luc, but you need to bloody discipline him."

"Listen, I'll be the one who fucking decides how to best reprimand my favorite, soldier." Lucius took a deep breath and smiled. "Anyhow, you'll be relieved to know my wife and daughter departed after the mid-day meal. I've dismissed all the servants save for the kitchen staff and, of course, Bryaxis. We'll save him for dessert. Now tell me, Gaius—how was the private inspection? Is your feral Dacian worth all that bloody coin? I want details, darling."

4

Gnaeus Decius's estate on the Quirinal Hill, Rome

SNORING SOFTLY ON THE OTHER SIDE OF THE SMALL ROOM, THE BARBARIAN slept soundly on the stone floor. The Dacian was attractive, for an uncivilized heathen, but nowhere near as beautiful as Nicomedes. Max leaned against the wall, closed his eyes and pictured Nic—his glistening bronzed skin, his mesmerizing sapphire eyes, his playful laugh, and his thick blond hair that fell in waves below his shoulders.

Beautiful, damaged Nicomedes. He'd been caged in that bronze contraption for two months now. Commander Fabius was furious when he'd discovered Nic's idiotic crime, but the punishment was less harsh than Max had expected. Surely the commander didn't want Nic permanently disfigured, did he? Max rubbed his eyes and shifted his weight on the squeaky wooden bench. So much had changed in a year's time.

Last summer, Dom had brought Max along to one of his secret dinner trysts at Counselor Petronius's estate. After he and Bry nibbled scrumptious morsels of meat and cake from their masters' outstretched fingers, the silver dinner plates were cleared and the wine poured freely. When the sky grew dark, they all retired to the master chamber and the pets performed an acrobatic sex show on cushions strewn about the floor. Bry was brilliantly flexible! And, other than Nic, Bryaxis was the only whore who could take every bit of Max's enormous cock down his throat. From up on the large bed, their masters watched the raunchy spectacle, shouting directions laced with profanities. After the slaves ejaculated over each other's sweaty faces—twice—Max crouched down on all fours and Commander Fabius fucked him like a rabid wolf. Not two feet away, Counselor Petronius bent Bry over a chair and hammered his arse, slapping his bum cheeks warm and ruddy between thrusts. Then the masters switched places.

Max's eyes crinkled as he smiled. What a fabulous party!

But Max wasn't a pleasure slave any longer; he was a freedman. And on this humid summer night, Commander Fabius had assigned him the dull task of guarding the shackled barbarian lying on the floor across from him. Yes, everything had changed. When Max took a deep breath, an unexpected whiff of fragrant stew tickled his nostrils.

A sandy-haired boy cowered in the doorway, his tiny white knuckles clutching the edge of a platter balanced against his concave, prepubescent abdomen. The rattling dishes bounced about and threatened to topple off the tray. "Please don't hit me, sir! Master Decius sent me."

Max unclenched his fists, shook his head, and scratched his day-old stubble. "Easy, lad. You can put the food on that table. What's your name?"

"Paulus, sir."

"Paulus?"

"I'm told it means 'little one.'"

"Is that so? It's an apt name for you. Are you a house servant or one of Decius's bed tenders?"

"A kitchen slave, sir. My father is the cook," the young boy squeaked in a mousy voice, as he bent over to the table to set the tray down. Max lifted his brows at the delightful curves of the boy's firm arse and frowned. "That's a shame. You're lovely. Perhaps, when you fill out in a few years, you'll be promoted to a pleasure slave."

Paulus fidgeted while he stared at the wall behind the table. After a moment, he cleared his throat and faced Max. "Um, Master Decius said to tell you… to tell you your dessert will arrive soon. He hopes you'll be pleased, sir."

Max laughed at his adorable stutter. "Ah, finally a bit of good news, then. I've a terrible craving for something sweet and luscious."

"Yes, sir. Enjoy your meal, sir." The boy stumbled and scurried out of the cell.

"Skittish little thing." Max walked over and stuck a thick finger in the rich lamb dish. He sucked it clean with a groan of pleasure. "Not Euphronia's divine cooking, but it's good. Let's hope this promised dessert will be even more satisfying."

Lucius Petronius's house on the Quirinal Hill, Rome

"Fabius is here," Bryaxis grumbled as he wandered over to the array of black pots resting on the grates above the cooking fires.

A tantalizing blend of delicious aromas filled the smoky air: seasoned duck crackling in a roasting pan, vegetables bubbling in creamy herb sauce and bread baking golden in the oven. After lifting a lid, he reached to steal a taste when a small but firm hand whacked him across the back of his head.

"Away from that! If you're a good boy, I'll save an extra portion for you, sweetheart."

Her shrill voice suited her colossal personality. She was short and rotund, with sagging breasts and a jolly, infectious smile that brightened up any room. She kept her crown of bright orange curls piled up high on her head, and had a habit of planting her pudgy hands on her prominent hipbones. Nearly sixty years of age, Euphronia had an aura of authority only a slave who had faithfully served Lucius's family for her entire life could carry with such warm conviction.

"They're dining in the garden, Euphronia. Dominus said to finalize the meal." Bry crossed his arms and slouched against the stone edge of the cooking surface.

"Should I march out there and give our handsome general a big hug and a sloppy kiss?" Euphronia asked playfully.

Bry winced as he rubbed his cheek. "The bastard's in another one of his foul tempers. He bloody hit me. See the mark here on my face from his fucking ring? Shit, I despise that arrogant prick."

Euphronia wagged a finger in the face of the man whom she'd basically raised as her own son for over sixteen years. "Shut your mouth, Bry. If Dominus ever caught you bitching about Commander Fabius, he'd have you whipped. And he'd let the general inflict the lashing! Now let me see that bruise of yours, sweetheart."

As Bry scoffed and shook her off, a skinny slave girl entered the kitchen carrying a jug of wine. She began gathering up the posh silver goblets from an unlocked cupboard when Euphronia walked over and interrupted.

"Daphne, give our poor Bry here a hefty cup of wine. Commander Fabius has arrived for dinner, and our boy needs to lubricate his throat before he sucks the general's foul-tempered cock." The freckled girl lowered her eyes and handed a plain ceramic cup filled to the brim to Bryaxis.

"You're so fucking thoughtful, *mummy*," Bry drawled, dragging out the last word with particular bite, before he slid into a seat at the kitchen table with a grimace. He cradled his chin in his palm, as Euphronia and the slave girl dashed to and fro, dipping ladles into the pots, tasting the sauces and adding a dash of spice or a splash of cream here and there.

"Do you think he hates me, Euphronia?" Bryaxis asked over the bustling activity.

"Who? Certainly you don't mean Dominus. He adores you."

"No, not Dom—Fabius." He swallowed a healthy gulp from the wine cup.

"No, of course not. Domina, on the other hand? Now she abhors you, dear. Commander Fabius just hates the idea of you, Bry. That's completely different." Euphronia looked over her shoulder and tossed him an exaggerated wink.

"What do you mean, 'the idea' of me?"

"Daphne, go fetch more fennel and salt from the storage room."

After the girl had left, Euphronia sat down across from Bryaxis, folded her hands under her chin, and smiled wistfully. "Bry, dear. You've been Dominus's favorite—his only bed warmer—for over twelve years now, right? You couldn't have been much older than twelve when the family purchased you, all arms and legs, tripping over your own clumsy feet. Remember when Dominus hired that Greek tutor for you? And look at you now, sweetie. And you're his invaluable legal assistant no less."

She leaned in closer and dropped her voice to a whisper. "But, Bry—Commander Fabius was here first, before you arrived. He and Dominus are..." She paused and blinked. "They've been close ever since they studied together in Athens. The general doesn't fancy having to share Dominus's affections, nor has he ever been pleased our master treats you more like a lover than property. Listen to me, Bry. Don't challenge that ferocious imperial lion. His bite is much worse than his roar."

She pushed up from the table. "Now, get your spoiled arse up! They'll want drink to start." Euphronia shoved an ornate gilded platter stacked with filled wine cups into Bryaxis' hands. "When Dominus permits, return to retrieve the first course. You know the drill."

"Yes, I know the bloody drill, *Domina*." Bryaxis rolled his eyes and kissed her chubby face, all the while balancing the tray so expertly none of the wine spilled. Not a single drop, even when Euphronia gave his bum a wickedly hard smack as he left for the garden.

"Cheeky bugger!" She wiped her hands on her dress, and picked up a short iron poker to rearrange the cooking embers.

WITH A GRUNT, GAIUS LIFTED TWO HEAVY LEGS OFF HIS SHOULDERS AND carefully pulled his spent, softening cock out of Luc's oiled hole. He collapsed on top of Lucius's broad chest with a thump. They lay motionless on the couch under the garden pergola lights, and their labored breathing slowed as they recovered.

Lucius straightened his knees as he lowered his legs, stretched his calves and groaned, "Loosen the bindings, darling. My arms are cramping."

"I'll decide when to release you, slut. Understand?" Gaius smiled against Lucius's thick wet neck.

"Yes, Dominus." Lucius looked up at the lights for a while before he grumbled, "But seriously, Gaius, my wrists hurt."

"Are you going soft on me, old codger? What happened to my filthy tireless whore who used to beg me to tighten the straps?" Gaius scooted up, rested his chin on Lucius's shoulder and tapped the tip of Luc's nose with his finger. "You are a bloody terrible negotiator. You'll pay me back in demeaning sexual favors for years, you know."

"Mmm, no doubt. And I'm only thirty-seven, arsehole—less than two years older than you." Lucius chuckled and closed his eyes.

Gaius leaned over and kissed him lightly on the corner of his upturned lips, before whispering, "And for that stunt at the auction, my foolish captive, you now owe our princess Publius a favor as well."

Luc's eyes shot open and his muscular arms pulled hard against the braided leather. "What?"

"How the fuck do you think I convinced him not to counter-bid your outrageous stupidity? He wanted my Dacian, Luc. I had no choice."

"Fucking lovely. Thanks for that, darling."

After Gaius removed the leather bindings and tossed them to the ground, he crawled back onto the couch and stretched out on his back next to his naked lover. Side by side, they looked up at the darkening night sky. The light from the suspended oil lamps illuminated the undersides of the thick cypress branches while brown bats flitted between the tall trees. It was peacefully quiet, except for the gurgling sounds of the fountain and the occasional shriek of a gull flying high overhead. The sweltering summer air had finally cooled to a comfortable temperature. Lucius reached down to the ground, grasped his discarded tunic, and pulled it over his satiated body like a blanket.

"This is perfect, Luc."

"Almost, but not quite. Next time, use the damn flogger with more force. You bloody well know how I like it. Your feeble tapping was tiresome, not arousing."

Gaius laughed and sat up, his tunic bunched up around his waist. "We're no longer carefree bachelors, love. How would you explain whipping marks? Ah, to be a bloody fly on the wall for that conversation." Gaius dropped his chin and adopted a comical baritone voice, as he clutched his tunic in supplication. "On the altar of my ancestors, my sweet Aurelia, I swear to you these crimson welts striping my arse and thighs are just a nasty rash!"

With his eyebrows drawn together, Lucius pushed up on his elbows. "All right, point taken. And I couldn't exactly blame any welts on poor Bry, could I? But, listen—you're skilled at covert military operations, yes? So, be creative and figure out how to punish me covertly, and harder. And for the record, I do not sound like that." Luc coughed softly and winked. "Shit, my throat's fucking parched. Bryaxis, bring us wine!"

Before Gaius had a chance to pull his damp tunic down over his hips, Bryaxis stood behind the couch holding a tray and beamed his crooked, charming smile. After he handed each of the men a silver cup brimming with one of the best vintages from Lucius's vats, Bry circled around to the front and placed the tray on a low marble-serving table. As he bent over, he arched his back and lifted his bum for optimal viewing.

"Are you ready to begin your meal, Dominus?" Bryaxis donned his most polite and submissive tone.

While Gaius moved over to the other couch, Lucius reclined on the cushions. "Commander Fabius, should we bathe before drowning ourselves in Euphronia's exceptional cooking?"

"I'm fucking famished."

Lucius shook his head and snorted. "Very well. Fetch the first course, Bryaxis, and dismiss the kitchen staff to their quarters. Do be sure to check all the doors to the garden are locked. We wouldn't want any unfortunate interruptions." He reached out for Bry's hand and squeezed it. "Thank you, pet."

As Luc rubbed the chafed skin of his left wrist, he added, "And Bry, bring back a freshly laundered tunic for this brute. He seems to have soiled his garment."

"That's a load of horseshit. After all these years, I still have excellent aim." Gaius's dimples dotted his mischievous grin.

While Bry strolled off towards the kitchen, Luc leaned over from his couch and whispered, "My aching rump agrees with you."

Suddenly, Gaius pushed himself up on his arm and shouted at Bry's back from across the garden, "Give my beautiful Euphronia a big, sloppy smooch from her favorite soldier, slave!"

5

Gnaeus Decius's estate on the Quirinal Hill, Rome

ALLERIX AWOKE WITH HIS HEAD PRESSED AGAINST SOMETHING COOL AND HARD and wet. Without moving a muscle, he kept his eyes closed and assessed the situation. His wrists were securely joined behind his back with what felt like rope chafing his skin. Both ankles were bound together by heavy shackles. No blindfold, no gag.

He opened one eye and realized his cheek was resting in a puddle of drool. He was naked, but a cloth of some sort had been draped over his body. His bladder was full and his stomach painfully empty.

Lying on the floor, he tried to recall what had happened after they'd been captured and carted to the enemy's capital. He and Gorgas had been separated from the other dozen or so prisoners and thrown in an empty cell. He'd been forced to swallow some bitter liquid; he could still taste tartness in the back of his throat. There was a stage of some sort, and a tent packed with faceless men shouting and laughing, a storm of noise and suffocating heat.

Allerix swallowed a rush of panic.

Where was Gorgas?

After their capture, his companion had been chained next to him on the floor of the wagon. They hadn't spoken for most of the journey from the mountains. What was there to say? That his young, headstrong friend was an idiot for thinking his horse could outrace a fucking deer? That Allerix was an even bigger idiot for chasing after him? Istros had warned them to hunt close to the camp and not stray beyond the river. Allerix squeezed his eyes tight and swallowed again.

He heard noises—animal-like grunts and groans—coming from somewhere close. His face half-hidden behind a curtain of dark hair, Allerix slowly reopened one eye. Although the room was fairly dim, he could see two figures over by the doorway. A pale, light-haired youth crouched down on his hands and knees, bobbing his head up and down between the bent legs of a giant man seated on a bench against the wall. In his short twenty-one years, Allerix had never seen an ebony-skinned man before. He stared at the man's glistening sable muscles and his dazzling white teeth.

After the black man's mouth opened wide and let out a deep, raspy moan, he gently lifted the boy's head up by his long flaxen hair. He reached into a pouch strapped to his torso and pulled out three pieces of bronze. "That was bloody wonderful. Here, take this. It's a modest amount, I confess. You certainly deserve more."

The blond held both his hands up and leaned back on his heels. "I can't accept your coin, sir. My master does not expect payment from his guests."

"Hush, it's for you. Your master will never know. Stash it away for the day when you are freed."

Wiping his flushed lips with the back of his hand, the sex slave cocked his head. "How do you know I'll be freed, sir?"

"We're all freed at some point, lad—either by our masters or by death." He glanced over at Allerix, who quickly shut his eye.

Shit!

"Go now. Be sure to tell your master how pleased I was with dessert." The metallic pings of coins and a gentle humming faded away down the hall.

"So, you're awake then. No need to pretend any longer, Dacian. Open those big eyes of yours." Several moments of silence passed. Perhaps the man would assume Allerix was an uneducated peasant who didn't understand their language.

"Hey!" the man shouted. Allerix opened both eyes wide but remained frozen in his bound position on the floor.

"Well, that's a start. You'll have to learn how to talk, you know." The man looked around the cell for something. "Shit, you're going to be a lot of work. You'd better hope Dom finds you worth all the trouble. And all that bloody silver."

Allerix blinked, but kept his eyes fixed on the black man until he walked out of his line of sight. Something metallic and hollow scraped against the stone floor. The man jerked him up to a standing position; Allerix struggled to keep his balance. Steadying him with a firm forceful hand, the man pushed a bronze pot up against Allerix's bare thighs and barked, "Empty into this before you piss all over the floor!"

Allerix stood still, despite the pressure threatening to burst his bladder.

"I said piss in the pot!"

He didn't move and said nothing.

The black man lifted his own tunic and pointed inside the vessel with the exaggerated gestures of a teacher instructing an ignorant child. Within a few moments, he drained into the bowl and shoved the container under Allerix's limp prick. "Piss!" Allerix nodded and relaxed his muscles. As his heavy stream splashed into the basin, he leaned against the man's broad shoulder.

"Good. You learned your first word. Now, let's see if you'll eat this stew I saved for you. It'll be cold by now, but it's good."

After he discarded the pot, the man pushed Allerix down to a seated position in the corner and rewrapped the cloak around his naked body. He held up a bowl and stared as Allerix hungrily wolfed down the meal. When he finished, the man wiped the residue off Allerix's mouth and wooly chin with the edge of the cloak and sat back, studying him carefully. After a few moments, the black man shifted his position and spoke.

"I am called Maximus," he said slowly, pointing at his chest. Then he pointed at Allerix. "What is your name?"

Without uttering a sound, Allerix just stared blankly, his heavy-lidded eyes following the exaggerated movements of the man's hands. To his relief, this pathetically confused, bullshit expression was easy to fake. After a couple more tries, the man called Maximus finally tossed his hands up in frustration.

"Shit, you're a thick one. How will I ever figure out your bloody name, Dacian?" Maximus mumbled, as he shuffled backwards and leaned against the wall, rubbing his temples. "All right, let's get some sleep. Dawn will arrive before too long."

Allerix closed his eyes while he tested the rope binding his wrists behind his back.

Lucius Petronius's house on the Quirinal Hill, Rome

• • •

Captivated by Luc's steely blue eyes and his perfect physique, Gaius washed down another piece of roasted duck and studied his dinner companion. Shit, he'd missed this gorgeous fucker and his daft jokes. And that sexy, deep voice. And those incredibly talented hands. It was good to be back in Rome.

Lucius never joined him on campaign anymore. Not that they ever enjoyed any time alone together while in the field, but at least he could watch Luc's bum bounce up and down on those nights when they shagged camp whores in the same room.

"You've already described his face, soldier," Lucius grumbled, reaching down to grab another bite of food. "What about the rest of him?"

"You were at the auction, Luc. You've seen the creature—firm and lean, not too tall or too short, bit on the hairy side, fucking delectable arse." Resting his chin on his fist, Gaius smiled.

"Ah, but what about his mind? Is he clever, like my Bry?" Lucius reached his thick forearm down the length of his thigh and raked his fingers through Bry's honey-brown hair, massaging his scalp vigorously. The slave lifted his chin and moaned softly, pressing his cheek into the side of Luc's leg.

"Hard to say yet. He was still dazed and floppy from the dealer's drugs, those lazy parasites."

Lucius chuckled. "He's bound to be feral."

"True. He'll be untamed and fiery. And yet, I'd wager good coin my Dacian will wind up more disciplined than your pampered Caledonian brat there."

Lucius looked down into Bry's devoted gaze, tossed his head back and laughed. "I'll take that bet. My brilliant Bryaxis is a rare gift from Fortuna."

Propped up on his elbow, Gaius took another sip of wine. Bry's long and perfectly bronzed body, dressed in a skimpy lime green costume, stretched the length of the couch beside his master's legs. A gold band spiraled around his arm above the swell of his defined bicep. Traces of coal rimmed his golden-green eyes.

"Fortuna's gift is getting moldy, Luc. You need to purchase something fresh, you know. This slut of yours must be close to Max's age by now. You should free him, set him up in some sort of trade like I did with Theodorus, and find a younger thing to warm your cock."

Bry narrowed his eyes and bit his lip as Lucius took a long, slow swig and cleared his throat. "Don't be a prick, Gaius. He's mine for as long as I say he's fucking mine. I'll free Bryaxis when I'm damn well ready." Luc took another gulp. "But why did you buy yet another lad? You already have that blond Greek, and your pretty little Simon."

Gaius peered over the lip of his wine cup. "I wanted him. That's fucking why."

"Admit it, Gaius. You're mercurial, always searching for the next shiny thing. That Dacian won't satisfy you for long. They never do. Isn't that right, pet?" Luc pulled Bry's head up by his hair and devoured his pet's mouth with blatant pleasure, pushing his tongue down his throat.

Gaius curled his upper lip in a snarl. "So, Lucius Petronius, your precious, loose-lipped whore here tells me you've been anxious and preoccupied of late. Is that true? Perhaps Aurelia is finally getting on your nerves, eh?"

Lucius chastised Bryaxis with a glare before he spoke, his voice shaky. He was hiding something, something important. Gaius could see the worry on his face.

"There's a curious case of embezzlement. Far too many talents are missing from the imperial coffers." Lucius lowered his voice. "The most likely culprit, in my opinion, is one of those slimy associates of Publius. But the evidence is spotty and Emperor Trajan wants this resolved. Yesterday."

"That's bloody serious, not to mention risky, Luc. You'd best tread carefully."

Lucius leaned forward and cupped Gaius's face in his big palm. "It'll be fine, darling. True, it's a difficult and delicate situation—more so since both our Emperor and our Greekling are involved. But I can handle it. Trust me."

Luc pulled away and conversation stopped. They both finished picking at Euphronia's sumptuous fare on the table, stealing glances at each other and tossing affectionate but strained smiles back and forth.

"I'm leaving," Gaius announced, after finishing another bite.

"I know. You always fucking leave in the morning." Luc huffed, tossing down a half-eaten piece of bread.

"Rome, Luc. I'm leaving the capital tomorrow, at first light. I need to get my Dacian cub down to my villa and begin his training before the triumph celebrations begin at the end of the month." Gaius didn't look up. He couldn't face the hurt he knew he'd see in those hypnotic blue eyes.

Lucius looked down into his cup and mumbled, "Leaving me for your Dacian mongrel, then?"

"Oh, for shit's sake!" Gaius grabbed his lover by his short, dark hair and smothered his mouth with a long, hot kiss. Luc's tongue fought back, wrestling with Gaius's as they held onto each other's shoulders for leverage. Gaius broke the kiss, panting.

"I'm not leaving you, you bleating twit. It won't take long. I'll be back before you even miss me. You've your lovely wife and your slut to keep you entertained in the meantime." He nodded towards Bryaxis. "How about we have that dessert you promised, if you're ready for another round so soon, old man."

With an eyebrow raised, Lucius looked from Gaius to Bry. His expression was a mixture of lust and anger and frustration. "Dessert might assuage my poor, forsaken heart, Commander Fabius. But, I have one condition."

"A condition? Well, spit it out then."

"We enjoy him..." Lucius leaned over and waggled his eyebrows. "Together."

Gaius's leer melted into a grin. "At the same time? It's been a while since we played that game, darling. You'd better prepare him. We wouldn't want to break your precious gift from Fortuna."

"He's already prepared. Isn't that right, pet?"

"Yes, Dominus." Bry smiled nervously, wiggling his hips.

Gaius rolled back and grabbed his prick through the woolen fabric of his fresh tunic. Bum fucking Luc's beautiful whore together was an infrequent but exquisite indulgence. Gaius could already feel himself sliding along Luc's throbbing length while they were both wrapped inside the tight heat of Bry's hole. They'd have to try this sport with the Dacian someday, both of their cocks pounding the round, plump arse of his beautiful new cub. Gaius curled his fingers around his girth and pulled hard.

A deep groan snapped Gaius out of his daydreaming and back to the garden. He looked over at the other couch. Swollen and shiny with spit, Luc's enormous prick slipped out and then back into Bry's wide and talented mouth. The arrogant slave did have one fucking incredible mouth. Gaius would admit that much. Without warning, Lucius pulled Bry off by a fistful of the slave's thick hair.

"Strip and serve up that perfect arse of yours, Bry."

Bryaxis immediately peeled off his skimpy, expensive costume and bent down over the marble server, dishes and scraps of food crashing all over the garden dining floor. He lifted his bare bum, reached back with both hands and spread his cheeks wide and stayed still, panting softly. Gaius cocked his head and gaped when Lucius grabbed hold of a cord and slowly pulled a thick, ribbed leather plug out of Bry's arse. The slave whimpered wantonly while blobs of liquid grease oozed out and dribbled down the backs of his smooth thighs.

"A new toy, counselor?" Gaius raised his brows.

Luc nodded. "Custom made. Not cheap, but no doubt well worth the cost. It's been stretching him nicely since this morning."

"He rose from his knees like a dancer in the vestibule earlier with that fucking monstrosity packed up his arse? I'm bloody impressed."

After tossing aside the plug, Lucius stretched out on his back, pulled up his tented tunic, and wrapped two fingers like a ring around the base of his rock hard erection. "All right, dove. Let's not leave you empty. Climb up here."

Bry rose to his feet and squatted with his back to his master, hovering over Luc's thick shaft. He pressed his hole against the head, and lowered his body down, slowly. He moaned and mewled, delivering a chorus of enchanting guttural noises. When his length was finally buried up to the hilt, Luc grabbed Bry by the hips and held him down.

"Fuck his beautiful sassy mouth, soldier."

Gaius lifted Bry's face with his forefinger. "Someone's master is being a right bossy twat today."

His eyes glazed over, Bryaxis smirked, licked his lips and parted them. After he stood up, Gaius braced Bry's head with one hand and slid his cock down Bry's throat up to his balls until the slut gagged noisily. Gaius almost laughed out loud at his dramatic horseshit choking. After years of swallowing Luc's massive member, Bry could easily handle Gaius's more average-sized equipment.

Bry rode his master's engorged shaft while slurping Gaius's hard prick until two strong hands grabbed the slave by the shoulders and pulled him backwards, slamming his back against Lucius's broad chest. Both Luc and Bry remained still for a moment. The angle was awkward and uncomfortable.

Lucius gasped over Bry's left shoulder. "Gaius, get in him. Hurry."

"Patience, counselor. Get your whore into position." Gaius grabbed a glass bottle of lubricating oil, as Lucius hooked his brawny forearms under Bry's knees and pulled the slave's long legs up to his shoulders, spreading his thighs apart.

"Come on, open nice and wide. That's good, Bry. Relax and enjoy it."

Gaius lubed and stretched the upper curve of the slave's rim, as he rubbed two fingers up and down the swollen vein of Luc's buried cock. He pulled his fingers out, stood up and slathered oil over his shaft. "Breathe in, nice and deep."

Bryaxis wrapped both of his hands around Luc's hefty biceps, let his head fall back and inhaled through his nose. When he exhaled, Gaius plunged into him in one continuous thrust. Gaius felt his balls draw up and shook his head to regain some control. Drops of sweat fell from the tips of his curls and sprinkled over Bry and Luc's faces. He braced himself with his palms against the backs of Bry's upper thighs.

"Ready, love?"

Lucius nodded, and Bry squeezed his eyes shut.

Gaius set the pace, pulling halfway out and then plowing into Bry's packed bum. His hardness rubbed up and down against the sensitive underside of Luc's pulsing shaft as Bry groaned from the excruciating pleasure and the burning pain.

"Easy there, soldier. Don't tear my pet in half."

Gaius bent down, and cupped Luc's sweaty face in his hand. "Let's reward him. I want to feel his tight arse wring us dry."

Luc lifted his head, kissed Gaius's mouth passionately and mumbled, "You're so generous with the boys."

Luc reached down and wrapped his fingers around Bry's prick, while Gaius closed one hand around Bry's long neck and bent down to nibble on his nipples. Bryaxis mewled and squirmed. A few final pulls of Luc's skilled slick fingers brought Bry to the brink and then over the edge, as he exploded into his master's hand. Gaius released his brief chokehold; Bry gulped for air before wailing in ecstasy. As his legs trembled in spasms and his toes curled and clenched, the constricting waves of his orgasm squeezed their encased cocks.

"Fuck, it's tight. I can't hold it," Lucius whimpered against Gaius's lips.

"Let it go. I'm there. Come with me."

In a furious tempo of alternating thrusts, they both cursed and groaned while they unloaded into Bry's quivering body. Sweat and semen and oil covered their bodies, as Luc's desperate sloppy tongue fucking gradually melted into soft kisses.

"Shit, that was brilliant," Lucius stammered, dragging his fingers through his damp, dark hair. Gaius collapsed and nuzzled his face into the crook of Luc's neck, while Luc hummed into his soaked auburn curls and rested his shaking hands on Gaius's shoulders.

With his head pushed to the side, Bry choked back a sob as tears rolled down his sculpted cheeks. "Hey…" Gaius reached over, cradled Bry's face and looked into his wet green eyes. As he wiped Bry's tears away with his thumb, he smiled and whispered, "You're well past your prime, Bryaxis—but, by the gods, you're still a damn amazing piece of arse to fuck."

Bryaxis' glassy eyes crinkled at the corners as he grinned. "So are you, Commander Fabius."

"Why, you cheeky tom. I should fucking cane you for that crack." Gaius squished Bry's face and kissed his puckered, smirking lips before he slid his cock out and pulled him off of Luc. He hauled Bryaxis over to the other couch, lowered him onto the cushions, and smacked his bare bum. After turning around, Gaius flashed his blinding dimpled smile and extended his hand. "Time for that long bath, Counselor Petronius."

"Overdue, I'd argue, soldier." Having pulled himself up to his feet, Lucius walked over to the other couch. He gently re-inserted the lubed plug into Bry's sore bum and covered his shivering pet with a light bedcover.

"You'll sleep here tonight, pet. Leave this beastly thing in for a while to ease the ache, but remove it when you're feeling better. There's no need to wait for my permission. And enjoy some of that leftover wine. Do you understand me, Bryaxis?"

The night sky was eerily still. Even the noisy gulls had long gone to bed. Bry looked up and smiled, his hair a tangled rat's nest and his face lightly streaked with dried tears. "I understand, Dominus. Thank you." Bry's abused bowels began to twist in angry knots; he curled up into a ball and shoved his knuckles in his mouth.

"Hush, Bry. You'll recover by morning. I'm very proud of you. Sleep well." Luc stroked his back and kissed him tenderly on his temple, before he stood up and took Gaius's hand. They flung their damp tunics over their shoulders and headed off to Luc's opulent private bathing suite.

Gnaeus Decius's estate on the Quirinal Hill, Rome

"Wake up, Maximus!"

The familiar bellow echoed from the direction of the hallway connecting the cells in Decius's slave quarters. Max jumped up and rushed out into the windowless corridor. Commander Fabius marched towards him, a small sack slung over his right shoulder. It was just before dawn and most of Decius's servants still slumbered in their cubicles.

"Commander." Max bowed slightly and waited for instructions he knew would fly at break neck speed off of the commander's tongue. He noticed his patron looked rested and well fucked. He should be in a good mood, Max hoped.

"How did you sleep, Max? Decius took care to provide you with a suitable diversion?"

"Yes, Commander. I slept very soundly."

"And the Dacian? Was he trouble?"

"No, sir. He's still weak and disoriented. But he appears healthy and rested quietly through most of the night. The auction drugs left no noticeable damage."

"Excellent. You'll prepare him for travel." Gaius affectionately slapped Max on the shoulder and pulled him down the corridor, away from the cells and out into a poorly lit courtyard. The sun barely peered over the edge of the horizon. Gaius lifted a small glass bottle from the sack and lowered his voice to a hush. "This contains honeyed milk laced with a strong dose of opiate. That should quiet him until we get out of the city. We need to leave Rome without drawing unwarranted notice." He gingerly placed the vial back in the cloth bag and lifted the strap off his shoulder.

"Yes, sir."

Gaius pointed to two burly armed blokes standing off to the side, their heads lowered in deference. "These men are two of my most trusted estate guards here in Rome. Despite our emperor's efforts, there are still rogue bandits attacking travelers along the roads. They will accompany us for the journey down to Campania."

The larger of the two bowed to Max. "It will be our pleasure to serve you, sir." Shocked at their deference, Max took an awkward step back.

Gaius continued to spew orders while he pulled Max over to a waiting wagon. It had a bench seat up front occupied by a squat driver, heavy leather reins resting in his filthy hands. The back of the wagon was a large wooden, box-like structure with a curved roof, a gated window and an arched door at the back. It looked like a small house on wheels.

"Decius has offered me use of this sturdy traveler's wagon with a good team and ample supplies. Carry the boy out when he's fully sedated, keep him shackled and place him inside the compartment, carefully. Blindfold him and latch the cart door when you've finished. My horse is ready, so I'll be waiting for you by the back gate of this estate. To avoid the center of the city, we'll head east on the salt road first and then cut back around south to the Appia."

"Understood, Commander."

Gaius handed over the sack containing several containers of the innocuous but potent sedative liquid and turned to collect his tacked mount, when he hesitated. "Maximus?"

"Yes, sir?"

Gaius turned back around, his brows furrowed. "What's the barbarian's name?"

"Um, his name is—Paulus, sir."

"I don't care what his fucking slave name is, Max! What's his birth name?"

"I don't know yet, Commander. He doesn't speak our language. And he doesn't seem all that bright either, sir."

"So that's your report? He's dumb and dull-witted? I expected more, Max."

"Yes, sir," Max mumbled, casting his eyes down to the brick herringbone pattern of the courtyard floor.

"Well, let's see if our mute little Paulus has the fortitude to survive a long, bumpy ride."

6

The Via Appia, Rome

Several miles south of the city, the supply wagon rolled along the basalt pavers of the Appian Way. With each revolution, the iron wheel treads scraped against the shallow ruts in the road and squeaked in rhythm with the gentle bounce and sway of the compartment. The mid-morning sun beat down mercilessly on the vaulted roof. Shit, it was warm. After he propped himself up on the blankets covering the plank floor, Gaius gnawed his bottom lip and stared down at the Dacian's sweaty, blindfolded face.

"Paulus is an odd name for a slave, but it suits you somehow. Perhaps I'll keep it."

His full lips slightly parted, the Dacian slumbered peacefully on his back, wrists tied above his head to the base of the wagon's frame, ankles still bound together loosely with shackles. He was dressed in an oversized, shit-brown tunic with no belt; Max must have found the ratty sack in the stores of Decius's barracks.

Gaius slowly pulled his ten-inch-long dagger from its sheath and ran the carved ivory handle over the curves of the Dacian's full cheeks, through the bristles of his black beard, and down the length of his sinewy neck. Fast asleep from the opiate, the slave didn't stir. Gaius smiled and leaned down.

"I paid an appalling amount for you, more coin than I'd spent on Max and Nicomedes combined, and then some. No doubt you'll be a defiant and bitter little shit for a while, but I'm tenacious. And I'm very patient. It's in my blood. We Fabii are justly famous for protracting our battles and wearing down our opponents. Victory achieved through strategic attrition. You will eventually surrender willingly, cub. It's only a matter of time."

Gaius wiped his brow and rubbed his eyes before he nestled the lion's paw handle into the hollow above the slave's collarbone. The ornamental knife held so many memories of his first deployment. Had it really been only ten fucking years since he'd served in Numidia? All those days and nights spent far from home at various remote garrisons, making frequent sojourns through the North African deserts to the vast imperial quarries. Maximus had been barely nineteen, a convicted delinquent forsaken by his kinsman and condemned to the brutal marble yards of Simitthus. He'd saved Max from certain death that day. And the brave beautiful fool had saved his life in return.

When the wagon hit a bump in the road, the Dacian rolled his head to the side and mumbled a string of incoherent complaints.

"Time for you to wake up, cub." Gaius pressed the ivory handle against his windpipe; the slave's wrists jerked against the bindings as he coughed and tried to sit up.

"Easy, Paulus. You're safe now, pet. We've left Rome."

Gaius slid the dagger handle over the Dacian's mouth and forced it between his lips.

"By the gods, you have a fucking luscious mouth. Let me have another gander at the rest of my expensive property."

Gaius carefully drew the handle out and reached down to hook the ivory paw under the hem of the slave's baggy tunic, slowly pulling the rough cloth up and over his narrow hips to just below his neck. A patch of black hair filled the dip of the Dacian's breastbone, while another dusting encircled his navel and trailed down to thick black pubic curls framing his flaccid dick. Gaius ran the handle over the slave's dark plump nipples, one at a time; they swelled and hardened. With a satisfied leer, he stroked the Dacian's soft shaft with the underside of the carved paw, pressing more firmly with each lingering pass until the lad's prick responded to the teasing friction.

"Ah, very sensitive and gloriously compliant. Perfect. Let's hear how sweet you sing, Paulus."

The Dacian's breath hitched before he spat, *"Ce vrei de la mine?"*

"Ah, so you do speak. I've never found your barbaric babble very pleasant to the ears, but your voice is lovely. Sonorous and sensual. You want to know what I want from you, cub?"

Gaius rested the dagger on the slave's bare stomach and wrapped his fingers around the Dacian's cock. He rolled his thumb pad over the swollen crown, teasing the slit with languid strokes. The lad arched his back, and a soft guttural groan escaped from between his quivering lips.

"I take what I want, Paulus, and now every inch of you belongs to me. Your moans are delightfully melodic, even more mellifluous than I'd hoped for."

After rolling the Dacian's balls carefully between his fingers, Gaius traced two fingers back and forth across the sensitive skin between his sac and his hole, pausing to rub circles around his rim. "We're headed down to my villa on the coast. You'll like it there. The weather's lovely, and you'll have companions to play with when I give permission. Nicomedes and Simon can be naughty scamps, but they're good lads, really. You'll learn to adore them."

When Gaius pushed the tip of his index finger against his puckered wet ring of muscle, the Dacian gasped before he clenched his jaw, clearly struggling against the urge to cry out.

"I am your master now. Your—what do you call it—your *stăpân*? You will address me as Dominus. I own you. You are mine, mine to protect and cherish and defile. Mine alone. Now, tell me your name, Dacian—your birth name."

After a long pause, Gaius removed his hand from between the boy's firm sweaty cheeks and picked up his dagger. He lightly rubbed the cool flat of the steel blade over the sensitive peaks of the slave's hard nipples until the boy squirmed against the restraints and whimpered in frustration.

"I confess I'm soft when it comes to punishing my boys. But discipline is necessary—and obedience is an absolute." Gaius snatched a fistful of dark hair and pressed the blade against the barbarian's exposed throat.

"Sadly, I'd never managed to become fluent in your language, but I picked up a few words here and there during the wars." Gaius tightened his grip and growled, "*Spune-mi numele tau.* I will not ask again so nicely."

The Dacian took a deep breath and parted his lips, when the wagon suddenly lurched to a halt.

"Why the fuck did we stop?" Gaius impaled the sharp point of the knife into a floor plank, inches from his new slave's perspiring face.

"Commander, come quick!"

With annoyed grunts, Gaius scooted to the front of the wagon compartment and pulled open the shutter of the small square window. "This had better be bloody important, Maximus!"

"Look, sir—ahead!"

They'd left behind the tracts of denser woodlands and reached the summit of a hill. From up on high, an expansive view of the surrounding verdant landscape opened up all around them. Down the paved road, several miles to the south, a large group of men on horseback were headed in their direction.

Gaius squinted into the blinding sunshine. "Twenty, perhaps twenty-five riders, by my count."

"Who are they, Commander?"

Flashes of light reflected off the group's metal trappings and polished armor. Near the front of the throng, surrounded by riders carrying long bundles of bound rods, a man wearing a vibrant purple cloak sat tall astride a dappled grey charger.

"Shit, they're carrying the imperial fasces. It's the emperor. Max, tell the guards to bring my horse around to the back door." After slamming the shutter closed, Gaius wrenched his dagger out of the floor, sheathed it, and shoved his weapon beneath the strap wrapped around his chest. He covered the Dacian's body with the ragged tunic and gently carded his fingers through the lad's thick disheveled hair.

"*Stai liniștit sau ești mort.* Do you understand my pathetic garble or do I need to gag you?"

The Dacian gritted his teeth and complied with a nod. "*Liniștit.*"

"Good. You're a smart pup. Stay quiet, *cățel.*" Gains kissed the tip of his nose as he ran his fingers over the soft mounds of the slave's lips. "We'll continue our playtime later, my pretty Paulus."

~

As the rapid clatter of hooves faded away, the wooden wagon door slammed shut and a metal bolt locked with a sharp click. Allerix pulled on the ropes, testing the strength of the bindings around his wrists. They were tight and unyielding.

He collapsed and cursed under his breath, "Fuck you, you savage son of a bitch."

~

Even after some twenty years, the imposing sight of his childhood guardian still threw him off kilter. Although Marcus was much older now, a few years past fifty, his natural aura of authority was dazzling. Marcus Ulpius Traianus was perfect, in an impressively imperfect way—a larger than life but sensible man whom Gaius coveted to imitate, success after glorious success. But the great man had also taught young Gaius other lessons long ago—when best to surrender, and what Gaius would have to endure to navigate the treacherous waters of the imperial court. He idolized his mentor; he despised the prick. It was complicated.

"My most warm greetings, Emperor." Gaius bowed his head, pulling back on the reins to steady his excited, sweaty horse pawing at the ground and snorting wet globs of mucus.

As he narrowed his brown eyes set deep below his prominent brow, Marcus kicked his enormous steed forward through the wall of attendants until he was alongside his former ward. "What are you doing down here, Gaius? You're supposed to be joining us in Rome."

"Yes, sir. I'm on a brief trip to transport much needed supplies down to Campania."

Marcus raised a thick eyebrow. "What sort of precious cargo requires the personal escort of my second in command?"

"Imported fabrics, some weapons, and farming equipment for the harvest, Father. I will return to the capital shortly and pay the court a long overdue visit." Gaius blinked and dropped his gaze. He still couldn't look Marcus directly in the eyes when he lied to him.

"Nonsense. You have my permission to send your supply wagon down to your villa. But you, Gaius Fabius, are returning to Rome. You'll accompany me for the journey. We've spent far too little time together lately, and I need your assistance with some preliminary matters concerning my construction projects in the capital."

Gaius glanced at the distant wagon and swallowed. "Yes, sir."

"Come." Marcus tapped his horse forward to a slow walk. "Tell me all about your latest adventures. I'm forced these days to live vicariously through you and Publius, and his debauched escapades are a tad predictable and tedious. How I wish we were still on campaign together, you and I, smiting the barbarian hoard. Peace is such a fucking bloody bore."

As they neared the supply wagon, Gaius asked, "May I deliver instructions to them for the journey, sir?"

"You may. By the gods, is that your Ethiopian sitting next to the driver?" Marcus tilted his head towards the bench.

"Yes, that's Maximus. I granted him conditional freedom shortly after I returned from Dacia, sir. He's been my devoted servant ever since I served as your tribune in Numidia, and I expect he'll be a trustworthy client for the remainder of his days."

"It's wise to reward loyalty, Gaius. I've taught you well. Your pretty lad certainly has grown into an impressive hulk of a man."

When the imperial entourage reached the wagon, Max climbed down off the seat and bowed low to the ground before the emperor. He held his respectful, suppliant posture until Marcus addressed him. "Greetings, freedman of Gaius Fabius Rufus. You may rise."

"Greetings, our most esteemed Emperor Trajan. It is a great honor to be in your presence, sir," Max spoke with perfect tone and diction, a far cry from the heavily accented, choppy slang he spewed a decade ago. Gaius grinned with pride as he nudged his horse forward.

"Maximus, Emperor Trajan has kindly granted permission for you and the guards to transport the supplies down to the villa. I am returning to the capital. Be sure to safeguard my property and store it properly when you reach my estate."

"Yes, Commander. Do you wish me to manage anything in particular during your absence?" His head cocked to one side, Max stared wide-eyed and hopeful. "Perhaps Nicomedes' situation, sir?"

Gaius narrowed his gaze. "Simply see my new purchases are secured with care and protected from damage. Have Simon assist you. I'll dispatch further instructions shortly. Do you understand, Maximus?"

Max clasped his hands behind his back and lowered his chin. "Yes, Commander. We will await your orders, sir."

"Have a pleasant and uneventful journey, Max."

~

The imperial residence on the Palatine Hill, Rome

Surrounded by lush formal gardens and the green canopies of tall stone pine trees, the grand imperial palace stood on the summit of the sacred Palatine, high above the stench and disease infesting the lower quarters of the capital during the oppressive summer months. Here in a private apartment on the southern side of the hilltop residence, reflections of ornate furniture, sumptuous woven fabrics, and gilded candelabra bounced off the polished marble walls. The cavernous space glowed in ethereal hues of crimson and gold.

Restless as a caged tiger, the emperor shifted his weight on a high, cushioned stool by one of the large windows. The heavy purple curtains were pulled aside, permitting just the right amount of late afternoon sunlight to illuminate Marcus's robust aquiline features. Down in the valley below, the sandy arena of the enormous chariot-racing track was quiet. The seats of the Circus Maximus were empty today. Races would not be held again for another fortnight, not until the opening ceremonies for the triumphal games.

"Aren't you finished with that bloody damn thing yet? My arse is getting sore!" the emperor hollered in his commanding bass voice. A few feet away, an artist's fingers shaped a chunk of reddish clay on a table, an assortment of metal carving tools at the ready.

"Almost done, Emperor Trajan. Just need to get your nose right. A bit more of a curve here on the bridge, I think. Just—one—more—moment."

"Rubbish! I'm finished, and so are you, maestro."

"Only a few more moments, sir. I implore you. We need the model finished in time for the bronze casters at the foundry. Your victory celebrations are less than twelve days away, sir."

"The sculptor's right, you know. The magistrates have already set up the statue bases for your triumphal parade. They're expecting a new image for the festivities, not that your face ever ages in those portraits. You could just as easily recycle last year's model, sir," Gaius interjected, chuckling. After he readjusted the heavy folds of the cloth draped over his arm, he walked over to the window and bowed. "Greetings, Emperor."

Marcus grinned from ear to ear. "Gaius, my boy, you've come to my rescue! I knew you were my favorite son for a reason. Yes, last year's portrait model would work splendidly. Reusing it would save me the tiresome ordeal of sitting here all afternoon doing fucking nothing. He can just rearrange my hair a bit or change something else trivial so the traditionalists in the Senate won't know I've reneged on my duties." Marcus laughed and rose to his feet as he wrapped his arm around Gaius's shoulders. The emperor leaned in close to his ear. "And besides, who wants to age? I thought I was rather dashing in my mid-forties. Didn't you think so? Or perhaps you preferred me in my lusty, youthful thirties?"

Gaius forced an unenthusiastic smile. "Be mindful, sir. The gods disapprove of vanity." He fidgeted with his toga folds and winked cheekily, before stepping away. Still taller by a head, Marcus grabbed Gaius by the bicep and pulled him closer. In the background, the dejected sculptor scurried about, wrapping up the clay and collecting his tools.

"Never fear the gods, Gaius Fabius. They've stood beside us, victory after victory. Don't ever forget mighty Jove has blessed us with his divine favor. And don't forget that I, your most generous Emperor, promoted you through the ranks and taught you how to be a successful and respected leader of our troops. And, lest you forget, I was the one who protected you and your mother after your father's senseless death at the hands of that madman, Domitian."

Marcus moved closer and lowered his face, practically brushing his lips across Gaius's mouth. His breath reeked of sour wine and garlic. "Don't ever forget it was me, your beloved sovereign, who taught you how to be a man, my sweet boy."

His nostrils flared, Gaius pursed his lips and looked to the floor. As much as he'd tried all these years, he could never forget the months following his father's murder. He would always remember that terrifying trip to promised sanctuary in that distant province with little more than the clothes on his twelve-year-old back—and that fateful day when his mother gladly handed guardianship of him to a complete fucking stranger. He was handed over to a frightening monster with callused and lecherous hands.

Gaius raised his eyes and clenched his fists. "I will never forget, Dominus."

"Good. Those were important lessons, you know. I made you who you are." Marcus kissed his forehead. "Come, I want to show you the latest designs for my new forum."

He pulled Gaius over to a large oak table with papyrus scrolls half-unrolled strewn over its smooth golden brown surface. "Apollodorus has added some extraordinary details. The man's a fucking genius!"

"You heard that, Commander Fabius. You'll testify as my witness the next time Aelius Hadrianus questions my abilities." As Apollodorus swept into the room, his reddish-orange and blue robes swirling around his slight frame; the brightly colored fabrics contrasted handsomely against his dark olive skin and cropped beard. His fingertips were stained from draughtsman's ink.

With a joyful grin, he bowed. "Greetings, Emperor Trajan and Commander Fabius."

"Apollodorus, what fortuitous timing! Show Gaius the changes you've made to the porticos. Those statues of humiliated captive Dacian beasts are bloody magnificent. And, by the gods, he's created this triumphal column,

Gaius—well, you just have to see the drawings. Apollodorus has outdone himself. We knew he was a clever engineer, but who knew our Greek associate here was such an innovative designer?"

Gaius pulled out of Marcus's grasp, rushed over and hugged the architect in a tight emotional embrace. He spoke softly into Apollodorus' ear, "Appy, my old friend. I'd heard you were in Rome." Gaius's voice cracked and his arms refused to loosen their grip.

"My dear Gaius Fabius." Gaius was shaking. Apollodorus pulled him in closer and whispered, "Is everything all right, sir?"

After one more affectionate squeeze, Gaius placed one hand on Apollodorus' shoulder and stepped back. As he wiped at his wet eyes, he flashed a forced smile. "Things are as they've always been. Shit, but it's bloody good to see you. Publius said you were staying here at the palace. For how long?"

Two attendants bowed and entered the chamber, carrying armfuls of scrolls threatening to spill out of their grasp and onto the floor. Marcus grunted and waved them over to the desk.

"I'm a guest here at our emperor's pleasure. I'll be in Rome until we all leave for the next war, I suppose." Apollodorus grinned, and squeezed Gaius's left forearm. "I am surprised to see you here, though. I ran into Lucius Petronius this morning, and he told me you'd left the capital for Campania."

"My trip south was interrupted," Gaius replied, his voice low and his jaw tight. "My dear guardian had decided my presence was required at the court."

Apollodorus cupped Gaius's face in his hands and smiled. "Well, allow me to be selfish and say I'm delighted our Emperor thwarted your plans. You'll accompany Helen and me to dinner tonight. Our host says it will be an intimate group, lots of laughs. I won't take no for an answer, sir."

"Cocky as ever, I see. It would be my pleasure to flirt shamelessly with your enchanting wife, Appy."

"Ha, wonderful! Should I invite Publius Aelius Hadrianus to join us as well?" Apollodorus lifted an eyebrow and smirked.

Gaius pulled his face out of Apollodorus' hands and dropped his sarcastic smile for a hard, sober glare. "Invite him and I swear I'll never fucking dine with you again, engineer."

"Hey, you two love birds—get over here!" Marcus tapped an unrolled scroll with his pointer finger, a confused scowl twisting his face as he scratched his ear. "Explain these new changes, Apollodorus. I swear just when I think I've finally grasped what you're doing, you bloody alter the design again."

Apollodorus grabbed Gaius by the elbow and winked. "Come, let me show you the forum plans. The damn thing is over the top and blatantly megalomaniacal, just the way you Romans like your memorials."

7

Gaius Fabius's seaside villa, Campania

ALLERIX BENT DOWN AND PLACED THE DISH ON THE FLOOR. THAT MEAL HE'D just wolfed down had tasted better than anything he'd eaten in a long time; only a scattering of breadcrumbs and tiny slivers of cheese were left on the red ceramic platter. He'd almost licked it clean but stopped himself. He smiled, his eyes glassy with tears, as he envisioned his beloved tutor, Istros, tugging his long grey beard while wagging a bony, crooked finger. *"Stop that, Allerix! Princes do not lick food scraps off plates like common mongrels."*

Allerix wiped his face with his forearm, and hoped somewhere Gorgas was eating decent fare, assuming the idiot was still alive. He'd dreamt about the boy last night, recklessly racing ahead, with his bobbing tangle of rich brown hair and that wide toothy smile, galloping right into the enemy's hands. The soldiers yanked both of them right off their fucking horses. If the bastards had known any mercy, they would have killed him and Gorgas right there in the grass.

He swallowed a gulp of water and rolled his shoulders, trying to forget, trying to focus on something less painful, like his brutally sore muscles. It was damn near impossible to massage his shoulders with his hands bound together, but he found a bit of temporary relief when he raised his arms and looped his shackled wrists behind his stiff neck.

For most of that endless, bouncy wagon ride along paved roads and dirt paths, he'd been flat on his back, wrists tied to the floor of the stuffy covered compartment. Twice a day, that man named Maximus had fed him; twice a day, he'd allowed Allerix to relieve himself in a chamber pot. Allerix counted five times they'd stopped for the night. Each time, two men had chatted outside the wagon's back door about the weather, women, and the public baths, whatever those were, in some place called Neapolis. They never mentioned that Roman fiend, the monster who'd ordered the slaughter of his kinsmen, of his friends—of his brave and handsome Brasus.

Allerix lifted the cup up to his lips again, and choked back a sob as he sipped another drink of cool water.

There was no point in crying any more.

They were all dead now—his cousins, his mates…

Brasus.

They'd all gone on to the afterlife, leaving him behind to face the humiliation of defeat alone.

When the wagon had stopped late last night, the pungent sweet stench of horse manure hung heavy in the air. Maximus carried him to a small room on the upper floor of a building next to the stables. Carefully, he'd deposited Allerix on a cushioned bed, removed his blindfold, and secured the chain attached to the shackles binding his ankles to the sturdy bronze frame.

Daybreak had brought bright sunshine, and the piercing cries of sea birds, and that plateful of delicious food on the floor by the couch. The only window in the room faced a vast expanse of crystal clear water. Through the metal window grates, the blue-green shimmering surface crested here and there, dipped and finally crashed against a rocky cliff. He'd heard tales of the enemy's great sea to the south, but Allerix never expected this. Back home, lakes were small, dark, and mysterious. And they didn't fucking move. Lulled by the sounds of the battering surf, Allerix closed his eyes and inhaled the fresh salty air. It was so different here, wherever here was.

So odd, and yet so strangely enchanting.

Peaceful.

"Greetings."

A young man stood by the doorway, dressed in a thin, creamy-pale tunic cinched with a wide leather belt. The pretty lad was shorter than Allerix by a hand and looked to be couple of years younger—nineteen, maybe eighteen. He had a similar build, lithe but nicely muscled.

"I'm Simon," he said in a soft voice, as he took a couple of tentative steps forward.

A thick quiff of honey-brown curls dangled just above Simon's emerald green eyes. His face was sun-kissed, a faint sprinkle of freckles above his cheeks, his features strong and perfectly proportioned. He was too damn beautiful for a boy.

"I see you've finished all of your first meal. Plautus is a good cook, isn't he? Bit of a stodgy old grouch, but he bakes the best bread I've ever eaten. Not that I leave our villa much."

Allerix relaxed and tilted his head, as he tried to appear bemused and ignorant. This fetching lad carried no weapon and seemed harmless enough. He reminded Allerix of Gorgas.

Rolling his eyes, Simon pressed his palm to his forehead. "Shit, I'm daft. You can't understand a word I'm saying, can you? Well, that's why I'm here." Simon walked over, plopped down on the bed and sat cross-legged next to Allerix. The brunet leaned back against the wall, resting his hands on his knees, and stared at Allerix's face.

"You have amazing eyes—they're like an owl's eyes—with those big droopy eyelids and those long feathery lashes." When Simon reached out to touch his face, Allerix made a low noise in the back of his throat and pulled back.

"Hush, I won't hurt you. You are called Paulus. *Pau-lus,* understand? I am Simon. Max—you know Max, right? He was Dom's favorite for a long, long time. He's been freed, and now I'm Dom's favorite. Everything's a bit upside down and confusing lately." Simon raked his fingers through his thick hair and scratched his scalp.

"Anyway, what was I saying? Oh, right. Well, Max—who, by the gods, has the biggest fucking prick you've ever seen—sent me here to teach you how to talk. Dom had me schooled properly when I was a boy, so I can read and write both languages, although my Greek is spotty. Sometimes I get to copy Dom's correspondence and read stories to him." Simon leaned forward and rested his chin in his palm. He blew a rogue curl out of his seductive eyes and pointed to Allerix's wrists.

"Do those shackles hurt? Those are called *sha-ckles*." Simon rubbed one of the embossed golden bracelets adorning his own wrists and grimaced dramatically. "Do they hurt? The *sha-ckles*?"

Allerix looked down at the heavy iron bands binding his hands together with a few inches of chain. He lifted them from his lap and shook his head back and forth.

"Good gods, you understood me, didn't you?" Simon clapped his hands softly and brought his fingers up, pressing the tips against his rosy lower lip. "That's wonderful! I taught you some words, didn't I? Max said I'd make a fabulous teacher."

"Should we petition the town council to erect a statue of Pedagogue Simon, Tutor of Bearded Barbarians? Would you prefer it stood in the forum or the gymnasium, oh great learned twat?"

Allerix looked over at the doorway and his breath caught in his chest. Wearing a wicked grin on his handsome face, a man leaned against the jamb, his sculpted arms crossed high and haughty. Crinkles framed the corners of his tapered eyes, eyes that sparkled bright like blue stars against his bronzed skin.

Simon jutted his chin out and pointed. "And this, Paulus, this shit head is Nicomedes. He's a cunt."

Simon made a smooching noise and blew a kiss at the striking man. With a sultry infectious laugh, Nicomedes cupped his balls through his dark green tunic with one hand and made a gesture with the other. Allerix didn't recognize the two-fingered motion but he could guess its obscene meaning.

After he tossed his long, wavy blond hair back, Nicomedes strode over to the window and sat down on the wide stone sill. "Simon, are you sure he's to be a cock warmer? I mean, really—look at him. Our Dom couldn't possibly want to fuck this hairy, illiterate cur."

Simon shrugged. "Max says he's a Dacian."

"No shit! A Dacian?" Nic sprang up and squatted in front of Allerix, peering at his face with skeptical, wary eyes. "I thought they killed all those crazy savages in the last war. So he doesn't understand what we're saying then?"

"Max doesn't think so. That's why he's put me in charge of teaching Paulus some basic words."

Nicomedes cocked a brow and cautiously extended his left hand to touch Allerix's ebony beard. "Well, that should be simple enough. Once furry face here understands—let me count—*strip, kneel, cock, suck, down on all fours,* and *bend over,* he should be all set, right?"

When Allerix jerked out of reach, Nicomedes lost his balance and toppled back on his sandal-clad heels. He cursed and winced, sucking air in between his clenched teeth.

"Shit, Nic. Are you all right?" Simon asked.

"I'm fucking fine, twerp. No! Get away. I don't need your useless sympathy."

Simon rolled his eyes and huffed. "Whatever. Be a bastard, but I know that hurt. I was just trying to help. See, Paulus—he is a cunt." Simon leaned down, pursed his lips and cooed, "But we love him just the same. Don't we, lamb? That's what Dom calls Nic—his naughty lamb."

"You obnoxious, adorable little—" After he rolled back up onto his knees, Nic reached up and cupped Simon's face, and kissed him passionately on the mouth. The younger slave smiled, parted his lips and returned the wet, frenzied caress. As their tongues darted and twirled in a sensual dance, fingers tangled in each other's hair, Allerix felt blood rushing to his groin. He rubbed his palms against the fabric covering his cock and lost himself in the lovely friction.

Sneaking a peek out of the corner of his eye, Nic chuckled into Simon's mouth. "Our Dacian here's a watcher."

Allerix froze. Within two breaths, his pale neck and creamy-white cheeks flushed to a splotchy pattern of rose and crimson. He yanked his bound hands off his engorged shaft and looked away.

"S'all right, Paulus. You can watch us." Simon giggled. He wiggled his right arm out of Nic's lusty grasp and pushed Allerix's shackled hands back down to his crotch. "Go on, touch yourself. Dom fancies that. And he fucking loves when his boys blush all pink and warm like you're doing."

"And, if you're lucky, he'll spank your arse cheeks red hot before he pounds you." Nic snorted, tilted his head and traced a lazy line with the tip of his shiny talented tongue from Simon's shoulder up to his jaw, up over his cheeks and back down to the boy's supple mouth. Allerix couldn't keep from staring. They were so beautiful, the way they kissed deep and heated without fear, without any hesitation or shame. They were spectacular and fucking mesmerizing. Without thinking, Allerix stroked his shaft again through his tunic.

Simon closed his eyes and grinned, as Nicomedes spider-walked his fingers up the inside of his thigh. "Let me swallow you, Simon. Right here. Let's give the lad a real show."

"Nic..."

"Come the fuck on, twat. I haven't had cock in years. Be a good sport."

Laughing and shaking his head, Simon shoved Nicomedes off him and pushed the blond down to the floor. "No fucking way, Nic. And don't exaggerate. It's only been a couple of months, not years. You, my naughty friend, are up to your balls in trouble as it is for breaking Dom's rules. No blowjobs without permission, remember? Now, if you're offering a hand job—"

"Simon! What's going on here? I gave you clear and simple directions, pup." Max marched in and jerked Nic to his feet by the collar of his tunic. "And who, on earth, gave you approval to come in here?"

"I just wanted to see Dom's new whore, sir. No harm done." With an apologetic smirk, Nic ducked as he half-heartedly tried to pull away.

"You're a bloody distraction, slut." Max brushed his lips along the curve of Nic's ear shell. "Get your gorgeous rump out to the exercise yard and do something useful. I need this Dacian mongrel to understand the commander's orders as soon as possible."

"When's Dom coming home?" Simon looked up, his green eyes wide and yearning, while Max smacked Nic's bum and shoved him out of the room. Nicomedes stopped just outside the doorway and dawdled within earshot.

As he rubbed his knotted brow with his thumb and middle finger, Max sighed. "I don't know, Simon. We should get word from Rome in a few days. Until then, quit larking about and teach this savage our language. After I tend to a few chores, I'll be back to take him for a wash." Max eyed Allerix with disgust. "I expect you fucking stink by now, don't you?"

Simon crinkled up his nose and pinched his nostrils. "Yeah, he's a bit, um, ripe. Can I help?"

"Focus, Simon. One task at a time."

Simon lowered his chin and mumbled, "Yes, Max."

When Max had left the room, Simon turned to Allerix and rubbed his palms together. "So, Paulus. What should we try next? Some words for colors, perhaps?"

~

MAX TURNED THE KEY AND PULLED OPEN THE HEAVY PINE DOORS OF THE TALL cupboard standing against the far wall of the commander's office. He lifted the top off the supply box he'd placed on a nearby table and removed the expensive objects from the cushioned layers of black fabric, one at a time. Three new acquisitions from Rome this trip: a bronze scabbard from Syria, a long heavy Germanic sword, and a shorter Celtic dagger with a handle shaped like a sea monster's head.

After he placed the rare scabbard on the top shelf of the storage chest, he noticed it. Affixed high on the back of the storage rack, the two-handed Dacian falx took pride of place in the commander's collection. Gaius Fabius had been awarded the exotic curved weapon by the emperor; the blade was a priceless trophy acknowledging the commander's valor during the first war. At one point it had belonged, so the rumor went, to the supreme and now very dead Dacian king. Max studied the bizarre instrument and shrugged. As far as he was concerned, the falx resembled an ordinary farmer's sickle.

"When did you get back?"

Max wasn't surprised he hadn't heard her enter Dom's office. She moved about the villa quietly, her footsteps softer than a cobra's hiss just before the lethal strike. As always, she wore a gauzy silk dress that hugged the curves of her breasts and hips before it flowed down in sheer waves of fabric to the floor. Dom's old whore strolled about the villa with the haughty attitude of an untouchable Vestal.

"Last night. Late. Atticus reports all has been blissfully dull down here. Is that true, Callidora?"

"There's been no trouble I'm aware of. Of course, the boys aren't my responsibility, are they?" Callidora sashayed over to the cabinet and gingerly picked up the scabbard, turning it over to inspect the intricate inlay designs.

Max took two steps towards her, his arms crossed over his broad chest. "Simon's your own damn son, or have you forgotten?"

"Simon was my child, Maximus—was. Past tense. Just as you were once Dom's favorite plaything before you grew too old and predictable. Our roles in this charade are in constant flux, my dear boy, apt to morph before we even realize what's happening. Tell me, did you enjoy your brief time in Rome?" Callidora lifted the Celtic weapon off the second shelf and pointed the dagger at Max's chest. "I see Dominus accumulated more precious war crap."

"Rome was sweltering." Max swallowed before he dropped his voice. "I saw Theo. You do remember him, right? Simon's father."

Slow and deliberate, Calli placed the knife back on the cupboard shelf. She walked up to Max, stood up on her toes and peered into his eyes. "How is my sweet and meek breeder these days? I'd heard rumor he took a young wife."

"Perhaps. He didn't mention a wife. But he seemed to be faring well, as well as can be expected. Theo runs a shoe shop for Dom. Profits are good. The commander was pleased."

"That's lovely. Our timid mouse deserves the pretense of happiness." She chuckled.

Max's hands tightened into fists. "What Theo deserved was to live his days out here at the villa with the family. You had no right to have him sent away."

"I did no such thing! Dominus asked for my opinion on the situation, and I was honest. It would have killed Theo to see Simon promoted to Dom's favorite, to see his son replace you in our master's bed. Theodorus became too attached to the boy. He had to go. It was best for Simon, and for Dominus."

"You are so bloody full of shit. You wanted him out of the way, out of your sight. So you fucking manipulated and harangued Dom until Theo was gone."

Calli waved her hand and yawned. "That's all in the past, Maximus. No one is irreplaceable. No one is safe from the whims of the Fates."

"Unlike you, however, Theo and I are now safe from the slave auction block."

Callidora's red-stained lips twisted with twitches of bitterness. She flicked one side of her long brown hair over her shoulder, pushed a few stray strands behind her ear, and cleared her throat. "There's word there is a new pet at the stable house. A barbarian."

"Dom bought a new slave. A Dacian."

"Well, well… it seems Nicomedes' days are numbered. Dom will never free him, not after that idiotic stunt he pulled. He'll sell Nicomedes to a brothel in Neapolis, I expect. The slut's tattered hole might fetch twenty pieces of silver, tops. Atticus can buy a fattened hog for the coming harvest festivities with the coin. Seems a fair trade, don't you think? Nic's used arse for a juicy swine?"

Every fiber in Max's body twitched in fury. "Watch it, Callidora. Nicomedes has endured enough suffering already."

She gulped and shook her trembling pointer finger. "Don't you dare threaten me, savage."

He slapped her face hard and shouted, "I am a freed man now, slave!" She fell backwards, tripping on the folds of her long dress, a thin trail of blood trickling down the side of her mouth.

Max folded his brawny arms and grinned, looking down his nose into her defiant eyes. "Your charms have withered, woman. Dom will sell you soon, and while Theo enjoys his new status and perhaps even a loving wife, you will die a slave. That's *your* fate."

After she wiped her split lip with the back of her hand and spat on the floor by his feet, Max grabbed her by the arm and pulled her up. "Be disrespectful to me again, and this free savage will whip your slave hide raw, with Dom's blessing no less. I'll do it out in the courtyard so the stable hands and field laborers can enjoy the show. Where Nicomedes can watch. And Simon. Now, get out of my sight, you fucking callous hag."

Callidora snarled through her teeth, "Yes, sir."

She bowed curtly, before lifting the hem of her long dress. As she shuffled backwards out of the office, she chanted a silent curse under her breath.

~

JUST WHEN IT SEEMED THE DACIAN MIGHT ACTUALLY DROWN, MAX YANKED HIS head up out of the bath. Struggling against the bindings tying his wrists and ankles, the slave opened his eyes wide, coughed and sputtered before gasping for air. Waves of hot, turbid water splashed over the sides of the deep pool. Max tightened his grip around a large clump of the Dacian's sopping black hair and pushed him under the surface again before pulling him up one last time.

"There, that should kill most of the lice. I'd fucking cut it all off if I had a choice, but the commander prefers long hair on his pets."

Max did not enjoy this, not one bit. In all his years, he'd never had to bathe a foul-smelling, wooly barbarian. Sure, he'd bathed and fucked Nicomedes, and Simon, in the more opulent private baths of the main villa house for Dom's viewing pleasure, but that was entertaining for everyone involved. Never before had he been forced to wash a full-grown, shackled heathen. It was sloppy and time-consuming. Here in the modest, sparsely decorated bathing room of the stable house, he was a soaked wet nurse. At least he didn't have to flush the Dacian's bum plumbing. Not yet.

"Simon, hand me that reed scrubber... no, not the oil scraper, boy—the one next to it hanging on the ring."

As Simon placed the bristled tool in Max's huge, outstretched palm, he asked, "Are you going to shave his face, sir?"

"Not without orders, Simon. Greek fashions are becoming more popular with Romans lately. There's a chance—a slim one, mind you—the commander fancies his whiskers." Max pinched a clump of the Dacian's beard and rubbed it between his fingers. "His beard is so much softer than I'd imagined."

"Can I touch? Oh, that is soft, like fine sheep's wool. Hey, if Dom likes whiskers, why has he never allowed me or Nic to grow a beard? And you've never had—"

"Simon." Max smirked as he rolled his eyes. "Get in the water and help me reposition him. Between the bath oils and his furry limbs, this mongrel's as slippery as a squid."

Simon stripped off his tunic and gracefully stepped into the water to straighten the Dacian's folded legs. Once they were rearranged, Max wrapped his arms tightly around the barbarian's narrow waist, lifted him up and dropped his round bum down onto his lap.

"Zeii mei!"

Max mumbled into the Dacian's right ear, "I have no fucking clue what you just said, but that is my very large and now very hard cock jammed between your plump cheeks."

As he knelt down to wash the slave's slender calves, Simon threw back his head of curls and laughed. "Oh, it's hard to miss that colossus, Max. Uh—I mean, sir."

Max winked. "Settle down, pup."

The Dacian's entire body tensed up as tight as a coiled snake when Max gently swirled the scrubber over his chest and down his abdomen to his lean thighs.

Max paused, and placed the instrument on the tiled ledge. "Listen, I'm not allowed to stick my huge cock up your little virgin arse. You are Commander Fabius's property. None of us, including me, can fuck you without his permission, so bloody relax. I'm going to clean your wee barbarian balls now. Simon, pass me that rag."

"He's a virgin?" Simon's jaw dropped, the corners of his lips upturned in delight.

As he ran the washing cloth over the Dacian's squishy sac, Max lifted an eyebrow and lowered his chin. "Well, that was what the slave dealer claimed, Simon. But I'm not convinced of it." Max's experienced hand stroked the lad's prick under the water until it twitched and stiffened. "And truth be told, Dacian, I'm not all that convinced you don't understand more of what we're saying than you're letting on."

"Do you really think he understands us? Well, I have taught him about thirty words today, sir. Perhaps he's just bright, a quick learner and all."

"Let's hope so. Dom paid a fucking fortune for this alleged virgin, thanks to Counselor Petronius. And, as we know, the commander has no patience for stupidity."

"Or disobedience," Simon added in his softest voice, before asking, "But I'm confused, sir. What does Counselor Petronius have to do with his price?"

"The auction was—um, a bit odd. It's a long story, Simon." Max turned and studied the Dacian's profile. He ran his fingertip down the gentle slope of his small, perky nose. "Now that I've a closer look at him, he is a pretty thing, isn't he? Underneath all that hair, I mean."

"He's, well—different, you know. He's sort of exotic. Not at all Greek like me and Nic. He's more like you, Max. He's unusual. Special."

His face blank, Max stared at Simon for a few moments in silence. He slowly closed his eyes and swallowed as he nodded. Shit, Callidora was wrong—this cub wasn't purchased to replace Nicomedes. How the fuck had he not realized it earlier?

Max snapped his eyes open, cleared his throat, and barked in a brusque tone, "All right, we're done here. We can't sit in the fucking bath all day. Let's get this one back to his room and finish up our chores before our meal."

"Did I say something wrong, sir?"

"You're honest, Simon. Brutally honest sometimes, but that's an honorable trait."

Simon grinned and ducked his head. "No one's ever called me honorable before. Thank you, sir."

Max reached over and ruffled Simon's damp curls. He would never tell Simon how much and how often he reminded him of Theodorus. There was no point, and it hurt enough just thinking those thoughts, let alone saying the words out loud. Theo was gone. He pulled Simon forward by his hair and kissed him on the forehead. "We all love you, sweetheart."

"Plautus doesn't. He fucking hates me, Max."

Max laughed as he wiped his eyes. "That old curmudgeon of a cook hates everyone, pup. Always has."

When he glanced over at the Dacian, Max swore he saw the barbarian flash a slight smirk.

8

The Circus Maximus, Rome

"CAN'T YOU SEE IT'S A TRAP?"

A strong gust blew from the south and whipped the crimson canopy shading the imperial box. The heavy fabric flapped violently like a ship's sail in a storm. Gaius leaned forward and wrapped his fingers around the bronze railing. With a groan, he dragged his other hand through his spiraling amber curls.

"Don't let those bastards crowd you, idiot!" He threw his hands up and slammed against the back of his seat in frustration. "It's a fucking ambush."

For most of the seven laps, four chariots had been out front, jostling for the lead. They flew by, charging down the circus track at full gallop, kicking up the fine sand. The three chariots of the Blue faction had maneuvered into position. They tightened ranks and pushed their outnumbered rival close to the high wall splitting the wide elliptical course into two broad lanes.

"Gaius, what on earth are they doing to that charioteer?" she asked calmly, though he detected concern in her voice.

"Swarming the poor fool—it's a dirty tactic but effective," he answered out of the corner of his mouth while he kept his eyes fixed on the race. As the Blue chariots closed in for the kill, Gaius shook his head. He'd always had a weak spot for underdogs.

The three Blues slammed their opponent's two-wheeled vehicle into the stone partition, and then rammed it again, as they struck the Green driver with their long whips.

His wife gasped in horror and clutched his hand. During their seven years of marriage, Marcia had attended the races only once, and that time with reluctance. Today, however, she had no choice but to be by his side. For the opening events of the emperor's triumphal celebrations, the presence of the entire imperial family was mandatory. He'd reminded her of that unfortunate fact just this morning over breakfast when she started bitching about the heat.

The chariots reached the conical posts for the last hairpin turn into the final stretch. The Green driver had managed to put some space between himself and his harassers when the Blue at the front of the battling pack steered too tight and lost control, flipping his vehicle on its side. The other three carts smashed into it; a thunderous cloud of shattered wood and mangled metal exploded into the heavy summer air.

Before the debris settled, the awe-struck mob jumped to their feet and roared in deafening unison. Another charioteer from the Greens raced around the wreckage and the mutilated remains of horses and drivers. Furiously slicing their flanks with his lash, he drove his chariot team across the finish line. From the spectators' stands came a second, less raucous cheer of approval.

Gaius gently squeezed Marcia's white-knuckled grip on his hand and mumbled, "They died instantly."

Publius, on the other hand, clapped and hooted like a mad man. After he'd sat down, he elbowed Gaius in the ribs and pointed. "Shipwreck! That—now *that* was bloody fucking spectacular!"

"You always have enjoyed a fatal crash more than anyone I know, little brother."

Marcia sighed in exasperation before she leaned over Gaius's lap, one palm pressed against his thigh. Even through the stench of well over a hundred thousand sweaty bodies, he caught a whiff of her light perfume. A dangling gold earring swung back and forth like a pendulum, brushing against the soft skin of her neck. Gaius fancied this new hairstyle she'd adopted during his absence—her dark brown wavy hair parted in the middle and loosely tied back in a braided bun. Thanks to the gods she'd finally abandoned that stiff, absurd fan-shaped fashion favored by her older, more conservative friends.

"Publius, I can't for the life of me understand why you are so happy with the results of that race. Are you no longer a devoted fan of the Blue faction? Have you switched sides on us, again?" Marcia asked, her sarcastic tone in no way hiding her disgust with Publius and the entire lurid scene.

From his seat two rows behind her, Lucius snorted out loud. Luc always did get a good chuckle out of Marcia's fierce dislike of the Greekling.

"Of course, Marcia. I've adored my Blues since I was a small boy. Gaius, tell your skeptical wife how much I love my team." Publius fidgeted with his toga and lowered his voice. "But I had a consultation with my astrologer yesterday, and he convinced me to wager on the Greens for this contest. Damn good thing too. That was the most spectacular smash up I've seen in ages."

"And where is your lovely wife, Publius?" Marcia lifted her chin and nodded towards the empty seat beside him.

"Sabina's not feeling well, I'm afraid. The suffocating weather and all."

Gaius leaned far back to allow his wife a clear line of attack. The last fucking thing he needed was to get caught in their bitchy crossfire. Marcia could be a malicious vixen. To say she didn't care for beautiful Sabina was putting it mildly.

Marcia cocked her head and smirked. "She is such a delicate, young flower. So very, very fragile. Do send our wishes for a speedy recovery, won't you?"

Apparently Publius wasn't in the mood for a spat today. He simply nodded as he wiped the sweat from his brow, and stretched forward to shout down the row of seats.

"Fabulous race! Wouldn't you agree, Emperor Trajan?"

"Marvelously entertaining!" Marcus bellowed back and slapped his legs just above his bony knees. "Ah, there's nothing as satisfying as a good afternoon at the races before a feast." He softened his tone. "Are you enjoying yourself, beloved?"

Plotina dabbed the pool of perspiration under her lower lip with her yellow silk cloth, and covered Marcia's hand with her weathered talon. "You do need to control your jealousies, my dear. Envy is not virtuous. And as for that race—well, my clever Publius doesn't allow his loyalties to slave charioteers to interfere with a sure victory."

After she finished chiding Marcia, Plotina answered the emperor with no particular rush, "These spectacles are wonderful, Marcus. But you deserve even grander celebrations for your brilliant triumphs, my esteemed husband. For the next festival, I shall organize more lavish events, personally." She patted her husband's forearm with a lazy smile.

Marcia turned to the side and rolled her large hazel eyes at Gaius as she murmured, "Oh, for the love of Minerva."

He whispered into her ear, "Save it, sweetheart. In case you've forgotten, we've an entire fucking night of this horseshit ahead of us." Gaius shot her a pained grin before looking down at the gory aftermath of the collision that had stained the arena of Rome's enormous track.

How was his new Dacian pet faring down at the villa? Had Max started training his luscious mouth yet?

Shit, he was fucking horny. Ever since he'd been forced to return to the capital, Lucius had been unavailable, even for a quick tryst.

Fuck Luc, and his time-consuming duties at the law courts, and his shrew of a wife!

Of course, Marcia's slave girls were readily available, but bedding her compliant dolls was bloody boring. He'd give anything right now to be down by the seaside, playing sweet and rough with his beautiful naughty boys instead of trapped at the palace for more victory celebrations and tedious dinner parties.

From beneath a large archway, a gaggle of race attendants wheeled a salvage wagon out onto the track. When they reached the baking wreck, one fellow tossed a severed leg into the back of the cart while two others grappled with the carcass of the Green faction's champion stallion. In a few moments, all traces of the broken chariots and the dead beasts, horses and slave charioteers alike, would be permanently erased and duly forgotten. Another race was to start soon, the next group of contestants already taking their places in the starting gates down below.

And so it would go on, lap after treacherous lap, for the remainder of the scorching afternoon until the final race of the day was decided and the last victor crowned.

It was the cyclical nature of the contests—the rhythm of life in Rome.

Gaius lifted his cup above his shoulder and barked in resignation, "Wine!"

~

Gaius Fabius's seaside villa, Campania

"What did Dom's letter say again, Max?" Simon's busy mouth was stuffed with half-chewed bread. Crumbs fell from his rosy lips and landed on the floor beneath the dining table in the stable house common room. When he brushed his cream-colored tunic, another scattering of crust bits flew down to the herringbone brick tiles.

"It said to tell sloppy Simon to stop eating like a fucking pig," Nic chimed in. "Learn some bloody manners, twerp, or you'll never go with Dom to one of those dinner parties in Neapolis."

"Sod off," Simon grumbled, more crumbs spilling out.

"Nic's right. We'll resume your etiquette lessons tomorrow, Simon. Your kneeling needs work as well. And as for Dom's letter, it's safely stored away at the main house, scamp. But the short of it is Commander Fabius will be home in about fifteen days. No doubt he'll send word ahead before he departs from Rome." Max sopped up the last puddle of tangy fish sauce from his saucer with a piece of bread and popped the bite into his mouth. "And no—Dom didn't say anything about ending Nic's punishment."

With a frustrated grunt, Nic crossed his arms on the tabletop and cradled his forehead in the crook of his right elbow.

Seated across from Max, Allerix drained the last drops of water from his cup. The food here was flavorful but too damn salty. For most of time he'd been at this villa, he'd been thirsty. All the time. That fucking briny fish sauce these people slopped on damn near everything was nasty.

Allerix held out his ceramic vessel between his bound hands and tilted his head.

Be demure and adorable. Appear harmless.

The key to any chance of escape was clear. He had to win Maximus's trust.

Fast.

The Roman monster would be home soon.

"Water please, sir."

Grinning with pride, Simon bumped his shoulder. "That was much better, Paulus. Next time say, 'May I have more water please, sir,' all right? And remember you have to ask permission to ask a question before you ask the question. Dom's pretty strict about that."

"Except in bed." Nic flicked his long blond braid over his shoulder and smirked, before sitting up to hold out his cup as well. He puckered his lips and complained, "Max, I think Plautus's latest batch of fish sauce sat in the sun for too long. It tastes rancid, don't you think?"

Max lightly cuffed Nic's ear. "You are bloody spoiled. Too many of those posh parties in Neapolis, I suspect. Be thankful you get three meals a day, brat."

"May I ask question, sir?"

"Almost perfect!" Simon yelped.

Max rolled his eyes but stayed calm. "You're taking this tutoring assignment a bit too seriously, Simon. Yes, Paulus—what is it?"

Allerix chewed on his lip before stuttering, "What is Nic's pun-ishment?"

While he filled Allerix's cup and then Nic's to the brim with fresh water, Max hesitated before speaking. Finally, he said, "Show him, Nicomedes."

"What?"

"You heard me. Show Paulus what you earned for breaking the rules. Now!"

Nic put his cup down, stood up and lifted his tunic, exposing his crotch. Allerix gulped and raised his eyebrows. He'd never seen anything like whatever the fuck that was before. It was some sort of metal torture contraption strapped to Nic's groin.

"Explain what you're wearing and why you were disciplined, Nicomedes." Max's voice was deadly serious.

Nic looked down at the lattice of interlocking bronze loops that cut into and strangled his limp prick. "This is a cage. I can't do anything, not even with my own hand. Understand? I'm being punished for fucking Zoe without Dom's permission." Nic turned to Max. "I promise it will *never* happen again, sir."

Max cleared his throat. "Nic has been caged for two months now. And I, lucky bastard I am, must stick my fist up his arse and milk him every fifth day. Not all that pleasant a task for either of us. But that cock cage is a mild penalty, given the other options. Nic's lucky he still has his balls. Shit, he's fortunate to still be fucking alive."

Max waved his hand impatiently. "All right, you can cover that up now, lamb."

Allerix swallowed and scrunched his brows. "Zoe?"

"She's another whore slave. Dom fancies girls as well. Zoe lives with my mother at the main house." Simon continued in a whisper, "She's a quiet and pretty blonde bird—same age as me—but don't fucking touch her. Ever."

"I understand. No Zoe." Alle nodded enthusiastically. He had no interest in girls and never had, much to his father's displeasure.

"No fucking *anybody* without Dom's permission," Max corrected as Nic sat back down.

After a few moments of heavy silence, Simon changed the subject. He rocked back and forth on his hands he'd shoved under his bum cheeks and asked, "How long does Paulus have to be in shackles, Max?"

"The commander left that decision to my judgment. I have to admit our furry barbarian here is doing much better than I'd anticipated. I'll decide about the restraints after I see how well our Dacian handles his cock sucking lessons." Max reached across the table, lifted Allerix's bearded chin with a finger, and looked him straight in the eyes. "Your training starts tonight, pretty cub. Do you understand what I'm saying?"

Allerix stared back and batted his long lashes, before dropping his gaze with a quick nod.

He'd be one step closer after tonight. He could practically taste his freedom.

The imperial residence on the Palatine Hill, Rome

Ten large windows, five on each side, pierced the long walls of the grand formal dining hall of the imperial palace. Outside, two identical courtyards each held a massive fountain resembling a boat at sea. The gilded ceiling of the two-storied space soared high above the opulent room, its polished tiles reflecting the colorful marble slabs on the floor.

As he looked down at his red patrician shoes, Gaius recognized the golden stone colored by streaks of blood crimson covering the floor beneath his feet. The precious marble was native to Numidia, exported from the quarries where Maximus had once labored—where Max had nearly died, alongside the dozens of slaves who perished in the quarry pits every day.

Over in the corner of the room, loitering by an archaic sculpture of Dionysus, Lucius Petronius and Apollodorus were sharing the latest scuttlebutt, while Aurelia was doing her best to ignore Appy's sweet but lower ranking wife.

Pompous bitch.

Helen had more class in her little finger than that weasel-faced woman and her entire clan of gold-digging kin. Her fortuitous marriage to Lucius certainly hadn't included a personality upgrade. Aurelia was still a greedy, uptight wretch.

A striking young boy approached him, bowed, and silently filled Gaius's half-empty wine cup. He didn't recognize the nearly naked slave —probably one of Marcus's latest acquisitions. The boy couldn't have been much older than ten years.

When Plotina hissed in his ear from behind, Gaius flinched. "He's lovely, isn't he? I can have Marcus send the boy home with you for a second dessert, if you like. I'm sure Marcia wouldn't mind."

Gaius hunched his shoulders and cringed. "I don't fuck little boys, Domina. That proclivity belongs to your esteemed husband."

He glared at her wrinkled face, covered with a cracked crust of bright cosmetics. "But, then again, you know all about Marcus's preferences for wee lads. You always have."

Plotina's laughter shook the rigid stack of hair artfully pinned high on her head. She patted his shoulder and pursed her lips in displeasure.

"Such crude language, Gaius. I've always said you think too highly of yourself, dearest. Constantly judging others and so quick to point out the most trivial of faults. I wonder—is hubris a common defect of the Fabii? By the gods we all know your unfortunate sire suffered from his share of unwarranted pride. I pray to Juno every morning that you, my sweet boy, don't suffer a similar fate."

As Plotina swaggered off to find her next victim, waves of golden silk fabric flowing in her wake, Marcia moved over to Gaius's side and squeezed his forearm. "Is everything all right?"

"No."

She sighed. "You just need a distraction. You always turn into a grumpy bear when you're away from your villa pets for too long. Let's greet the proconsul, Senecio. I've never actually met our magistrate. Introduce me, will you?" Marcia tugged on his elbow.

"He's a dullard, dear. An incompetent boob. Quintus Sosius Senecio should never have been awarded that command in Moesia during the war. And now the Senate's honored the fool with a portrait statue in the forecourt of Jove's sanctuary. A fucking bronze statue for that buffoon? On the bloody Capitoline Hill?"

"Lower your voice, Gaius. He'll hear you. Come—boob or not, I need to meet the man. He has influence with certain stubborn elders in the Senate. A friendly connection with Senecio would help us both. Indulge me."

He placed his hand over hers and grinned. "You know, I've long admired your balls, woman."

She pulled him towards a small group chatting by one of the windows. Introductions were made, and Senecio—like most men—was quickly charmed by Marcia's noble carriage and subtle flattery. Unfortunately, the dolt had the worst ear-rattling cackle of a laugh. Gaius tasted bile burning in the back of his throat when a bell rang out, echoing through the hall.

"Greetings, everyone!"

Marcus was in rare form, already swaying a bit from the day's oppressive heat and one too many cups of wine.

"Tonight's sumptuous feast is ready to be served. The guest of honor for this evening who will receive the place of distinction on the couch beside me for the meal is our most noble…"

Not bloody Publius again. And where the fuck was Princess Publius? Arriving late to bask in his dramatic solo entrance, no doubt.

"Gaius Fabius Rufus!" the emperor shouted. "Our most esteemed master of the Lucky Fourth Lions, and my talented second in command for our victories over the Dacian scourge. And, of course, my devoted former ward." The emperor offered out his elbow. "Come, Gaius Fabius—accompany your emperor to the couches."

Shit.

Gaius froze and blinked twice.

He hadn't been honored with the prized seat at a formal palace dinner in years. Cheering with abandon, Apollodorus led the round of applause, while Lucius shot him an obscene gesture of congratulations. Perhaps Gaius Fabius Rufus had a chance at winning the imperial throne after all.

Gaius held Marcus's arm and together they strolled over towards the prime seats on the dining couches.

"I've heard my chief counselor recently purchased a pretty Dacian boy at an auction on Decius's estate. Quite a bidding spectacle, according to the reports."

Gaius stiffened and lowered his chin. Of course the emperor would have found out about the auction. His spies were everywhere. And Publius had a big fucking mouth.

"I was in attendance, sir."

The emperor's jovial tone dropped to low and lethal. "And you examined the beast for royal markings, yes? There's no chance it's a Dacian princeling?"

"There were no tattoos, only calluses. The mongrel was a common peasant, nothing more. Completely untrained, of course. Lucius has already sold it and lost coin on the transaction." Gaius swallowed hard. "My most esteemed Emperor."

Marcus sighed and pulled Gaius closer. "You should have warned your friend not to make such a foolish purchase in the first place. Because you, better than most, understand Dacians are ruthless and conniving savages, not concubines to be pampered and coddled."

"Yes, Dominus."

"And, Gaius—"

Marcus pulled Gaius to a sudden stop and whispered, "You're a Roman patrician, not some bloody Greek catamite. Put an end to this dishonorable dalliance with Petronius Celsus. Do it immediately, or I will be forced to stop it myself. And that, I promise you, would be most unpleasant for all of us."

Marcus stepped back and smiled. "The gods bless those who venerate their esteemed ancestors. Tend to your marital duties, Commander Fabius. Produce an heir, secure your immortality."

After Marcus turned and walked to the imperial couch draped with purple coverlets, Gaius muttered under his breath, "You hypocritical son of a bitch."

The diners reclined on the ornate plush couches arranged around two circular silver tables, and a group of lyre and flute players struck up a soothing dulcet tune. When everyone was comfortably settled, the palace steward snapped his fingers and a flurry of attractive slaves in skimpy outfits brought out trays of appetizers and pitchers of honeyed wine.

Gaius glanced at the platter placed by his spot. It was loaded with stuffed dormice and an assortment of black olives, ripe wild plums, and boiled quail eggs with pine nut sauce—all of his favorite delicacies. As the guest of honor, he was offered first taste. He picked up a serving of dormouse and bit into the spicy rodent treat.

The perfect balance of succulent and crunchy.

Next to his couch, the steward stood at attention, waiting for the signal. Gaius lifted a brow and nodded his satisfaction. As everyone dove into the appetizers, he licked his fingers and tried to relax as he mulled over the emperor's directive. Lucius's reputation and authority were at stake, as well as any fucking chance Gaius might have to inherit the throne.

But thanks to the grace of Fortuna, hundreds of miles away, his Dacian trophy was safely hidden.

Gaius Fabius's seaside villa, Campania

"Come on, then!"

Clearly impatient with the slow totter of Allerix's bound ankles, Max practically carried him down the footpath connecting the stables to the main building. "This is how we access the villa house. Do not use the large doors on the east—not that you'll be allowed to venture anywhere unaccompanied for quite a while, Paulus. Understand?"

Allerix nodded.

The night sky glowed with the waning light of dusk. Allerix tried to get his bearings, but high boxwood shrubs on either side of the path blocked his view of the surrounding landscape. He could hear the crashing waves of the sea to his left. Or was the water on his right? Which direction was east?

Once inside the house, they moved down a long hallway, turned a corner, and kept shuffling along until they reached a door at the far end of the wide corridor. A large man approached them from a side passageway.

Max nodded to the burly brute, close to the size of an ox. The armed guard carried a short sword, not that he needed it. His gigantic paws could easily strangle even Max. The bald-headed man's flat face was grossly disfigured. A deep scar zigzagged from his forehead, over the bridge of his nose, and down to his jawline. His wide nostrils flared as he narrowed his eyes at Allerix.

"Greetings, Maximus."

"Greetings, Varius."

"This is the commander's new pet, I take it?"

"Yes, sir. The slave's name is Paulus."

Max shoved Allerix a step forward and continued, "Varius is an esteemed veteran and a client of Commander Fabius. He's in charge of security here. If you fuck up, Paulus, Varius will most likely be the one who ties you to the post out in the yard and whips you bloody until you black out."

Varius's broad smile revealed he'd lost a few teeth. Arms crossed, he leaned down uncomfortably close to Allerix's face. Allerix tried to say calm, but his mouth started to quiver.

"Our friend Maximus exaggerates."

Varius moved another couple of inches closer. Allerix bit down on his trembling lower lip.

"You're not frightened of me, are you? I'm just a big old pussycat.

Though, let me be very clear. I will snap your little neck like a dried twig if Commander Fabius gives me the orders."

He pinched Allerix's plump cheek. "So, be a good boy, right? Good boys don't get flogged. Good whores don't get their necks broken."

Varius chuckled and stepped back. As he readjusted the wide leather belt cinched below the swell of his protruding stomach, he looked Allerix over from head to toe.

"He is a pretty thing, isn't he? All right, then—I'm off to make my rounds and check the perimeter, Maximus. Are Simon and Nicomedes tucked safely in their beds?"

"Yes, sir."

"Very well. Goodnight, you two."

Max waited for Varius to leave before he pulled a ring of keys from his pouch and unlocked the heavy wooden door. Allerix imagined Max must have had a key for nearly every lock at the villa.

"This is Dom's playroom. You'll be spending quite a bit of time in here."

Against the crimson back wall between two flickering oil lamps, an enormous bed dominated the center of the space. On the left, a wide balcony opened out over the sea, with sheer red curtains draped between slender white marble columns. To the right of the bed, a shallow alcove contained a bronze chest. Allerix stared at the large metal box.

"That's where Dominus stores his toys. You'll find out all about those soon enough." Max walked over to a bench near the balcony, sat down and waved his hand. "It's late. Let's get started."

After Allerix hobbled over, Max asked, "Can you strip without assistance?"

"Yes, sir."

Allerix reached behind his neck, grabbed the back of his tunic with both hands, and pulled the tan cloth up over his head. The cool ocean breezes blowing in through the curtains tickled his creamy skin to goose bumps. His fleshy, brown nipples tightened into hard nubs. He looked into Max's eyes as he sank to his knees.

"Your form is quite graceful. You won't need much more training as far as kneeling goes, will you?"

Allerix smiled wide. His round cheeks swelled above the bristles of his short beard. Max hoisted his ivory tunic up around his waist; his long, thick cock bobbed and bumped against his firm stomach in anticipation.

Max reached out and cupped Allerix's furry chin. "Shall we see what you already know?"

Allerix nodded with a slow blink and leaned forward.

Win his trust.

When he wrapped the fingers of his bound hands tight around Max's hard shaft, Max grabbed a fistful of his hair and yanked his face up. "You bite me, Dacian, and I'll send for Varius. And, trust me, he's no bloody pussycat."

"No biting, sir. I understand," he replied, and Max released his grip.

Allerix began tracing lazy lines with his wet tongue and soft beard over the vein running up the underside of Max's cock. He pulled back, took a deep breath, and swallowed as much of Max's length as he could manage until he gagged.

"Whoa—easy there." Max chuckled, gently brushing his fingers along the nape of Allerix's smooth neck. His chin already damp from saliva, Allerix relaxed his mouth, and Max's ebony cock slid out slowly from between his full pink lips. With a flick of his tongue, he licked a pearl of precum from the sensitive slit. After he languidly swept his lips and beard over the curves of the engorged head, Allerix inhaled sharply through his nose and swallowed Max's thick shaft back down his throat, more slowly this time.

Max growled, "That's very good. Dom will be fucking pleased with you. He prefers slow, noisy sucking. Shit, I hope he keeps your delightful beard."

Firmly holding the stout base of Max's cock with both of his hands, Allerix moaned around the throbbing hot girth. His tongue and cheeks vibrated and then sucked with each sloppy stroke. Up and then back down. Hum and squeeze. He increased the tempo and relaxed his jaw to take Max as deep as he could without coughing.

Max let his head fall back against the wall and closed his eyes, lost in the exquisite pleasure.

"Fuck, yes—you are a sweet, sweet boy. Dom loves when his whores moan around his cock low and deep like that. We'll get those shackles off you before our next lesson. See what spectacular things you can do with your hands free, hmm?" Max groaned and laughed at the same time, his long fingers tangled in Allerix's messed hair.

Allerix glanced up from beneath his thick lashes and grinned, just moments before Max cried out and shot waves of warm semen down his throat. Max rode out the intense orgasm as he dug his fingers into Allerix's pale shoulders. When the last of the aftershocks finally subsided, he carefully pulled his softening cock out and gently pushed Allerix down on the floor until he lay flat on his back.

Allerix looked up with heavy, dazed eyes and licked his swollen lips in slow circles.

Be submissive. Appear pretty and harmless.

The slave handler dropped to his knees beside him and whispered, "Paulus, that performance earned you a special treat. Let me show you what Dom really likes, yes? Hush, though—don't tell the other lads. It'll be our special secret." Max winked. He lowered his face, and smiled one more time before he engulfed Allerix's aching prick all the way down to his Dacian balls in one smooth swallow.

After a loud gasp, Allerix squeezed his eyes shut and softly mewled and squirmed, arching his back, thrusting up into Max's mouth.

He'd be home in the mountains of Dacia before the first snowfall of winter.

He could already taste fresh roasted venison.

9

Gaius Fabius's mansion on the Caelian Hill, Rome

WITH A CONTENT GROAN, HE ROSE FROM BENEATH THE SURFACE OF THE steaming hot water and smoothed back his drenched chestnut-red curls with both hands. Droplets fell from the tips of his spiral locks and rolled down the muscular curves of his broad back. His wet hair hung down well past his shoulders. It was growing too long. One of Marcia's nymphs would give him a proper trim before he left for the Senate deliberations tomorrow morning. The session was scheduled to start early, but there should be time for a quick haircut. The girls had already laundered his formal toga and left it neatly folded over a chair in his bedchamber.

Through the haze clouding the vaulted bathing suite, Pyramus crept out on his long legs from some dark hiding place. The large spotted cat padded cautiously around the small puddles scattered across the mosaic floor before settling behind Gaius's shoulder on the blue tiled ledge of the sunken soaking tub.

"There you are, my sweet puss." Gaius reached up, scratched its cheek and cooed, "I've hardly spent any time with you, Pyramus. I'm a derelict master and you're such a good, lovely boy. Listen, sweetheart—I'll be leaving Rome soon, and you, my friend, will be in charge once again. Only three more fucking days of these wearisome obligations and I'm finally going home."

Ah, blissful, breezy Campania. Not this ostentatious colossal house on the Caelian Gaius's father inherited after grandfather died. Less than a year after the mansion had been renovated and redecorated, a gang of the despot's butchers broke down the door and dragged dear old dad, the accused traitor, away to his death. Gaius and his mother barely escaped Rome alive. And yet, somehow, through all the suffering and fear that strangled the city during the tyrant's reign, this monstrosity of brick and stone survived, still dwarfing its neighbors on the hill.

This place was fucking spooky, a temple for the ghosts of his ancestors. More than a few times, he'd walk down a corridor or enter a room and a strange, frigid blast would tickle his skin, causing the wispy golden hairs on his forearms to stand on end. Sinister ice-cold gusts of outrage mixed with despair. Gaius made all the proper sacrifices at the family mausoleum on the holy days, but it never seemed to help. The house was cursed. Perhaps the Fabii were cursed as well.

The flame of the oil lamp hanging from a bracket on the back wall of the bath suddenly tripled in size and flickered violently. Pyramus froze and stopped purring.

"It's all right, puss—just a visit from Father's pissed off ghost. There's nothing to avenge anymore, old man! They're all dead now, those bastards who murdered you. It's over, so stop haunting me, Quintus. I can't do a fucking thing to retaliate."

Gaius rubbed his eyes and grabbed his silver cup off the ledge of the tub. After he washed down the lump in his throat with a sip of overly sweet Gallic wine, he pursed his lips in disgust and looked down into the vessel. He should have ordered some Falernian grape instead.

Pyramus' whiskers drooped forward and his enormous tufted ears folded back as he closed his eyes and relaxed into the touch of his master's damp fingers. When Gaius pulled his hand away, the exotic African feline lifted one of its paws in protest.

Gaius chuckled. He rubbed the soft underside of Pyramus' furry chin and whispered, "Can't ever get enough loving, can you? You're as bad as Simon, Pyramus."

Over the sound of a small waterfall gurgling in a corner, a faint shuffling of fabric rustled behind Gaius's head. Pyramus' prominent ears pricked up. The cat turned its head towards the noise and stared unblinking, its pupils round and dark.

Gaius exhaled silently and pulled back his hand, slow and steady.

His dagger was right there, resting by his discarded clothes on the edge of the pool.

Right fucking there.

When Pyramus hissed and leapt away, Gaius lunged across the bath. Water splashed everywhere. The lion's paw handle was almost in his grasp when the leather sole of a sandal crushed his right wrist, pinning his arm to the wet polished tiles.

"Too slow."

A large hand grabbed his knife off the floor while another clenched a fistful of Gaius's thick sopping hair and jerked his head back. The blade hugged just below his larynx.

"You're out of practice, Commander."

Gaius stared up into the man's upside-down silver blue eyes. "How did you get in here?"

The grip on his hair tightened. "You underestimate my talents."

"Not likely."

After he shoved the dagger away from his throat, Gaius twisted around and clamped on to the intruder's ankle. He pulled the squatting giant off balance and dragged him, feet first and fully clothed, into the heated pool. The dagger flew across the room and landed with a loud clink. They grunted and grappled, wrestling for control in the shallow water. When Gaius found himself pinned with one arm twisted behind his bare back, he kicked the larger man's feet out from under him and watched a head of dark hair sink below the surface. A flurry of air bubbles came up from the bottom of the pool. Gaius stuck his hand under and yanked him up by his ear.

"How exactly the fuck did you get in here?" Gaius barked, as he released his fierce pinch.

"Ow! Shit, Gaius—that bloody hurt."

"Did Marcia see you?"

Breathing hard, Lucius raked back his dripping mop of short hair with his fingers and laughed. "Yes, your wife saw me." After he pulled his soaked tunic over his head in one clumsy motion, Luc settled his muscled, naked body into the water across from Gaius. "She was most gracious under the circumstances. You're a lucky man."

Gaius leaned back against the edge of the bath pool, crossed his arms and gnawed on his lower lip. "I'm waiting for an explanation."

"Hmm? Oh, why am I here? Well, it seems our empress decided it was time for one of those daft bird gatherings of hers. Aurelia wanted Marcia to accompany her to the bash, so I escorted my bride all the way over here to fetch your lovely wife. Beautiful afternoon for a stroll." Lucius coughed and pointed to the wine cup. "May I? I'm bloody parched."

Gaius nodded once with a sneer. He gritted his teeth in a sorry attempt to mask his smile, as Luc crawled over on all fours, the mounds of his glistening toned bum bobbing above the bath water. Lucius took a healthy swig of wine and wiped his mouth with his forearm.

"Blech! Terrible wine, Commander Fabius. So, anyway, your guards are now escorting the ladies to the palace." Luc leaned over, waggling his thick, black brows. "We're alone, soldier."

Gaius took the cup back, finished off the last swallow with a grimace, and threw it against a wall. Blood rushed to his aching cock. He scooted closer, and playfully flicked one of Luc's dark brown nipples.

Gaius asked, "How long do you think we have?"

"I have…" Lucius cupped his chin and brushed his mouth with parted lips. "Absolutely no fucking idea."

He shoved both hands under the younger man's arse and pulled him up close enough to force Gaius to part his legs and straddle Luc's crotch. They both plunged their hands under the water and rubbed their shafts against the other, pulling and stroking and groaning.

"Fuck, I need more than a cock rub," Luc cried in frustration, before snaking his hungry tongue between Gaius's lips. Their mouths fought for dominance, biting and sucking with gasps and growls. When Gaius grabbed Luc's lower lip with his teeth, Luc pressed his nose against Gaius's forehead and mumbled, barely coherent, "Let me have your arse, darling. Let me wear the laurel wreath for a change."

Gaius let go and leaned back, his face twisted in amused confusion. "What?"

Lucius descended on his neck, sucking and nibbling, close to bruising the skin in spots. "You heard me. I want to fuck you. Pretend we're back in Athens—insane and insatiable. It's been forever since I've been the Zeus to your Ganymede." Lucius blew a warm breath against the sensitive spot behind Gaius's left ear and nipped his squishy earlobe, as he stroked Gaius's throbbing cock under the water.

The sensation was intoxicating. The gorgeous bastard knew just how to suckle on his ear lobes. He'd definitely have to teach the Dacian that technique. Gaius let his head fall back, and closed his eyes. His thick lashes fanned out like wet feathers. Every inch of his skin tingled with excitement.

"You have your Caledonian whore to pummel, counselor."

"True, I have Bryaxis, but…" Luc's tongue licked a trail along Gaius's jaw from his ear to his chin. "I want you, soldier."

"All right, then. Argue your case."

Lucius shook his head and rolled his eyes, before purring, "Your tight fortress craves to be breached by my battering ram."

With his heavy eyelids now half-open, Gaius furrowed his brows and smirked. "Come again?"

"I want to impale you to the hilt of my steel sword."

"Not convincing me, Luc."

Sticking the tip of his tongue out of the corner of his mouth, Lucius tickled his lover's sides with his long fingers. "Let me assault your bastion with my iron spear."

"Shit, that was fucking awful!"

"Surrender or I'll keep going. I've a long list of scintillating military metaphors to seduce you, soldier. Let's see—I want to pierce your sweet portal with my robust…"

Gaius pushed Luc's hands away. "Enough! You're fucking relentless."

"Hey, I'm a lawyer." Luc raised both hands and winked.

"And a damned persuasive one at that."

"Wait—what was that? Quiet in the court! Did our esteemed Commander Fabius, Lion of the Lucky Fourth, just confess his desire for my sorry old prick up his delicious arse? This calls for a victory celebration."

Gaius grabbed Lucius's face in both hands and snapped, "I've sat through enough fucking triumphal festivities to last me months, you son of a bitch." As he kissed Luc with every bit of force he could muster, Gaius rubbed his groin against Luc's thigh, and lifted himself up on his knees, teasing the engorged head of Luc's cock with his slippery crack.

Panting for air, Lucius broke off the brutal kiss. "Slow down, darling. Turn around and let me warm you up. It's been a long time since you've been ridden." Luc paused. "It has been a long time, right?"

"Well…" Gaius squinted.

"You've let someone else—" Luc covered his mouth with his hand and cleared his throat to muffle the pained crack in his voice, but Gaius heard it.

"Luc, really? For shit's sake, you claimed my unsullied schoolboy arse before our studies even started. I wore your heavy gold chain in plain sight for my whole first year in Athens, didn't I? You're the only one who's buggered me, counselor." Gaius looked him straight in the eyes, before cracking a grin. "Now kiss my buttress, you filthy plebian."

Lucius sighed with relief and laughed at the same time. "Oh, shit—what a pompous arse I was back then. You were barely off the boat when I told those other third year prats the new, red headed kid was mine. By the gods, you were so beautiful—so young. *We* were so young." Lucius kissed him softly on the lips.

Gaius ran his fingers through Lucius's thick, short sable hair. His temples were peppered with a few grey strands. "That was nearly twenty years ago. Everything's different now, isn't it? I mean, we're still mates—best friends, right? We always will be, Luc. Nothing will change that."

"I know, darling. Leave the past in the past. Act like a proper, respectable citizen and all that rubbish." Luc stared down at his twiddling fingers and swallowed.

Gaius moved closer and lightly brushed Luc's cheek with his thumb pad. "We can't be together here anymore, not in the capital, not within sight or earshot of the court spies. But you'll come down to Campania for a visit when you can. We'll find time for a romp here and there. Don't toss out those bindings and floggers, right?"

Lucius's crinkled eyes grew glassy wet. After he wiped his perfectly straight runny nose, he looked up with a forced smile.

"I've been expecting this, of course. And yes, I'll keep the toys. Listen, I know it can't be like it was between us back in Greece, but just once more for old times' sake. I need to fuck you so hard you'll hobble around the Senate chamber tomorrow morning."

Gaius pressed his lips together in a smirk and turned around to bend over the ledge. "Ah, so that's it! At last, the truth comes out. You want to pummel my arse and then mock me?" He snorted, as he raised his bum and braced himself on both elbows.

"You're leaving soon. I want to send you off good and sore for the long ride to Neapolis. Gaius, whatever happened to that gold chain anyway?" Luc asked, before he spread Gaius's cheeks with both hands and lapped warm circles with his tongue up his crack from his sac to his sensitive hole.

"I still have… oh, fuck. Yes. Yes, exactly like that." Shit, he hadn't realized how much he'd missed this. Gaius squirmed against Lucius's strong hands and wiggled his hips, trying to get something—anything—inside of him. It had been years.

After several languid, teasing licks, Luc pushed his long tongue into his hot tightness until Gaius cried out, his fingers curled into tight fists. Slowly Lucius pulled his tongue out and mumbled into the curve of Gaius's wet cheek, "Mmm, I think I'll make you come first, just eat you out until you spill your seed into the bath."

"Fuck that. Screw me with your cock. Do it, now!"

Lucius raised his powerful arm and slapped Gaius's bum hard; the sharp smack echoed throughout the dim room.

His eyes and mouth wide open in complete surprise, Gaius's shock quickly morphed into delight.

"Well, that was unexpected. Perhaps I have underestimated you, Counselor Petronius."

"You want the cock, you play nice. Do not order me around like some barbarian slave, first year. I'm in charge here, *Eromenos*."

Ah, that wicked passionate term of endearment. A rush of vivid memories ripped through Gaius's heart.

All those chilly winter nights in Athens spent cuddled in Luc's warm bed in the dormitory.

The scent of that Egyptian oil they would buy at the market by the port, and the smooth flavor of that delectable Chalkidian wine.

And the weight of Luc's ownership chain around his neck as Gaius fidgeted in the auditorium of the lecture hall while some grey-bearded, wrinkled Greek codger expounded on Euclid's theorems.

And that time Luc had cradled his dazed shivering body in his strong arms after Gaius suffered that endless, terrifying fit in the library after hours. Thank the gods the place had been deserted and none of the other lads had witnessed him thrashing about on the floor, frothing at the mouth like a rabid dog.

But, most of all, he remembered Luc's passionate, tearful promise to never say a word to anyone, ever, about the fact that Gaius Fabius Rufus, ward of the imperial court, had the fucking dreaded 'sacred disease.'

The lunacy.

That's what Publius had called it after a violent attack knocked him to the ground when they were both young boys playing swords in the shadows of the formal gardens.

Lucius and Publius—what an odd pair to be safeguarding his grave secret.

Gaius swallowed, and looked over his shoulder. "Yes, my *Erastes*."

After gently kissing the warm, ruddy handprint on Gaius's bum, Lucius snarled, "I'm no Greek, pretty slut. We're in Rome now. Remember? Try again."

Gaius covered his sob with a chuckle. This would likely be the last time he and Lucius played their forbidden game. It was bittersweet, but it had to be done.

It was time to end this.

End them.

"Yes, Dominus," Gaius whimpered.

He rested his cheek against the damp cool floor. Soon his whole body quivered with pleasure under the caress of Lucius's talented mouth, while his mind drifted off to Campania.

He couldn't wait to get back down to the seashore. Go home and play with his beauties. A salacious vision of Paulus's alabaster body folded over the edge of his desk in his villa office drifted into his head. He would seduce his feisty Dacian into sweet submission. It was only a matter of time.

10

Gaius Fabius's seaside villa, Campania

As he walked down the corridor on the second floor of the stable house, Allerix scratched his short black beard and chewed on his lower lip. He stopped just half a step outside the open door. Through the iron bars of the lone window, beams of late afternoon light flooded Nicomedes' room, painting the stone grey walls with a brilliant wash of orange. From where Allerix stood, Nic's private cell seemed ordinary enough; there was a cushioned bed and a small table and chair, and a wooden storage box against one wall. Seated on the edge of the bed, the blond man's eyes were downcast, his hands folded gracefully in his lap. Allerix couldn't decide if Nic was sad or bored or perhaps a bit of both.

"What do you want?" Nic asked without looking up.

"Simon—" Allerix cleared his throat. "Simon said ask if you need help with your chores."

After he pulled apart his long, intertwined fingers and leaned back on his elbows, Nic slowly lifted his eyes. Shit, those vibrant blue orbs always caught Allerix off guard.

"I finished early. So, no—I don't need any help, Paulus," Nic answered flatly and stared at the floor, rolling a pebble around under the sole of his sandal. "Must be easier for you to move about the place now, huh? Your cock sucking must be fucking impressive for Max to release you from those irons so soon."

Without thinking, Allerix raised his hands. The shackles had been gone for close to four days. The dark purple bruises wrapping his wrists and ankles were far less visible now.

"Um, I…"

His mind raced as he tried to think of a reasonable way to prolong this rare conversation. Since he'd arrived, he'd barely spoken with Nicomedes. Although they lived on the same hall in the same building and shared the same meals, they'd never spent any time alone together. He needed to talk to him, tease out Nic's story. Allerix needed as much information as possible if he had any chance of escape.

"Simon went to stables," he blurted out, deliberately fumbling over every word and pronunciation of the enemy's language, a simple language he'd mastered as a boy. "To water horses. What are your chores, Nicomedes?"

"Why do you care?" Nic kicked the pebble and it bounced off the wall across from the bed.

He stared blankly at Nic, and Nic stared at the pebble, before the blond grumbled, "I take care of Dom's fish. And the mice."

Allerix had no fucking idea what he'd meant, but he moved closer, putting his foot on the threshold. "Can I enter?"

"I suppose." Nic shuffled over and patted the feather-and-straw mattress.

Maybe an appeal to his ego would work? After a few moments of silence passed, Allerix mumbled, "You are very attractive, Nicomedes."

Nic tossed his long, wavy hair over his shoulder with disinterest. "Save your bullshit flattery, fur face. I'm caged—remember? And besides, Simon's the favorite, not me. That's what you're aiming for, isn't it? To be Dom's new favorite?" Nic's tone was direct and bitter.

"What does favorite mean?"

"The favorite pet sleeps with Dom in the main house when he's here. Not every night, but a lot of the time—sometimes in the bed, sometimes on a mat on the floor. And Simon gets more attention from Dom. And more presents and…"

"So it's good to be the favorite?"

"Very good, especially if Dom takes you along to parties, buys you expensive clothes, lets you eat from his fingers and kisses you in front of his posh friends."

Allerix nibbled on his thumbnail and arched an eyebrow. "Friends?"

"You know, other fucking rich aristocrats—army officers and magistrates and court types and people like that. But Simon's still too boorish and spastic to go with Dom to those dinners. I expect he'll learn. He's a sharp and eager little shit."

"Were you the favorite before Simon?"

"No. I've never been…" Nic's voice trailed off.

There was more uncomfortable silence, except for sea gulls screeching outside as they fought over a late day meal.

"Does that metal thing on your cock hurt?" Allerix pointed to Nic's covered groin.

"The cage? No, not as long as my pathetic dick stays soft and useless. If I get hard, it hurts like mad. There's sharp little points on the inside, so don't get flirty with me, all right?" Nic chuckled, but his forced laughter didn't mask his despair. "Max was right though—I'm lucky to still have my damn balls."

Allerix nodded, and quickly looked around the room for another potential topic, one less prickly. He spotted a large lidded clay jar over in the shadows of one corner. It was strange; its sides were pierced with randomly placed small holes.

"What is in that container?"

"You're full of questions, aren't you? I keep something very special in that jar." Nic shot him a genuine, eye-crinkling smile and his voice softened. "My friend's in there. Want to meet him?"

"Um, all right."

Nicomedes walked over to the round, red earthen pot and lifted the lid off by its handle. Crouching down, he carefully lowered his hand inside the vessel and scooped up something.

"We have to keep our voices down. I mean, we can't really wake him up right now, but still…"

Shit, Allerix hoped it wasn't a snake. He loved animals, but he fucking despised snakes.

After he sat back down on the bed, Nic leaned over and opened his fingers. "Here he is."

"What *is* that?" Allerix asked with wonder, his lips parted and turned up at the corners.

"He's a dormouse. They normally hibernate after the autumn harvest, but I've trained him to sleep during the summer because I'm usually stuck indoors during the winter. He keeps me company. We play and we talk, and I've even taught him a few tricks."

"Did you catch him?"

"No, nothing like that." When he let his guard down, Nic had a charming laugh. "He was the runt of this big litter and his foot was all mangled. Deformed, you know. So I asked if I could keep him since it was clear he'd never amount to much of a snack. And Max said yes. Well, it was Dom who gave permission for me to keep him, of course."

"Um, what do you mean by snack?" Allerix regretted the question as soon as it rolled off his tongue.

"They eat dormice like him. Break their tiny necks and then stuff their guts with meat, spices, and other shit and then cook them. Max says they're pretty tasty and Dom fucking loves them. That's why we raise dormice here at the villa—so there's always a fresh supply."

Allerix twisted his face in disgust. There was no sport in feasting on helpless little creatures. Except for rabbits. They were delicious roasted to a crisp on a spit with vegetables.

"Yeah, I'd never eat one either unless Dom or Max told me to. Caring for the mice, feeding them—that's one of my chores. And so one day, I opened up one of the breeding jars and found this little fellow squashed under its mother and, well, you know the rest."

Curled up in a ball on its back with its eyes shut tight, the golden-brown mouse opened its mouth, wiggled its long black whiskers and snuggled deeper into Nic's cupped palm.

"It's—" Allerix gently rubbed the sleeping rodent's soft, fluffy tail with his pointer finger. "Adorable. Is that... is he snoring?"

"Yeah." Grinning ear-to-ear, Nic's muscles relaxed. "He snores like a little old man when he's hibernating."

"Does he have a name?"

"'Course he does. I named him Achilles—you know, cause he has the bad foot and all."

Allerix caught himself just in time. "No, I don't know. Who is Achilles?"

"He was a Greek hero who could only be defeated...shit, never mind. It's a long story. A really long bloody story."

"Can I... I mean... will Achilles let me hold him?"

"Sure. Just be gentle. Yeah, that's right—bend your fingers in and curl your palm into a pouch."

As Allerix cradled the dormouse in his hand, he pressed on. "Are you a Greek like the hero Achilles, Nicomedes?"

"First of all, call me Nic. I'm so fucking tired of hearing you stumble over all the letters. And a Greek? Fuck if I know. My mother was a prostitute, perhaps she still is, so who knows what I am. Nobody at the brothel cared about that. Cared about me. When I was born, those sons of bitches named me *Culus*. Do you know what that name means?"

Allerix shook his head.

"It's slang for anus, bum-hole. Lovely, right? 'Come here, my tight, sweet little Culus.' Fuckers. When Dom became my master, he changed it right off to Nicomedes. He said Nicomedes means 'dwell on victory.' And then he went off to war and he won. Dom says I'm his good luck charm."

Allerix swallowed, but stayed focused on the tiny ball of fur slumbering in his palm. Exchanging grins back and forth, they both petted the mouse's white underbelly, and Nic completely dropped the last of his defenses.

"I was born in Neapolis. That's the port city down the road, not all that far from here. Fucking place is filled with filthy whorehouses. Anyway, I started working as soon as I could walk, fetching water and scrubbing the dried cum off the beds—whatever needed to be done. Then, when I turned nine or so, the pimp started whoring me out. Mum couldn't say anything. I don't think she wanted to stop it. I was popular and I made good coin. She was proud of me."

"Is that where…" Allerix almost choked on the loathsome title. "Is that where Dominus bought you?"

"What? No, no. Dom doesn't go to fucking brothels, Paulus." Nic snickered until he coughed into his fist. "So, this pimp got sick of my shitty attitude and sold me to a nasty, fat bastard when I was, I dunno… thirteen or something. The prick was a merchant and bloody cruel, with clumps of hair all over his disgusting body except on his thick ugly skull. He got off on whipping us bloody before he fucked us. I watched two other whores die while I lived at his slum of a house."

"Die?"

"Yeah. He beat them to death, poor lads. They were nice kids. But I survived, scarred but alive. See?" Nic pulled down the collar of his loose green tunic and exposed his right shoulder. A crisscross pattern of deep, silvery pale lines disfigured his otherwise smooth tanned skin.

"But then one day, me and my former master were at the main market by the docks and Commander Fabius marched right over to us, out of nowhere, and took me away from him. I mean, that prick didn't want to sell me; he loved the way I could take the flogger. But when Dom wants something—anything—people don't say no. Or they can't." Nicomedes shook his head with a smile. "Shit, that was a long time ago. I was nineteen, which was pretty old for a street whore. It still seems like yesterday."

They were both quiet for a while, until Allerix asked, "Does he flog you for fun?"

"Who? Dom? No. Never. He's never once whipped me to get off. Not for real. Spanking, sure—but that doesn't count, right?" Nicomedes winked, and a slight flush colored his bronzed cheeks.

Allerix smirked and added, "That Varius fellow is scary, though."

"Yeah, I know—what with that nasty scar across his face! But Varius isn't that bad. His wife and children died from a sickness while he was away at war, so Dom hired him, you know, to be the guard here. He's as strong as a fucking bull, but he can't move fast. Something about a battle injury. Just stay out of trouble, and he'll leave you alone."

"Here." Allerix handed the mouse back to Nic. "Thank you."

"For what? It's just a fucking mouse. No one will miss it when it's dead, except for me."

"I will. Can I play with Achilles when he wakes up?"

"Yeah, sure. I'll show you his tricks. Mice are smarter than most people realize, you know."

"I believe you."

A flurry of steps came from the hallway outside Nic's room. Simon skidded to a stop, bracing himself against the doorpost.

"Nic, a letter's arrived!"

Nicomedes raised his brows and cocked his head slightly. "And I care about this because…?"

Simon bent over and pressed his palms against his thighs, fighting to catch his breath. Finally, he raised his head and pushed his brown curls away from his eyes.

"It's a letter. From Dom. He'll be home in five days."

"That's good news." Nic let out a long sigh and nuzzled Achilles with his nose. "I might not be around much longer, Achilles. C'mon, let's put you back in your nest."

Simon rolled his eyes as he put his hands on his hips. "Dom's not going to sell you, you daft shit!"

Nic got up and walked over to the jar in the corner, mumbling over his shoulder, "You don't know that, Simon. Dom could sell me. He could sell you. Fuck, anything could happen."

"Dom would never sell me," Simon responded defiantly.

"You know—you're right, twat. He wouldn't sell you."

Wringing his hands, Allerix closed his eyes and swallowed.

Only five more fucking days until the Roman returned—and anything could happen.

Gaius Fabius's mansion on the Caelian Hill, Rome

The spacious balcony off their winter dining room looked out over a dense landscape of buildings crammed together down in the valley below. From up here, the view of the cityscape was spectacular, especially during the first rays of morning sun. The early light reflected off the polished, creamy-white marbles, the terracotta roofs, and the red brick facades, bathing the center of Rome in a warm rosy glow.

"There you are. You're up extra early," Marcia mumbled, as she held her hand up to her mouth and yawned. She pulled her thin summer mantle around her petite frame before reclining on a couch. A few feet away, Gaius sat motionless, gazing at the scenery. Equipped with scissors and two combs, Marcia's favorite nymph, Melissa, was busy trimming his thick auburn hair, snipping off the tips of his curls here and there. In the cool morning breezes, clipped red ringlets swirled about over the black-and-white mosaic floor.

Without turning to greet her, Gaius answered, "There's a Senate meeting this morning regarding the final appropriation of land for the emperor's forum complex. I'm expected to be in attendance to demonstrate support for Apollodorus' outrageously expensive project."

Marcia furrowed her brow in confusion. "The emperor's construction plans actually require the elders' consent?"

"Not at all, but our Emperor prefers to secure a gesture of approval from the powerless farts. You know Marcus. He's extremely cautious when it concerns public perceptions, at least here in Rome. Doesn't give a fucking damn what people think of him on the battlefield, as long as his officers obey him, his enemies fear him, and the troops love him."

Marcia accepted the glass offered to her by another graceful sprite. She took a tiny sip of the undiluted wine and asked, "What about your hoard of clients? I didn't see any of those hapless fools lurking in our reception hall on my way out to the terrace."

"This morning's salutations are over, dear. I handed out the appropriate favors and pretended to listen to all of their horseshit requests. By the gods, Titus Manlius is a fucking buffoon! Did you know that witless twit closed his baths on the Quirinal without consulting me?"

"Gads, the horror! Did you chop off his head?"

"Do not mock me, wife. After these never ending celebrations and loving exchanges with my court family, I'm in no mood for ridicule."

She got up and rubbed Melissa's shoulder. "That's enough, pet. Go to the master's bedchamber and fetch his toga." After Melissa left, Marcia raked her fingers through Gaius's hair, fluffing his silky curls and massaging his scalp. "I woke up alone in a cold bed."

"I had to prepare for this early meeting and didn't want to wake you. Besides, the mattress should still have been plenty warm, given how hard and long I fucked you into it for half the night."

"Mmm, yes—that was an unexpected surprise. What on earth made you decide to visit my bed?"

"I'm your bloody husband and I was horny—as were you, my darling, if I remember our dinner conversation last night correctly. By the gods, do I need a formal invitation every single time?" Gaius leaned his head back to look up at her. "I'll admit I was relieved to find you alone."

"And if I hadn't been?"

"Simple. I would have screwed you and your girls, multiple times in every possible combination—and then I would have no doubt overslept, missed the Senate meeting, and climbed to the very top of Marcus's shit list."

She pecked his forehead and bent down to whisper into his ear, "Well, it was a good thing then I was companionless for a change, wasn't it? Gaius, darling, there's a dinner party at Aulus Spurius's estate tonight and I thought..."

He cut her off mid-sentence. "I won't be here."

"Is that right?" Marcia untangled her slender fingers from his locks and leaned her hip against the stone balustrade. "Care to tell your beloved wife where you'll be, Commander?"

"On the road to Campania, at long last."

"You've changed your plans? I thought you weren't leaving Rome for at least two more days."

"Our dear and generous friend, Lucius Petronius, offered to cover my obligations so I could depart the city earlier than scheduled. I would have implored him to attend this Senate rubbish in my stead as well, if I could have escaped Marcus's wrath." Gaius winked at her with a smirk.

Marcia crossed her arms under her small breasts and narrowed her hazel eyes. "So you're leaving the capital immediately after the Senate deliberations?"

"My travel bags are packed and the horses are ready. Will you miss me, darling?"

"No," she answered without emotion before cracking a coy grin. "Well perhaps just a little—especially after your stellar performance last night. But I won't miss your surly foul mood of late. Come back satiated and cheerful, or I won't let you in the door. You'll be forced to sleep on the entrance steps, alongside that grouchy watch dog."

"You're a cruel warden, woman. I trust you'll be dutiful while I'm gone. Spin baskets of wool and weave a new tunic for me in the atrium like a proper matron?"

"Not on your life, bastard. But I promise to be prudent, as always."

She walked over and cupped his face in her hands. "All right, I'm off to make my morning sacrifices, and then I intend to enjoy a leisurely bath before *my* obligatory business at the palace. Who knows—perhaps we'll have a baby of our own next year. I'll pray to Juno and Diana at our garden shrine and implore them for fertile blessings."

"Give those spiteful bitches my warmest regards."

"Blasphemy will never get us a baby, Gaius. A son would secure your chance to succeed Marcus as the next emperor. You should make offerings before you leave the city. Stop by the altar on the Aventine and beseech the goddess for an heir." She lifted his chin and asked, "Are you even listening to me?"

Sneering, Gaius raised an eyebrow in contempt. When Marcia leaned down and kissed him softly on the mouth, he wrapped his thick freckled arms around her waist and pulled her closer. His lips were tender but his tongue demanding. She melted into his forceful kiss. He slid his hand down her curves and pinched the soft flesh on the sensitive underside of her bum.

"Stop that!" She chuckled into his mouth. "I won't miss you at all, barbarian."

He was leaving, again. She wouldn't see her gorgeous ornery general for some time. But at least now that the wars were over, the odds were far better he'd come home alive and unharmed.

Perhaps they would be fortunate this time. Perhaps the gods would finally impregnate her barren womb. She couldn't accept it if they steadfastly denied her a child—denied Gaius the rightful heir he needed. He'd wind up being forced to adopt someone else, most likely an adult, to be the inheritor of his estate and his clients.

And there was no way on this earth Lucius Petronius would be named Gaius's heir. If he did, she'd never be rid of her husband's handsome but insufferable ex-lover. Besides, Lucius was a bloody plebeian and a lawyer, no less. And his jokes were awful.

She pulled back with a smile, her small left hand resting on Gaius's broad shoulder, and stroked his sun-kissed cheek with her right thumb. "I wish you a speedy meeting and safe travels, Commander Fabius. Have a wonderful time at the seaside, and do remember to write me once in a while. And please, whatever you do, fucking relax and try to have some fun."

"You're adorable when you curse." Gaius grinned, revealing his deep dimples. "Trust me, Domina. I intend to have cartloads of fucking fun."

11

Gaius Fabius's seaside villa, Campania

ALLERIX PRESSED HIS BACK AGAINST THE PRICKLY HOLLY BRANCHES AND HELD his breath. Varius was just on the other side of the thick, tall hedge—his heavy steps crunching the gravel on the path, the raspy wheeze of the guard's labored breathing.

"Where are you, boy? I saw you take it, so let's save us both some trouble and show yourself."

Think.

"That's why you ran, isn't it? Pets aren't allowed to play with knives, slave."

Allerix stayed completely still and tried to ignore the pounding in his chest. Sweat soaked his scalp and poured down his neck. He wanted to brush his dripping forehead with his forearm, but he didn't dare move. He'd been foolish to think he could simply run away without anyone noticing, and now here he was, within a hair's breadth of being caught and whipped within an inch of his life.

Think, for shit's sake!

In his left hand, he clutched the wooden handle of the knife he'd stolen from the stable house kitchen. It had been sitting right out on the table, ripe for nicking. It was small and blunt, but it would have to do. He'd find a more suitable weapon along the way somehow. The Roman could be here as early as tomorrow, if Allerix had calculated the distances correctly. He had to leave, now. As he gripped the weapon tighter, his knuckles paled to white and his fingers ached.

On the opposite side of the large lawn, Max and Simon were heading to the main house. Max carried a bundle of fabrics in his arms and said something to the curly-haired lad. Simon laughed and skipped up the steps right behind Max. The service door opened. No one closed it.

"Just give old Varius the knife, and I'll go easier on you."

Leather straps slapped against flesh.

"No? Very well, then. I've slaughtered hundreds of vile Dacian vermin in my time. You're cowards, all of you. I'll round up the stable hands to flush you out of whatever rat hole you've crawled into."

Allerix swore under his breath and gnawed on his full lower lip—both habits he'd had since boyhood—and squinted at the oppressive sun, high and bright in the midday sky.

It won't work.

He looked to his left, and to his right. There was no one around—only that scar-faced ox on the other side of this leafy hedge. The grinding of Varius's boots on the gravel path grew quieter until the sound faded away. Any moment now, the field slaves would return from the orchards and assemble in this yard, hungry for their first real meal of the day. And Varius would be back, but this time with a gang of armed stable hands.

It has to work.

With a deep breath, Allerix took off running across the soft grass towards the house and slipped in through the service door. Although he'd been in the main villa building before, the twisting maze of hallways confused him. Dashing through the narrow, colorfully painted corridors, he moved blindly but quickly, until he reached the open door of one of the more sparsely decorated guest rooms. Max and Simon were inside. His back to the door, the slave handler was arranging the blankets on a couch at the other end of the room as Simon babbled excitedly, gesturing with his hands, about his master's imminent return.

Allerix wiped the sweat from his upper lip with his tunic sleeve and made his move. He grabbed Simon from behind, one arm wrapped around the boy's slender torso, the blade's edge pressed against his neck. With a shaky voice, he whispered into Simon's soft brunet curls, "Don't fight me, Simon. I won't—I don't want to hurt you."

Simon didn't move or utter a word. Instinctively, he lightly pressed his arse against Allerix's thighs in a nearly imperceptible gesture of submission. The blade rose and fell when Simon swallowed.

No doubt bewildered over the sudden silence, Max turned around. "What the…? Paulus! Put that bloody knife down!"

Allerix shifted his weight to get a better grip on the boy and the weapon. Simon closed his eyes and started to cry.

"Stay back, Max! I won't hurt Simon if he follows my orders. We're leaving."

"Leaving?"

"I can't stay here. I can't fucking be that bastard's slave. His whore."

Max shook his head and sighed, before speaking soft and low, "Listen to me. You fought them and your people lost. You're a spoil of war, just another slave, and a lucky one at that. Your master's not a cruel man. Now give me the knife and let Simon go." Max took a cautious step forward, holding out his huge palm, his jaw squared in determination.

"Not a cruel man? He fucking killed my kin. My friends. He destroyed my lands!"

"Exactly. The fighting's over, and the Romans won. There's no place to run to anymore, Paulus."

"You're wrong. Some of us escaped to the mountains. There's a port near here, down the road. There must be ships. I'm leaving, and Simon's coming with me until..."

"Until?"

"Until I can get far enough away, until I can fucking find my way home. You used to be free, Max. Remember? I need to go home. Let us leave, Max—please."

"And then what? Whether you kidnap Simon or kill him, Commander Fabius will hunt you down, on or off a damn ship. He'll stop at nothing until he finds you. Simon will only slow you down. What on earth are you thinking, boy?" Max paused and rubbed his temples. "And then there's Varius. How do you imagine you'll slip by him, hmm? You think you can hold off an experienced veteran soldier with a cook's knife?"

"I can fucking try." Allerix's voice cracked. He sucked on his upper lip as his eyes began to water. "I have to try."

"Listen to me…"

Max's jaw dropped when he glanced over Allerix's shoulder.

Before Allerix could react, an arm came around from behind and clamped like a vise around his throat. A powerful bicep and thick forearm pressed against the sides of his neck and cut off his air. Cut off everything.

Allerix couldn't talk. Shit, he couldn't breathe.

The kitchen knife dropped to the stone floor, as Allerix grabbed and clawed and tried to pull away, but the steady pressure only increased. He grew dizzy and thrashed his legs in desperation. After being kicked to the floor, Simon scrambled to his feet and scurried over behind Max. The stranglehold around Allerix's neck became tighter and tighter, when a silky voice murmured softly into his ear.

"I'm home, *căţel*. You're not going fucking anywhere, Dacian. You're mine."

THE POTENTIALLY LETHAL WRESTLING MOVE GAIUS HAD MASTERED LONG AGO in the gymnasium was both efficient and quick. There would be some bruising, but no permanent damage. Terrified and confused, the Dacian's arms dropped and dangled helplessly by his sides. He sputtered incoherent nonsense right before he blacked out.

"Well— it's good to see everything's fucking under control in my absence, Maximus." Gaius twisted his thin lips into a ferocious snarl.

"Commander, I…"

While Gaius lowered the Dacian's limp body to the floor, Max tried to collect his jumbled thoughts. "Sir, I have no excuse. I was careless, and the Dacian is… well, he's cagey, sir. And scared and…"

"Damn right you have no excuse!" Gaius yelled. He took a deep breath to control his temper before softening his tone to smooth honey. "Simon. Come here, pup."

With as much grace as possible on weak legs, Simon ran over and fell to his knees at his master's feet. He moaned gratefully as he brushed his wet cheek against Gaius's dirt-speckled calf. While he fluffed the boy's thick luxurious locks with his right hand, Gaius glared at his freedman.

"I warned you he would be a handful, Maximus—until I break him, this feral mongrel requires close supervision."

"I…"

"Enough! Haul the Dacian to the playroom and bind him to the ceiling ring. Leave him dressed. And close the shutters and extinguish the lamps in there. I'll school the savage myself after my bath."

"Yes, Commander."

After he'd tossed the barbarian over his left shoulder like a sack of grain, Max headed straight for the large suite in the other wing of the house. Gaius raked his fingers through his hair, still damp and dark with sweat from his travels.

"Simon."

The boy looked up, his wide eyes peeping through his mop of curls, his cheeks streaked with tears and dirt. Gaius lifted his chin with a gentle finger and turned Simon's head back and forth, inspecting the boy's sinuous neck for any signs of a wound. Once he was confident his favorite pet was unharmed, Gaius's fierce amber eyes relaxed at the succulent vision of Simon's quivering full mouth. Fuck, he missed his Cupid.

"You did well by not struggling and getting yourself injured, pup. Are you all right?"

Simon nodded.

"You may speak, Simon."

"Thank you, Dominus. Yes, I'm fine. Is… is Paulus badly hurt?" Simon immediately flinched. He hadn't been given permission to ask a question.

"No, sweetheart. He's not seriously hurt. He'll be punished for his actions, but that's not your concern, now is it?" Without warning, Gaius's gentle touch turned harsh. He grabbed a clump of Simon's thick hair and twisted the brown curls with his fingers. "Apparently, discipline of all my pets, including you, has become rather lax during my absence."

Simon tried not to wince as he pressed his head into his master's fist. He didn't dare open his green eyes or move a muscle. A few moments passed before Max returned, panting.

"The Dacian is shackled exactly as you specified, Commander."

Gaius pulled Simon's head back by his hair. "Simon, open those beautiful eyes for me. Go tell Atticus to prepare my bath. It was a long, shitty ride from my client's stinking hovel, and I need a good soak and a cup of our best grape. See that it's done correctly."

"Yes, Dominus."

After Simon scampered out of the room, Gaius fumbled with the stubborn knot of his riding cloak. When he finally had it untied, he threw the garment on the couch with a disgusted huff and walked over to the window, his hands curled into fists, his back to his freedman. After a few moments of silence, Gaius turned around slowly, his nostrils flaring.

"Max."

Max stood with his hands crossed behind his back, his gaze fixed to the floor. "Yes, sir?"

"Damn it, look at me, Maximus! Are you certain the Dacian's bindings are fucking secure?"

"Yes, Commander. I'm positive."

"Good." Gaius marched over, roughly gripped two fistfuls of Max's tunic and yanked him down until their faces were inches apart. "Go find Varius and have him mete five lashes to your negligent arse and five more to your careless back—out in the exercise yard where I can witness the flogging. Or would you rather I take away your freedom?"

"No, sir."

Satisfied, Gaius released his hold. Max's shame was palpable as he swallowed and bowed before he silently left the room.

Gaius collapsed in the chair by the small desk and rubbed his tired, bloodshot eyes. He leaned back and lifted his filthy legs, propping them up on the smooth surface. Letting his head fall back, Gaius sighed as he dragged both hands through his dusty, matted hair.

"Ah, yes. Fucking cartloads of fun."

~

"Yes, right there. Shit, yes."

In the far corner of the room, an elderly slave ducked in the doorway and tossed another ladle of water over the hot rocks in the bronze brazier. With a loud hissing noise, fresh clouds of steam filled the small chamber. The walls of the sweating room located just off Dominus's private bath suite were covered in colorful paintings of marine life and dramatic episodes of Odysseus' sea voyage. Rivulets of condensation slowly dripped down the plaster frescoes, pooling along the edges of the mosaic floor.

Undressed and face down on the firm couch, Dominus reached under his hips and readjusted his full, aching balls. Simon hoped a good, hard fuck was next on the menu; at the moment, his master seemed satisfied with a soothing rub down after having spent too many hours baking in the saddle. When Dominus lifted his head for a swallow of Spanish wine, Simon dribbled another splatter of warmed oil over the skin of his lower back.

On his knees, naked and soaked with sweat, Simon straddled his master's muscular thighs, expertly kneading away the stiffness knotting his back and shoulders. Despite his lithe and lightly muscled frame, Simon's wide shoulders offered perfect leverage. With every push of his talented fingers and every firm press of his palms, he elicited a delightful chorus of muffled grunts and appreciative raspy moans. Max had trained Simon in many arts long before he was old enough to be fucked. Massage had turned out to be one of his treasured talents; with each steady stroke, he felt his master's tension gradually melt away.

"Dominus, may I ask a question?"

"Mmm… yes, Simon. What is it, love?"

Simon hesitated before he spoke; this was potentially dangerous territory, especially for a slave, even if he was the master's current darling. He brushed away the curls sticking to his sweaty forehead with the back of his hand and gathered his thoughts before asking the question that had been tormenting him ever since Nicomedes had stupidly earned Dom's wrath.

"What will you do about Nic, Dominus?"

"Why do you…? Wait—is there something wrong with him?" Dominus stiffened with worry. He abruptly raised himself up on his right forearm to look back over his shoulder at Simon.

"No, he's well. It's just that, um… he's been behaving much better, Dominus."

With a sigh of relief but clearly annoyed at the misunderstanding, his master lowered his head back down on a richly colored pillow.

Simon had an odd protective streak when it came to Nicomedes, despite the fact that Nic was older and more experienced—and much more of a shithead. He wondered when his master would realize he'd also grown quite fond of the raven-haired Dacian.

"Max's letters have kept me updated on Nic's behavior adjustment. So, you believe our blond slut has learned his lesson then, Simon?"

"I think he has, Dominus."

"Did Nicomedes ask you to speak to me on his behalf?"

"No, Dominus!" At the audacious sound of his response, Simon immediately shut his mouth and lowered his chin. He swallowed hard before speaking another word. The last thing he wanted to do was to get Nic in even more trouble.

"Then what's your concern, pup?"

"Dominus, I… I think Nic's frightened you've lost interest in him—that you're going to sell him."

Dom chuckled. "Good. Nicomedes should be fucking worried, though not because I intend to peddle him off on another owner. That damn cocky attitude of his needs some serious tempering, despite how often it amuses me."

"May I ask another question, Dominus?"

"Chatty today, aren't we, pet? There are much better uses for that lovely mouth of yours, you know."

Simon smiled affectionately at his master's mess of auburn locks spread over the blue pillow at the head of the couch. He cleared his throat, waiting for permission to ask another question.

"Well, what is it then?"

"Did Nicomedes make the right choice?"

"Ah, yes. Fuck—that feels bloody good." Dominus stretched his arms out as Simon rubbed and squeezed his taut, tensed biceps. "What choice, Simon? You mean the choice between prostituting for my profit at Sirius's brothel or the chastity cage? Yes, Nicomedes made the correct choice. He's a sharp lad. You both are, pup."

"Thank you, Dominus."

Simon hopped off the couch, easily catching his balance before he slipped on the wet floor, and began massaging his master's tight hamstrings and calves, paying special attention to the soles of his feet as well. His face broke into a bright proud grin whenever Dom groaned in relief. When the grunts and moans stopped, and Simon wondered if his handsome owner might have fallen asleep, Dom asked a question.

"Simon, what do you make of the Dacian?"

"Paulus? He's all right, I guess. He keeps to himself much of the time. I've been teaching him how to speak our language, Dominus. He's a good student. I think Paulus is very bright, sir."

"So you believe he's worth my fucking trouble?"

Simon froze, both hands wrapped around his master's right calf. He had unwittingly entered more dangerous territory. He'd have to pick his words carefully.

"He needs training, Dominus. Given what happened to him, he'll require some patience as well."

"Explain."

"Well, what I mean is… he's not like me or Nic, Dominus. Max told us he was captured not that long ago. So, if he wasn't born a slave, he has no real understanding of… well, what he is now. He's confused and scared, I imagine. Sir."

"Good boy." Dominus slowly rolled off the couch with a labored groan and moved behind Simon to whisper in his ear, "That was a difficult question, and you handled it well."

He ran his right palm over the curve of Simon's arse as he pressed two fingers lightly against the small of his back. Simon's heart raced at the subtle but familiar signal. Seductively and without a word, he bent face first over the couch, stretching his hairless arms forward and curling his fingers over the edge of the sturdy piece of furniture. Without another prompt, Simon spread his legs wide, arched his back, and offered up his round bum.

"Such a good lad," Dom cooed as he tenderly stroked Simon's sensitive underside. Suddenly, his master turned towards the door and shouted, "Slave! Water!"

A flutter of footsteps followed by slurping sounds, and then two thick, oiled fingers pushed hard into Simon's hole. Simon gasped before he moaned at the slick, burning pleasure; no one had fucked him since his master had left for Rome. Dom had given him a dildo and he could finger himself if he wanted to, but it wasn't anything like this. Simon needed to be filled by his master's cock, to be completely owned by his ferocious desire.

More thirsty gulping, as Dom's fingers twisted and opened him. Out of the corner of Simon's eye, the old slave held up the silver cup of water, his blank expression showing no sign he noticed or cared their master's fingers were sliding in and out of Simon's exposed pucker.

After a few more moments of drinking and fingering, Dominus snapped. "Leave, slave."

Before the servant had a chance to depart the sweating room, Dom impaled Simon in one demanding, rough thrust. Simon cried out and whimpered into the thin fabric of the couch, squirming and pushing back for more.

His master leaned down and mumbled against Simon's damp skin, "You've missed me, haven't you?"

"Very much, Dominus," Simon groaned into the cloth. His slender legs started to shake when his master began pounding into him hard, slapping his bum with his bare hand every now and again. Dom pulled nearly all the way out and slowly drove back into Simon's greased entrance.

"Shit, I've missed your sweet arse, pup." Dominus slid his hand between the couch and Simon's stomach and lifted him up, setting Simon down on the cushion on his knees, all the while his cock buried deep inside his tight body. Dom pulled his torso back against his broad, hairless chest and lightly stroked Simon's dripping prick. "When I give you permission, come for me. Shoot your seed as far as you can, dove. Understand?"

With his eyes closed and both hands clinging onto his master's muscular arms, Simon grinned and nodded.

Dom grabbed him by the jaw with his free hand and snarled into Simon's damp curls, "That was a fucking question, pup."

"Yes, Domi—"

He slipped three fingers into Simon's open mouth.

"There's my darling, obedient boy. Now suck… that's right, be noisy while I fuck your sweet cream right out of you, pet. You'll be lucky if you can walk back to the stable house when I'm finished with you. Would you like that?"

With three thick fingers tickling the back of his throat, Simon laughed as he gurgled around their girth, "Yes, Dominus. Very much."

12

Gaius Fabius's seaside villa, Campania

When Allerix regained consciousness, every muscle and fiber ached from strain and fatigue. His long arms were stretched taut, his biceps pressed against the sides of his head. With each thumping beat of his heart, a painful lump at the back of his head pulsed.

He opened his heavy-lidded eyes; his vision gradually adjusted to the low light. Several feet in front of him was a fuzzy, large rectangular shape —probably a bed. There were smaller silhouettes in the large space, furniture of some sort or other. But no lamps lit, no windows open, only a few faint streaks of orange light seeping in through the narrow crevices between the closed shutters.

How long had he been here, wherever here was?

Allerix looked up at the leather straps ensnaring his wrists. He pulled and jerked them, but the restraints were tight and sturdy.

He was trapped, vulnerable to whatever happened next.

It suddenly occurred to him perhaps nothing would happen. Perhaps the monster would leave him here, like a helpless calf strung up at market until he died from thirst. He licked his chapped, cracked lips and tasted blood.

To die from thirst would be slow. Perhaps the Roman would be merciful and return with a sacrificial knife, slice open his abdomen, and pull out his liver. Would his eviscerated guts reveal a favorable omen, a divine sign from their sadistic gods?

Shit, he was going mad.

He looked down at his bare feet, bound at the ankles, and wiggled his toes. He'd been wearing a pair of flimsy sandals when he'd dashed across the yard to follow Max and Simon into the main house. They were gone. He closed his eyes and thought back to that tenth birthday, when he received his first pair of hunting boots. He could still see his father's beaming smile as he tied the final knot of the thick string with a proud harrumph.

There was nothing left now, was there? No mines of gold, no stockpile of weaponry, no future, no honor—nothing, except a few useless baubles packed away by the surviving elders on the day before their frantic escape to the mountains. His city, his home, and his past—everything was gone, razed to the ground and destroyed forever by these ruthless savages.

At least he would die clothed. Fuck, he despised this shapeless slave costume from that very first day Max had pulled the scratchy fabric over his head. His favorite woolen shirt and his long trousers had been left behind in the field where those soldiers had raped him. And Gorgas. Allerix tried to shake the memory of that brutal day from his aching skull, but all he could see was the anguish in Gorgas' tear-filled eyes, pleading for help that would never arrive.

Shit, his head hurt.

Allerix temporarily lost his balance as the room began to spin. He leaned to the right, pulling against the bite of the bindings. Dizzy and disoriented, he watched dumbstruck as a vision of Tarbus's ruddy face materialized like a cloud of smoke in the dim air. The hallucination of his bastard of a half-brother rolled a section of his long, full beard between two fingers and laughed in that deep, mocking voice of his.

"Well, well. Look at this. Trussed to the ceiling like a holiday hog, little brother? Quite fitting, really—considering how you disgraced our father and offended the gods, you filthy cock sucking deviant."

The apparition of Tarbus faded as quickly as it had appeared. Goose bumps broke out over Allerix's thighs; he shivered as the forest of black hairs on his legs stood on end. With the short tunic hiked up over his narrow hips, the humid air tickled his bare arse and danced across the sensitive skin of his dangling sac.

Allerix licked his dry lips again and shouted into the shadow-filled space, "Kill me, you Roman cunt!"

The words ricocheted off the walls and reverberated throughout the dark room.

And then, nothing.

Just silence, save for the sound of his own heavy breathing.

His head dropped forward between his shoulders, as he prayed, "Oh great Zalmoxis, protector of all that is true and just, take pity on your foolish child and guide me to my next life."

And still there was nothing. Only silence.

Allerix, second son of Thiamarkos, had been forsaken.

"GREETINGS, LADS!" SIMON YELLED, AS HE SKIPPED CHEERFULLY INTO THE common gathering room of the stable house. His brunet curls flopped about in every direction, and a satisfied shit-eating grin was plastered across his happy face. It was late in the day; the stone hall was ablaze in hues of red and gold from the waning sunlight, the air hazy from the lingering smoke of the cooking fire in the nearby kitchen. Simon's stomach growled when he caught a tantalizing whiff of the afternoon meal he'd missed: roasted pork, greens with fennel, and fresh bread.

Wired and fidgety, Simon plopped his well-fucked bum into a chair. Seated next to him on a low cushioned stool, Max cradled his head in his folded arms on the table as he shifted his flogged body back and forth. When Simon reached for a piece of fruit from the red ceramic bowl filled with treats from the orchard, Nic smacked his hand, hard.

"We need to address Max by his proper title all of the time now. Dom is home. No more fucking sloppy mistakes, got it?"

With a look of disbelief, Simon recoiled and groaned at the stinging pain. Across the table from him, Nic scraped off the last bits of food from his plate, his eyes cast down and his face hidden behind his shoulder-length hair.

Simon protested, "What Paulus did is not my fault, Nic. He could have killed me!"

"But he didn't. Pity, isn't it?"

Chewing the last morsel slowly, Nic pushed back from the heavy oak table and crossed his bronzed athletic arms.

"How is Dom, then?" Nicomedes' normally lush voice was weak and unsure.

"He's well. Tired from his travels, but well. Do you think there's anything left for me to eat? I'm starving."

Nic picked a piece of ripe fruit out of the bowl and took a bite. "I would have thought your little belly was full of Dom's seed, twat."

Peering out from beneath his long curls, Simon smirked. "Nah, Dom didn't want my mouth. Mine's too small and nowhere near as talented as your golden gob, Nic. Isn't that what you always say? That you're Dom's favorite cock sucker?" Simon winked in jest, and then ducked to avoid being clocked in the head by the partially eaten apricot.

Max growled. "Fucking quit, both of you. Should I send for Varius? I'm sure he has plenty of energy left."

Before either pleasure slave could protest, the rotund cook waddled into the room carrying a plate of steaming food. Plautus dropped a generous meal down on the table in front of Simon with a rude thud, shot Nic an annoyed glare, and left to mind the kitchen without saying a word to anyone.

"Friendly fellow, that Plautus," Simon mumbled as he tore off pieces of crusty, warm bread to soak up the spicy sauce. "Shit, I forgot how hungry I get after Dom fucks me."

"Slow down, Simon. You'll choke—argh, shit!" Max winced.

"Sir, are you all right?"

Max waved Simon off and groaned across the table, "Nic, love—I need more of that salve."

Nic jumped up and grabbed a wad of boiled wool and the bottle of ointment out of a shallow tray resting on a side table.

"May I lift your tunic, sir?" he asked.

Max grunted as he nodded. With nimble fingers, Nic delicately dabbed the herb-infused numbing cream on the raw stripes stinging Max's skin. "There, that should help. Is it better?"

"Much better. Thank you."

Nic kissed the back of Max's thick neck. "You'll heal quickly, sir. Looks like Varius delivered a light hand."

"I suppose so. Dom must have signaled for Varius to go easy on me. I have no fucking idea why, though."

"Dom loves you. Besides, you couldn't have predicted Paulus would pull a knife on Simon, sir. No one could have foreseen that."

"I bloody well should have, Nicomedes. I suspect I'll be paying for that major mistake for some time." Max cleared his throat. "Simon, did Dom give you any instructions before he sent you back here?"

"He told me to eat better and get more sleep. Dom was pissed off I'm skinnier and pastier than he remembered."

"Shit." Max dropped his head in his cupped hands and grumbled, "Was that all he said?"

"Um, I think so, sir." Simon grabbed his cup and closed his eyes as he gulped down a mouthful of water.

"Sir?"

"Yes, Nicomedes?"

Nic leaned down and spoke softly into Max's ear, "Do you have another task for me?"

"No, sweetheart."

"May I have your permission to return to my room?" Nic's voice was shaky. The cage punishment had broken his spirit. Worse, Dom was finally home but there hadn't been the usual immediate demand for Nic's mouth —no sign at all the blond had been forgiven.

Max turned around and prodded gently, "Are you all right, Nicomedes?"

"Dom's lost interest in me, hasn't he?" Nic whispered, as he gnawed on his thumbnail. "S'all right, though. I'll serve another master, like before."

Nic pulled his thumb away and bit the inside of his cheek, trying to maintain his composure.

Max rubbed his face with a sigh. "There's nothing else, Nicomedes. You may retire to your cell."

Simon suddenly piped up, "Oh, there *was* something else."

Welling up with tears, Nic's eyes opened wide at the twinkle in Simon's mischievous voice. Simon put his cup down slowly and, with an impish grin on his face, looked straight into Nic's bright blue eyes.

"Dom said to tell you, Nicomedes, to get all cleaned up and hightail your pretty arse to the playroom before it gets dark."

Simon crumpled against Max's shoulder in a fit of giggles fueled by his buggered-arse euphoria. He rarely pulled a prank on Nic and when he did, it almost never succeeded.

Nic grabbed Max's shoulders for support as he collapsed with relief, before reaching over and thwacking Simon's ear with a loud pop. "You little prick!"

After grabbing a fistful of his chestnut curls, Nic pulled Simon up from his chair and latched onto the boy's soft mouth, drowning him in a harsh, punishing kiss. No doubt the lad wanted to punch Simon in the face, but Nic couldn't afford another cock up. When Simon struggled to breathe, Nic dropped the stunned sprite and sauntered off to wash up, cheering with obscene hand gestures.

Simon coughed and wheezed, before finally blurting out, "Max! He can't—Nic's not allowed to do that to me! Sir."

"You deserved much worse, Simon. I would have strangled you." Max smirked and winked. "And don't fucking whinge. It's not attractive."

~

THE ECHO OF STEADY FOOTSTEPS FILLED THE SPACE BEHIND HIM.

Allerix cautiously opened his eyes. At first he didn't move in a pathetic attempt to feign sleep, but temptation and his military training defeated that cowardly strategy. He tried to turn around when a hand grabbed his hair by the roots and held his head firmly in place.

"Keep your eyes forward, Dacian, or I will snap your fucking neck."

The warning was calm but venomous.

Allerix recalled that unforgettable hypnotic voice from the arduous trip down to the villa. He'd been bound and blindfolded for the entire journey, but for a short stage of that uncomfortable, bumpy ride on the hard floor of the wagon, that same haunting voice had washed over his sweaty face.

"You're safe now, pet. We've left Rome."

"You are mine to protect and cherish and defile. Mine alone."

Behind them, someone held up a lamp. Flickering light from a flame illuminated a small portion of the dim space. The Roman adjusted his grip and tightened his fist, as he angled Allerix's head back. Allerix cried out in pain when his hard knuckles pressed against the tender lump on his scalp.

~

GAIUS STUDIED THE CONTOURS OF THE DACIAN'S PROFILE: LONG DARK LASHES; a slightly curved, small nose; luscious full lips; that round cleft chin and those gracefully arched eyebrows, clenched in agony. He loosened his hold until the Dacian's pained expression softened.

As lamplight flickered across the walls, Gaius brushed his other hand over the black scruff of the slave's short, soft beard. Shit, the lad was even more attractive than he'd remembered. Once the mongrel was rid of his thick cover of whiskers, his face would be absolutely exquisite. This new plaything might actually be worth every bit of silver spent at Decius's private auction.

"Put the lamp on the table by the bed," Gaius ordered.

~

A ROGUE REDDISH CURL OF HAIR BOUNCED INTO ALLERIX'S VIEW BUT QUICKLY disappeared. He'd never seen the face of this fucking bastard—he'd only heard that velvety voice and felt those strong hands. Late one restless night at the stable house, Simon had described with blatant delight the details of his master's appearance, but Allerix needed to see the prick with his own eyes. His ignorance about something so basic, so necessary, was driving him mad.

The servant carried the lamp over to the right corner of the room, lighting up the space. Allerix shut his eyes tight. His suspicions had been correct.

The playroom.

With one hand gripping him firmly by the hair, the Roman drew his weapon and held the shiny blade high enough for the reality of the dagger to be crystal clear.

"I see you like to play with knives, cub. So do I. Perhaps we'll play together some time."

Allerix could hear the monster's smile.

Light from the flame danced off the polished steel surface, casting random patterns of pale reflections over the painted walls. After catching his breath, Allerix opened his mouth to speak. The sharp metal point pricked the tender skin on the underside of his hairy chin. He flinched while small drops of warm blood trickled down his pale neck.

"Rule number one, Dacian: Do not speak unless I ask a direct question. Simple enough, yes?"

Allerix swallowed and said nothing.

"That was a fucking direct question. Do you understand rule number one?"

Allerix stammered, deliberately fumbling his words, "I speak not your tongue."

"I see. My tongue, did you say?" The Roman chuckled and lowered his voice. "Let us hope for the sake of those lovely barbarian balls of yours you're a quick study, cub."

He pressed the cool flat of the steel blade against Allerix's thigh, a mere hand's width below his exposed groin. "Do you understand rule number one, *cățel*?"

"Yes. I understand."

"Excellent. I don't fuck eunuchs." The monster leaned in close and whispered, "But perhaps I'm being selfish—a terrible habit of mine. Would you prefer a quick castration, Dacian?"

"No."

"Maximus must have taught you how to properly address your master. Let's try that again, shall we?" He grazed the edge of the dagger blade across Allerix's wrinkled sac.

"No, Dominus," Allerix conceded through clenched teeth.

GAIUS'S SCOWL MELTED INTO A SMILE. WHAT A BLOODY LOVELY VOICE FOR A vulgar barbarian.

After sheathing his dagger, Gaius pulled out a strip of black cloth. He released his hold on the lad's thick hair, but only long enough to tie the rag securely over those big dark eyes.

A soft shuffling sound came from the direction of the doorway behind them.

"Dominus, you sent for me?"

"Nicomedes, you gorgeous rascal. Strip and get on the bed, scamp. I need to have a word with you."

Nic quickly unbuckled his leather belt and pulled his tunic up over his head with the grace of a dancer. He reclined, face up, atop the mattress and folded his arms under his head as he spread his knees wide apart. Gaius spied the magnificent bronze device Nic had endured for months.

With a firm farewell pat to the Dacian's bare bum, Gaius strolled over to the foot of the bed. The polished surfaces of the mesh cock cage ensnaring Nic's shaft shimmered in the flickering light of the oil lamp. The metal casing was secured to Nic's groin by thick leather straps belted around Nic's waist and arse. The cage itself was a deceptively simple design of overlapping, tight-fighting bronze bands linked together by a sturdy curved rod.

Gaius cocked his head and licked his lips at the vision of his blond slut's prick wrapped in those shiny bronze bangles. What a remarkably well-crafted and strangely beautiful device—like a fine piece of precious lattice jewelry. Another visit to that talented bronze smith's shop back at the capital was in order.

He reached down, grabbed Nic's ankles, and dragged the pleasure slave towards the foot of the bed.

"Maximus reports you've been on your best behavior, pet. So, why on earth did I lock your prick in that cock cage? Remind me."

"Dominus, I..." Nic's sultry voice cracked from nerves as he blurted out his offense, "I earned my punishment for fucking Zoe—outside of your presence and without your permission, Dominus."

"I'm curious, Nicomedes. Did you think the punishment was too harsh? Have I been cruel?"

"No, Dominus. I should have been castrated for my inexcusable crime."

"Castrated?" Gaius smirked and scraped his teeth across his lower lip. "I should have killed you, lamb—or sold your whoring arse to the fucking mines." Gaius looked away and exhaled, before looking back into Nic's desperate, glassy blue eyes. "I'm far too soft when it comes to you. You do know that, don't you?"

"Yes, Dominus." Nic tried not to weep even though tears were close to the surface. With his hands still wrapped tightly around Nic's raised ankles, Gaius felt the boy's legs trembling from fear.

"I should have killed you, Nicomedes. Do you understand me?"

Nic gulped. "Yes, Dominus."

"Do you remember where I store the key to the lock for that chastity contraption? Get up and fetch it now."

After Gaius released his ankles with a thump, Nick hurried over to the vaulted alcove holding the storage box and lifted the lid. His eyes wandered over the impressive collection of dildos, plugs, cock rings and braided leather restraints. Finally, he spied the brown woven bag and dug out the small key tangled in the dark threads at the bottom. Returning to Gaius's side, Nic collapsed to his knees and pressed his forehead to the floor. He raised his left arm, the metal key to the cage lock cradled in his palm like a sacred offering.

After he sat down on the side of the mattress, Gaius plucked the small piece of iron from Nic's hand.

"Over my lap, on your back. As exquisite as it looks on you, lamb, it's time to remove that heinous apparatus."

Shaking, Nic rose and arched his long back over Gaius's thighs. He stared at the shadowy upside-down image of the Dacian's bound feet a few feet away. After Gaius opened the lock with a sharp click, he slipped off the leather straps and heavy scrotum rings before placing them on the table. He carefully pulled off the linked metal bands and inspected Nic's flaccid member. His pet's shaft was marked with indentations, scrapes, and slight bruises, but otherwise he was only superficially disfigured. Nicomedes' young equipment would recover quickly.

"When was the last time you had a pleasurable release, pet?" Gaius asked gently, knowing full well the answer, while he reached over and dipped his left hand in a jar of oil on the table by the lamp. Drops of the slippery liquid splattered across Nic's legs.

"Not since you caged me, Dominus—two months ago." With his sandy-flaxen hair pooled on the floor around his head, Nic groaned in bliss when Gaius wrapped his right hand around the base of Nic's cock and began stroking him—gently at first and then more firmly.

"Maximus milked you regularly, correct?" Gaius's breaths were controlled, although his eyes were not on Nic, but instead fixed on the Dacian's luscious mouth. The blindfolded beauty was panting, heavily—a promising sign.

"Yes, Maximus milked me, Dominus." Nic squeezed his eyes tight. According to Gaius's instructions, he'd been bent over a wooden rack in a dusty stall in the stables while Max pushed his greased hand up his bum to force his semen to dribble out through the tip of the cage. Nasty business, milking.

Gaius kept stroking Nic's hardening shaft. "That must have been unpleasant for you. There's no pain now, is there?"

"No, Dom…" Nic gasped when two of Gaius's oiled fingers penetrated him, pushing deeper until Gaius located the lad's swollen prostate.

"You are so bloody sensitive under my hands, lamb—glistening with sweat and lust, responding to my every caress."

Nic's release took a while; his neglected body had to catch up with his raging need. Gaius was patient and steady, pumping Nic's engorged prick with one hand, rubbing firm against his bumpy nub with the other.

"Come for your master." Gaius leaned down and flicked his tongue across Nic's wet slit. "Let it go."

Nic babbled incoherent nonsense as his back arched and his balls pulled up. He cried out when thick ribbons of semen shot out and splashed over his abdomen and his chest, a smattering of milky cream landing on his face and his neck. Nicomedes was covered in pools of bliss.

Gaius chuckled softly. "So fucking perfect every time."

Nic's ecstatic moans gradually changed to heaving sobs as he covered his sweat-drenched face with both hands. Gaius slipped his forearm underneath Nic's back and pulled the blond up on his lap. After a deep, slow tongue fuck, Gaius stopped to comb out Nicomedes' matted wet hair with his fingers.

"I've missed you, Nicomedes. It was torture forcing myself to ignore you. Make sure I never need to cage you again, pet. Understood?"

Humming and giggling, Nic nodded, shut his eyes and leaned against his shoulder while Gaius traced lazy circles in the pearly puddles mixed with sweat on Nic's smooth chest. Gaius scooped the slave up in his arms and gently placed his slack, shivering body on the soft mattress.

"All is well. I'm home now." Gaius pressed a loving peck to Nic's soaked temple. "But mind my words—I will not forgive you a second time."

After Gaius pressed the tip of his finger against Nic's full lower lip, he slowly pushed himself off the bed. An eerie silence filled the room.

Gaius strolled over, glanced at Allerix's bobbing, half-hard prick, and smiled. He cupped his bristly chin in his palm and said, "It pleases me you enjoyed listening to Nic's pleasure, cub. Will there be a day when I forgive your idiocy? Will I ever find reason to trust you?"

13

Gaius Fabius's seaside villa, Campania

As he stood there studying his raven-haired purchase bound to the ceiling in his playroom, Gaius's freckled skin flushed and his cock throbbed with arousal. The blindfolded Dacian inhaled and exhaled through parted lips. After every third or fourth rapid breath, his luscious mouth quivered, his rosy lips framed by that black scruffy beard. Gaius stepped closer and reached his right hand around the boy's slender waist, running his palm over the curve of his bare arse, and fingered the cleft between his damp, tensed cheeks.

The barbarian swallowed, but made no sound.

After slowly removing his hand from the lad's crack, Gaius brushed his knuckles under his slave tunic and over the smooth skin of his stomach, tracing the line of soft black hair traveling from his navel to his groin. He stroked the barbarian's thickening cock before cupping the Dacian's supple sac with his other palm. His new trophy gasped softly, but didn't move a muscle.

"I paid that sniveling Egyptian dealer a foolish amount of silver for an unsullied arse. Are you a virgin, *căţel*?" Gaius's tone dripped with amusement.

"You wasted your coin, *asasinule*," the Dacian spat back with a sneer, his teeth clenched in terrified rage. Sprawled out on the mattress, Nic instinctively flinched as if he were the one about to be hit. But Gaius didn't backhand the arrogant beast across the face; he chuckled and leaned in closer.

"Trust me. I'll recover my investment tenfold, one way or another." Gaius tightened his grip on the Dacian's balls as the words rolled off his sharp tongue like thick syrup. "Now open your mouth for your murderer of a master."

Gaius traced his fingertip over the full mounds of the boy's lips before he slipped two thick fingers, still a tad sticky from Nic's salty release, into the Dacian's snarling mouth. When Gaius felt teeth graze his skin, he squeezed the barbarian's balls hard and warned, "Do not fucking bite me. Open wider."

The beauty pursed and then separated his lips; Gaius pushed his fingers until they bumped against the back of the lad's throat.

"Suck my fingers clean. Show me what you can do, besides cocking up a simple escape."

As tears rolled down his cheeks from beneath the lower edge of the blindfold, the Dacian tried to force his fingers out with his tongue, but he wound up only drooling and gagging louder when Gaius pressed in even farther. Defeated, the barbarian drew in a deep breath through his nostrils and surrendered; his whiskered jaw slackened and relaxed as he hugged the girth of Gaius's probing fingers.

"There's a good, obedient slave. You have potential, my dear new bauble." Gaius pulled his hand out and gently wiped off the Dacian's tear-streaked cheeks with the side of his thumb.

"Atticus!"

The playroom door opened with a slight squeak of the metal hinges.

"Yes, Dominus?"

"Send for Maximus. Tell him to bring the shaving tools. It's time to barber this wooly creature." Gaius dropped his voice as he stroked the back of his hand over the lad's beard. "So bloody soft. I imagine these whiskers would feel exquisite against my balls. It'll be a shame to see them go, but I need to see your entire face, Dacian."

Gaius brushed his lips over the boy's ear shell. "Do you know how this feels—this moment right now? It's that same thrilling tingle of expectation that buzzes through a child right before he unwraps a precious gift on the Saturnalia."

Gaius stepped back, crossed his arms and narrowed his eyes; the shackled Dacian licked his lips as he swayed back and forth blindly. A series of rapid knocks on the door interrupted the heavy quiet of anticipation.

"Enter."

The door swung open. "Commander."

"That was bloody quick. Did you race a rabbit here from the stable house, Maximus?"

"I marched as fast as possible, sir," Max garbled out between panting breaths. "Apologies for my tardiness."

Gaius rolled his eyes as he uncrossed his arms and nodded towards the Dacian. "Remove his beard—but do it slowly."

Max hesitated for a moment before grabbing the barbarian's face with his left hand. He lifted one of the sharpened iron knives from a leather pouch attached to his belt, stretched the Dacian's skin taut, and began shearing off the thick bristles. Back and forth, up and down. No oil, no lubricant of any sort to safeguard his skin from the searing burns of the scraper. The blade snagged and nicked his jaw and neck; tiny drops of blood bubbled up from the cuts.

"Nicomedes!"

Naked and spent, Nic sprang off the bed and knelt at his master's feet, his perfect nose pressed against the stone floor.

"Taste my new dark-haired cherry."

Without hesitation, Nic rose up on his knees and took the Dacian's prick down his throat, sucking and slurping feverishly.

With his eyes fixed on the lad's face, Gaius absentmindedly tangled his fingers in Nic's damp, wavy hair as the blond bobbed up and down, engulfing and undoing his new slave with each slobbery stroke.

Scrape after burning scrape, Max's razor revealed the pale glow of ruddy skin as the Dacian pressed his lips together. Cropped ebony hairs littered the floor, some stray bits fluttering down to land on Nic's blond mane. Languidly following the gentle slope of the lad's flawless nose with his finger, Gaius growled, "Sing for me, Dacian. I want to hear you enjoy Nic's talented mouth, savage."

~

ANOTHER STINGING RAKE OF THE HONED BLADE ACROSS ALLERIX'S CHEEK; another wet stroke of Nic's exquisite tongue along the pulse of his vein.

Trying to keep his head still against the pressure of Max's shaky grip and the iron razor, Allerix fought the urge as long as he could until a low, raspy whimper forced itself out from between his vibrating lips.

~

"Fucking exquisite," Gaius exclaimed.

With a last flick of the cutter, Max stepped back, returned the razor to the pouch, and cast his gaze to the floor, both hands quickly crossed behind his back.

Gaius sighed. "So you enjoy pleasure with a bite of discomfort, *căţel*. That's delightfully fortunate."

The Dacian sputtered and buckled against the restraints in vain, desperate for release. Nic's mouth was talented. The dark-haired lad was close to orgasm.

"Stop," Gaius commanded.

Nic pulled his mouth off, wiped his spit-covered chin with the back of his hand, and resumed his kneeling position on the floor by Gaius's feet. As the Dacian's discarded cock jerked and dripped, an anguished cry of frustration and torment spilled out of his mouth. Gaius grabbed him by the hair and noticed a lump on the back of his skull.

"Listen to me, pretty heathen. You'll fucking earn any crumb of pleasure I might give you." Gaius drew his hand back and smacked the boy's dangling balls with his half-closed fist.

The Dacian's cries rose to a scream.

Gaius stepped closer. "Never lay a hand—or a blunt kitchen knife—on my whores without my fucking permission!"

Breathing heavily, Gaius dragged his hands through his curls. He reached down and cupped Nic's face between both of his palms, along with a few stray wisps of Nic's golden locks. "Nicomedes, my lamb."

He lifted him up and kissed Nic passionately on the mouth before releasing him, breathless.

"Get dressed. Those bright blue eyes of yours will light up the foot of my dining couch. You and I will return here for dessert, so don't waste my time gathering up your sandals."

~

Although the sounds of their footsteps faded, through the walls Allerix heard the Roman bark more orders at Max.

"You, Maximus—not Varius—will deliver twelve lashes to his back. You miscalculated, so you will administer the beating. Apply the cane carefully, and soothe his wounds with ointment. No permanent scars—no lasting damage—or I'll flog you myself. Is that clear?"

"Yes, sir."

Shit.

Allerix had wondered not if, but when, he'd be beaten. The reality of an imminent thrashing was strangely comforting.

"Then strip and bind him to that column by the balcony. I'm not finished with the gorgeous son of a bitch."

Allerix fought to control another surge of tears. His arms and shoulders hurt like mad and his tormented balls ached with pain.

"Yes, sir," Max answered.

Blinded by the dark cloth wrapped around his head, Allerix gnawed on his chapped lower lip as shreds of his shorn noble beard lodged themselves in the spaces between his sweaty toes. He lost his last scrap of self-control and wept, beseeching his impotent gods for an end to this nightmare.

~

As he reluctantly emerged from a deep blissful sleep, Gaius stretched his arms above his head and growled with satisfaction. That was the best rest he'd enjoyed in fucking forever. He slid his hand under the covers to investigate the warm head resting on his stomach, blowing ticklish breaths against his skin. He recognized the sensuous feel of that thick wavy hair—yes, his gorgeous naughty Nicomedes.

Shit, it was good to be home.

Last night, after they'd returned to the playroom, he'd fucked Nicomedes' gorgeous body, over and over—first draped across the edge of the bed, then face down on the mattress, then on his back with his knees drawn up to his shoulders. Gaius loved to watch Nic's blue eyes roll back as the lad emptied his balls. As ordered, Nic was extra loud, begging and moaning with every brutal thrust. After months in the chastity cage, Nicomedes craved his touch, needed his attention. Perhaps Nicomedes even realized his noisy command performance was ordered for the benefit of the Dacian. Nic may have been permanently injured by abuse as a child, but he was no half-wit.

Yes, Nic understood the Dacian was the new shiny thing until his temporary sparkle wore off. Within a few moons, perhaps less, the exotic barbarian would be just another whore waiting impatiently for his turn in Gaius's bed.

Gaius lifted up the thin sheet and snaked his fingers through his pet's flaxen hair, as Nic opened his lazy narrow eyes and smiled, humming against Gaius's abdomen.

"Good morning, Nicomedes."

"Morning, Dominus. Thank you for allowing me to sleep in the bed, sir."

"Come here," Gaius said softly, tugging Nic up by his mane. After a lingering kiss, Gaius whispered, "I let you spend the night with me because I bloody adore your arse, lamb. Don't misbehave again, understand?"

"Yes, Dominus." Nic's smile melted into a shy grin. He batted his long, dark blond lashes and basked in Gaius's blatant affection. "Thank you, Dominus."

Gaius chuckled as he pushed his thumb pad against Nic's lower lip. "Go back to the stable house and enjoy a hearty morning meal. And tell Maximus to report here immediately."

After one last peck on the mouth from his master, Nic threw on his crumpled tunic, bowed and left.

The Dacian.

Passed out on his feet and bound to the rightmost post of the colonnade, the young man's body was backlit by the morning sunshine like some mystical vision—his head and shoulders slumped forward, his dark hair obscuring his blindfolded face. With his wrists and ankles tied to hooks attached to the back of the sturdy column, the Dacian stood in a half-squat position. He'd been flogged as directed, but Gaius hadn't yet inspected Max's work. Nic's tight rump had been too distracting a temptation.

Gaius threw back the rest of the bed covers and pushed himself up off the mattress, not bothering to dress. This year's summer mornings were unusually warm; no doubt the afternoon would be scorching. In no rush, Gaius circled around the column, admiring the barbarian's nude form. He didn't want to wake him—not just yet—so he resisted the urge to touch and instead allowed his eyes to caress every supple curve and sinuous line.

He moved closer to judge the condition of the Dacian's lacerated back. There they were—twelve distinct reddish-purple stripes. Not deep, but not too shallow either. Perfect technique, just as Gaius had ordered. The healing salve had reduced the swelling nicely; no scars would mar his new prize.

As Gaius had intended, the Dacian enjoyed little relief while bound on his feet to the stone column. When the lad pressed his back against the cool surface of the marble, the pressure aggravated his tender whipped skin. And if he leaned forward, away from the column, the strain on his tired leg muscles was excruciating. So he oscillated blindly throughout the night, leaning forward and then back, all the while listening to Gaius pummel his noisy Greek whore mercilessly.

"So, our fierce Dacian captive finally surrendered to exhaustion," Gaius whispered. "You need more stamina, cub. We haven't even begun to play."

Standing at attention over in the shadows of the doorway, Max coughed. Gaius looked over and nodded as he picked up his discarded tunic and then pulled it over his head. Guiding Max by the elbow, he led his slave handler out into the hallway.

"Excellent touch of the cane, Maximus. Tell me, how did he react?"

"Admirably stoic but inexperienced. I don't think he's ever been caned before, sir."

"A coddled barbarian stripling, then. All right, time for him to return to the stable house to be washed and fed. And be mindful of what you say around him, Maximus. He certainly knows our language much better than he's let on—and he probably understands some Greek as well, if my suspicions are correct. Do not underestimate him again."

"Understood, Commander."

"Maximus, I'm curious about something. How did the Dacian acquire that bump on the back of his head?"

"Um, I dropped him while he struggled during the initial binding, sir. I'm afraid he slipped and hit his head on the floor."

"Not unexpected, given the circumstances."

"And well, sir… I might have hit him. With my fist, sir."

Gaius arched an eyebrow and smirked. "A blow to succor your injured pride, was it?"

"Yes, Commander. I suppose it was."

Gaius shook his head and laughed. "I'm confident both your pride and your flogged backside will recover fully. Tell me about his cock sucking. You've been training him?"

"His skills were already exceptional. The Dacian required little instruction, sir."

"Hmm, then there's no need for more fellatio lessons. That should eliminate any further distractions and keep you focused on your primary responsibilities."

"Yes, Commander."

"Let's take him down. I'm fucking famished and I need a bath."

Gaius and Max returned to the playroom and stood on either side of the sleeping beaten boy strapped to the marble post. As Max reached behind and quietly unfastened the rope that bound the Dacian's wrists to the iron ring connected to the column shaft, Gaius moved in front of the lad, held out his arms and waited. His new toy would likely collapse and wake in the same instant; their first face-to-face meeting had to be vivid and fucking unforgettable.

After his wrists were freed and the strain on his arms and shoulders released, the Dacian gasped in a near scream. His fatigued, wobbly legs gave way, but his ankles were still bound to the post. He fell, face first towards the hard stone floor. Gaius grabbed him and broke his fall.

"Easy, Paulus. I have you now."

Gaius held up the Dacian's sluggish weight, as Max twisted the boy's long arms behind his back and tied his wrists together above the curve of his bare bum. After his ankles were released from their hook, Max untied the blindfold and slowly pulled the dark fabric off of his eyes.

Squinting at the bright morning light, the Dacian sucked in gulps of stuffy air. His lips were cracked and bloody. Gaius released his grip to cup his razor-burned cheeks and hold his trembling face steady. The Dacian blinked twice and then fixed his gaze on Gaius's eyes.

"Good morning, Paulus. You've had a terribly rough night. Do you know where you are, Dacian?"

The barbarian stared; Gaius stared back, a smirk lifting the corners of his mouth. The Dacian's queasy expression hardened into an icy, lethal glare. Gaius grabbed him more firmly and stepped closer.

"After all that, you're still a defiant, fiery little shit, aren't you? I'll ask you again. Do you know where you are?" Gaius cocked his head and smiled, and decided to wait for a few moments—see how long this feral mongrel could hold his tongue. They stood there, locked on each other's eyes, battling without words or weapons, until the Dacian stuttered a hoarse reply,"I know where I fucking..."

His weak, scratchy voice collapsed into an alarming fit of heaving coughs. He fought to catch his breath, wheezing and thrashing. When Max lunged to grab him, Gaius's fascination turned to concern. He jogged over to the bed and snatched a silver cup from the side table. It contained stale, watered-down wine from the night before, but it would have to do.

"Drink this." Gaius's eyes lingered on the Dacian's swollen, rough lips.

The barbarian gulped the bitter liquid down as he struggled to clear his dry throat. When he could finally breathe more easily, he closed his eyes and relaxed. After a few moments, he slowly lifted his heavy, sultry lids and mumbled, "Thank you, Roman."

The insolent, little prick!

No deference at all. The savage showed no fucking hint of supplication.

Gaius should have slapped the disrespect off his face, but he didn't. No point in killing the cub's rebellious spirit just yet. No, not when the lion wanted to swat his fascinating prey about for a bit longer.

But that could wait. His stomach was empty, and after all that sweat and sex, he needed a fucking soak in a cool pool. Taming the Dacian would take time. Gaius wanted it to take time. No need to hurry this along. He stepped back and looked the boy up and down, from head to toe.

"Take him back to the stable house and clean off the filth. After he's fed and shackled at the ankles, bring him down to the smith's workshop."

"Sir?"

"I've ordered Felix to fashion a fugitive tag. I do not want our barbarian tempted to run off again. I've already selected a collar for him. Understood?"

"Yes, Commander."

"All right, I'm off for a wash and a meal. Atticus mentioned Callidora requested an audience with me. Apparently it's an urgent matter, but there were no further details. Have you any idea what our mysterious Calli might want to discuss, Maximus?"

Max swallowed and stared at the floor. "No, sir."

"I'll find out soon enough, I suppose." Gaius strode within a few inches of the Dacian's face. "And as for you, cub—we'll start serious training when I'm damn well ready. In the meantime, rest up. And let's have no more fucking daft dreams of escape. You're my property now. I own you."

Gaius pinched the lad's plump ashen cheek and flicked the tip of his small perfect nose. "I will discover who you are, you know. The sooner you tell me your birth name, the easier it will be for you."

As he sauntered towards the corridor, Gaius whistled a cheerful tune while he vigorously scratched his satisfied balls through the fabric of his tunic. He hesitated a step and laughed over his shoulder.

"It is bloody damn good to be home, Maximus."

"Yes it is, Commander."

14

Gaius Fabius's seaside villa, Campania

AFTER TOTTERING DOWN THE PATH FOR SOME DISTANCE WITH BOTH OF HIS ankles shackled together, Allerix stumbled over the chain and fell to the ground. He turned his shoulder and landed on the soft grass instead of slamming into the sharp gravel of the walkway. Max reached down and hauled him to his feet.

"The smith's workshop is over there. Move and let's get this over with."

They shuffled down the crunchy footpath leading from the stables to the craftsman's quarters. The stench of manure gave way to fragrant fumes of burning wood. The horses' whinnies and snorts faded, replaced by the sharp pings of metal striking metal. The new smells and sounds were comforting somehow. Allerix had grown up serenaded by the songs of the forges that had dotted the towns and fields of Dacia, the music of blades being sharpened for battle against these unmerciful savages. There had always been war. As long as he and his kinsmen fought, there had been hope. Peace meant defeat.

When they turned a corner, a small brick building with a high vaulted roof came into view. A thick clay pipe at the top billowed white smoke into the midday air. The wide wooden door was propped open; light from the forge illuminated the ragged, ruddy features of a large man swinging his hammer down onto a glowing metal rod, bending it a bit more with each violent blow. In the shadows, a young man whose face was obscured by soot—a slave, no doubt—wrestled the unwieldy bellows.

Max pushed Allerix over the threshold into the ash-filled air.

"Felix!"

His hammer held high for the next strike, the smith spied them and carefully lowered his tool. "Greetings, Maximus. Is this the slave I'm to collar?"

"Greetings, sir. Yes, this is the Dacian."

"The Dacian coward, you mean." Varius picked at his few remaining teeth with a sliver of wood as he stepped into the low light of the shop from behind a stack of harvesting equipment.

"My dear Varius, is this the scamp you've been grumbling about?"

Felix reached for his clay cup and swallowed a hefty swig of wine; red bubbles spilled out of the corners of his downturned mouth. His face was etched by an intersecting pattern of wrinkle lines and sagging flesh. "The fool who nicked the kitchen knife?"

"The very one, mate. Bastard stole the blade and snuck into the main house. He threatened the Commander's favorite whore—you know, that spastic lad with the floppy brown curls. Show me the fugitive's back, Maximus. Let's see if it's been properly caned."

Max held Allerix firmly by the shoulders and turned him around, pulling him into an awkward embrace. "Commander Fabius ordered this slave collared with a tag, sirs."

"Atticus visited me earlier with the commander's instructions. What a bloody round and tight rump on this one. Shit, I'd love to shove my prick into that cushion. Perhaps when the commander tires of him, he'll give us a turn." Felix's shrill cackle resembled the pathetic cry of a trapped animal.

His face pressed against Max's broad chest, Allerix winced when rough callused fingers scratched the tender lashes crisscrossing his back.

"Excellent patterning. Not as harsh as I would have delivered, but effective." Varius slapped Allerix's arse, hard enough to force a whimper from his lips.

"Is his collar ready, sir? I have other chores to finish before daylight disappears."

"Lay it face down on that table. Varius, be a good fellow and bring me that leather hood. We wouldn't want to scar Commander Fabius's new toy, would we?"

After Max pushed him flat on his stomach over the length of the wooden worktable, Varius snaked the musky tan covering over Allerix's head.

Blackness. Suffocating blackness. Allerix flew into a panic, flailing his long legs and yelling smothered obscenities. The muffled hiss and crackle of the fires grew louder.

Max gripped his ankles. "Easy, Paulus! The hood's to protect your skin. Stop thrashing about or you'll get burned."

Two gigantic hands pressed firmly down on Allerix's shoulders. "Tie up the laces at the back, Maximus."

The leather hood tightened around his head, mashing Allerix's face. He fought for air as blood coursed from his ears to his toes. With every rapid, shallow breath he inhaled, the leather pulled in, crushing his nose and lips.

"By the gods, what is that?"

"It's an antique neck ring old Atticus brought down from the house. Commander Fabius ordered it refashioned into a slave collar. Feel the weight of that silver, Varius. Worth a basket of coin, I reckon."

"I recognize this. It's that Gallic relic from the commander's collection. He showed it to me once, told me his ancestor received this silver torque as a gift from the divine Julius Caesar himself. Can you imagine that? It's as old as the Republic, probably older. Look at that bloody intricate craftsmanship. A work of art, really."

"What a shame to waste such a treasure on this Dacian scum. All right, hold the slave still while I secure this around its neck." After the torque was wrapped around his throat, something metal was placed on the back of Allerix's neck.

"Ah, shit. Wait!" Felix cursed. "I nearly forgot the fucking fugitive tag. I have to be sure the lettering is facing out. All right, it's on there correctly. This is the tricky part. Make sure the fugitive stays still."

Varius held him down; the side the Allerix's hooded face pressed against the surface of the table.

"I've never witnessed a slave collared," Varius said.

"Watch, friend. Take the rivet from the fire and set it upright on the plate. Then slip this hole in the flattened end of the torque over the rivet. See what I'm doing here? Now finish off with the other end of the collar. Aim and...."

The hammer smashed down; Allerix choked when the torque was locked tight around his neck.

"Gotta be quick, though. Secure the rivet before it cools too much to set properly."

The smith slid the metal plate out and the collar loosened. "I suspect if this scoundrel does run off again, it won't be returned. What damn fool wouldn't lop its head off for that thick braid of silver?"

A hand snaked under the flaps of the hood; chapped fingers grazed the back of Allerix's neck.

"Either way, the slave is dead. Commander Fabius won't tolerate another escape attempt."

"There, good and snug but loose enough for cleaning. Sit the vile savage on that stool and leave the leather in place until the metal cools."

While Max carried Allerix over to the stool, Varius mumbled with disgust, "I thought I'd seen the last of these vicious heathens after the last war."

"Aye, you fought hoards of them on the battlefield, Varius. Always good for a war story, you are. My favorite is the one about the blue-eyed Dacian prince who begged you to kill him."

Allerix forced his breathing to slow down to quiet the drumming of his pulse.

"That wretch was daft enough to think I'd defy the commander's orders to capture any and all royals alive." Varius chuckled. "Did I tell you that Dacian offered its arse up like a bloody prostitute, if—and this was fucking unbelievable—if I promised to slit its throat when I was finished. As if the bastard was in a position to bargain!"

"What happened to that sad tart?"

"It was carted off to the capital with the rest of the captured royals for execution in the amphitheater. Commander Fabius did allow me to keep that barbarian's gold handled dagger as a trophy. Haven't I shown it to you, Felix? It's that dagger with the intricate wolf's head design engraved right on the blade. I sometimes carve up my food with that knife. Bloody marvelous utensil."

Could it be possible? The dagger sounded like Allerix's prized weapon, but what were the odds?

As the veterans bantered, Max loosened the laces and lifted the leather hood off. Allerix opened his eyes and gasped for air, tears streaming down his cheeks. Backlit by the light from the doorway, all three men looked him up and down in silence until Varius finally spoke.

"Well, now. Aren't you a fetching slut with your pretty new silver necklace."

"Du-te dracului!" Allerix hurled a gob of spit; it landed with a splat on the stone floor just short of Varius's sandal.

His fist was swift and ruthless, slamming as hard as an iron hammer against Allerix's mouth. Running his tongue over the edges of his still intact teeth, he shook off the blinding pain and stared back defiantly at the Roman brute. Blood dripped down Allerix's chin as his muscles tensed in anticipation of another punch.

Max grabbed Varius's raised forearm. "Sir! The Dacian is Commander Fabius's property. You've no permission to beat him."

"Did you see that?" Varius pulled his arm free and pointed. "This slave —a fucking filthy barbarian—spat at me, at an honored veteran soldier. I was awarded the oak crown for valor in battle, you know."

"You are most honorable, sir. But the commander spent a cupboard of silver for its face, among other attributes. Dominus would be furious if he saw any unnecessary damage to his new pleasure slave's expensive features. Trust me." Maximus softened his eyes and smiled. "Please trust me, sir."

Varius lowered his arm and crouched down until his scarred nose was directly in front of Allerix's angry eyes. "When Commander Fabius finally does order you castrated, Dacian, I vow before Mars I will be the fortunate bloke permitted to wield the blunt blade. Shit, I'll use Plautus's fucking kitchen knife to cut off your balls."

When Varius grinned, the battle scars on his weathered face widened to grotesque crimson fissures. "I didn't hit you that hard, did I, Dacian? You still have your fucking teeth, don't you?" Varius pinched Allerix's cheek, rose to his feet and marched towards the open door. "Keep that foul mongrel out of my sight, Maximus. Farewell, Felix."

Felix waved his iron tongs as he shouted, "And good health to you, my old friend!"

~

Outside the bars of the only window in Allerix's cell on the second floor of the stable house, white caps rolled along the dark rough seas. Although the welts on his back were less tender since Max had applied ointment to them before chaining him up for the night, his mouth was fucking sore. He'd managed to sleep on his side for a while, but now, as the sun disappeared from the sky, his empty stomach growled.

Allerix's gold handled dagger?

Did that Varius brute have his ceremonial dagger—the weapon he'd gifted to Brasus for his twenty-fifth birthday? Could Brasus still be alive and imprisoned somewhere in their capital city? Rome couldn't be that far a distance to travel. Allerix recounted the number of nights on that journey in the wagon down to this villa when a vision of his friend's gentle blue eyes filled his heart. Those warm, romantic eyes filled with kindness, so different from the Roman's leering gaze.

Gaius Fabius scrutinized him like a hungry lynx on the prowl in the dead of winter. Predatory amber eyes flecked with flakes of gold and green. Eyes that declared, "I own you," and, "You are mine to devour."

Brasus had never looked at him that way. No one had ever stared at Allerix with such possessiveness and desire.

Could he surrender to this fate? Would he be able to endure those lethal hands stroking his body? Could he survive the butcher's cock fucking him?

When a pair of sandals tapped lightly across the stone floor of his room, Allerix covered his crotch with his hands before he turned away from the window.

"Greetings, Paulus."

"Simon? I'm surprised to see you. Maximus sent you in here alone?"

"You're stripped and shackled to the bed frame. Shit, you're no danger to anyone like that, even me. Here, catch! I swiped an old horse blanket from the stables. The stars are bright tonight, so it's bound to grow cold."

When Simon leaned in closer, Allerix covered himself with the scratchy fabric.

"Ouch. Varius delivers one nasty punch. But, by Minerva's tits, that's a bloody gorgeous rope of silver. I've never seen a slave collar anywhere near as grand as that before."

Allerix touched the twisted coils of the refashioned Celtic torque. Did the Roman monster know more about Allerix's family than he'd let on? No, that was impossible. It had to be a coincidence. Shit, this thing was heavy. Although the silver torque was relatively loose around his neck, it still felt as if the fucking thing was choking him.

"Shit, I want a beautiful collar like that. I knew it—Dom's already spoiling you with fancy jewelry." With a grin, Simon placed a tray of steaming food on a nearby small wooden table. "Listen, I know you tried to run away because you were scared. But you didn't hurt me. To be honest, I really didn't believe you'd cut my throat, Paulus."

"Why?"

"Because we're friends, aren't we?" Simon scrunched his brow as he tilted his head. "We spent all that time together on lessons. You're the first friend I've had anywhere close to my age."

"I wouldn't have hurt you."

"See, I was right. You're not a violent type, just frightened and confused. But it's safe here, and you'll understand that some day."

"Have you ever been to war, Simon?"

Simon grabbed the single chair in the room and dragged it over. "No, of course not. Dom hardly ever permits me to leave the villa grounds. You must have fought, I imagine. Did you?"

"Yes, in the second war—towards the end."

When his stomach growled again, Allerix stretched down to pluck a piece of soft bread from the plate; Simon grabbed hold of him just before he toppled off the mattress.

After a quick nod of thanks, Allerix shoved the bread in his bruised mouth, mumbling between chews, "I didn't fight in the first war. My father wouldn't allow it. He said I was too young and inexperienced with weapons. I trained hard after that—practicing every day until he was forced to admit that I'd mastered our weapons well enough to fight."

Smiling his bright slanted smile, Simon poured water from a small pitcher and offered out the cup. "Is your father still alive, Paulus?"

Allerix took a long drink, long enough to weigh how best to answer. As he wiped off a few drops from his lips with his forearm, he noticed a slight movement in the hallway outside of his room. It was brief but distinct, like the shadow of a wolf darting between trees in waning light of dusk.

He looked down at his reflection on the surface of the water in his cup. Simon hadn't come alone after all. No one could be trusted.

"My father is dead. He was only a simple farmer trying to protect his crops and his family from the Roman invaders. I never saw him again after the day he rode off on his mule for another battle—his last battle. We never found his body, so I never honored him with a proper burial. They're all gone now—my father, my brother..."

Simon blinked slowly and cleared his throat. "Um, have some of this fish stew. It's not Plautus's best fare, but it's not bad. Here, try some." Simon lifted a spoonful. Allerix paused before he relaxed and wolfed down a hefty mouthful.

"I'm surprised I'm being fed at all."

"Dom's a generous and kind man, Paulus. He'll feed and shelter you for as long as he decides to keep you."

"Kind? I was fucking beaten, Simon, and I was—touched."

"You were punished for breaking Dom's rules. And having Nic suck your cock is hardly abuse, even if Dom didn't allow you any release. I know, I heard. But I am sorry about your father." Simon's voice cracked as he returned the spoon to the bowl. "It's hard to lose family, especially both a father and a brother."

There was a long silence before Allerix asked, "What about your father?"

"Theodorus lives up in Rome, last I heard. I don't remember him well. Dom inherited him from his other father, the Elder Fabius. When he was young, Theodorus was the old man's favorite whore."

"So your father's a slave as well?"

"Not anymore. Dominus gifted him freedom a while back and sent him off to the capital. He works for Dom—runs a shop for him, I think."

"They free slaves?"

"Sometimes. But, by the spirits of the most holy Penates, I pray Dom never frees me."

"I don't understand. Isn't it better to be free?"

The shadow in the hallway shifted again.

"I suppose it might be, but I don't want to run a business or work in the baths or whatever the fuck freedmen do. I love it here at the villa and I love getting fucked by Dom, although once in a while I dream about going on adventures and seeing new places. Daft, childish fantasies." Simon ducked his head when a light rosy tint spread over his cheeks.

"I don't think that's daft, Simon. Where would you go?"

"Um—to Egypt, I think. I've read stories about those gigantic stone pyramids built by the ancient pharaohs, as tall as mountains. First I'd sail to Egypt and then to Troy. Where would you go, if you could?"

"I'd go home, but..."

Simon lifted his chin. "But what?"

"But there's nothing left there anymore. The Romans destroyed our cities and burned our fields—razed everything to the ground."

Simon placed a gentle hand on Allerix's blanket-covered calf.

"You can come with me to Egypt. We'll go on a grand adventure together, like Orestes and Pylades. No one can topple the mighty pyramids, not even the Roman legions."

Max marched into the room and lightly cuffed Simon's ear. "Simon, that's enough. Gather up the plates and take them back to the kitchen, boy."

"Yes, sir. Farewell, Paulus. I wish you pleasant sleep."

"Thank you, Simon. And thanks for—for being my friend."

~

MAX AND SIMON WALKED SINGLE FILE IN SILENCE DOWN THE NARROW WOODEN steps towards the kitchen. When they entered the main gathering room on the first floor, Simon placed the tray filled with dirty dishes on the table and dropped his face into his hands.

"Oh, sweetheart." Max wrapped him up in his arms and leaned down, kissing him on the temple. "I know facing the Dacian alone wasn't easy, but Dom needs us to gather information, although you damn well gave more than you gathered. But you did fine. I'll report back to Dom about how brave you were."

"I'm not brave, sir. Deceiving someone—pretending to be their friend—well, that isn't brave."

Max lifted Simon's chin with his finger. "Nonsense. What you did was courageous. You need to maintain this ruse. If the Dacian trusts you, he might share information with you vital for Dom's purposes."

"I'll do whatever Dom wants me to do, of course, but lying is dishonorable, Max."

"Listen to me, pup. Who's your favorite of all the epic heroes?"

"Odysseus, sir."

"And wasn't it Odysseus who was forced to trick people to secure the safety and good fortune of his companions?"

"Yes. But, he..."

"Hush." Max kissed the boy softly on his full mouth before planting a second gentle peck to his forehead. "You did well, my brave little Odysseus. Dry those tears, go wash up and then off to the playroom with you. I'll be there to collect you when Dom's finished with you. Considering Dom's temper earlier, I doubt you'll have enough strength to walk back here on your own."

~

Gnaeus Decius's estate on the Quirinal Hill, Rome

After Bry licked the sauce made from pulverized dates and raisin wine from his master's long thick fingers, he felt the pleasant tingle of pepper as it danced over his tongue. The tangy spice only enhanced the virile taste of Lucius's skin.

Bryaxis had never eaten ostrich before Lucius offered him that bite-sized nibble; it tasted like cow. Or maybe it was goat. Euphronia rarely cooked luxurious imported meats. Bry could already hear her dismissive laughter in the morning after she urged him to tell her all about the outrageous concoctions served at this posh event. Strangely enough though, his usually gregarious master had been avoiding these social gatherings of late.

Yet, here they were, spending a breezy summer evening at an exclusive dinner party in the grand dining room of an estate high atop the Quirinal. It was a small affair as these things went. Reclining on ornate gilded couches arranged around a low marble table, seven gentlemen jabbered on about the recent triumphal games and the unusual hot weather. The trio of pipers playing soft tunes in the background looked as if they wished to be elsewhere.

In front of his master's couch was an extravagant feast of ostrich, oysters, and crispy songbirds offered up on a golden tray. The host—a portly man named Decius whose round face always reminded Bry of a fattened holiday pig—had clearly spent far too much coin on this gathering in order to impress his fellow aristocrats. No doubt Gnaeus Decius had been inspired to pry his purse wide open after he'd learned his patron, Lucius Petronius, had agreed to attend the party.

And as often happened at these events, every man had left his wife home and brought along his favorite concubine instead. Around the enormous serving table, boys and girls knelt on cushioned footstools beside their masters, lifting their faces only if they were offered small morsels of food. Some of the pleasure slaves wore garish costumes, while others were naked save for their glittering jewelry.

Bryaxis, on the other hand, wore a near transparent, sleeveless ivory tunic, cinched tight around his abdomen by a simple but elegant sash. The sheer clingy fabric accentuated every tanned cut and curve of his long, muscular body. It was sexy, but tasteful. Lucius had approved of the outfit with a surprise gift—two gold bracelets in the shape of menacing cobras now spiraling up Bryaxis' lean, hairless forearms.

As he sucked and slurped the golden date sauce off of Lucius's fingers, Bry looked up at that gorgeous face. The wrinkles at the corners of his master's adoring grey-blue eyes grew more pronounced as he seductively pushed his fingers in deep between Bry's wet lips before pulling them out, slick with traces of sauce and saliva. When Bry opened his mouth like a baby bird, a cheeky smile tugging at the corners of his lips, Lucius leaned down and whispered, "What a greedy boy you are tonight."

"Insatiable, Dominus."

Laughing, Lucius scooped up another dollop of sauce. Before he could slip his fingers back into Bry's waiting mouth, a guest interrupted their food play.

"Counselor Petronius, have you any news about the scoundrel who pilfered the state coffers?"

It was an impolite question to ask at a most inappropriate venue. Bry blinked and lowered his chin to his chest. Lucius never suffered fools.

"It seems highly unlikely a lone villain could have choreographed such a theft, my dear Gellius. But let us save those sorts of tedious discussions for the basilica. Your nymph is most lovely, my friend. Do you deliberately have her hair dyed that most extraordinary shade of yellow?"

Bryaxis lifted himself up and wrapped his lips around Luc's dangling fingers to gag the chuckle threatening to burst from his chest. With an innocent grin, Lucius waited for an answer while he caressed the roof of Bry's warm wet mouth.

"Why yes, Lucius Petronius. Her locks are doused regularly with a mixture of oils and Egyptian yellow ochre. A pricey cosmetic but worth the expense, wouldn't you say?"

Lucius arched a brow as he pulled his fingers out of Bry's mouth to grab his silver wine cup. "Indeed. You spoil her."

After he enjoyed a generous swig, Luc lowered and tilted the vessel to offer Bry a taste. Pleasure slaves weren't normally allowed wine at these functions, but Lucius was an indulgent rebel. Bryaxis had enjoyed many fine wines over the years. Dry Falernian was his favorite, and Lucius made sure to have an ample supply in his cellars.

"Dear Jove, is that truly the same brunet slut you've bedded for all these years, Lucius Petronius?" Publius Aelius smirked, one hand rubbing the bristles of his curly beard as the other ruffled the blond fringe of his latest disposable pubescent faun.

Publius Aelius Hadrianus, former ward of the emperor and tactless twat extraordinaire.

"Yes, my most noble Aelius Hadrianus. I've owned Bryaxis since he was fifteen years of age." Luc lifted Bryaxis' chin. "And you grow more alluring with each passing season, my sweet Caledonian pet."

"Yet you never share your whore with your esteemed associates. Bloody selfish of you, you know," another crank grumbled; Bry didn't know the man's name, but he'd seen the greasy-haired fart at these sorts of gatherings before.

"Most uncharitable, I'd say," Publius added, raising his cup in agreement. "I'm tempted to order you to lend him to me, my dear Lucius. You owe me a favor or two."

"According to your brother, I owe countless favors to all the members of the imperial court." Lucius lowered his cup and winked. "Alas, in this instance, I would be forced to defy your command, my most honorable Aelius Hadrianus."

While he stroked Bry's hair, Lucius dropped his already deep voice another octave and continued, "I do not share Bryaxis."

"Except with Gaius Fabius, of course. Rumor has it you share much with my older brother."

A fleeting chorus of muffled chuckles and gasps drowned out the flute music.

Lucius tossed back his head and laughed loudest before clearing his throat. "We do share much, including a deep affection for you, my little Greekling."

The room went dead quiet.

Even the musicians lowered their instruments, as all eyes focused on Publius and waited for his reaction to the nickname no one dared to say out loud, except for Lucius Petronius, of course. Bryaxis' master had an enormous pair of brazen balls.

When Publius blinked for the third time during the staring match with Lucius, Gnaeus Decius pushed his large mass up off his couch and tried to defray the tension with a distraction. "It's time for tonight's entertainment, gentlemen. Bring out the dancers!"

It worked, as distractions with half-naked beauties often do. Publius turned his attention towards the open stage of the hall decorated with a circular pattern of colorful floor mosaics. The empty space was quickly filled with sleek dancers dressed as forest creatures gyrating about to loud whirling music.

Lucius whispered to Bry, "Do you remember our discussion about Rome's early wars against the Greeks? Well, what just happened now with my impudent joke made at Publius Aelius's expense was akin to a Pyrrhic victory. I've won the verbal tussle, but at a cost. Time for me to yield."

"Lu..."

Lucius pressed his forefinger against Bryaxis' lips before lifting himself higher on one elbow.

"My esteemed Aelius Hadrianus. Please accept my deepest apologies for my insulting outburst. I've imbibed more than my share, I'm afraid."

Publius paused before he waved his hand in apparent indifference. "Apologies are unwarranted. You are among friends, Lucius Petronius. And besides, you're Gaius's client, yes?"

"No, I'm not his—not exactly. I would be honored, however, to serve as your client, Aelius Hadrianus."

Bryaxis' fingers dug into the muscle of Luc's calf, while Publius's incredulous grin collapsed into a laugh.

"What a generous offer! But I believe you are a treasured client of our Emperor. That is true, isn't it?"

"Yes, I serve the court at the pleasure of Emperor Trajan, sir."

"Then you, my dear Lucius, have your cart hitched to the most demanding patron of all. Certainly we both can agree you've no need for a second patron. But I thank you for your fidelity nevertheless."

Lucius flashed his warmest flirty smile. He'd played these dull obsequious games for as long as Bry could remember. "As you wish, sir."

After he rose from his seat, Publius fussed and fiddled with the thick folds of his embroidered Greek-style tunic as he sauntered towards them. Bryaxis cringed and fixed his gaze to the floor while his master shuffled over to clear a place on his couch for the dandy's imperial arse.

"Lucius Petronius, will you join me for dinner at the home of Gaius Plinius on the evening before the Ides? It promises to be an intellectual gathering, stimulation of a more cerebral sort than this frivolous affair. You and our esteemed host could entertain us with tales of your adventures on the judicial council. Perhaps we'll convince Pliny to retell that marvelous story of Mt. Vesuvius's murderous eruption. Please say you'll come, Lucius."

"How could I refuse? Is there a special party frock you'd like me to wear?"

Bryaxis looked up; a cheeky sparkle twinkled in Lucius's steel blue eyes.

Publius chuckled and winked. "Why you coy and incorrigible scamp. No wonder Gaius Fabius adores you so. Don't misjudge me—I love my ward brother—but I do enjoy when he's away from the capital and we can chat about more intellectual pursuits. Our dear Gaius can be such an insufferable dullard, droning on and on about war logistics and military intelligence. I swear by Castor's balls if I never hear the bloody word 'Dacian' again I'd die a happy man."

"I would agree, my dear Aelius Hadrianus. 'Dacian this' and 'Dacia that.' It's simply exhausting."

Publius sighed before he leaned in closer and dropped his voice to a whisper. "Don't you believe, my dear and most attractive counselor, that you deserve a more cultured playmate? Perhaps someone who can caress your mind as well as your cock?"

Lucius's playful smile faded.

The pompous prat knew about Lucius and Commander Fabius. Shit, quite a few people did. More than once while assisting his master at the courts, Bryaxis had overheard speculative whispers in the far side aisles of the basilicas.

"Lucius Petronius Celsus, whore of the imperial ward."

"So it's all settled then." Publius spilled an oyster onto his tongue and swallowed the briny meat down his throat. "I'll collect you on my way to the party. An arrival with the potential heir to the throne will even further enhance your authority."

"I have a capable entourage, Publius." Lucius lowered his chin and raised his brow. "And the Quirinal is far off your path. Your escort services are not necessary, sir. I will meet you at Plinius's residence and we'll gorge ourselves euphoric on intellectual nourishment without that boorish word 'Dacian' uttered once."

Publius leaned back as a blush erupted across his cheeks and his hands began shaking. Lucius could charm a fucking corpse. Shit, he'd once charmed that prickly Fabius into serving as his cock sucking catamite.

"Very well. It's been arranged. Now let's enjoy the dance."

"I have enjoyed it so far, sir." Lucius winked, and drained another gulp of diluted wine.

15

Gaius Fabius's seaside villa, Campania

GAIUS MIGHT NOT HAVE NOTICED HER AT ALL IF HE HADN'T CAUGHT SIGHT OF the fringed edge of her long wispy mantle fluttering down to the floor. Once again, Callidora had entered his office without offering him a proper greeting. His first fuck and the mother of his beloved Simon enjoyed certain privileges. The freedom to move about in silence was one of them.

Without turning to face her, Gaius muttered, "Atticus informed me you'd requested an audience. What by the gods compels you to enter my office before I summoned you, Callidora?"

"There is a situation, Dominus."

Gaius's nostrils flared as he turned around and propped his right elbow on the back of his chair. "I'm in no mood for games. What is it?"

Callidora lifted her dark brown eyes. By the gods, even after all this time, she was a bewitching beauty. A charmer of serpents.

"Maximus struck me, sir. He hit me across the face."

"I see." Gaius smirked for a moment before switching to that expressionless mask he often wore. "Maximus is a freedman now, a freed man with powerful hands and limited patience. For future reference, I suggest you not piss him off."

"Then he is permitted to hit me? Can he strike our Zoe if he so pleases?"

"Maximus understands the responsibilities and boundaries of his new freedman status. Do not try to wedge yourself between us. It won't work, my darling. Not this time, not with Maximus. Is that all?"

"There is more, Dominus." Callidora's haughty demeanor disappeared. Was the proud harpy he'd known for most of his life actually unnerved?

Gaius crossed his arms and waited.

"Zoe is with child, Dominus."

After he rubbed his face, his broad shoulders slouched in resignation. He shouldn't have been surprised—these things happened—but the news grabbed him by the balls and squeezed. Hard.

A child.

"Who is the father?"

"I believe the odds are in your favor, Dominus."

Gaius pushed out of his chair and marched across the office, his eyes burning from the rising storm of anger and suspicion boiling in his gut. "The odds had bloody fucking well be! Zoe is in your charge. You were supposed to see to it this never happened."

Calli ducked her head and mumbled, "I've prepared and watched her drink the herb mixture every morning, but I am not divine, sir."

"That's an understatement. I need to speak with her. Where is she?"

"She's waiting outside in the corridor, Dominus."

"Zoe, get in here!"

The lithe blonde tiptoed into the room, her gigantic blue eyes wide with fear. Fighting to stifle her sobs, Zoe dropped to her knees beside Callidora and crossed her tiny hands behind her back. She was a delicate gift from Venus. His girl. The one Marcia had tossed out her bed and rejected as too meek and shallow.

Gaius sighed before raking his fingers through his curls.

"Zoe, my dove. Who is the father of the child you carry?" He cupped her small, pointed chin and lifted her pale face streaked wet with tears.

"I believe the child is yours, Dominus."

"And what about our Nicomedes? Have you forgotten you fucked him without my permission?"

"Dominus? I..." Her full pink lower lip quivered. She glanced sideways at Callidora for reassurance, but her brunette warden offered little more than a dismissive curl of her lip.

"I... I don't remember much from that night, Dominus."

"Callidora, leave us."

Calli gathered together the folds of her mantle and gracefully walked backwards out of Gaius's office, her head downcast. Gaius clutched a thick plait of Zoe's straight golden hair and tugged. "Stand up. Let me have a look at you."

He ran his palm over the soft fabric covering the gentle curve of Zoe's abdomen. "There's no swelling. Are you sure you're with child?"

"Yes, Dominus. At least, I think so. I feel different, and Callidora says my stomach will begin to grow soon."

"Then I have time to consider the options." Gaius brushed back the unruly locks flopping over his face and walked back to his seat. "Come here, Zoe." He patted his lap.

She shuffled over but hesitated by the side of his chair before bending at the waist.

Gaius put his hand up to stop her. "I've already caned you for your transgression, dove." He smiled as he caressed and cupped her round bum cheek through her light summer dress. "The welts should be healed by now, yes?"

"Yes, Dominus."

"Good," he said, as he squeezed her hard enough to elicit a birdish squeak from her lips. With his right arm extended, Gaius tapped his thigh with the other hand. "Sit down."

She settled into his lap and snuggled into his tight embrace, resting her head against his shoulder.

Gaius mumbled against her temple, "Nicomedes was disciplined as well. A punishment well suited for his crime."

She flinched in his arms.

"What's the matter?" he asked.

"By the grace of Juno, is he… Is Nicomedes a eunuch now, Dominus?"

Gaius pulled back, his lips parted in a surprised grin. "What? No. Nic's naughty balls are still attached for the time being."

Zoe started to speak before quickly covering her mouth.

"Go on."

"I was going to say Nicomedes loves you with all of his heart, Dominus. He would never disobey you if..."

Gaius lifted her chin with one finger while he coiled a strand of her hair around another. "Yes?"

"It's just... I'm confused about what happened that afternoon."

"What do you mean?"

She hesitated, nibbling on her thumbnail.

"Answer me, Zoe."

"It's odd, that's all, Dominus. Nicomedes and I never cross paths outside of the times you summon us to the playroom. What I mean is, we're never in the same place at the same time. And then the wine..."

Gaius sat back to listen, his left arm draped over the back of the chair.

"The wine was tainted, Dominus. I couldn't taste it at first, but..." Zoe looked down at her lap and rubbed two folds of cloth between her fingers.

"Finish."

"Well, it seems a strange coincidence Nic and I would both go into that storeroom at the same time, and there was that jug of tampered wine on the cupboard... I don't think it was a coincidence, Dominus."

"Why didn't you inform me of this earlier?"

"I don't know. I was scared I was wrong. I still am."

"Have you shared your suspicions with Callidora?"

"No, no I haven't, Dominus."

"That's my girl." Gaius leaned forward and kissed Zoe on the plump curve of her cheek before he grabbed her by the chin. "But then there's that troublesome part of this conspiracy story of yours, isn't there? Did someone force you and Nic to fuck as well?"

His rough fingertips pressed into her flesh as he growled, "Zoe, if you break my rules again, you will be sold. Any of my rules. Understood?"

Zoe closed her blue eyes and nodded before she mumbled, "Yes, Dominus."

Gaius waited a moment before continuing, "I suspect the father's identity will become quite clear once it's born. Whatever the outcome, this child belongs to me. I decide if it lives or dies. I decide what becomes of it, whether it spends its days as a slave or not, and you will obey my decision without so much as a hint of question. Is that understood as well?"

Zoe's fingertips grazed the back of Gaius's hand resting on her stomach. "Yes, Dominus."

She glanced down at his signet ring. "I received a portent, sir. The fair-haired goddess visited me in dream the other night and smiled as bright as the midday sun. My whole room lit up from her radiance and the good goddess proclaimed I would give birth to a healthy, strong boy. Your son, Dominus."

"The gods often speak to us in our dreams." Gaius kissed her forehead. "Return to your quarters and rest. You will join me in the playroom tonight. No boys. Just you and I."

Zoe raised her eyes; they were filled with desire tempered by apprehension.

He ran a fingertip down the gentle slope of her petite nose. "There'll be no harm to the child. You have other delightful orifices that require my attention. I've been shamefully neglectful."

He kissed her one last time on the mouth and nudged her slender frame off his lap with a gentle pat to her backside.

WHEN THEY CROSSED THE THRESHOLD, THE ROMAN'S BACK WAS TO THEM. Scribbling across a sheet of papyrus, he sat hunched over a large wooden desk. As he wrote urgent words, the fingers of his left hand alternated between twirling and scrunching his auburn curls. Allerix had never seen anything as striking as that man's shiny soft hair, colored every shade of copper from the lightest strands of golden bronze to dark chestnut.

"The Dacian as you ordered, Commander." Max's powerful hands pushed Allerix down to his knees on the polished marble floor.

They had entered this large bright bedchamber after walking down a long unfamiliar passageway. Unlike the playroom, the vaulted space was decorated with restraint—in addition to a large desk and cushioned chair, there were several tall silver lamp stands, a long table along one wall, and a high raised bed covered with white linens and plush furs. An unlit massive bronze brazier stood on a tripod over in one corner. The walls were cream-colored and decorated only with slender vegetal motifs. Despite its size, the room felt cozy.

Comforting.

Without acknowledging their presence, Gaius Fabius rose from his chair and walked over to a row of marble columns by a balcony. His fingers interlocked behind his head, he finally turned around. Late afternoon sunrays filtered through his unbelted white tunic, silhouetting every curve of his muscular contours. He said nothing for a few moments, staring as if deep in thought, until he smiled and said, "There you are, Paulus." Suddenly, the Roman furrowed his brows. "Wait, what is that?"

He marched over, grasped a fistful of Allerix's thick black hair and pulled his head back. Gaius grazed his lower lip with his hand; Allerix flinched when the Roman's fingers brushed across the bruise left by that ox's punch two days earlier.

"Why is there damage to his mouth, Maximus?"

"The Dacian spat at Varius, sir."

The Roman shook his head with amusement. "Would I be right then to assume our Varius wished to inflict much more damage than this bruise?"

"I stopped him, Commander."

"You stopped Varius? Good work, Maximus. I'll have a few words with our pugnacious soldier about spitting barbarians and controlling one's temper."

The general released his grip and ran his fingers over the twisted rope of silver coiled around Allerix's neck. "I knew the torque would look spectacular on him. And did you see this finely engraved lettering on the tag? *Paulus. To be returned to the house of Gaius Fabius Rufus.* That's solid craftsmanship."

He stepped back and crossed his arms.

"Remove the shackles, Maximus."

"But, Commander..."

"The irons won't be necessary while he's with me. Isn't that right, Dacian?"

His wrists chained together behind his sore back, Allerix clenched his tender jaw. He couldn't go through with this. He couldn't surrender.

A finger lifted Allerix's lightly stubbled chin; the Roman spoke softly, his voice silky but stern, "That was a direct question. Answer me."

After he gnawed on the inside of his cheek, Allerix cleared his throat. He needed to do this. If by some slim chance Brasus were still alive, this monster might know where to find him. And then there were other possible advantages to consider.

Several.

"No, sir."

While the Roman waited, he scratched his fingernail across the bristly underside of Allerix's chin.

"I do not need to be shackled," he stated clearly and then swallowed. "Dominus."

Gaius Fabius's tapered leonine eyes relaxed a bit at the corners.

"Release him and leave us alone, Max. Before you go, hand that sealed letter sitting on my desk to Atticus. Instruct him to have it sent immediately to my wife."

Allerix furrowed his brow.

Wife?

The Roman walked across the room to the long marble table positioned against the wall; an array of sculpted metal cups and a jug of wine sat on a tray at one end. He poured two cups, while metal locks clicked open and chains rattled on the marble floor tiles.

When Max was finished, he warned, "Stay down on your knees."

After nodding twice, Allerix rotated his stiff shoulders and rubbed his chafed wrists together. Searching for a second exit, he looked around the room when something flew at him in a blur of dark blue, hitting his face before covering his head.

"Wrap that around you."

Allerix pulled the indigo cloth off and opened his eyes. Max was gone. He froze for a moment before he wound the unwieldy folds of fabric over his naked body.

Gaius Fabius barked over his shoulder, "Get up and sit on that footstool by my chair."

That wasn't a question. Allerix cursed silently but scooted over to the only stool in the room, rewrapped the cloak and waited as the general took a sip from one of the cups.

"I haven't tasted this delicious grape in a while. You Dacians certainly have mastered the art." He strolled over and offered Allerix a two-handled drinking cup, one of an identical pair.

"Here, enjoy some wine from your fertile region of our empire. What's the matter? Are you worried I've tampered with it?"

"Is that a direct question?" His plump lips slightly parted, Allerix slowly raised his heavy eyelids; it was time to use some of the only weapons he had left.

Mesmerized, the Roman stared at Allerix's face. Finally, he chuckled. "I suppose it is a direct question. Here's another one. Why are you hesitant to accept my gift?"

"I've been poisoned through drink before. Sir."

"That's true." Gaius Fabius lifted the cup and tossed back a large swallow. "You'll learn in time I would never deliberately spoil such a fine nectar. Now if this were shitty Numidian swill, you might have cause for suspicion." He offered Allerix the cup again. "Take it. I don't allow my slaves such luxuries often."

Allerix took a sip and let the smooth burgundy liquid roll over his tongue. The lingering tartness reminded him of those splendid solstice feasts, feasts he'd never celebrate again in the king's great dining hall. The hall had been burned to ashes. King Decebalus was dead. Allerix savored the taste of his past, the flavor of life before enslavement.

Gaius Fabius turned his large armchair, settled into it and took another swig, this time from his own silver cup, before dragging over the small wooden table beside his large desk.

"I need to know your birth name, *căţel*, for practical purposes. But I'm growing bored with floggings and iron shackles and all that crude, time-consuming nonsense. There's no sport in it. Let's have some fun." After he'd placed his cup on the table, he rested his elbows on his knees, crossed his forearms and leaned down.

"Do you fancy a wager?" The Roman's grin widened to a gorgeous dimpled smile. "You and I are going to play a game, cub. Though I must warn you—there's a strong probability you'll lose. Again."

Allerix bit his tongue. Protest at this moment and in this place was worthless. It wouldn't get him what he needed. He'd exact revenge in his own time. Eventually.

The general lifted a slender wooden box off the desk and opened it flat on the small table.

"Do you know the game we Romans call Tabula?"

"No." Allerix furrowed his brow as he studied the board. It appeared to be the same game he'd mastered under Istros' tutelage. There were several strategies to score a win. "I do not know this game, Dominus."

The butcher dumped a handful of metal discs from a tan fabric pouch into his cupped palm. "I'll teach you. You'll pick it up quickly. It's simple."

"Roman kings seem to prefer simpler challenges."

As he sorted the game pieces into two piles, Gaius Fabius smirked without looking up from the wooden board decorated with lines and numbers. "First, unlike you lot, Romans don't have kings. Second, I'm surprised to learn your peasant father schooled you on the gambling vices of our Divine Claudius. Careful, cub—your purple pedigree is showing."

Allerix tightened the mantle around his shoulders. The edge caught on the silver fugitive collar.

"We will play the game by my special rules. I won't repeat them, so listen carefully, Paulus."

Allerix swallowed.

"Each player receives three types of tokens with numbers on one side, five of each type. Fifteen for you, fifteen for me. You will play the numbers three, five and eight." The Roman carefully placed fifteen bronze discs face down and pushed them towards Allerix's side of the board. Each had a large number stamped on its upturned surface.

"Keep them face down or else you forfeit the game. I'll play the twos, sevens and nines."

After pulling the other pile over to his side, he lifted Allerix's chin and asked, "Are you paying attention to my instructions, *cățel*?"

The man's amber eyes were filled with volatile mixture of lust and curiosity. Allerix couldn't look away. He felt himself melt into them, as if he and the Roman were two divergent streams merging into one dangerous torrent.

"Yes." Allerix smothered a cough with another swallow of Dacian wine and garbled out an unenthusiastic, "Dominus."

"The goal is to get one of your men to the finish first. We throw these dice to move the tokens." Gaius Fabius unfurled his right fist; three ivory dice rocked back and forth in his palm.

"This position is the starting point." He tapped the first narrow compartment on the board labeled with the numeral one. "I prefer to play Tabula as if our men were chariot rivals, jockeying for position, until one of our tokens crosses that line for the victory. It's much like a circus race, in fact, though with more calculation and less bloody carnage."

"What is the reward for winning?" Allerix's deep voice was strong and confident until it cracked. "Dominus."

"That..." The Roman extended his palm. "That is a surprise. You are the guest, cub. You may toss the tesserae first."

"I am a prisoner of war," Allerix countered, as the dark blue cloak he was wearing fell open to reveal his thick but small patch of black chest hair.

"The wars are over and your people lost. You are a slave, Paulus." Gaius Fabius placed the three ivory dice on the board, leaned back in his chair and drew a hearty gulp from his wine cup. "You are my property now, *cățel*, but for this game on this day I prefer you play the part of my honored guest. Now cast the fucking dice."

Allerix picked up the incised cubes and threw them across the wooden tray; they bounced off the lip on opposite side of the board and came to rest.

"Io, the gods have granted you eleven moves. Good throw. It's best to divide up your moves between two or three of your men."

"Why would I do that?"

The Roman raised an eyebrow at first but softened his annoyance with a smile. "This is a game of strategy, not a fool's race to finish. All fifteen of your playing pieces must find a spot on the first half of the board—in these boxes marked one through twelve—before your men are allowed to advance to the second half of the playing field. Understand?"

Allerix nodded and moved three of his discs: two threes and one five. His red-haired opponent picked up the dice and took his throw.

"Sixteen."

The Roman stared at the board for much longer than seemed necessary; he perched his chin on his fist as the tip of his tongue darted in and out between his thin lips. With casual indifference, he spread his thighs apart.

It was impossible not to notice the shadow of his sac hanging down between his legs.

Allerix was transfixed, again.

With a chuckle, Gaius Fabius hoisted his tunic up around his waist and spread his thighs wider to fully expose his naked groin. "I am flattered, but you'd be wise to stop drooling and focus on the game instead of on my colossal balls."

Allerix blinked and turned his attention back to the board.

The Roman enjoyed a slow drink and said, "I purchased a lad once who turned out to be ill-matched, a twitchy timid little thing that never enjoyed a good pounding, let alone having my cock shoved down its throat. No interest at all in a hard arse fuck. Pity, since it was rather pretty. Though not nearly as attractive as you, cub."

"What did you do? I mean, what happened to him?"

"I sold it, of course, and made a decent profit on that sale, as I recall. Your people don't own slaves, do they?"

Allerix snapped. "My people own nothing now, Dominus."

The general slammed both palms down on his armrests. "Blame your dead and unreasonable prick of a king for that!" He took a deep breath and lowered his voice. "But, if I understood your society correctly, Dacia did have a proletariat class who lived off the land, beholden to royals and priests."

Allerix fought back the tears. He'd be damned if he'd let this monster see him weep. "Yes. But no one, certainly not a child, was ever forced into slavery."

"You had no slaves because Dacians never won a real fucking war. We've built the greatest empire to ever rule the seas on the backs of slaves. Slaves and some damn fine soldiers." After a satisfied grunt and a vigorous scratch of his sac, the Roman leaned down and moved one of his tokens until it landed in the same compartment as Allerix's number five.

"Ah, how very unfortunate for you, my beguiling guest. Now that token of yours must start all over again from the beginning."

His mouth open wide, Allerix watched the Roman pick up his coin and drop it on the game board's starting point.

"That's horseshit!" Allerix shouted.

"No, that would be my fucking rules. Back to the starting gate for you, sport." He grabbed Allerix by the jaw. "You're even sexier when you're angry. I'll remember that."

The game continued as the waning daylight grew dim. The Roman ordered a house servant to light the lamps, and they played on, roll after roll of the dice, bronze discs moving around the board, some bumped back to the starting position. During one of Allerix's longer deliberations over which token he should move, Gaius Fabius stood up and poured them both more Dacian wine.

Allerix tentatively touched one of his pieces with his fingertips. He changed his mind briefly, before reaching for the same token again.

The general quietly sidled up behind him, crouched down and purred into Allerix's left ear, "Remember, a soldier can't claim victory unless all fourteen of his comrades stand beside him on the same side of the battlefield."

Allerix hesitated and rubbed his fingers together. He exhaled and moved the bronze eight piece instead, bumping his opponent's nine back to the starting position.

The Roman nuzzled Allerix's ear shell. "You've won the game, *căţel.* I must find another strategy to learn your name. But don't worry—I have many options."

"I won?" Allerix turned around; Gaius Fabius caught Allerix's bruised lower lip between his teeth and sucked gently before letting go.

"Yes, you damn well fucking did." He smiled as he pointed. "Look at the board. It would require two throws of the dice at a minimum to move my nine back to where it was, and my other three tokens haven't even crossed to the second half yet. You, on the other hand, only need one more throw for victory. I surrender and acknowledge Fortuna is with you today."

They stared into each other's eyes, until Allerix asked, "What's my reward?"

"Let's take a look, shall we? Each one of the numbers on these brothel tokens has a different sex act on its front face." The Roman reached over, picked up Allerix's winning disc and flipped it over in his cupped palm. Allerix strained his neck to see.

The bastard licked his lips and smiled.

"What—what is it?" Allerix asked with more enthusiasm than he'd intended.

"A favorite of mine. But we'll have to save it for another day, cub. Tonight I have a special engagement. Perhaps I'll share this victory prize with you on the day when you address me properly, every damn time, without choking on the fucking syllables. Work on that, yes?" The Roman closed his hand around the token and hollered, "Maximus!"

Max must have been waiting just outside the door the entire time.

"Yes, Commander."

"Take our Dacian back to the stable house. Stop! Don't bind his ankles. Only shackle his wrists in front of him for now. And find my cub a proper tunic, a blue one. I like him in blue. The color complements his eyes."

Max wrapped his enormous hand around Allerix's bicep and pulled him to his feet. As Allerix spun around, the loose mantle he was wearing slipped off his shoulder and dropped to the floor.

The Roman walked up behind him and ran his hand up the curve of Allerix's bare bum; slowly he traced his fingers down the heat of his crack. He brushed the tip of his aquiline nose across the back of Allerix's neck and growled into his black hair. "So bloody edible, *cățel*—a smooth Persian peach, firm and appetizing."

A low moan rumbling in the back of Allerix's throat changed to a gasp when Gaius Fabius slapped his arse cheek.

"I'll save that feast for another time. Tonight, I'm fucking my girl. Max, see to it Paulus receives a hearty meal. He played a good game."

"Yes, sir."

~

ALLERIX WALKED IN FRONT OF MAX DOWN THE LONG CORRIDOR WHEN THEY reached a part of the main house he finally recognized. They'd said nothing to each other until Max asked over his shoulder, "Who won the game?"

"I did."

Max snorted. "You only think you've won because Commander Fabius wants you to believe that, Paulus. Dominus never loses."

16

Gaius Fabius's seaside villa, Campania

GAIUS LOWERED THE POINT OF HIS SWORD TOWARDS THE SAND COVERING THE exercise yard to readjust the stiff leather breastplate strapped to his torso. Other than basic chest protection and a practice shield, he wore a pair of scuffed bronze shin guards that had seen better days and a white linen loincloth. The beads of perspiration dotting his arms, legs and broad back glistened in the early morning sun.

After he wiped his brow with his forearm, Gaius pointed and yelled, "You're out of practice, soldier!"

They'd been mock sparring in the courtyard since sunrise. Varius looked as if he might vomit.

"Retirement will do that, sir," Varius hollered back, huffing and puffing as he tried to catch his breath.

"Shall we call it a draw and head for the baths, then?" Gaius jested.

Bent over from exhaustion, Varius lifted his head and laughed. "You are a generous competitor, Commander. A better man than most."

"Aye, that's true." Gaius winked even though Varius could not have seen the gesture, given the streams of sweat pouring down the veteran's forehead and stinging his eyes.

The sound of laughter echoed from the back entrance as Max escorted

Nic, Simon, and the Dacian into the courtyard for their daily exercise session. They walked in single file, Simon leading the way.

Max was adjusting well to his new position. He was now charged with insuring that Gaius's boys kept fit and lean with a bit of ball tossing and wrestling every day the weather was agreeable. The Campanian villa was a military camp in miniature, everyone assigned duties suited to their abilities and their unique position within the hierarchy of his family. Where would the Dacian fit into all of this, assuming he didn't sell the furry cur to the eunuch dealers for good coin?

Time would tell.

"Pardon us, Commander Fabius. I was unaware you were practicing this morning," Max apologized with a quick bow, while Nic and Simon dropped to their knees, their eyes downcast to the gritty sand. Simon's technique was clumsy and unattractive; that boy should have bloody improved by now.

The Dacian, on the other hand, stood tall with his wrists bound in front of his body. Shit, what long furry legs the beauty had—muscled but lean. And the new tunic Max had obtained for his raven-haired lad was perfect, a rich vibrant azure that suited his pale skin.

Gaius's face lit up with a genial smile. "Maximus, come over here!"

He threw an arm around his freedman's brawny shoulders, not an easy feat considering Max's substantial height coupled with the awkwardness of Gaius's mock armor. Gaius tipped his chin towards the old veteran and teased, "It seems I've tired out our most honorable Varius. How about you and I spar for a while?"

"Me? Commander, I'm a terrible swordsman."

"Nonsense, you just need more training."

"Commander, forgive the intrusion, but there's a much more interesting contestant standing right over there. Though be prepared—it spits." Varius nodded his head in the Dacian's direction.

"Ah, yes. Excellent suggestion." Gaius's jubilant tone grew serious. "Remind me to have a chat with you about your temper, Varius. I was not pleased with that bruise on his face the other day. For now, retrieve another gladius from my weapons cupboard. And the falx."

"The falx, sir?"

"Did I damage your fucking hearing, soldier?"

"No, sir."

"Maximus, unlock the Dacian's shackles." Anticipating protest when Max opened his mouth to speak, Gaius continued, "The lad can't be expected to swing a blade correctly with his hands bound, for shit's sake. Go."

~

MAX STRODE OVER AND UNLOCKED THE IRONS.

"What are you doing, sir?" Allerix asked.

"Commander Fabius wishes to spar with you. I have no idea if you can actually wield a weapon, Paulus, but assuming you can, do not harm him or I will kill you. Personally, with my fucking bare hands."

Allerix chuckled sarcastically. "Max, he's a professional soldier, the leader of the Roman army. So, after he kills me, would you please build a funeral pyre for me constructed of old oak and decorated with freshly-cut pine garlands, sir."

Simon said nothing, but Nic snickered.

"Shut up, go over there and kneel at his feet. Shit, lick his feet if you like. Perhaps he'll let you win, again."

~

THE DACIAN CROSSED THE SHORT DISTANCE OF THE SMALL COURTYARD; HE looked into Gaius's eyes while lowering himself to his knees. He only broke his defiant glare when Varius finally returned, a short Roman sword in one hand and a large Dacian falx in the other.

"Let's see how you handle a weapon. Stand up and choose one," Gaius ordered.

Mesmerized, the barbarian slowly rose to his feet. The ceremonial Dacian falx bore an intricate swirl pattern masterfully etched into the surface of its curved blade. The metal reflected a random pattern of sparkles that danced across the lad's captivated face. Within sight but out of reach, the weapon taunted him, teased him with its dormant power. The Dacian's eyes betrayed his lust to touch it, to hold its lethal weight between his hands.

Gaius pressed his palm hard against the white fabric barely covering his stiffening cock.

"How did you...?"

"I was gifted this exotic treasure by Emperor Trajan as a reward for my leadership of our valiant troops during the first war. It's a victory trophy, a bit like you. Now, chose your fucking weapon."

The Dacian bit his lower lip as he studied the cramped space of the exercise area.

"I choose the short sword."

"It's as daft as the rest of them, Commander!" Varius blurted out.

Gaius crossed his arms and smiled with pride. "The falx is an open field weapon, my dear Varius. You do remember that much, don't you? The courtyard is too small to brandish it correctly or effectively. A very strategic choice, cub."

He took the sword from Varius and handed the weapon to the Dacian, handle first. The lad tossed it by the hilt, back and forth between both hands, in order to assess its weight and balance.

"Are you finished playing with it?" Gaius quipped with a smirk.

"It's a fine sword, but an unfair match. I have no armor."

"For the fucking love of Mars." Gaius loosened the straps of his breastplate, pulling it up and over his head. After he tossed it to the ground behind him, he bent down, unfastened his bronze greaves and held out both hands. "Better? Or would you prefer I relinquish this last scrap of modesty and remove my garment as well?"

"No, you can keep your little skirt."

With a cheeky twinkle in his eyes, the Dacian tore his gaze off the prominent bulge tenting Gaius's loincloth and stepped back for a few practice swings. Gaius used the distraction to lunge, hitting the dark-haired lad's forearm with the flat of his blade. The sword flew out of the barbarian's hand and sailed end over end across the short stretch of the yard, only to hit the marble wall close to where Varius happened to be standing.

"Pay attention, Paulus. Swordplay is not a dullard's dice game of chance."

His eyes dark with anger and humiliation, the defiant lad stood his ground until Gaius growled, "Get over there and pick up your fucking weapon."

The Dacian clenched his teeth and jogged over to the wall. He picked up the gladius and spun around, pointing the gleaming tip directly at Gaius.

Idiotic neophyte.

Gaius strolled over and carefully pushed the sword to the side with his shield.

"Drop the sword! Varius, give the lad your fucking shield. His blatant lack of experience is bound to make this sloppy, and I don't want to damage my property without good cause."

The barbarian swore under his breath as he accepted the small round practice shield and adjusted its leather straps over his right forearm. After the shield was firmly in place, he picked up his sword from the ground and held it upright in his left hand.

"You're cursed, then?" Gaius remarked, as he took several steps back.

"What?"

Pointing with his sword, Gaius explained, "You hold the gladius with your sinister hand, cub. You're afflicted."

What a marvelous, sexy laugh the Dacian had. "You are correct. I'm a cursed wretch with nothing left to lose, Roman."

Gaius's smile disappeared. With his shield up and sword positioned for a strike, he charged at the Dacian and forced him to run backwards on his heels. Before he was pinned against the wall, the lad dodged the trap. Gaius followed his frantic steps, pursuing him as the barbarian backpedaled around the perimeter of the courtyard.

"Are you running away from me, cub? You no longer want this cunt of a butcher to kill you?" Gaius sneered and thrust his sword; the Dacian blocked it with his shield.

"No," the lad confessed, the sunlight blinding him momentarily.

"That would fucking be, 'No, Dominus.'" Gaius attacked again, too fast this time for the Dacian to evade his assault. His back slammed into the hard wall as Gaius pressed the metal edge of his shield against his throat. When he tried to swing his sword to knock Gaius off balance, Gaius wedged the boy's left wrist into a wide crack in the portico wall with the hilt of his gladius and pressed his lips against his long, damp neck.

"Surrender to me. Here. Now."

The Dacian struggled to break loose, writhing and pushing against Gaius's weight, but to no avail. He gritted his teeth and cursed a threat that sounded more like a whimper.

"Fuck off."

Gaius chuckled before shouting over his shoulder, "Leave! All of you!"

Max shepherded Nic and Simon out through the rear exit as Varius grabbed the falx and made a silent escape, only to stand at the ready in the shade of a nearby roof overhang.

Gaius twisted his sword handle, grinding it against the inside of the Dacian's wrist until the boy was forced to drop his weapon to the ground. Those fucking defiant young eyes; his cub was determined to fight on, although the war had already been lost. The barbarian leaned his head back against the wall as he tried to catch his breath.

Gaius pressed closer and nuzzled his nose along the edge of the Dacian's jaw. "Calm down, colt."

He opened his hazel eyes. "I'm not a colt or a cub or whatever other animal name you call me. I'm a warrior."

"A warrior?" Gaius snorted. "I thought you were a lowborn peasant, a poor virginal lad who toiled away his days shoveling shit uphill."

"I'm—I'm no one. And I'm not a virgin, you bastard. Your soldiers..." The Dacian bit his lower lip.

"I know what likely happened when you were taken prisoner, *cățel*. It's an unfortunate but common cost of capture. But those bastards who raped you were not under my command." Gaius brushed a thumb pad over the Dacian's flushed cheek and wiped away a tear-shaped drop of sweat. "How long has it been since you've been properly loved?"

The lad's knees wobbled, but he said nothing. Gaius lifted the hilt of his sword off of the Dacian's bruised wrist. The metal blade scraped along the stone of the courtyard wall as Gaius leaned forward, took hold of the boy's mouth and kissed him gently, but deep. The kiss lingered and the lad's long legs buckled, again.

Grinning, Gaius pulled back. "You *are* a virgin, aren't you?"

Gaius shook his practice shield until it slid off his forearm and fell to the sand. After he snaked his left hand between their soaked bodies, up under the hem of the lad's bright blue tunic, Gaius rubbed his damp palm along the shaft of the Dacian's hardening prick and whispered, "Relax. You're mine to protect now. No one can touch you."

"Except you."

"Except me." Gaius winked and flashed his dimples. "Should I order Max to return? Should I have him put those shackles back on your wrists and take you back to the stable house with the others?"

"No," the boy snapped, before lowering his lashes. "I want to stay."

Gaius lifted the Dacian's chin and waited until he capitulated.

"Please may I stay, Dominus?"

"Better. You're starting to get the hang of this, aren't you? Now would you be so kind as to untie my little skirt?"

The Dacian stole a quick glance at the fabric barely covering Gaius's protruding erection. With a smirk tugging at his lips, Gaius sighed against the Dacian's damp black hair. "Our cocks are starving for a proper introduction, cub. It's well past time, and by the gods, my patience is fucking exhausted."

With trembling fingers, the barbarian unfastened his shield and dropped it onto the sand. He then made quick work of the knot holding the loincloth in place across Gaius's hips. When it fell to the ground, Gaius threw his sword down and took both of their pulsing cocks in his hand, pumping up and down until a whimper burst from the Dacian's lips.

"We're nearly the same size," Gaius noticed, as he snatched a fistful of the lad's long hair and bent his head back to attack his delicious neck. He nibbled hard, intending to leave a mark, until the boy reluctantly let out a half-laugh, half-moan.

"Is that so, Dominus?"

The lad wasn't gagging on the fucking word now, was he?

"You're a tad longer, cub. See for yourself. Get your hand down here and join me."

The barbarian whimpered like a songbird caught in a silk snare. He didn't want this, but yet he did. He slowly wrapped his sweaty fingers around their girths beneath Gaius's fist and squeezed tight.

"You feel so..." The Dacian gasped when Gaius sped up the rhythm of his skilled strokes, every so often running the tip of his thumb lightly over his wet slit. The lad's knees shook as his prick grew impossibly hard. They pressed their soaked foreheads together, kissing and nipping, until Gaius growled, "Ah, you are so close and so fucking sensitive. You have my permission to come."

"I have your fucking permission?" The Dacian nearly laughed, the cocky little shit.

Gaius removed his hand from the lad's softening prick and wiped his sweaty, precum-covered fingers on the plump swell of the boy's cheek.

"And just when I feared this would be far too easy." Gaius pressed his lips together before hollering, "Varius!"

From out of the shadows, the veteran appeared and marched over to stand at attention.

"Escort this slave back to the stable house." Gaius didn't break his amused but determined glare. "And, Varius..."

"Yes, Commander?"

"Mind your fucking temper." Gaius's scowl melted into a smug smile. "Tell our dear Maximus to report to my office after the midday meal. Tell him it's time."

"Now *that* is one bloody impressive purple mark." Nic stared at Allerix's neck as he sat back in his chair and swallowed another gulp of honeyed wine. The Roman had sent a jug of a sweetened local grape to the stable house as a treat. It complemented the assortment of cheeses and fresh figs nicely.

"I've had nastier bruises," Simon gloated from across the table, crumbs of bread stuck to his full lower lip.

Allerix touched the sore spot on his throat just above the collar, the area where the Roman had ravaged him with his mouth, long and hard.

A stamp of imperial ownership.

Fucker.

Nic bumped Allerix with his shoulder. "So, what happened back in the exercise yard after we'd left, Paulus? Give us details."

"Nothing happened."

"Horseshit! Dom doesn't allow *nothing* to happen."

"He touched me, that's all."

Simon leaned forward and crossed his forearms on the table surface. He raised his brows in amusement. "Did you just say 'touched' again? By the holy Penates, you are a virgin."

Allerix pursed his lips. "Apparently I am."

"Not for fucking long, Dacian." Gorged and sleepy, Nic flipped his braid back over his shoulder and stacked their empty ceramic plates moments before Plautus returned to collect the dishes. The portly cook only grunted at them. As he left through the door leading to the stable kitchen, Max trudged into the common room and took a seat at the long table. He was tired, but then again Max always looked tired.

"Wine, sir?" Simon asked, offering out his cup.

"There's wine left? What's wrong with you lads? Are you ill?"

His bright blue eyes crinkled at the corners, Nicomedes choked out a laugh. "We saved you some, handsome. Um, Sir."

Max waved off Nic's flirtations and settled back into his chair as he balanced one ankle across his other bare knee.

"Simon, Dom's ordered you and Paulus to report to the playroom."

"When?" Bobbing up and down in his seat, Simon glanced at Allerix before asking, "Now?"

"Easy, pup. Not now—later tonight. I want both of you to get some rest and then it's a long, thorough cleaning for the both of you. Teeth and balls and bum holes and fucking everything had better be scrubbed and spotless. I'll shave both of you."

"I've had two shaves today already," Allerix said flatly.

Max waggled one brow. "Not around your barbarian ball bits, you haven't. One slip of the razor and...." With an exaggerated wince, he made a slicing sound before laughing, and pointed to the stairway that led up to their rooms. "Off for a nap, you two."

~

AS THE YOUNGER MEN MADE THEIR WAY UP THE WOODEN STEPS, THE CHAIN binding the Dacian's wrists rattling with every step, Nic rose and walked around the table. He wrapped his arms around Max's shoulders and kissed his neck.

"What about me, sir?"

"You?"

"Dom hasn't called me to the playroom in ages."

"I've noticed that. You do realize he doesn't call for me at all anymore, love." Max rubbed his temples before patting his thigh, inviting Nicomedes to sit. "Dom gave us permission to spend tonight together after my duties are fulfilled."

Nic's exaggerated pout melted to an enthralled grin. "He did?"

"Would you be averse to being mine someday, Nicomedes? I've been saving the wages the Commander now pays me."

"Max, are you serious? You really think Dom would sell me to you?"

"He's been hinting, here and there, that he might allow it. Or perhaps it's just my imagination. I'm really not sure what..."

Nic pressed his pointer finger against Max's mouth. "I would be honored to belong to you, Max."

Max pulled Nic in for a long tongue kiss and whispered, "I love you, Nic."

Nic lowered his gaze and traced his fingertips over the muscles of Max's thick arms. "I've loved you since time mattered, ever since I saw you strolling about that market by the docks in Neapolis. Tall and strong and so fucking gorgeous—a vision of the mighty dark Hercules come to life before my very eyes."

"You still remember those days?"

"I remember every moment. You visited our booth every market day, even when you didn't need to purchase a damn thing."

"Shit, was I that obvious?"

"You saved me."

"Commander Fabius saved you, Nicomedes."

"Dom was about to depart for another long campaign. He took me from that monster and welcomed me into his family so I could entertain you during his absence, and you know it. We all knew it, even though no one said it."

"There's much that's not spoken."

"Silence doesn't make it any less true."

"You are wise beyond your years, sweet sage." Max winked and wrapped Nic in a tight embrace until the lad squeaked out a sexy giggle. He pushed the blond's long braid out of the way and kissed the edge of his ear. "Come join me in my bed. You'll nap peacefully cradled in my arms. We'll need our rest. This night promises to be a fucking long one."

~

BRONZE LAMPS SHAPED LIKE STIFF CURVED COCKS HUNG FROM PEGS ON THE walls; their flickering light was enhanced by a few faint beams from the full moon sneaking into the room through cracks in the shutters. Together, they created subtle patterns that danced over the frescoed walls of the playroom. As ordered, Atticus had selected a fresh change of bed coverings to match the deep red color of the painted walls.

The stage was set, the equipment prepared.

Facing the door in anticipation of their arrival, Gaius stood with his arms folded across his chest. Every tantalizing shadow, every curve of his muscular frame, was accentuated by the lightly fragranced oil veiling his naked body in a delicious sheen.

He was ready for battle.

"Enter!"

The heavy wooden door creaked on its iron hinges. Both barefoot lads were clad in crisp, beltless whisper-thin tunics falling just above their knees. Simon shuffled forward and dropped to his knees, his hands clasped behind his back.

"Dominus."

It took a bit more effort to move the resistant but unshackled Dacian into the large room. Max was efficient and determined; he shoved the boy down on the marble floor beside Simon.

Gaius cupped Simon's face. The glistening head of his hardening cock bobbed just out of reach of his slave's pouty mouth.

"Simon, go retrieve two pairs of restraints from the storage chest—the leather ones. There's no need for any further bruising."

The lid of the bronze storage box in the alcove of the playroom was already propped open. With a submissive nod, Simon rose to his feet and strolled over to the box filled with all sorts of delights. The braided leather bands sat on top of the assortment of sex toys.

"While you're over there, pup, select a plug. For yourself."

Simon picked up the restraints and rummaged through the chest until he found the tan bag containing that special indulgence imported from Egypt—a smooth and thick plug with a sturdy silver pull.

"Maximus—strip our Dacian and carry him over to the bed."

Before Max could stop him, the Dacian sprang to his feet. At least the barbarian demonstrated a modicum of grace. He shook Max's hand off of his shoulder and protested, "I do not need to be carried like a fucking child."

Gaius glanced at Max, before nodding. "Very well, then. Take off the tunic and go lay on your back with your hands above your head. Understood?"

"I understand, *măcelar*," the Dacian cursed, as he yanked the loose garment over his head and hurled it to the floor.

"In case you're still fucking confused, if this butcher—as you're so fond of calling me—wanted to bloody rape you, I would have done so a long time ago," Gaius snapped. He picked up a delicate glass from the side table and stood by the side of the large bed. "Down on your back, now."

After Max took a pair of leather bands from Simon's outstretched hands, he tied them around the Dacian's wrists and fixed their straps to the hook on the wall above the bed.

Gaius sat down on the mattress and brushed away the strands of black hair that covered the lad's anxious, pallid forehead. He took a small sip from the cup and explained, "The nectar in this vessel contains a mild sedative mixed with a pleasant and tasty Phrygian aphrodisiac. I find it both soothing and stimulating."

Gaius looked over his shoulder. "You've always relished this elixir, haven't you, Simon?"

Simon knelt on the floor next to Gaius's feet and smiled in adoration. "Yes, Dominus. Very much."

"Would you like a taste, pup?" Gaius chuckled as he ruffled Simon's soft curls.

After Simon nodded coyly and opened his mouth wide, Gaius swirled his fingers around inside the ornate polychrome glass until they were coated with the delectable brew. "Show our Dacian here how pretty your pink tongue licks this juice off of my fingers."

Simon opened his sparkling eyes and looked up at Gaius while he seductively lapped every drop of the expensive liquid.

"Would you care for a drink, Paulus?" Gaius asked. "The potion's harmless and will help you relax and better savor tonight's game."

"Game?"

"Yes, another contest. There will be three players this time, since Simon will join us." Gaius dropped his voice. "Are you feeling fortunate again?"

The Dacian hesitated and furrowed his brow before finally parting his lips. Gaius offered him a healthy slurp and placed the vessel back on the table.

"Undress, Simon, while Max and I secure our Dacian's ankles."

Simon jumped up and quickly peeled off his sheer tunic as Gaius picked up the other pair of braided restraints and tied one around the lad's left ankle.

"Easy now, beautiful." Gaius unfurled and attached the chain-link strap to an iron ring fixed to the corner post at the foot of the bed. When the Dacian's right leg jerked and kicked, Max clamped it down. It didn't take much effort; the herbal potion had already begun to curtail the barbarian's instinct to struggle.

Gaius tossed the other restraint to Max.

"Make sure it's comfortable but secure."

When Max attached the strap to the opposite post and pulled it tight, the Dacian sighed with a mixture of resignation and despair and let his head settle onto the plush mattress. His only escape was to focus on the warm, tingling sensation Gaius guessed was now radiating from the boy's belly to his groin.

"Maximus, you may leave us. And be sure to open the shutters of your room at the stable house so I can hear Nicomedes scream with pleasure, yes?"

Max flashed a bright, wicked grin. "Yes, Commander. Thank you, and good evening, sir."

After Max had bowed and left, Gaius stood up and looked down at his bound pleasure slave. The Dacian's long, lean body was flush with the first drops of perspiration; his pale abdomen rose and sank with each deep breath, and his huge eyes were glassy from arousal he was already helpless to temper. As the drugged drink coursed through his veins, spreading from his limbs to his digits, the lad's prick began to stiffen.

Gaius laughed, deep and raspy. "By the gods, you're exceptional. I haven't even touched you yet, *cățel*." He reached down and traced two fingers over the curve of the Dacian's narrow hipbone, before brushing his fingers along the trail of dark fur leading from his navel to his groin. When his fingers skipped teasingly close to the thickening base of the lad's twitching shaft, Gaius removed his hand.

The Dacian's gasp melted into a groan.

"Simon, give me your toy and your arse, scamp."

Simon crawled onto the mattress on all fours, lifted his hips and offered up his perfect apricot bum. His head hung low between his shoulders as his thick quiff of brown curls flopped down and obscured all but his nose and mouth. The air in the playroom was toasty and growing turbid from the black smoke of the lamp fires.

Gaius picked up the cup again and poured a thin stream of the golden liquid in the crack between Simon's firm cheeks. As the nectar slowly trickled down, Gaius spread Simon's bum cheeks apart and swished his tongue in circles around the lad's hot rim, slurping up another dose of the tasty potion.

"You're mouthwatering, pet."

"Dominus, please. I need more," Simon pleaded in a high-pitched whimper, his hands clutching clumps of the luxurious crimson blanket.

Gaius chuckled and drove his tongue into Simon's arse, pulling out and pushing back in, mouthing and lapping until Simon squirmed and mewled into the bed covers. A few more drops of the drink, a few more moments of devouring and tongue poking, and Simon's entrance was soaked and begging to be filled.

Gaius dangled the thick plug in front of Simon's face. "Suck on it, pup."

The bulbous metal toy was quickly covered with Simon's shiny saliva. Gaius rolled its curved end around the loose muscle of Simon's ring before pushing the plug all the way inside of him in one smooth motion. Simon groaned and collapsed on his stomach. When he noticed the Dacian's heavy eyes fixed on him, Simon stuck his tongue out and winked.

"Better now?" Gaius teased with a gentle slap to Simon's arse cheek.

"Yes, Dominus." Simon's voice was more raspy than usual. "Thank you, sir."

"Get up and fetch the eagle ring."

With a slight hobble to his gait, Simon retrieved the toy from the chest and carefully placed the thick bronze ring decorated with bird wings on the mattress by Gaius's hand.

"What do you imagine it is I want you to do next, Simon?" Gaius asked playfully, his ragged voice brimming with lust.

"This, Dominus?"

Simon reclined on his back beside Allerix and wrapped his right hand around his own pulsing erection. The brunet closed his eyes and caressed his young cock for Gaius's viewing pleasure.

"Not too fast, sweetheart. Nice and slow."

Simon's lips turned up at the corners as he concentrated on falling into a more steady rhythm of smooth, languid strokes.

Gaius held the heavy bronze ring in front of the Dacian's face. "This is a cock ring, cub. It's designed to enhance your pleasure, and mine."

The barbarian licked his dry lips as his prick twitched in anticipation. He bit the inside of his cheek when Gaius carefully slipped one of his testicles through the opening, and then the other, before expertly snaking his shaft through the same hole.

"A perfect fit, and it looks so lovely on you." Gaius leaned down and brushed his lips across the boy's luscious mouth. "Now it's time for our game, yes? When you tell me your Dacian birth name, I win. And when I win, you win. Sing for me, and everyone wins."

Gaius started with lingering, feather-light touches using only the tips of his fingers, timing his teasing caresses to the slow tempo of Simon's lazy strokes. As he gently pulled and stretched the Dacian's foreskin, he made note of every muscle spasm and twitch that wracked the boy's body. The lad's prick was rock hard and jerking under his touch, desperate for more friction, the ring wrapped snug around the base of his shaft and his scrotum.

"I can't," the Dacian groaned between wheezes.

"You can't *what*?"

"I can't tell you my name."

"No? That's a terrible shame. I'm afraid I'll be forced to have you castrated, and you, my poor boy, will spend the rest of your life as someone else's effete eunuch."

"Someone else?"

"I've told you I don't fancy castrated lads. I've never understood the appeal, frankly. But other men do, trust me, and they'd be willing to pay me substantial coin for a particularly delectable faun with such a fuckable mouth." Gaius removed his hand and gestured. "And again, I win—either way, I win. I do so love this game."

From the other side of the bed, Simon half-moaned, half-giggled.

Gaius leaned down and kissed the Dacian, long and deep. He leisurely curled his fingers around the lad's shaft and lightly dragged his hand upwards, over and over, stopping every so often to graze his palm over his engorged crown, brushing his thumb pad across his dripping slit.

The teasing was effective. When the barbarian was near tears and drenched with sweat, Gaius stopped and asked, "What is your name, Dacian?"

The Dacian pulled on the bindings and gritted his teeth. His glazed hazel eyes implored Gaius for relief.

"Don't be shy now. Here in my playroom, you can make as much noise as you wish. Cry and scream and curse yourself blue, but I won't give you what you so desperately need until I get what I want." He lowered his voice to a purr. "Tell me your name, cub."

The lad swallowed several times, the lump of his larynx bobbing up and down above the silver collar. He was losing the thin remnants of any control he foolishly thought he might keep.

Gaius broke the silence. "Perhaps I should guess then. Let me think, what Dacian names do I still recall? Hmm, is it Dardanos?"

Nothing.

"Dairos?"

No answer, save a pathetic snivel and slight shake of the Dacian's head.

"Tarbus?"

"No!"

Gaius momentarily held his hands up and chuckled. "All right, so it's not Tarbus."

The end was close, victory within reach. When he was finished nibbling on the boy's sensitive earlobe, Gaius took one of the Dacian's plump brown nipples between his lips and sucked until the lad writhed against the unforgiving bindings.

"Alle."

Gaius let go of the boy's hard nub and lifted his head. "Come again? Did you say something?"

"Alle. Please, please—my name is Alle."

"A nickname, I assume. What is your full birth name, *cățel*?"

Tears spilled down the Dacian's cheeks as Gaius's torturous caresses grew even slower and more excruciating.

He swallowed once last time and choked out a string of syllables, "Allethodokoles."

Gaius removed his hand and cocked an eyebrow before rolling his eyes. "You have got to be fucking joking. How many damn letters is that? Well, one thing's for certain—that's not a name you could have fabricated on the spot, now is it?"

Gaius smirked before he said, "Simon, stop playing with your prick and come write this bizarre name down, for shit's sake."

When Simon returned, a reed-pen and a small piece of papyrus in hand, the Dacian repeated the same bizarre string of syllables in a shaky voice.

Gaius smiled broadly, hints of sarcasm spicing his words. "What is wrong with you Dacians? You heathens take perfectly reasonable Greek names and turn them into mangled gibberish. We'll stick with your nick-name: Alle. I like it much better than Paulus. And it's simple."

"Please..." The boy's plea was so soft Gaius barely heard it.

"Tell me what you want. Come on, ask for it."

"Please let me come, or I swear I'll fucking die."

Gaius narrowed his eyes, and the Dacian surrendered, again.

"Please, Dominus."

"Now there's a good lad."

Smiling as he pressed his teeth into his lower lip, Gaius pumped Alle's cock fast and hard. It didn't take long before the lad's thighs and calf muscles contracted and his toes curled in anticipation of the impending release.

Gaius increased the speed and growled slowly into the lad's ear, "You've earned your master's permission. Let it go."

The Dacian pulled on all four straps and arched his back as high as the bindings allowed, his scream no more than a strangled gasp. After several more moments, cords of milky semen surged up his shaft and erupted in thick, violent spurts, covering his stomach and chest with puddles of lustrous cream. He cried out again and collapsed into deep and heavy sobs.

"Simon, come lick our cooperative barbarian clean."

After Simon had enthusiastically lapped up most of Alle's release, Gaius grabbed the younger boy by his long curls, pulled him over the Dacian's spent body to his side of the enormous mattress and shoved his tongue down Simon's throat for a taste.

He pulled back and said, "Yes, he's as delicious as I'd hoped he'd be." Gaius reached down, pulled the plug out from Simon's hole and rolled him over on his stomach.

Gaius positioned his knees in the space between Simon's legs and spread them wide. "I'm going to ride your tight arse so hard you'll see the gods frolicking on the stars tonight, pup."

No hesitation, no more lubricating oil. Gaius impaled and pounded Simon in a furious, unrelenting pace that threatened to damage the sturdy bed frame. He roared like an animal when he emptied his heavy balls deep inside Simon's bum.

After he caught his breath and pulled out, Gaius rolled off the bed and stumbled over to a large table by the alcove for a healthy pour of wine. His throat was parched from the heat and the herbal aphrodisiac.

When Simon coughed sweetly for attention, Gaius took a slow, satisfying gulp before waving at the boy with a mixture of annoyance and indifference.

"Finish yourself off, Simon."

Speechless, Simon hesitated for a moment before he rolled over on his back and gripped his neglected, needy cock. After a few forceful, fast pumps, he exploded all over his own stomach without so much as a sound. He crumpled back onto the mattress.

"The game is over." Gaius wrapped himself up in a dark wool mantle before he tossed one of the discarded tunics over Simon's body. "Here, return to your cell at the stable house, pup."

"Dominus, I..." Simon appealed, but then shut his mouth. He slipped the tunic over his head and bowed. Gaius smacked his arse before Simon tottered out of the playroom, his dejected gaze fixed to the floor.

Gaius strolled over to the bed. "You've made the correct choice again, Dacian." After he slipped the cock ring off of the barbarian's shriveled prick and emptied balls, he offered the lad a quenching drink of watered-down wine from a blue ceramic cup. "I'm most pleased with my purchase. You will recover and rest here tonight, Alle."

The Dacian's heavy-lidded drowsy eyes were little more than slits. Gaius thought he saw the hint of a smile when the lad licked the wine from his lips.

"Sleep well. We'll play more tomorrow."

Gaius closed the door behind him, and found Varius standing at attention halfway down the long corridor. He rewrapped his cloak, walked over and handed the veteran the small piece of papyrus.

"This is the Dacian's birth name, or so the barbarian claims. It's not a royal name, but it's unusual nevertheless. I'm curious about its origins. Lock this scrap in my safe box."

Gaius combed his damp curls with his fingers as Varius departed for the office, the tiny sliver of writing clutched in his gigantic hand.

A rapturous wail came from the direction of the stable house and filled the night air. Gaius chuckled under his breath. "And pleasant dreams to you both as well, Max and Nicomedes."

He rubbed the golden stubble on his jaw and scratched his balls. He'd intended to return to his private suite on the other side of the main house, perhaps to finish reading that treatise before turning in for the night, but he couldn't shake the nagging desire gripping his chest.

He needed one more touch, one last taste.

Gaius cracked open the heavy wooden door of the playroom; the Dacian was snoring softly, his face serene and seemingly not bothered at all by the taut bindings around his wrists and ankles strapping him firmly to the frame. Gaius padded over to the bed and lowered himself down onto the edge of the mattress.

The Dacian was deep in dreams, perhaps far away on the snow-capped rugged mountains of his defeated homeland. Gaius brushed his hand up the handsome lad's naked torso and flipped the large fugitive tag attached to the collar out of the way. His wispy black chest hairs were so soft. As Gaius leaned down to feel his dark fur against his lips, the Dacian sighed under his gentle touch and his alabaster skin shivered with goose bumps.

But the room was warm. The summer day's stubborn heat still clung to the humid night air. After Gaius touched the shimmering silver collar, he retrieved a gauzy linen bed cover from the floor and carefully covered his new boy. When he'd finished untying the leather bands encircling his ankles, he loosened the straps attached to the Dacian's wrist restraints and kissed him on the mouth, running his tongue over the black-haired beauty's soft, swollen red lips.

So exquisitely brilliant, so bloody unlike anyone he'd ever savored before.

After a lingering peck to the Dacian's temple, Gaius smiled.

"You're mine, cub."

One more kiss and he whispered, "Goodnight, my fierce sweet Alle."

Gaius strolled quietly around the large space, opening the shutters and extinguishing the phallic lamps one by one. The ethereal radiance of silver-blue moonlight flooded the room. As he crossed the threshold, Gaius paused and turned around for one last look before closing the door.

17

Lucius Petronius's house on the Quirinal Hill, Rome

"I THINK I'VE AGED RATHER WELL."

Lucius tilted his chin and ran his palm over the slight creases around his neck. He pulled the skin until the wrinkly lines temporarily disappeared. "Older but still attractive. Shit, Bry, hold the damn mirror steady, will you? Do you realize I'll turn forty years of age before we celebrate the next Turian festivities?"

"You're more handsome than ever, Dominus," Bryaxis responded with an exasperated lilt as he tried to keep the long silver handle still, but his shoulder was cramping. This ornate mirror was fucking heavy.

His lips pressed together, Lucius scowled in jest. "Don't you remember what I said about your behavior when we're alone together here in the privacy of my suite?"

"Yes, I remember and I am trying. You're gorgeous and most distinguished—Lucius."

"I so bloody adore how my name sounds when you say it. I should have had you call me Lucius years ago. Come here, pet."

Lucius pulled the mirror out of Bry's hand and pulled him into a tight embrace. Nearly the same towering height, they leaned into each other until their foreheads touched.

"Bry, I know you're disappointed you can't accompany me tonight, but it's not that type of dinner party. This gathering will consist of nothing more than a flock of rotting, bitter politicians prattling on and on about dull administrative trivialities and procedures."

Bryaxis grinned, parted his lips for a kiss and was rewarded with Lucius's passionate talented tongue. When Lucius finally untangled his fingers from Bry's thick hair and allowed him air, Bryaxis cooed, "But I thought you aristocratic types listened to poetry and debated philosophy and all other sorts of cultured crap."

Lucius shook his head with amusement. "Fetch my formal cloak, the crimson one with that fabulous scroll stitch work."

As Bry sauntered over to the chair, Lucius explained, "No doubt there'll be some pompous erudite posturing during tonight's dinner, but the conversation never fails to come full circle back to politics. I fear I shall fall asleep."

"Aelius Hadrianus will keep you entertained." Bry fastened the embellished cloak over his master's right shoulder with a monstrous circular gold pin.

Lucius rolled his eyes and laughed. "I'm sure our Greekling will try."

As he leaned his shoulder against the wall, Bry inspected Lucius from head to toe.

"Something's not right." He tilted his head and arched a knowing brow. "That boring tunic needs an elegant accessory. Let's add a flashy belt, that dark leather one decorated with bronze studs."

"Whatever you deem suitable, love. Gaius gave me that belt as a gift years ago, you know. Of course, our incorrigible Commander Fabius had other uses for it in mind when he purchased that naughty strap on a whim while we were on holiday in Baiae."

Lucius winked and held both of his arms out to the side; Bry lifted Lucius's right hand and kissed his master's knuckles. As he walked over to the wardrobe to retrieve the belt, Bry thought about Max. He couldn't imagine Maximus had ever been so audacious as to suggest clothing for Fabius to wear to an official event.

That red-haired bastard was right about one thing.

Bryaxis was most certainly one fortunate, pampered son of a bitch.

Bry meandered back, his long chiseled body swaying like a dancer's with every step. After he reached underneath Lucius's posh cloak and buckled the belt around his waist, Bryaxis kissed the side of his master's neck and said, "Time for shoes. Those fancier sandals of yours with the fringe would be perfect. Go sit on the bench by the window while I find them."

As Lucius settled back on the plush bench cushion, he growled at Bry's back, "I'd prefer you at my feet in all your spectacular natural glory. Be a dear and spoil me, won't you?"

Bryaxis crossed his long arms behind his head and pulled off his pale summer tunic. Bronzed and naked, he turned around wearing only his crooked grin. Lucius's posh sandals hung down from his curled fingers by their thick brown laces.

"Found them."

Bry's big soft cock swung back and forth in sync with the dangling shoes as he padded over and dropped to a crouch before Lucius's bare feet. He lifted the left one, kissed his master's toes and slipped the bottom of one sandal over his large foot. He wrapped the laces around Lucius's calf, marking each turn with a loving peck to his master's warm skin.

Then right shoe, and more kisses up Lucius's leg. Bry raised his gaze, his lusty eyes peering up from beneath his bangs. "Do we have time?"

"We always have time. A fucking eternity for you, pet."

Bryaxis rose to his knees. "I love you, Lucius."

Lucius snatched a fistful of Bry's golden-streaked brunet hair and pulled him up for a deep, dominating kiss. When he broke it off, he sweetened his deep rich voice. "Make me forget for a fleeting while that I must leave you and walk halfway across bloody Rome to attend to this tedious horseshit."

"You'll feel the sweet ache of release for the rest of the night. I can guarantee you that much, Dominus."

His master tugged his hair, and Bry corrected himself, "Lucius."

Lucius rolled the folds of his formal tunic up and around his waist; his throbbing erection sprang free and brushed across Bry's chest.

After he ran his fingers up the prominent vein of Lucius's thick shaft, Bry smiled. "Forget, relax, and enjoy my mouth." He licked circles around the rim of Lucius's swollen head before swallowing his enormous length in one uninterrupted motion.

Lucius let his head fall back against the wall as he mumbled, "We have only the time the white-robed goddesses gifted us long ago, Bryaxis. Let us hope they were generous."

~

BRY OPENED HIS LARGE EYES WITH A START AND PEELED HIS CHEEK OFF THE sticky papyrus leaf. He'd been reading through the legal papers Lucius wanted him to review in preparation for another long day at the courts tomorrow. Squeeze Mars' balls as dry as the Nubian Desert—this current inquest was duller than a dormouse's tit.

After rubbing his face with the bedcovers in case any of the ink had wiped off on his skin, he took a drink of water before snuggling back under the fresh summer blankets. His handsome master's bed had been his home for well over ten years now, sumptuous and warm and safe.

Through the shutters at the far end of the suite, the full moon was high in the sky. It was late.

Where was Lucius?

He would have politely excused himself from that party as early as possible, no? Bry had expected him back before the sixth hour, and it was well past the middle of the night now. Bathed in silver light, the elegant room was eerily aglow but dead quiet.

A loud bang of wood against stone echoed through the corridors, followed by the low rumble of men's voices.

Bry sat up and rubbed his drowsy eyes as he listened. Convinced the noise didn't concern him, he lay back down.

A blood-curdling wail ripped through the moonlit air.

Bry threw the covers off and jumped out of bed. After he'd bundled his naked body in one of Lucius's mantles, he sprinted from the master suite to the front of the mansion, zigzagging through the maze of familiar frescoed passageways, past a blur of painted mythological panels and floating Muses. When he crossed the mosaic threshold of the reception room, he skidded to a stop.

Four men were carrying his master through the torch-lit cavernous hall on a makeshift plank litter. Lucius's face was twisted in agony, his gasps raspy and labored. Blood drenched the front of his formal white tunic, glistening wet in shallow pools on either side of his posh Campanian belt. Most of the household stood huddled together in the shadows of the atrium, helpless as they held their breath.

"Take Dominus to that guest room." The steward pointed, his normal confident voice cracking with panic. He turned to an estate guard. "Get the physician! Hurry, man!"

Domina's screams gradually deflated to slobbering whimpers. The bitch knew how to fake a cauldron of emotions. The crowd stepped aside as Bryaxis snaked through the throng of people gathered by the door to the small spare room.

Everything was spinning. Even the air hurt. Bry could hardly breathe.

Lucius's long body was stretched out on the modest guest couch, his blood-soaked crimson cloak hanging down to the tiles. His face was pale, except for the shadowed hollows under his eyes. On one side of the bed, Domina sat on a chair and observed her dying husband with an unblinking reptilian glare.

"Lucius, my beloved husband, speak to me," she pleaded, though her posture remained stiff and cold.

Bry fell to the floor on the opposite side of the bed and grabbed Lucius's right hand. It was damp and cold.

"Dominus." A cascade of tears streaked down Bry's face.

As he babbled garbled noises, Lucius slowly turned towards Bry's voice. Bryaxis squeezed his hand hard.

"A doctor's been sent for, Dominus. He'll be here soon. Hold on and stay with me."

"Bry..."

Bryaxis grazed a forefinger across his master's lower lip. "No talking, sir. Save your strength. Everything will be fine."

"Pet, come closer."

Bry leaned down. Lucius's eyes were cloudy, blurred with the fog of looming death. Without warning, his voice rose to a high pitch as if he were suddenly transformed into a prepubescent boy.

"You're here, right in front of me. I can see you so clearly. Greetings, Father."

Bry pulled back. "I don't understand what you're saying, sir."

Blood bubbled up and rushed down from the corner of Lucius's mouth. He cried out again.

"Father, I've failed you. I've betrayed my ancestors. Please forgive me. Allow me to come home."

"Dominus?"

Lucius blinked a few times; his eyes cleared as he regained his wits. He reached up and pulled Bry down by his hair as more blood gushed out from between his quivering lips.

"Beg him to forgive me. Beg him, Bryaxis. Promise me you will."

His face splattered with specks of Lucius's blood, Bry asked in desperation, "Who? Forgive you for what, Dominus?"

"Gaius—tell Gaius that I never wanted to get involved. I had no fucking choice. Tell Gaius I'm so—so sorry. Implore Gaius to forgive me. Promise me."

Shocked and confused, Bryaxis whispered again, "I don't understand, Dominus."

"Swear to me!"

"Yes, of course I'll tell Commander Fabius. I promise, Dominus."

Lucius collapsed back on the thin mattress with a grunt of torturous pain. Holding onto Lucius's hand for dear life, Bry stared into his sunken eyes. What had been bright blue gems filled with mirth and passion were fading to dull grey.

Lucius was leaving.

Bryaxis fought to speak through his anguish. It couldn't end like this—all those years of devotion couldn't end like this.

"Don't go. Please don't die, Lucius."

Lucius squeezed Bry's hand with his last bit of strength and whispered, "It sounds so perfect—so pure and true. Say my name for me one more time."

"I love you, Lucius."

"Thank you for allowing me to love you, my sweet Bry."

Lucius's fingers released their grip as his chest rose and fell—one last breath, one final gurgling gasp.

It was over.

Bry's prayers and pleading had failed him. Still holding his master's hand, he crushed his face into the mattress cushion and wailed.

Lucius was gone, and Bryaxis was alone in a crowd of onlookers.

He was abandoned.

Left behind unprotected.

Domina reached across Lucius's body, clutched a fistful of the cloak around Bry's neck and asked, "I couldn't hear him. What did he say? Did he mention me? Did he say something about his final testament?"

Wiping his face with his mantle, Bry jerked out of her grip. "Yes, he did mention you. Lucius said you are a fucking heartless, greedy viper, and he hopes you choke on your own forked tongue, Domina."

With her jaw dropped, Domina glared at Bryaxis until she regained her composure and squawked, "Get this worthless slut out of my sight! Did you hear how it spoke to me? Did you hear what it said?" She pulled her painted lips into a thin, angry line. "How dare this thing, this worthless slave, refer to Counselor Petronius by his familiar name."

She looked over at the stunned family members clogging the doorway and pointed to Lucius's corpse.

"Our kindhearted and most generous Dominus never understood the immeasurable value of a strong hand. He pampered this barbarian cur as if it were an eastern king's courtesan. Seize this impudent vermin!"

Lucius's estate guards hesitated at first, but finally capitulated to her orders. They moved in unison towards Bry's side of the bed.

Bryaxis scooted up the couch and carefully closed Lucius's half-open eyes with gentle swipes of his thumb pad. After he wiped his master's lifeless, bloodied mouth and chin with the edge of the cloak, he kissed the tip of Lucius's perfect nose and mumbled.

"I'll join you soon, Lucius. She'll have me killed before the sun rises. Please—" Bry choked back another sob. "Please wait for me. I don't belong here anymore. I don't belong anywhere without you. You are my home."

As the guards pulled him from the bed and off of Lucius's chest, Bry went limp and surrendered to the terrible Fates.

"By the gods, wait for me. I love you, Lucius."

Domina walked over, stood up on her toes, and slapped him across the face as hard as she could muster.

"Enough! Whip this filth until it's broken and lock it in the library. No food, no water! It can rot there along with the rest of Counselor Petronius's useless scrolls and legal records."

As they carried Bry down the hallway, his feet dragged along the polished marble tiles. Out of nowhere, a figure stepped from the shadows of a vestibule into the corridor, her eyes fierce as she wagged her finger.

"Release him."

"We have orders, Euphronia."

"And now you have new orders. Escort Bryaxis to Dominus's library, but there will be no beating."

"We don't answer to slaves."

"Fair enough. But you do answer to Dominus."

"Dominus is dead."

Euphronia took a deep breath and fought back the tears. "I know—I know he's gone." She raised a fold of her dress and sniffled into the cloth before collecting herself to continue.

"I also know Dominus left specific written instructions for a tragic event of this sort. Bryaxis no longer belongs to this household. If you beat him, his new guardian will be furious to learn his property has been damaged."

"My new guardian?" Bryaxis' head jerked up as he questioned her with terrified wide eyes.

"But—" The taller guard looked at his companion for reassurance. "Counselor Petronius's will was deposited with the courts, wasn't it? His testament couldn't have possibly been unsealed yet."

"No, of course it hasn't," she answered. "Dominus's last testament will only be unsealed in front of the inheritance magistrates and in the presence of Commander Fabius and the other witnesses. But Dominus left an official document for an emergency in the safe box in his library. He wrote a letter before his marriage, and he shared its general contents with me some years ago. I will show it to you."

Euphronia gave them a moment to understand before she warned.

"With his dearest friend stabbed to death like a feral dog, all of Rome will soon face the wrath of the Lion of the Lucky Fourth." Euphronia held her upturned hands towards the ceiling and beseeched her goddess, "Great mother, we pray you will spare the innocent from perishing in the carnage of the lion's revenge."

No one moved as they all stared up at the plaster-covered vaulted ceiling.

"Perhaps—" She redirected her gaze. "Perhaps you gentlemen should be damned afraid of Commander Fabius's anger. Perhaps you should think twice before you volunteer to climb up on the sacrificial altar. But why listen to me? I'm just an old, fat slave—and a crazed woman no less. I'm nothing more than the servant who prepares the meals."

After the pair glanced at each other, the guards loosened their tight grip on Bry's arms and stepped back.

Euphronia swaddled Bry up in Lucius's mantle and cradled his wet, ashen face with both of her hands. "Commander Fabius will be here soon, Bry. Until then, we'll do what we must to survive. Dominus would want you to survive. He'd want you to be brave. Do you understand what I'm saying, my dear boy?"

Bryaxis nodded. His tears, colored with drops of Lucius's blood, flowed in red-stained rivulets down his jaw, down the length of his long neck.

"I made a promise. No matter what happens, I will find a way to fulfill my vow to Lucius."

~

Gaius Fabius's mansion on the Caelian Hill, Rome

Marcia sat at the desk in her bedroom and reread Gaius's letter by the flickering light of an oil lamp. When she'd finished digesting his words for the third or fourth time, she pushed her loose hair behind her ears, sighed and leaned back in her chair.

A child would grace their home soon after the Saturnalia.

The child was his bastard spawn with that aloof blonde tart, but the baby was Gaius's child nevertheless.

She glanced at his near-illegible scratchy scrawl again.

Gaius was right. This predicament could work in their favor and all but guarantee them supreme power. Gaius would secure the throne in a mere seven months, assuming the baby was born alive and healthy. Assuming it was a boy.

Juno had answered Marcia's repeated prayers in a most unexpected but brilliant way, as she was often wont to do. Marcia rolled up her husband's letter, tapped her chin and smiled.

"You seem happy, mistress." Melissa sat up on the bed, her full milky-white breasts revealed as the blanket slipped down. "You've received pleasant news, I hope."

Marcia turned in her chair.

"I thought you'd fallen asleep, my love. Yes, we've received marvelous news. It appears Commander Fabius and I are having a child, but I'll need your assistance. Do you remember that meek girl who lived here once named Zoe?"

Melissa pursed her lips. "You mean that snobby waif who preferred Dominus's cock over our attention? Didn't he move her down to his villa near Puteoli, mistress?"

"Yes, after I allowed him to buy her from me. Melissa, sweetheart, I'll need your help. It'll be tricky but—"

A loud knock on the bedroom door interrupted their conversation. Marcia questioned Melissa with her eyes before she granted permission.

"Enter."

As Melissa pulled the blanket to her chin, the house manager crept in, his shoulders slouched and his aged eyes cast to the floor.

"Forgive me, Domina, but you have a visitor, and he claims it's most urgent he speaks with you."

"By Juno's sacred grove, who would have the audacity to call at this late hour?"

"Apollodorus of Damascus, the emperor's architect, Domina."

"What on earth could that Greek possibly want?" Marcia stood up and wrapped a heavy cloak around her slight frame. This was most odd. Apollodorus was a prudent fellow, the last man who would dare disturb her over some trivial nonsense. Her heart raced as she mulled over the awful possibilities.

"He didn't give specifics, Domina. Shall I send him on his way?"

"No. Show our friend from the emperor's court to Commander Fabius's office, and offer him a cup of one of our local vintages. I'll be there momentarily."

Marcia padded over to the bed and cupped Melissa's cheek. "Is there some untoward gossip flitting about the servants' quarters of the palace I'm not privy to, pet?"

"I've heard nothing out of the ordinary other than the normal catty chatter, Domina. And certainly nothing that involves you, or Commander Fabius."

"Then this must be serious. Apollodorus is a sensible and loyal client, not a man prone to hysteria. I'll return soon."

When Marcia entered Gaius's office, Apollodorus had his back to her; he was hunched over, inspecting an unfurled scroll resting on the desk.

"I never knew you to spy other peoples' private papers, Apollodorus."

Apollodorus jumped and spun around. "My deepest apologies. Pardon my curiosity, but are you aware that—did you know your husband is writing a commentary on the wars?"

"Yes. His history scribbling keeps him occupied." Marcia walked over to the serving table and poured herself a glass of wine.

"Now tell me why you've decided it proper to call on our home in the middle of the night? Are you aware Commander Fabius is down in Campania?"

"Yes, I know he's left Rome."

"By the gods, has something happened to Gaius?"

"No, Marcia. I'm afraid, however, I have brought tragic news. Our mutual friend, Lucius Petronius Celsus..."

"Yes, what is it?" She chuckled nervously. "Has our dear Lucius offended someone else with his tasteless humor again?"

"Lucius Petronius is dead." Apollodorus took a long breath. "He was murdered earlier this evening—stabbed by a vicious gang of miscreants while walking to the Quirinal with his guards after attending Gaius Plinius's dinner gathering."

Marcia dropped her glass; it shattered across the stone floor. Streams of red wine seeped through the shimmering slivers of broken glass. She froze, unable to speak, until finally she raised her hand to her mouth and whispered through her fingers, "Were you there?"

"I attended the dinner, but I did not witness the crime. Otherwise, I would be dead as well, no doubt. Bloody savages."

"Have the criminals been captured?"

"The emperor's forces searched the neighborhood, but the killers seem to have vanished into the dark maze of the city. Emperor Trajan plans to resume the manhunt at first light. The poorer districts of Rome are crowded with a slew of hidden holes to shelter such sewer scum."

She turned towards the window, wiped her eyes and sighed. "Oh, my poor Gaius."

"Allow me to deliver the news to Commander Fabius in person. Our Emperor has granted me permission to travel to Campania and inform him."

"I would be most appreciative, Apollodorus. A visit from you would be more appropriate and much more respectful than for him to hear such horrific news through a written dispatch."

"Of course. Commander Fabius is a dear friend."

Rubbing her abdomen, she spoke soft but low. "Travel with speed and be careful. When he discovers Lucius has been murdered, Gaius's fury and his anguish will explode greater than Vesuvius. Let us all pray his blood-lust for vengeance is quenchable."

Her heart pounding in her throat and her fingers twitching, Marcia marched out into the corridor.

She had to do something. Anything.

"Wake up and make preparations! Dominus will be coming home!"

18

Gaius Fabius's seaside villa, Campania

Simon and Allerix wandered into the common room after an afternoon spent cleaning the nearby horse stalls. Mucking horseshit was a challenge since his ankles were shackled again, but Alle had adapted. At least he could walk more comfortably now that the chain attached to his irons was longer.

Everyone at the villa had a regular chore or two, including the whores.

Alle enjoyed working in the stables. The pungent odor of fresh hay mixed with horse sweat and manure reminded him of the Dacian refugee camps high up in the Carpathian Mountains. Only the scent of smoke from the cooking fires was missing.

Nic sat at a narrow serving table pushed up against one of the stone walls of the common room; when he pulled the lid off of a small cosmetic box cupped in his left hand, his homemade mirror—a polished old metal dinner plate—wobbled and tipped over with a clang.

"Shit! Simon, get over here and hold this damn thing for me, twerp."

"I'm not your servant."

Simon plopped his bum on the bench, propped his legs up on the long wooden table, crossed his ankles and picked at stray bits of filth lodged underneath his short fingernails. He nodded towards Allerix. "Tell him to do it."

Alle looked over and scowled.

"You want another job, Dacian?" Nic spun around on his stool. "Come here and hold this mirror steady so I can coal my eyes for tonight."

"Looks like you're wearing your finest frock. Where's Dom taking you?" Simon asked, his monotonous tone doing a poor job masking his jealousy.

"We're attending a dinner party in Neapolis, at the house of Appius Valerius or Titus Valerius or whatever. Fucking Romans have too many damn names."

Allerix huffed before walking over to Nic's makeshift dressing area, while Simon pestered on, "And you're wearing eye paint for this?"

"Max told me to primp. He said it's one of those sorts of parties."

Simon fidgeted until he couldn't stand it anymore.

"What sort?"

"An orgy, you twat—pummeling and sucking and wicked times all around. Dom fucks me while we watch everyone else play, after the meal is finished, of course." Nic waggled a brow. "My favorite kind of bash. Good food, great sex."

Careful to temper the curiosity in his voice, Alle picked up the mirror and asked, "Who attends these sex parties?"

"When Dom attends, the leading men of Campania make sure to attend as well. Dom's the commander of a fucking legion; he's the Lion of the Lucky Fourth. He draws a crowd. And if we go to—"

Simon interrupted, "Does he share you?"

"No, Simon. And stop pulling your pecker at the thought." Nic laughed and lined the bottom rim of his right eye with the black soot on the tip of his pinky finger. "Dom doesn't share—well, unless he spots another pretty young whore who catches his eye. Then we all play together. But no one fucks his boys' bums at these gatherings. He's damn possessive."

"But I thought that..." Simon's full lips pursed with confusion.

"What? You mean up in Rome?"

"Yes."

"The parties at the capital are special; different people and different rules, or so I've heard."

Allerix piped up. "Who goes to those parties in Rome?"

"Watch it, pretty lad—too much curiosity killed the barbarian." Nic grinned and continued, "Same sorts, Paulus, just way more fucking powerful. You know, senators and magistrates and all the other filthy rich pricks who own the rest of us and rule the world."

Simon added, "I've heard members of the court attend."

"Hmm? Yeah, sometimes Dom's brother shows up, and Counselor Petronius is usually at those parties in the capital. Lucius Petronius and Dom go to most of the same events. Or, that's what Max has told me."

Beneath his thick fringe of hair, Alle furrowed his brows. "He has a brother?"

No answer.

"Shame Dominus hasn't brought you to one of those exceptional affairs up in Rome, Nic. You'd be a bloody star." Max snorted, as he carried over a bowl of figs and berries from the kitchen. "Here, have a piece of fruit. You'll need your strength for the ride." Max plucked out a ripe, juicy red cherry and handed it to Nicomedes. "And don't forget to use this to stain those pretty lips of yours, love. Scoot over so I can braid your hair. Simon, bring me that basket of ribbons."

Simon passed over the collection of colorful fabric strands organized in neat bundles in the woven container. "Max, you've been to many posh parties up in Rome. Tell us about one of them."

"You've heard all my stories before, Simon."

"But Paulus—um, I mean Alle— Alle hasn't heard them. Besides, I want to hear about the palace again, about the walls and floors all wrapped in sheets of gold and colored marbles, and the outrageous food and the gorgeous silk outfits and the jewelry and the music and dancing. Such grand adventures you've had, sir."

"Calm down and fetch me that other stool, pup. My days attending dinners with Dom in Rome are over." Max's voice cracked with ache.

Nic peered over his shoulder. "Last winter wasn't that long ago, sir."

"It's been an eternity since that party, sweetheart. The wars are over and everything's changed. Lean back for me."

As Max raked his fingers through Nic's long wavy locks, Alle switched the polished disc to his other hand and said, "I'd like to hear a story, sir."

Max ignored him.

He divided Nic's hair into three sections and started to braid, wrapping his golden tresses with ribbons of blue linen. As Nic relaxed and surrendered to his strong hands, Max murmured, "Dom's granted you a second chance, Nicomedes. Do not give him the slightest reason to regret that decision."

"I'll make you proud, sir."

Max kissed the back of Nic's head and smiled.

Cutting through the somber silence, Simon asked, "What about that dinner at the palace when they served crocodile from Egypt?"

Max whispered into Nic's ear, "He's not going to fucking quit, is he?"

Nic stifled a chuckle as he shook his head.

"Ha, yes! They served crocodile soup, Simon, in these huge tortoise shells with live baby eels swimming about in the broth. That particular party I remember."

"Who was there?" Alle mumbled, nonchalantly.

Max tied the ends of the final ribbon; he gazed off at nothing in particular as he recounted that night, "Shit, that was a glorious event—the festivities started with these gorgeous dancers in exotic bird costumes and a troupe of talented Lesbian acrobats. Imagine that! Even the emperor attended."

"He dines with the emperor?" Allerix asked.

Max dropped his voice and replied, "Commander Fabius is our Emperor Trajan's ward, or he was before he came of age. I'm not sure how all the details of this Roman ward business work exactly."

"I'm confused. I thought the emperor was Dom's father. I've heard Dom call him his father. So then, what's a ward, sir?" Simon wondered.

"Simon, I've gone through this with you before." Max sighed in exasperation. "A child becomes a ward when his parents relinquish guardianship to a trusted friend or a relative. Dom's mother gave guardianship of Dom to our Emperor when Dom was a boy."

"Why did she do that, sir?"

"I don't know, Simon."

"But what happened to his real father? Did he die on the battlefield?" Allerix asked.

"Fabius Senior wasn't a soldier. He was murdered." Max patted Nic's shoulders as he turned to speak to Allerix, "And that's enough questions from you. Go change into a clean tunic and wash up, Paulus. Dom wants an audience with you before he leaves."

"Is that what Dom's calling it now? An audience?" Nic laughed as Allerix put down the mirror and reluctantly doddered up the steps to the second floor of the stable house. Once he was out of sight, Alle stopped on the landing, sat down and clasped his hands around his knees to eavesdrop for a precious few moments.

"Was there sex at that dinner in Rome, sir?"

"It wasn't an orgy, Nicomedes. Our Empress Plotina does not permit lewd parties at the palace."

"That sounds terribly dull."

"Well, there was this one time when the empress was away at her country estate. It was a year or two before the wars started. Only the men of the court were in attendance and the wine flowed freely." Max paused and chuckled. "I remember I wore nothing at that dinner save two thick gold arm bands. All of the pleasure slaves were naked. Shit, everyone was plastered, including Dom. Many of the masters shared their pets. And I can confirm without a doubt our noble and most proper Emperor Trajan appreciates a good blow job as much as the next chap."

Simon gasped. "Holy Penates, did you suck off the emperor, Max?"

"No, not me, pup. Counselor Petronius's favorite sucked the imperial purple cock, right there in front of every man and whore in the dining hall. Magnificent performance—slow and slobbering. No one sucks as fierce and as hot as Bryaxis. And his master rarely shares Bry's talented mouth. It was a huge honor for Bry and, more so, for his master. If I remember correctly, Counselor Petronius received a coveted promotion soon after that bash. And I distinctly recall Dom was blatantly envious."

"Dom wanted the promotion?" Simon questioned.

"The blow job, Simon."

~

"Your elixir as scheduled, Dominus."

Gaius took the clear glass from Callidora's outstretched hand, paused and raised his brow before he swallowed the small amount of drink in one gulp.

"It might only be one dose every month, but I'll never grow fond of that potion's noxious flavor," he said as he shuddered in disgust and handed the cup back to her.

"I added clover honey this time."

"Yes, I could taste it. It doesn't help."

Gaius unwrapped the white cloth slung around his hips, kicked off his bath sandals and lowered his naked body into the steaming hot water of the soaking pool.

Callidora licked her red lips. "But you find the cannabis oil to be beneficial, don't you, Dominus?"

"I haven't been wracked with the lunacy in years. We do have ample stock of that foul nectar in the storerooms, yes?"

"Yes, sir. And a fresh batch arrived all the way from the Kushan hills last month. The merchant assured me it's high quality and very pure."

"And he gauged me a ridiculous amount of silver for it as well, no doubt. See to it our supply never runs low, Calli, and be sure to prepare vials for travel. I will not endure another violent fit, here or anywhere." Gaius settled back in the water with a blissful groan.

"Why are you still here, Callidora? Is there something you wish to discuss?"

Calli's mouth twitched before she blurted out, "What will you do about Zoe's condition, Dominus?"

"I've made a decision. I'll share it with you, my dear, when I wish you to know."

Gaius stared, his expression cold and blank.

Calli gathered up the folds of her mantle and bowed. "Thank you. Enjoy your bath, Dominus."

She departed the opulent room with no further nonsense. Calli might have aged into a conniving bitch, but she was a bloody well trained and obedient bitch. Always had been.

Gaius closed his eyes and sank into the fragrant water.

~

THE WALLS OF THE SMALL VAULTED CHAMBER WERE SHEATHED IN POLISHED green and blue tiles with bits of sparkling glass. No less impressive, the floor was covered in tiny cubes of colored stone carefully arranged to form lifelike pictures of fish and other bizarre marine creatures. Allerix parted his lips in awe. If he bent down to touch one, would it swim away?

"This is the changing room of the commander's private baths."

Max pulled the tunic up and over Alle's head and pointed straight ahead.

"That door leads to the next room. The marble floors in there are scorching hot. Slip your feet into those sandals. Your master is waiting."

"He's in there, Max?"

Max hit Allerix in the back of the head. Not hard, just enough to smart. "You're forgetting your fucking place again, Dacian. You refer to me as 'sir,' always. And 'he' is Dominus. Move."

Max steered Alle through the doorway. Thick clouds of steam filled the dark room. Only the geometric border designs of the mosaic on the nearest wall were visible.

Allerix flinched when the Roman's thunderous voice sliced through the heavy blanket of steam.

"There you are, cub. I was beginning to think you'd run off once more, but you're too sharp to pull that daft stunt again, aren't you?"

The monster's raspy chuckles were followed by loud sloshes of water.

When Max released his biceps, Allerix glanced back over his shoulder. Max always seemed to disappear into the shadows.

Alle blinked a few times while his eyes adjusted to the low light. The edge of the pool was only a few feet in front of his toes. He stared down into the dark water and waited for the beast to emerge. He nearly jumped out of his skin when two muscular arms wrapped around his waist from behind. The Roman's hard wet cock pressed into the crack between Alle's bum cheeks.

"Welcome to my humble baths, *cățel.*" Gaius Fabius pulled him closer and lightly nibbled on his right earlobe.

Allerix gasped. "This place is amazing."

"Manners, cub."

"Dominus."

"I'm pleased you like it. There's little more satisfying than a good hot soak in the bath. Slip off those sandals and join me in the pool."

When the Roman took hold of his right hand and squeezed, Alle jerked out of his grasp and stumbled backwards over the chain connecting his ankles.

The man caught Alle before he fell down, and held him in his arms.

"You're scared. Your fear is unwarranted, but understandable."

Alle's eyes widened. "Unwarranted?"

"All right, perhaps a touch warranted." The butcher grinned as he rubbed his fingers along the stubble covering Alle's jaw. "Your bristles return earlier in the day than they do for most lads, cub."

"I'm a feral, hairy northern barbarian. I could attack you right here in your splendid baths."

"A word of advice—it's unwise to share your strategy with your enemy, Dacian. Fortunately for you, I'm no longer the enemy. I am your master. I own you. Are you planning on attacking me? I am, as you can clearly see, unarmed."

He traced a finger over Alle's eyebrow.

"You mock me. Aren't you afraid of me at all?" Allerix asked.

"No, but perhaps I should be. Brazen confidence is a fault I share with many a dead Roman soldier. Let's have a soak before you strike, hmm?"

Gaius Fabius took Alle's hand again and led him down into the delights of the sweet-smelling warm water. It wasn't long before Alle's sore, tired muscles relaxed. He leaned backwards and submerged his entire head beneath the glassy surface. When he rose, his black hair drenched long and shiny, his captor's grin melted into a broad smile.

Shit, the Roman's deep dimples were too sexy to be real.

He flicked a few drops of bath water at Alle's face and asked, "Enjoying yourself?"

"This water is soothing. What's the faint fragrance I smell?"

The Roman sat there, arms crossed and one eyebrow cocked, until Alle added, "Dominus."

"Flowers from our gardens and rare aromatic lavender imported from Arabia." He put one hand in the water and lifted it; two white rose petals floated side by side in his cupped palm like twin boats on a calm lake. After he gently returned the petals to the bath water, the Roman lifted a silver jug from the tiled ledge of the pool and slowly poured a cup half full of the crimson red drink.

"Would you care for some wine? A client of mine owns vineyards close by the slopes of Vesuvius. His grapes are exquisite."

"May I ask a question first, Dominus?"

"Much better." The bastard flashed those dimples again. "Yes, you may."

"Is that drink drugged?"

"No drugs. Just wine."

"Yes, then. Thank you." Alle smiled back. "Dominus."

"Very polite." The Roman offered the bronze vessel decorated with winged cupids and nymphs. "We'll share."

When Allerix leaned down, he tilted the cup for him. "Do you care for it?"

"It's good, Dominus."

"Do you remember that board game we played in my chamber?"

Alle opened his mouth for another sip, and the Roman allowed it.

"Tabula?" Allerix smacked his full lips. "Yes, I won."

Gaius Fabius laughed. "Yes, you did indeed. And you've made impressive strides since that day. You've learned to address me properly, most of the time, and Simon tells me you're working hard in the stables. So, I've decided I will award you the prize for your Tabula victory."

"Here? In the bath?"

"Here will work quite well." The Roman picked up the playing piece with the number eight hidden behind the wine jug and tossed the brothel coin to Alle. "Look on the back. There's an image."

Allerix flipped the coin over in his palm and laughed. "My reward is to suck your cock?"

"No." The Roman grinned as he placed the wine cup carefully on the tiles. He lowered both hands into the water, grabbed Alle around his waist, and hoisted him up until Alle sat perched on the smooth edge of the pool; Allerix yelped in surprise as water splashed over the mosaic tiles. His gasps dissolved into moans of disbelief as the man's tongue danced up the inside of his thigh, his teeth tugging on Alle's dark leg hairs.

"Shit," Allerix groaned.

The Roman looked up from beneath his thick wet lashes, his amber eyes twinkling with mirth. "Don't tell me you haven't had your prick sucked before."

Allerix swallowed; Max had told him to keep that ball-sapping blow job a secret. Alle's mind raced to craft a lie.

"Once. I was drunk. It was during a holiday celebration, in a dark storage room. I don't remember much to be honest, Dominus."

"I value honesty." He nuzzled Alle's balls. "Boy or girl?"

Alle hesitated for a while before whispering, "Boy."

"Why did you pause? There's no shame in playing with other lads, cub."

"Dacians consider it a crime, an offense to our gods."

"Ignorant heathens." After the Roman licked a lazy line up Alle's shaft, he asked, "Did you have a wife, Alle?"

"Before the wars began, my father had arranged for me to marry a girl from our village. She and her family were massacred by Roman troops."

"Pity. A loyal and fertile spouse is most useful." Gaius Fabius mouthed the head of Alle's prick until he forced a whimper.

"Is that why you have a wife, Dominus?"

When the Roman laughed, his lips vibrated against the sensitive skin of Alle's throbbing vein. "Every ambitious Roman man takes a wife, cub. The wise and fortunate marry well." He dragged his tongue up and over Alle's tender slit and said, "And I have been most fortunate. Now, be quiet while I devour your exquisite prick. Trust me, *cățel*. You'll remember it this time."

When he swallowed Allerix's cock down his throat with ease, Alle ran his fingers through the man's wet curls. The Roman slowly lifted his mouth off, his lips upturned at the corners, a thick string of saliva stretching from his lower lip to the tip of Alle's prick. "You may touch my hair, but do not fucking pull my locks or push my head down. Understand?"

The garland of spit swung back and forth as he spoke. Alle snickered through a groan. "Yes, Dominus."

Despite Alle's attempts to hold back his release and relish the intense pleasure for as long as possible, the Roman took control. Again. Up and down, teasingly slow and then fast and demanding. With one final squeeze of his cheeks and stroke of his tongue, he moaned around Alle's girth until Alle cried out and emptied his balls. Gaius Fabius rose up and took hold of Alle's face, snaking his tongue through his lips to share the taste of Alle's semen.

"Delicious, yes? Your nectar is more flavorful than any wine."

Panting through his tremors, Alle fought to catch his breath. When his breathing had slowed down enough to speak, he asked, "Why—why did you buy me, Dominus?"

"You were the one trophy of those brutal wars I hadn't yet managed to acquire. You complete my collection, Dacian."

"What about Nic and Simon? Aren't they resentful?"

Gaius Fabius chuckled. "They're accustomed to sharing my affections."

"They love you."

"They're loyal to a fault. I treasure my boys' devotion, but neither of them fulfills my cravings these days."

"Nic is bloody gorgeous."

"Nicomedes is damaged. The trauma of his past wounded his mind permanently, but he understands I will always protect him, whether I fuck him or not."

The Roman kissed Alle deeper before pulling back to add, "I had great expectations for my beautiful Simon once, but he's a simple lap dog—adorable, obedient, and completely fucking predictable. I care for the pup, but I bore easily."

"What about Max? He was your favorite for years. Why did you free him?"

"It was time. Maximus is more valuable to me as a freedman than as a pleasure slave. Don't mistake me—Max will always hold a special place in my heart."

"He didn't want to be freed."

The Roman snapped, "I'm fucking aware of that! Enough questions. You will keep my words in confidence, understand?"

"Yes, Dominus."

He took hold of Allerix's hips. "I've tasted your juice, now roll over like a good lad and let me enjoy your sweet arse." Gaius Fabius flipped him over onto his stomach and licked leisurely strokes across the firm curves of Alle's round bum, lapping and nibbling as he hummed with pleasure. He spread Alle's cheeks with both hands and traced his tongue up his cleft.

Alle's legs trembled from nerves and lust, when suddenly the faces, the voices, the stink of his attackers in that field came rushing back as vividly as if the assault had happened yesterday.

The Roman caressed his lower back. "I won't hurt you. Don't be afraid."

Alle clenched his teeth, but he'd already lost control. A powerful wave of anger and fear raced though his body, twisting his gut. Bile stung the back of his throat. "I'm not afraid of you, butcher."

Gaius Fabius pressed his fingers into the smooth flesh covering Alle's hipbones. "Relax, I'm not a monster. I am your protector."

Allerix squirmed under his grip.

"You fucking ordered the slaughter of my people."

"I did what I was ordered to do. I did what the gods expected of me, *cățel*. My victories magnified the glory of my emperor and my family."

He rolled Alle over on his back. "Look at me. Look into my eyes. Back when Rome was little more than a village of huts, my esteemed ancestors journeyed from their homes to Campania to consult the oracle of Cumae."

Tears welled up in his eyes, but Alle said nothing.

"The prophetess declared when the coffers of Rome spill over with rivers of barbarian riches, a Fabius would soon rule the empire. Our treasury is now bursting with Dacian gold. I fought valiantly during those wars for my emperor, and I won to secure my destiny and wield the imperial scepter."

"You directed your soldiers to murder thousands of men, women and children. Thousands more were condemned to slavery. Others were mutilated for sport. You're a savage."

"Lucius was right. You are a fucking colossal project." He pulled Alle up by his hair. "Your fierce spirit and your undeniable beauty intrigue me, slave, but I will not tolerate disrespect."

"Kill me."

"How bloody noble of you."

The Roman stood up, his body dripping wet and shimmering in the low lamplight—a bronzed god rising from the sea.

"You're my property to keep or to sell, and I will not forfeit one fraction of my investment. A gorgeous lad like you is worth substantial silver."

"Then sell me."

Gaius Fabius grabbed hold of Alle's chin, lifted his face and glared, unblinking until he smirked. "I'll find a buyer."

Neither man broke eye contact.

Neither man backed down, until Alle closed his eyes. He had to stay in control. He had to play this game to the end.

He had to win.

And in order to win, he first had to surrender.

"Please forgive my stupidity. Please allow me to stay. I don't wish to be sold, Dominus."

The Roman exhaled. He unfurled his fists, waded through the shallow water to the opposite side, and stepped out of the bath. After he slipped his feet into his sandals, he said, "Convince me you're not a fool. I will return from Neapolis in two short days. When I do, persuade me to keep you."

Alle swallowed. "I will, sir."

"We shall see. And to be perfectly clear, I had no intention of plowing your arse tonight." The Roman grasped his still erect shaft and stroked it. "You haven't come close to earning my cock, boy."

He let go of his prick and walked back to the edge of the pool. "If you wish me to keep you—" He squatted and lightly ran his fingers across Alle's damp facial scruff. "Then seduce me, Alle."

Allerix clutched the edge of the pool to catch himself from falling into his irrational but ferocious desires. This man had destroyed his people and razed his capital, and yet he was the most handsome and seductive son of a bitch Allerix had ever known. Even his boyhood idol, Brasus, paled in comparison.

The Roman was so powerful, so perfect, in such an imperfectly ruthless way.

Gaius Fabius turned and yelled into the shadows of the changing room, "Maximus!"

"Yes, sir."

"Hand me that dry bath cloak on the peg. Is Nicomedes ready?"

"He's waiting by the main vestibule, Commander."

Gaius Fabius wound the soft white fabric around his broad shoulders and growled, "Be sure our naughty lamb is dressed in a heavy cloak for the ride into town. There's a bitter chill in the air tonight. Come, I have instructions for while I'm away in Neapolis."

"Yes, sir." As Max followed Gaius into the corridor, he warned over his shoulder, "I'll be right outside. Don't move, Dacian."

Alle lay back, clasped his hands behind his head, and stared up at the beads of condensation clinging to the pale domed ceiling.

"I'll seduce you, you bastard. I'll persuade you to prefer me, to choose me to kneel by your couch at the palace in Rome within arm's length of your beloved ruler. And at one of those dinners, your king will die and I will earn immortality."

Allerix sat up and reached for the wine cup. "On that glorious day, I will join my god and my slaughtered kinsmen in the majestic afterlife. All of Dacia will celebrate my courage. And you, Roman, will inherit a throne soiled with the blood of your murdered father-king."

He turned his gaze towards the dark doorway. "Your oracle foretold our fates long ago. Our destinies are intertwined, Dominus."

After raising the cup in salute, Alle gulped down the remaining splash of ruby red wine.

19

Gaius Fabius's seaside villa, Campania

THE HORSE CANTERED PAST HIM; COOL, SLIMY RIBBONS OF MUD SPLATTERED through the wooden fence of the riding arena and coated Allerix's bare shins. Dawn had broken that morning with a heavy rain, the first cleansing downpour since he'd arrived at this villa. The oppressive heat was gone, the humid air washed away. Alle inhaled the sweet and fertile fragrance of the nearby green pastures.

"She's finally found her stride!" Simon shouted with unabashed joy, waving both of his arms in the air, as he drove the dark brown mare around the exercise ring for the third time. "Just needed warming up!"

"He's talented," Allerix noted.

"Simon took to horses when he was a young boy, always hanging around the stables making a nuisance of himself. He has a natural way with these animals," Max replied, as he tentatively stepped closer to the railing.

"He doesn't use a bridle to guide her, just leg pressure. See?" Allerix pointed. "Right there he used his inside leg to change her lead. That's the mark of a skilled rider."

"You seem to know a lot about horses. Do you ride well?" Max asked.

"Dacian boys learn to ride before they can walk." Alle turned his head and stared into Max's deep brown eyes. "Or we used to, before they destroyed us."

"Perhaps if he doesn't sell you, Dom might allow you to assist Simon with exercising the horses, Paulus."

"You'd have to convince him to remove these shackles around my ankles, Max. I'm collared, so there's no need for them. I know I can't escape. And—why do you still call me that? You know that my name is Alle."

"Paulus is your slave name. You're a slave, a sex slave. It's dangerous for you—for all of us—to think otherwise."

"Dominus calls me Alle." The words came out cockier than Allerix had intended.

"So I've heard." Max grinned. "Listen, Commander Fabius does whatever the fuck he wants. He owns all of this, he owns you. I, on the other hand, will call you Paulus because that's the name written on that fucking fugitive tag, Dacian. As long as you wear that collar, you are Paulus."

Just as Alle looked down at the metal disc attached to the silver collar around his neck, Simon raced his horse over to the fence. The mare skidded to a sloppy stop; a wave of mud flew up and coated Allerix and Max's legs.

"Fuck Minerva's withered fanny, Simon!" Max bellowed as he wiped off some of the muddy filth. "Get down from there, wash that horse and put it back in its stall. We've other chores in the main house to tend to after the midday meal."

Beaming from ear to ear, Simon slid off the horse's back and panted. "Yes, sir."

"Paulus, help Simon. And I expect you two rascals to return to the stable house as soon as that's finished. Understand?"

Energized from the ride, Simon nodded with enthusiasm; his brunet curls flopped like dog's ears to and fro in the light breeze. Alle chuckled before he answered, "Yes, sir."

The two young men headed down the roofed aisle separating the rows of stalls in the stables, the charcoal brown mare plodding obediently behind them, when Allerix stopped and asked, "You love horses, Simon, don't you?"

"Riding is my second favorite activity in the whole world." Simon winked and smirked coyly. "I feel free when I'm on the back of a horse."

"I'd wager you've ridden most of these mounts, right? Which is your favorite?"

"That grey gelding in the back stall on the right. His name is Glaucus. He's sweet, obedient, and he has the smoothest gait."

"Which is the fastest?"

"The fastest?" Simon paused, as he looked around and finally pointed. "That would be Dom's prized stallion over there. Dom bought him as a colt from a racehorse dealer before the last war. He's of Thracian stock and that bastard can run circles around anything. He could chase down a leopard."

Allerix took a few steps towards the stallion's stall. "This one here?"

The pitch-black horse lifted his statuesque head. The whites of its huge dark eyes glowed menacingly. It snorted, daring Alle to come closer.

"Careful, Alle. Don't get too close. He's a wild beast with a volatile temper. Dom's the only person who's ridden him. Don't say anything, but once he threw Dom off—reared up and tossed Dom, arse first, right into a heap of horseshit. I honestly don't know why Dom keeps him. He's a handsome steed and all, but..."

Simon didn't understand the first thing about the Roman, did he? Perhaps none of them really did.

Alle cleared his throat and replied, "Dominus keeps him because he relishes a challenge. Why didn't he ride him to Neapolis?"

"That horse isn't completely tamed, and Nic's with Dom. Nic can't ride, so Dom shares his mount with him when they travel together. Nic's scared of all horses, the skittish prat, but he's especially terrified of that stallion."

Alle considered Simon's words before asking, "What's the horse's name?"

"Ferox. It means fierce. Come on, then—let's get this mare washed and head back for our meal."

"I'll be right there," Allerix mumbled. He walked up to the stallion, his hand extended as a peace gesture. "So you're a Thracian, are you? I suppose that makes us cousins, then."

The stallion looked down at Alle's shackles and swooshed its long, thick ebony tail.

"I'm the bastard's property as well." Alle reached into a nearby sack hanging from a nail and pulled out a handful of grain.

As the stallion happily gobbled up the treat from Alle's flattened palm, Alle whispered, "I'll ride you one day, Ferox. Then we'll see how fast you can really gallop." Alle winked and stroked the horse's broad nose before heading off to catch up with Simon.

The sunlight outside the stables was blinding. Alle shielded his eyes; a lanky silhouette of a man whom he didn't recognize at first walked towards him.

"Greetings, Dacian! Gorgeous day, isn't it? Where's Max?"

Alle smiled and said, "Nic, you're back."

Nic wrapped an arm around Alle's shoulder. "Yeah, we just returned home, my little furry friend. Fuck, I'm bloody starving. It's midday meal about now, right?"

"It is, and Max should be in the common room. Did you have fun at that orgy?"

With a baffled expression, Nic cocked his head. "The dinner was pleasant enough, but a couple of the other whores acted weird around Dom and me, all twitchy and guarded. There must be some gossip flying about the slave quarters. Slaves' loose lips carry news faster than the fucking imperial courier service, for shit's sake."

As Nic looked down at his feet, lost in thought, Alle asked, "Where's Dominus?"

"Dom headed straight for the main house, as he always does after a journey. You do have a plan, right?"

"What?"

"You don't want Dom to sell you, do you? He told me about your daft behavior in the baths."

"He did?" Alle absentmindedly reached up and touched his silver slave collar. "No, I don't want to be sold, Nic. And I don't have a plan."

"You should get one."

"I..." Alle reached out and grazed his fingers across Nic's tunic-clad chest. "I need help. Your help."

"Ah, you've come to the right slut for counsel, barbarian. I call it: 'How to seduce a Roman master in ten licks or less.'"

Nicomedes chuckled and squeezed his shoulder before leading Alle towards the stable house. "Let's eat, and afterwards we'll feed Achilles and Dom's fish and I'll share with you the great Nicomedes' idiot-proof seduction techniques. But you have to promise me you'll unclench that tight, virgin bum hole of yours and mind my advice."

~

GAIUS BELCHED AS HE THREW HIS RIDING CLOAK ACROSS THE ROOM; IT DRAPED half-cocked over his chair by the desk. He'd enjoyed a tasty meal and some good wine but he was too damn exhausted to soak in the baths. He hadn't slept save a few winks since he'd left the villa; despite the delicious spread of sexy, compliant distractions at that wicked party, the Dacian had dominated his thoughts for two days and nights.

He couldn't get the feisty, beautiful lad out of his mind.

Just inside the threshold, his tidy villa steward rocked back and forth on the balls of his feet, pretending not to notice when Gaius's riding mantle slipped off the chair and fell to the floor. Rubbing his fingertips together anxiously, Atticus asked, "Can I bring you something else, Dominus?"

"There's fresh water in that jug?"

"Yes, sir. And I've changed the bed covers, of course."

"Then I require nothing more. Everything's been calm in my absence, Atticus?"

"Yes, Commander. All has been quiet. Maximus is waiting in the corridor to speak with you, sir."

"Send him in."

Gaius unbuckled his wide leather belt and draped it over the back of his chair.

"Greetings, Commander. Welcome home. I hope you enjoyed your time in Neapolis."

"Greetings, my sweet and handsome Max." Gaius stalked over, stood up on his toes, and cupped Max's square jaw. "Wasn't that thunderstorm this morning bloody marvelous? Thank fucking Jove we've been gifted some relief from the sweltering summer heat. How are my boys?"

"They are well, sir. The Dacian has requested an audience with you, Commander."

"Has he now? Excellent. Bring him to me."

"Here, sir? To your master suite? Not the playroom?"

"Maximus." Gaius kissed him soft on the lips. "I realize I've imbibed more wine than is prudent this early in the day, but I'm quite sure my speech is not impaired."

"Yes, sir. I mean, no, sir." Max rubbed his face. "I'll fetch him."

"And remove the shackles on his ankles. There'll be no need for them."

"Yes, Commander."

Gaius reached under his tunic to unclasp the leather strap of his scabbard. Carefully, he unsheathed his ivory-handle dagger and placed it along with the scabbard on his desk.

Another test for his Dacian.

He staggered over to the bed, flopped down on his back and lifted his right leg to unbind his sandal. After three attempts, he gave up and threw his freckled forearm over his tired eyes.

"Fuck, it's too bright in here."

~

"Greetings, Dominus. Thank you for agreeing to see me, and for having those shackles removed."

Ah, that sultry singsong voice. Gaius propped himself up on both elbows and grinned.

"My most attractive and noble heathen." Gaius lay back down and covered his eyes. "Close the shutters, cub. As lovely and refreshing as this day is, my head can't take the sun's glare."

Alle quickly closed the wooden panels one by one. No doubt the Dacian would spot his weapon lying out in the open. Would the lad have the fucking nerve to touch it? Gaius lifted his arm and glanced over.

Alle closed the final shutter over the desk and rushed over to kneel on the floor by the edge of the bed.

"You must have seen that dagger, but you defeated the temptation to take it. I'm pleased with your self-discipline." Gaius covered his eyes again.

"May I untie your sandals for you, Dominus?"

"Yes, take these damn things off. My entire fucking body aches. Nicomedes squirmed like an eel during both legs of our trip. I should have just released my grip on the nervous nit and let him fall off our horse. Would have taught him a lesson. You do know how to ride, correct?"

"Yes, Dominus."

The Dacian unknotted the first pair of laces, slipped off Gaius's right sandal, and rubbed his foot for a moment before he scooted over to untie the left one.

Gaius covered a yawn as he mumbled, "Can I assume you've mulled over my ultimatum, *cățel*?"

"I've considered your words and the consequences, Dominus. I'm begging you not to sell me and I'm..."

~

A rumbling snore interrupted Alle's plea.

"Dominus?"

The Roman shifted his weight on the mattress. His dark amber eyelashes fluttered when he snored again.

Allerix whispered under his breath, "Shit."

~

"WHAT DID YOU TELL HIM, NIC?"

Simon's mouth hung open in anticipation, while across the table, Max stared at Nicomedes with a mixture of disbelief and pride.

Nic took a long drink of water before he declared, "I told him to lie down on the damn bed, spread his hairy legs, and take Dom's cock up his arse like a man."

Nic raised the red ceramic cup towards Max and winked, as Simon doubled over in giggles. Max shook his head with a snort. "I suppose we'll learn if our Dacian has some fucking common sense."

"He'll do what he must. He's terrified of being sold."

"Good. He should be. Dom's patience is as famously limited as his attention."

"Max, sir?"

"Yes, Nicomedes?"

"Have you heard any rumors lately concerning Dom? What I mean is—has something happened up in Rome?"

"No, I've heard nothing. What's troubling you, darling?"

"A couple of the whores at that dinner seemed anxious when they were sent to our couch. Shit, one even spilled wine while he was serving Dom a drink. Dom just laughed it off. Dominus was more relaxed and cordial than he's been at one of those bashes in a long while. Those slaves had no cause to fear him."

Max stood up and walked around the end of the table. He sat in the chair next to Nic and placed his large hand on Nic's shoulder.

"And the guests? Did they act different?"

"No, just the slaves. I'm sure none of the men in attendance noticed anything, and Dom didn't seem bothered. He never said a harsh word about it."

"Listen, Nic, Dom's a formidable and influential aristocrat. He's one of the highest-ranking members of the imperial family. I suspect their masters warned them to be on best behavior. Those slaves were likely worried they'd be punished severely for some daft mistake, no?"

"I suppose. It was just—well, odd."

Max hooked a finger around Nic's sculpted jawbone and turned his face so he could smile into Nic's bottomless blue eyes.

"The best orgies are always a tad odd, love."

~

Gaius awoke and winced. Shit, his shoulder hurt.

What the fuck was jabbing into his collarbone?

He opened his eyes and looked down to find a disheveled mess of ebony locks. Careful not to wake the sleeping faun, Gaius shifted Alle's body until the slave collar was no longer crushing his clavicle. He caught a whiff of the Dacian's freshly washed hair.

Alle mumbled something incoherent before he sighed and snuggled closer.

What a delightful, albeit unexpected development.

"Sir?" A deep voice carried across the dimly lit room.

Varius stood just inside the doorway of the master suite, his burly arms crossed and his wrinkled eyes focused on the dozing Dacian. A faithful guard dog at the ready. Gaius pressed his finger to his lips. With a quick flick of his wrist, he ordered his protective veteran to leave.

The Dacian's left arm was wrapped tightly around his waist, his bent left leg draped across Gaius's bare thigh.

Gaius stared up at the ceiling and blinked a few times.

This was a most pleasant surprise.

He chuckled as he nuzzled Alle's forelocks and twisted his lustrous, ink-black hair with his fingers.

"Wake up, cub."

With a mild groan of protest, the Dacian pressed into Gaius's touch and fell back asleep.

"Nap time is over. Wake up, Alle."

Roused from his drowsiness, Alle slowly peered up at Gaius. He swallowed before he asked, "I shouldn't be here, should I?"

"You requested an audience and I granted it, *cățel*. This is exactly where you should be. Where you belong."

Gaius brushed his knuckles across Alle's jaw and pulled him closer. With his left hand still tangled in the lad's black hair, he wrapped his other hand around Alle's throat. He ran his tongue over Alle's parted lips, then his teeth, before driving into his wet warm mouth. The Dacian surrendered to his demanding kiss; the sensitive skin covering his long sinuous neck shivered under Gaius's fingertips.

Gaius withdrew and asked, "Now what exactly do you wish to discuss with me, cub?"

His huge eyes darkened from nerves and desire, Alle whispered, "I'm here to seduce you, Dominus."

"You've been seducing me from the very first day I'd laid my eyes on you, beautiful."

The Dacian sat up and pulled his blue slave tunic over his head. Goosebumps broke out over his pale skin; he was trembling and on fire. Gaius let his gaze wander over the vision of the lad's naked body.

"I want to persuade you to keep me." Alle leaned down on one elbow and kissed Gaius, at first hesitant but then firm. "Do I have your permission, *stăpân*?"

Before Gaius could answer, Alle straddled his master's hips and slid down the length of his body; with the tip of his nose, he traced a line from Gaius's breastbone to his navel.

Gaius shoved a plush pillow underneath his shoulders, laced his fingers behind his head, and watched as Alle picked up the hem of Gaius's tunic between his perfectly white teeth.

The Dacian looked up from underneath his black lashes to seek approval with his eyes.

"Permission granted," Gaius growled.

When Alle smiled, the hem of fabric fell from his mouth. He snaked both his hands underneath Gaius's tunic and pushed it up halfway. After Gaius sat up and raised his arms, Alle lifted the cloth over his head until a flood of reddish-brown spiral curls spilled out from the neck hole.

The Dacian tossed the tunic to the floor. "Your copper hair is remarkable, Dominus," he said as he wrapped a rust-colored strand around his pinky finger. "So vibrant and soft."

The lad might be a virgin, but he was one seductive little kitten.

"My nickname, Rufus—the epithet given to me at birth—means red-haired. I despise it."

"Then that's what I shall call you." Alle playfully barked like a dog. "Ru-fus."

"No." Gaius twisted a fistful of Alle's long locks until he grimaced. "You will not."

The Dacian jerked out from Gaius's grasp and grabbed hold of both of Gaius's wrists with one hand. Like a coquettish courtesan, he batted his long lashes and asked, "Perhaps then only when we're alone, Rufus?"

"You've got balls, cub."

"And I want to keep them, sir."

"They are lovely. It would be a bloody shame to geld you." Arching a brow in amusement, Gaius flashed his dimples. "You enjoy rough play, then?"

"I've never played much of anything. I want to try, to feel..." Alle tightened his grip. "I'm not damaged or wearisome. I want everything, Dominus."

"Fortuna is with you, *căţel*. I'm terribly fond of everything." Gaius stroked his tongue languidly up the length of Alle's neck. "Start by worshipping my cock."

"Would you prefer my hands or my mouth, *stăpân*?" Alle flirted.

Gaius grinned, just enough for his dimples to tease. "Give me your everything, Alle."

The Dacian released Gaius's wrists and crawled backwards towards the foot of bed until his mouth hovered over his master's crotch. He wrapped his left hand around the thick base of Gaius's cock as he traced his lips over his engorged shaft, peppering his solid length with light kisses.

The lad's mouth was talented, soft but fervent. Max had taught him exactly how Gaius preferred to be sucked. But it was those heavy-lidded hazel eyes looking up for approval as he licked and swallowed that drove Gaius insane.

"Stop," Gaius demanded.

"Dominus?"

Gaius pulled the lad up by his hair and groaned. "Roll over for me. I need to finish what I started in the baths before I left for Neapolis. I need to fucking taste your perfect arse, cub."

Alle closed his eyes and turned over onto his stomach. He clutched the fresh bed covers, squeezing until his knuckles turned white, as Gaius spread his cheeks and wondered with palpable yearning, "Do you trust me, Alle?"

The Dacian nodded. "Yes."

Gaius licked sloppy circles around his rim of muscle and tongue fucked his hole until Alle writhed in desperation. As he squirmed and moaned, lust building with every twist of his torso, the Dacian lifted his hips and cried, "Take me! Please, for shit's sake, fuck me."

"I fuck what is mine at my leisure. I'm in control. Breathe deep and calm down."

Allerix squeezed his eyes tight and collapsed. He gasped when Gaius bit down hard on the firm flesh of his left arse cheek. He shrieked again, louder, when Gaius took a mouthful of the right cheek and bit down even more savagely.

Gaius kissed the purpled skin and growled, "By the time I'm finished with you, *căţel*, your pristine alabaster body will be mottled with imperial porphyry marks. Everyone will know I own you, that I've devoured you and that I cherish you."

Alle exhaled and welcomed the exquisite pain, moaning and whimpering deliriously into the plush fabric as Gaius bruised him with his teeth. He marked the lad from his bum up to the curve of his serpentine neck.

When he was finished, Gaius blew cool air on the final indigo bruise on his shoulder blade. "Now you are a work of art, Alle. My masterpiece of a trophy."

The Dacian didn't answer.

"Căţel?"

Worried, Gaius sat back and rolled Alle over on his back to study the lad's eyes; they were clouded and dazed. The Dacian had capitulated completely.

Gaius reached over and dipped his fingers in the jug of water on the nearby table. He sprinkled a few drops of cold water between Alle's parted lips, caressed them and kissed them. "Are you all right, Alle?"

The Dacian half-opened his heavy lids and pleaded, "Please, I need—"

"What do you need?"

"You."

Gaius's pulse raced like a chariot horse's hooves charging down the circus track. Shit, he'd never felt this rush before—this dizzying energy coursing through his body, pounding in his chest and his groin. He'd never felt more alive and more vulnerable.

Was this what the poets called the inextinguishable poison of Eros?

Gaius shook his head; beads of sweat dripped down from his forehead to mingle with the dewy sheen that veiled Alle's divine, young face.

After pouring a thick stream of oil over his rock hard prick, Gaius hooked Alle's knees in the crooks of his elbows and lifted the barbarian's furry legs high. As he pushed them apart and down, he held both of Alle's wrists above his head with one hand.

"You're mine."

Alle grimaced and cried out as Gaius penetrated his tight warmth and slowly drove into his body.

"Oh, shit! You're... it's fucking big." The Dacian's wails soon quieted to pathetic moans.

"Relax. The discomfort will subside." Gaius stilled and allowed Alle's body the time it needed to adjust to his girth. "There, that's right. I won't move until you're with me."

Panting, Alle opened his eyes and groaned, "It's better. Please, please move."

Gaius smiled and kissed him. He started slowly, until their bodies rocked back and forth in passionate rhythm. He impaled him, faster and more punishing with every drive. Gaius reached down and stroked Alle's dripping erection and said, "You've a gorgeous prick. Come on, fuck my fist while I fuck your arse."

"This is... Dominus, I'm going to come. I can't hold it back."

"Go on and let go. There'll be more." Gaius ravaged his mouth. "We've the entire night ahead of us—as much loving as I demand, cub."

As his trembling fingers and toes curled tight, the Dacian's cock grew impossibly rigid under Gaius's touch. He arched his back and squeezed his eyes shut. His balls drew up as his cock ejaculated cords of milky semen over his stomach and chest.

Alle screamed and crumpled into sobs of ecstasy.

Gaius kissed him with abandon, sucking and nipping and chuckling, until he snarled into the lad's mouth, "You are no longer a virgin. You're mine. Forever, Alle."

~

Allerix awoke to a shrill symphony of chirping songbirds. When he tried to rub the sleep from his eyes, he realized his left wrist had been chained to the bedframe.

A familiar syrup-thick voice caressed his ears. "Good morning, Alle."

Stretched out in a chair over by the balcony of the master suite, the Roman's bare feet were propped up on a stool, a silver wine cup in his hand. His bronzed body was barely draped in a whisper-thin white robe.

"Morning." Alle squished his face and scratched his new beard growth with his fingernails of his right hand. "You felt it necessary to shackle me to the bed, Dominus?"

"I prefer not to have my throat slit while I sleep. Long ago, I learned to never underestimate a Dacian. So, how do you feel?"

Alle shifted on the mattress. "My arse is damn sore."

"But it's a pleasant ache, I'd wager."

"Yes." Alle yawned and then smiled. "Very pleasant."

"Good." Gaius Fabius smirked and took a long drink. "Would you care for some wine?"

"No, thank you. Do you have water, sir?"

"In that pitcher on the side table there."

Alle sat up and leaned over; he could just reach the bronze jug of water. As he poured himself a cup, he felt the heat of his captor's intense gaze burning his skin.

"Did I satisfy you?" Alle was genuinely curious; the Roman had enjoyed countless whores over the years, no doubt.

"You were spectacular. I selfishly wish I could take your virginity every night; an ever blooming rosebud to caress and pluck and savor, over and over."

Allerix snickered. "I could pretend, if you like."

"You're a terrible actor. Let's take, for example, this rubbish peasant ruse of yours. How long do you plan to lie to me, Alle?"

"I don't understand the question, Dominus."

The Roman scoffed. "By the gods, you're a stubborn shit."

Allerix needed a diversion, and quick. "Who is Lucius?"

"Classic evasive strategy. Not very effective, but at least you're quick on your feet—or arse, in this case. I have a dear friend, an old mate of mine named Lucius. Why do you ask?"

"Back in the baths, you said someone named Lucius was correct—that I was a colossal project."

"Luc is often right. He's a lawyer."

"Is he your lover?"

The redhead furrowed his brow. "Roman men of high rank aren't permitted to fuck each other, cub. It's considered unseemly and dishonorable."

"Ignorant savages," Allerix mumbled into his cup of water.

The Roman pressed his palm against his stomach as he burst out laughing. "By the gods, you're right! They're bloody everywhere, those fucking prudes." He took another swallow and crossed his ankles. "Many years ago—shit, I was younger than Simon is now—Lucius and I were companions during our advanced studies in Athens. Buggering was tolerated under those circumstances—no, it was encouraged. Most of the lads at school paired up and fucked each other senseless. It was the tawdry Greek thing to do in one's carefree youth."

"What happened after that?"

"I completed my philosophy instruction and left for military training in Macedonia. Luc eventually returned to Rome for his apprenticeship in the courts. We corresponded regularly through letters, but we didn't see each other again for a couple of years."

"And it was over, just like that?"

"No." He bit his lower lip and looked out towards the sea. "But it's over now. We've ended it."

"Do you still love him?"

"Love him? I'm not sure I've ever loved anyone. Or perhaps I love too easily. I honestly don't know. But a part of me will always adore that gorgeous bastard. Lucius, on the other hand, replaced me with someone more suitable shortly after he returned to Rome."

His lips parted in shock, Allerix remained quiet and waited.

Gaius Fabius sighed. A faint ghost of hurt swirled across the glassy surface of his golden-brown eyes. "Luc fell hopelessly in love with his pleasure slut, a bright and fucking breathtaking little son of a bitch from Caledonia. Well, Bryaxis is not exactly little. He's quite tall and nicely muscled with an exquisite face, a luscious mouth, and a huge cock. I couldn't really blame the counselor, could I?"

"I would have been furious." Alle quickly added, "I'm sorry."

"Don't apologize. Bryaxis gives Luc what my dear friend needs. The whore loves his master in a way I never could or would. Lucius and I recognize we're both better off being business associates and friends. Sex only complicated matters, and such illicit dalliances can be dangerous. He and I will always have a wealth of wonderful memories. Our loyalty and respect for each other has never wavered."

"I was infatuated once," Alle blurted out while his right hand fidgeted with the bed covers. The Roman looked over but didn't interrupt. "He was older—a skilled warrior—kind and strong and very attractive. Nothing serious ever happened between us, but I wanted something to happen. Something more than me sucking his cock when it was convenient." Alle lifted his sleepy hazel eyes. "I wanted him to want me, to love me. He never did."

Gaius Fabius gulped down another swallow of wine before asking, "Where's this daft fool now?"

"I don't know. He never returned from the last war."

"If you share his name, I will check our military archives the next time I'm in the capital. Perhaps he's still alive."

"Thank you, sir. I would be very grateful. " Allerix paused before mumbling, "Although, sometimes I think it might be better not to find out what happened to him, Dominus. Is it odd to feel that way?"

The Roman unwound his summer mantle, rose from his chair and strolled stark naked over to the bed. He lifted Alle's face and spoke softly.

"It's not strange at all. There are moments in our lives when the fog of the unknown is more comforting than the harsh light of the truth, *căţel*."

"I suppose, Dominus."

"Unfortunately, I have never found solace in such comfort. Treading into the unknown has and always will be a piss poor tactic, an idiotic strategy ripe with potential for disastrous failure."

He sat astride Alle's hips and pushed him back onto the mattress. "I prefer power over fleeting comfort." The man bent down until his lips were nearly touching Alle's mouth. "And the greatest source of power is information."

He kissed Alle one more time, before hollering, "Maximus!"

~

MAX RUSHED IN AND FOLDED HIS HANDS BEHIND HIS BACK. "YES, COMMANDER Fabius."

"Unlock this wrist iron and escort my beautiful barbarian back to the stable house. Be sure to give him a generous meal and a good wash. I'd fuck his mouth-watering arse one more time but I fear my sorry old prick would fall off."

"Yes, sir."

"And no more shackles for him during daylight; he's earned my trust, for now."

Max quickly unlocked the iron as Gaius rose from the bed. After Alle was freed from the bindings, Gaius extended his hand and lifted him to his feet. He pulled him close for a departing embrace and whispered into his ear, "Don't betray my trust. And don't ever fucking underestimate me, *Allerix*."

Alle froze. He blinked as he swallowed the lump in his throat. "Dominus, did you just call me...?"

"Did I call you what? Is there something troubling you, Alle?" Gaius cocked his head and smiled innocently.

Allerix paused and blinked again. "No, sir. Um, thank you for releasing me from the shackles, Dominus."

"Don't give me cause to regret my decision."

As he was led out into the corridor, Alle looked back over his shoulder in bewilderment. Gaius waved at him with a silly wiggle of his fingers and puckered his lips in a mock kiss.

"Let's move, Paulus." Max shoved him forward before he closed the heavy wooden door of the suite behind them.

Gaius picked up his discarded white mantle and secured the cloth at his right hipbone with a fat knot. He sat down in his chair, spread his legs apart and tossed back the last drops of wine in his cup.

"Your master spared you from a gruesome death in our great arena, my Dacian princeling."

He tossed the silver vessel to the floor. With a loud ping, the cup bounced off the marble tiles and rolled away.

"I am your savior, Allerix, son of Thiamarkos. Yes, I know who you are. I discovered your true identity long before your feet touched Decius's auction stage. And, as I'd expected, you lied to me."

Gaius pressed his fingertips together and smirked. "I also know you want something from me, Allerix—the chance to rescue your not-so-skilled, attractive Dacian comrade, perhaps? Ah, my foolish, gorgeous barbarian. We are going to have fucking cartloads of fun, aren't we?"

20

Gaius Fabius's seaside villa, Campania

SIMON GRUNTED AS HE HURLED THE WEIGHTED EXERCISE BALL AT THE DACIAN; he caught it with ease and tossed it over to Nic. The lithe barbarian was stronger than he looked. Appearances were often deceiving, Max reminded himself.

All three lads had been out in the courtyard for much of the early morning, wrestling and throwing the heavy ball about with a raucous chorus of teases and laughter. Nic berated Simon, and Simon mocked Paulus. And so it went, round and round, their taut skin shimmering with sweat; beads of perspiration accentuated every bulge and cut of their firm young muscles. Shit, Dom had accumulated a beautiful brood of boys.

Standing by the edge of the yard, Max heard a noise and glanced over his shoulder; a sleek wagon pulled up by the long paved path to the main entrance of the villa. After it came to a full stop, an attendant jumped out and held the compartment door open. It was a posh rig with elaborate bronze trappings. This visitor must be someone important.

As he peered through an opening between the stout marble columns, a slender bearded man wearing a swirling ensemble of dark wispy robes emerged from the carriage and stepped down.

Was that...?

Max screened his eyes with his right hand and squinted.

Why, yes it was.

He tilted his head and smiled as he clapped his hands together. Max always relished these rare but memorable visits of Commander Fabius's dear Greek friend. That man knew how to entertain a dinner crowd.

"Have we a guest, sir?" Nic yelled.

"Yes, come see."

Simon stopped mid-throw and dropped the exercise ball to the ground; all three curious rascals strolled side by side across the sand towards the outer colonnade.

"That's Apollodorus, the emperor's architect." Max tilted his chin towards the wagon. "You've never met him, Nic, but he's a dandy and talented fellow. Quite an amusing storyteller." Max slung his arm over Nic's shoulder and added, "Dom adores him."

"Why is he here?" the Dacian asked.

"I'm not sure. Perhaps he was in the area and is paying Dom a courtesy visit. They're close friends who served on several campaigns together."

WRINGING HIS CLAMMY HANDS, APOLLODORUS WAITED BY THE WAGON WHILE his attendant ran to the house to announce his arrival. He spied Gaius's tall Ethiopian freedman and three pretty lads—pleasure slaves, no doubt—watching him intently through the columns of a nearby courtyard. Could they tell how terrified he was? Apollodorus swallowed and looked away.

The trip down from Rome had been slower than anticipated. Sudden summer downpours and a flooded road crossing near Capua had hampered their progress. What should have taken three or four days at the most instead took five.

But here he was—finally—ready to face the wrath of the Lion of the Lucky Fourth. Of all the assignments he'd ever undertaken, this was by far the worst. He braced himself for the impending firestorm.

It wasn't long before Gaius Fabius Rufus emerged, his unique copper hair bouncing bright in the sunlight.

"Appy, you old goat! What, by the gods, brings you all the way down to Campania?" Gaius shouted as he hurried down the long walkway, his arms stretched wide for an embrace.

Apollodorus hugged him tightly and murmured, "Commander Fabius, my dear and most noble friend." His voice cracked. "I bring news from Rome."

"What a marvelous surprise. Let's go into the house and have a drink.

You must be parched from your trip. We'll talk over a cup of my best grape." Gaius took hold of Apollodorus' arm. "Come, be my guest. And why are you dressed in such bloody dour fabrics? Dark colors don't flatter your olive complexion, my friend."

"Commander..." Apollodorus didn't step forward; he couldn't stop his hands from shaking.

Gaius's broad grin dissolved into a concerned glare. "Apollodorus, what's the matter?"

"I don't know any other way than to deliver this awful news forthright." Apollodorus steeled himself before he said, "Lucius Petronius has been murdered."

Frozen with shock, Gaius's uneasy expression grew blank and cold. The light breezes that had blown all morning stopped and, in the distance, a crow shrieked. It seemed as though the all-powerful gods themselves gasped collectively in horror.

When he snapped out of his trance, Gaius grabbed Apollodorus by the neckline of his tunic and twisted. "There must be some mistake. Luc's not dead. That can't be true. It's not possible."

"Gaius." Apollodorus coughed. "You're choking me."

Gaius pulled his lips into a thin line as his golden-brown feline eyes narrowed and his nostrils flared. "When did this occur?"

"On the first night of the last full moon, the night before the Ides. Lucius Petronius was returning home from a dinner party when a ruthless gang attacked him and his guards." In desperation, Apollodorus clawed at Gaius's forearm.

The general's powerful grip only tightened. "How did he die?"

"He was stabbed, several times. A physician was called but he couldn't save him. Our dearest Lucius left this world at his home, Gaius, with his family by his side."

Apollodorus coughed again. He was growing dizzy. "Gaius, I am so sorry to deliver such terrible news. All of Rome is in mourning."

Gaius released the panicked architect and stormed towards the house. His clenched fists pressed against his thighs as his teeth cut into his lower lip. Apollodorus scurried after him.

Without turning around, Gaius growled.,"Give me some fucking facts, Greek. Who else attended this dinner event?"

Apollodorus panted as he tried to keep pace. "I was in attendance. And there was Gaius Plinius, who hosted the dinner at his home, our friend Caelius, Caecilius Strabo, the consul Minicius, and Aelius Hadrianus."

Gaius stopped dead in his tracks, his fierce gaze focused on the grand entrance portal. "Did you just say Publius was in attendance?"

"Yes, he invited Lucius Petronius to the dinner. Lucius was his honored companion for the evening."

Gaius's fury turned calm but even more lethal.

"Publius invited Luc? That's rather curious. Tell me, have the murderers been caught, Apollodorus?"

"No, sir. Not yet."

"WHAT'S HAPPENING, MAX? I THOUGHT YOU'D SAID DOM LIKED THIS architect fellow."

"I don't know, Simon, but it can't be good."

"Where are you going, sir?" Nic's voice trembled from fear.

"To assist however I can. Go back to the stable house, all of you!"

The Dacian stepped in front of Max and seized him by the elbow.

"I'm going with you." His determined defiant hazel eyes threw Max off guard. The lad gulped for air before gnawing on his upper lip. "Max, let me go with you." He squeezed Max's arm. "Please, let me help him."

"For fuck's sake, Dacian!"

By the most holy Penates, the wooly cub was falling for Dom. Max wasn't surprised, just baffled at the speed of it. Then he remembered that terrifying night in the African desert ten years past when he'd lost his heart to Gaius Fabius Rufus. He'd nearly died. Shit, they both would have been torn to pieces if it hadn't been for that damn dagger.

Max pulled his arm out of the barbarian's grasp and pointed towards the stable house. "You are not coming. Go with Nic and Simon, Paulus!"

MAX SPED THROUGH THE CORRIDORS OF THE MAIN HOUSE UNTIL HE REACHED the grand internal courtyard. From the square opening in the roof, beams of light streamed down, flooding the ornate space in a warm yellow glow. A display of marble sculptures of Roman men on tall pedestals, some dressed in togas, others garbed in military costume, stood around the perimeter of the garden. In the center was a decorative shallow pool.

Mute and unblinking, the statues basked without a care in the world in the sublime sunshine.

The general stomped through the bright space without so much as a glance in any direction. He snarled and laughed maniacally under his breath, clasping his hands together and shaking his head from side to side.

Commander Fabius was headed to his office.

Someone tapped Max on his right shoulder.

"You are Gaius's freedman, Maximus, yes?" Apollodorus asked.

"Yes, sir." Max bowed and continued in a hushed voice, "Please, sir—what has happened?"

"Commander Fabius's closest and most dear associate was murdered, struck down by a pack of armed thugs on the streets of Rome."

Max stared in disbelief. "By the gods, are you referring to Counselor Petronius? He's dead?"

Apollodorus nodded, closed his eyes and leaned against Max. The slightly built foreigner with the peculiar accent was shaking. Instinctively, Max wrapped his arm around him. His deep voice cracked from fear as he mumbled his dear friend's name, "Gods, Bryaxis."

~

GAIUS CLOSED THE WOODEN PANELS AND SLID THE BOLT UNTIL IT LOCKED INTO place. He pressed his head against the office door before he staggered over to his chair and collapsed.

This couldn't be true. Lucius couldn't have died; he would have known if his friend had passed. He would have felt the knife of loss cutting into his heart. After all those years with Lucius, he should have felt something, for fuck's sake!

He rubbed his eyes before resting his face in his folded arms on the desk. Across the office, something caught his eye: a bronze box embellished with copper and ivory inlays on a shelf in a small cupboard.

The letters.

The correspondence Lucius had sent to him after Gaius departed Athens. He'd saved every single one, storing them neatly in that keepsake chest for all these years.

Gaius pushed himself up and walked over to the storage cabinet. Such an exotic box; it had been a gift from Publius. Gingerly, he picked up the container and took it back to his desk. After lifting the hinged lid, he sorted through the pile of slender scrolls until he found the first letter Luc had ever sent him all those years ago. The dry papyrus sheet crackled as he unfurled it.

• • •

To my dearest Gaius

You won't receive this letter until you arrive in Macedonia. I can picture you standing on the deck of that ship, stirring up all sorts of mischief. Here I sit, alone in my room at the dormitory. You only left yesterday and already I miss you terribly. Our bed is cold and empty. Your scent lingers on my pillow, but that will fade with time.

Sappy, melodramatic oaf.

Shit, for a future court magistrate, Lucius had the sloppiest bloody handwriting.

A tear rolled down Gaius's cheek as he touched the ink, faded from the years that had passed —all the law cases that had been won and the battles fought, the marriages and the baths and the morning salutations.

The teardrop clung for a moment before it fell from Gaius's chin and landed on the sheet. The salty liquid blended with the aged indigo ink, blurring the first letter of Lucius's name.

Gaius selected another scroll from the pile and unrolled it.

To my dearest Gaius

In less than a month, I'll finish my studies and leave this mythical city to return home. I'm ashamed to confess it has been easier to concentrate on my work ever since you departed Athens last spring. I trust you are well and dazzling those army brutes with your sword skills. I hope you still hold me in your heart as close as I hold you, Gaius. I miss your dimples, your hair, and your naughty predatory eyes. I miss licking that constellation of freckles on your left shoulder. I miss everything. I miss us.

Shit.

Gaius rubbed his eyes again and read one final letter as his heart cracked and threatened to shatter. It was a more recent message sent from Rome.

To Gaius Fabius Rufus,

Warmest greetings from your associate and friend, Lucius Petronius Celsus. I've learned you shall return from Macedonia with mountains of accolades from your army superiors. What a grand arrival that promises to be! Euphronia will prepare your favorite dishes for a homecoming celebration. I pray to Jove and Mercury every morning for your safe return, my friend.

I have completed my first apprenticeship in our Emperor's civil courts. There is so much to learn I fear I'll never master this taxing job. Two months past, I increased my household. I have a slave assistant now, or I will once he completes his training. It's a lanky but sharp Caledonian boy I purchased from my father. It's not a full legal staff, but it's a start. My little brother, Gallus, assures me I shall be named a chief jurist before my fortieth birthday.

"YOU WERE AWARDED THE BLOODY RANK OF CHIEF COUNSEL BEFORE YOU turned thirty-two, you idiotic, brilliant fool."

Gaius choked back a sob. "I swear those filthy agents of the palace are behind this crime. If you had never met me, Luc—if I hadn't been a fucking ward of the imperial court..."

Clutching the letter, Gaius flung his other arm across the desk, knocking the ornate box to the floor with a loud clatter.

"Commander, are you all right? Is there anything I can do?" Max's plea was desperate.

Gaius took a deep breath and hollered at the locked door, "Leave me be, Maximus!"

His glassy eyes narrowed with a surge of red-hot anger. With a roar, Gaius gripped the edge of his heavy wooden desk and pushed it over on its side; piles of scrolls, an empty bronze cup, and a small gold statue of Victory crashed to the floor. Gaius grabbed the back of his chair and lifted it above his head when he spotted the portrait bust of his father, Quintus, staring at him from its display shelf up on the wall. He carried the wooden chair until it was positioned directly underneath the shelf; a quick climb up and he had the heavy stone head between his hands.

Gaius stepped down from his perch and stared into his dead father's painted stone eyes.

"You're responsible for this, Quintus. If you hadn't trusted the damned monster, Domitian—if you hadn't been such a naive fool and gotten yourself killed—then mother wouldn't have felt obliged to transfer guardianship of me to Marcus."

Gaius lifted the sculpted image closer to his face. "If you hadn't failed me, if you hadn't abandoned me to the Fates, then Lucius would never have met Marcus and Plotina and the rest of my ruthless family. He'd be alive and safe and ignored by those unscrupulous court spies. You, dear father, might as well have murdered Luc with your own hands."

Gaius lifted the sculpture and released his grip; the marble portrait head fell to the floor and smashed into pieces. A jagged stone chip ricocheted to the ceiling, slicing Gaius's cheek. He wiped the trickles of blood off with the back of his hand as he cursed the fragments scattered across the mosaic tiles.

"I am not longer your son, Quintus Fabius. I will no longer perform the customary rites at your tomb nor will I light the sacred lamps at the Parentalia nor will I pay the elegiac poets to sing your praises at the festivals. I fucking disown you, Quintus Fabius!"

"Dominus!" Max was close to hysterical.

Gaius raked his fingers through his hair as he calmed his deep, rapid breaths. After he unlocked the office door, he marched out and explained in a relaxed, smooth voice, "Everything's fine. Just an unfortunate accident, Maximus."

"You're hurt," Max said as he reached to touch the cut on Gaius's face.

Gaius pulled back, pushing Max's hand away. "It's a scrape, nothing more. Where's Alle?"

"The Dacian? He's in his cell at the stable house, sir. He begged to accompany me, but..."

"Of course, he did. Cocky little urchin." Gaius turned to his steward standing at the ready. "Atticus, fetch a broom and sweep my disgraced and forsaken father off the floor of my damn office."

"Where are you going, sir?" Max asked.

"To the stable house. Stay here and begin preparations for travel to the capital. We depart today. And Max—inform Callidora she and Zoe will accompany us for the journey. I'm relocating them to my ancestral mansion for the time being. Tell her to pack a few fresh vials."

"Vials, sir?"

"She'll understand. Go on, then."

Apollodorus stepped out from behind a pillar, his dark-tan cheeks stained with sorrow.

"Commander Fabius."

"Appy, my poor friend. You were burdened with a most difficult task, and I am deeply grateful for your courage."

"Gaius, what can I do to help? I feel positively impotent."

"Join us for the trip to the city." Gaius smiled through the pain. "Distract me with your outlandish stories."

"I would be honored, sir." Apollodorus bowed. "I shall share the fantastic tale of the sea monster covered in hooked spikes..."

Gaius held his hand up as he shook his head. "Save your storytelling magic for later. We'll need it to break the tedium of travel, Appy."

~

NIC AND SIMON SAT AT THE TABLE IN THE COMMON ROOM, WORDLESS AND baffled. When Gaius charged in, they dropped to their knees, hands clasped tightly behind their back.

"Greetings, pets."

"Greetings, Dominus," they mumbled simultaneously.

Gaius looked around—this place was shabbier than he'd remembered. He made a mental note to order Atticus to rectify that soon.

"Where is Alle's room?"

Simon lifted his head, his young face flushed with alarm. "Upstairs, Dominus. Down the right hall, the third cell on the left."

Gaius ruffled Simon's thick locks to comfort him. "You're trembling, Simon. Get control of yourself, lad—everything will be well. You're mine and you're safe."

Simon sniffled and cast his eyes to the floor. "Forgive my childish behavior, Dominus."

"It's time for you to grow up, pup."

"Yes, Dominus."

"Nicomedes, sweetheart—I'm departing for Rome. Do you remember my dark-haired associate, Lucius Petronius? The tall, handsome friend of mine with the huge cock who visited us here at the villa after the first war?"

"Yes, Dominus. I remember him well." Nic's bright blue eyes were soaked and bloodshot with distress. He'd always be beautiful; he'd always be broken.

Gaius paused to collect his thoughts and control his pain.

"My dearest friend has been brutally murdered. The magistrates of the inheritance courts cannot unseal his final testament until I'm present for the reading of the will. I'm bringing Max along for the journey to the capital. We should return soon after the Kalends, but until we do, you are in charge here at the stable house, Nicomedes. Understood?"

Nic looked as if he might faint. "Yes, Dominus. I won't disappoint you, sir."

"I know you won't, my lamb."

~

Hugging his knees to his chest, Allerix sat on his modest narrow bed and stared out the window. The sea was rough as it careened along, its white-capped waves swelling and crashing violently against the rocky shoreline.

Someone ascended the wooden stairs to the second floor. Max must have returned from the main house.

Perhaps he had news.

Alle rushed to the doorway.

He was almost to the threshold, when the Roman stepped inside.

"Greetings, *cățel*."

Alle bowed his head in deference without hesitation, but remained standing.

"Greetings, Dominus."

"Must I keep you in shackles for you to fucking remember to kneel in my presence?"

Alle slowly dropped to his knees and mumbled, "I was unaware you visited the stable house, sir."

"I rarely do," he said and strolled over to the bed, touching it apprehensively before sitting down. "It seems I've been a negligent master. This building is dilapidated and dreary. That will be remedied." He patted the thin mattress; a cloud of fine dust rose into the air. "Come over here and join me, cub."

After he took a seat next to the Roman, Alle brushed his hip up against him and gently pressed his weight into his shoulder. "May I ask what has happened, Dominus?"

With a sigh, Gaius Fabius rested his elbows on his knees and intertwined his fingers as he stared at the drab wooden floor. "I must return to Rome immediately to honor and fulfill my duties to—" He paused and swallowed as he shut his eyes. "To bid farewell to Lucius."

"Your friend from Athens? Is he going somewhere?"

"He's already left." After spitting out the words, the Roman rubbed his face and added, "He was murdered."

Silence.

The man cracked his knuckles and sighed again.

Finally, Allerix whispered, "I'm not sure what your rituals are, but I'll pray your gods grant him eternal bliss and glory."

"My gods?" The Roman cackled in disgust. "My so-called gods are selfish, cruel fuckers—the whole shitty lot of them."

More silence. Only the lulling sounds of the ocean filled the room.

"Please, Dominus. I can be of help. Take me with you."

"No, *cățel*. You will remain here at the villa—protected and unnoticed—while I visit the palace for a private audience with our Emperor. There will be little opportunity for sweet distractions once I swat the imperial hornet's nest."

With the back of his hand, the Roman rubbed the dark bristles sprouting along Allerix's jaw. "Stay out of trouble during my absence, cub." He tugged a thick lock of Alle's sable hair. "And no playing with knives, remember?"

Allerix smiled half-heartedly. "I remember, Rufus."

"Cheeky." He pinched the tip of Alle's nose before he stood up. "Nicomedes is in charge of the stable house while I'm gone. You and Simon make sure he doesn't fuck things up too terribly. Of course, Atticus and Felix will keep watch over all three of you scamps."

"Yes, sir." Allerix rose to his feet. They stood there, drowning in each other's eyes, until Alle pulled Gaius Fabius into a tight embrace and kissed him with his lips, his tongue, his scruff—his everything—until they both were forced to stop for air. As they pressed their foreheads together, Alle tangled his fingers in the Roman's long, brilliant curls.

"I wish you safe and speedy travels, Dominus."

"You are an incorrigible rascal, aren't you? I fear when it comes to you, *cățel,* I may have inadvertently opened Pandora's box." He kissed Allerix on the lips before he headed for the door. "I'll be back as soon as the Fates permit. You and I have much unfinished business to address, Alle."

"I'll be waiting, Dominus."

~

ON HIS WAY BACK TO THE MAIN VILLA HOUSE, GAIUS SPIED VARIUS IN THE rustic yard outside the stables. The veteran was loading supplies into a travel wagon. The draft horses were hitched; the preparations for the journey close to ready.

"Varius!"

Varius placed a wooden crate on the wagon bed and averted his weathered eyes to the dirt. "Commander, my deepest condolences. Maximus informed me about the villainous murder of Counselor Petronius."

"Varius, listen to me carefully. You will ride ahead of us to Rome. Tell my veteran clients in all the districts of the city to whet their blades and prepare for battle."

"Battle, sir?"

"If this comes to arms, I want my men readied in advance for rapid assembly in the old Forum. I will demand retribution for my murdered associate. I will have fucking justice for Lucius."

"Yes, Commander. I'll depart immediately."

"There's another task, soldier."

"Your orders, sir?"

"Pay a visit to my home on the Caelian and request an audience with my dear wife. Inform our Domina of my imminent arrival. Tell her I'm bringing Callidora and the girl."

Varius acknowledged the orders with a bow and lumbered as fast as he could manage to the stables to fetch a horse. Rushing past his house servants scurrying through the corridors like frightened mice, Gaius made his way to the posh internal courtyard. He unsheathed his dagger and pointed the tip of the blade at the colossal statue of the emperor on display at the far end of the garden. The marble portrait of Trajan, clad in ceremonial armor and a voluminous imperial cloak, towered like a living god over the smaller sculptures.

"Gird your loins, Marcus Ulpius Traianus!"

Gaius stared at the bronze scepter held upright in the statue's gigantic marble hand.

"Your favorite son is coming home, Dominus."

EPILOGUE

AD 2010

Piazza della Rotonda, Rome

After I'd ordered another over-priced beer, I glanced down at my journal. I only had about one more hour for this stroll down memory lane before I'd have to leave to meet him in time for dinner. There was another city bus strike and traffic was snarled; catching a taxi would take a while.

~

15 July 2007: The Ides of July and the day after our chance discovery of the hole in the well shaft. His cell phone rang.

"*Pronto*?"

I half-listened to Stefano's phone conversation as our waiter, a lanky seventeen or eighteen year-old kid with dark blond hair gelled into a curved point above his forehead, brought out our second course.

We were at my former colleague's favorite restaurant, a quiet establishment in a forgotten piazza near the Tiber River. Every evening, old men and women left their homes and gathered outdoors to catch up on the latest neighborhood gossip around the edge of the small square. There was never a t-shirt clad, sneaker-shod tourist in sight. Wisteria vines hung down from the surrounding apartment buildings, blanketing the plaster-covered walls in colorful tapestries of vibrant purple. An old stone fountain shaped like a pine cone gurgled while dulcet violin notes of a Vivaldi concerto wafted through the tepid summer air.

Stefano gestured wildly as his voice grew louder. The call was from someone at the archaeological ministry, no doubt.

Stefano shut his flip phone and sighed. "Bad news, *caro*."

"What is it?"

"The ministry is taking control of our project."

"What? They can't do that!"

"It's an exceptional discovery with high publicity potential and they have jurisdiction. It's their property, Charlie. It's politics."

"That's bullshit. What do we do?"

"All work must be stopped and nothing can be touched. There's little we can do, except—" Stefano arched a brow as he took a sip of his wine.

"Stefano?"

"Charlie, do you remember that debris pile?"

"The one we used to gain access to the Roman corridor? Of course, it's massive."

"Let's go have another look at it, *si*?" Stefano pulled out a flashlight from his man purse.

~

All right, so it wasn't really a purse, more like a fancy Italian leather messenger bag. Struzzo carried that damn satchel as if he were an Italian *principessa* flaunting the latest designer accessory during an evening stroll along the Via Veneto at sunset.

~

"Why do you want to go investigate that heap of debris now?"

"I have a suspicion it's more important than we initially thought." Stefano paused to light a cigarette. "Charlie, if the medieval well diggers saw those skeletons, why didn't they take the dagger? It's very valuable, no?"

"Shit, you're right. They should have taken it. They must have not seen the dagger, but why not? It was right there in plain sight once you went into the corridor far enough."

"We need to go back and have another look, Charlie. Tonight. Tomorrow, we may not be permitted access to the passageway. It won't be long before the ministry changes the locks."

"So, you're suggesting we drive all the way out to the Via Tiburtina and climb down our well in the middle of the night to re-examine a pile of Roman bricks and mortar near two intact skeletons? In the dark?"

Stefano reached into his bag and pulled out a kid's cartoon cat keychain; the key to the entrance gate at our excavation site dangled back and forth like a tempting piece of ripe forbidden fruit. "*Esatto*."

"You're crazy."

"*Sí*, but that's why I'm your partner."

"Good point, my friend. Let's get the hell out of here. I want to hear all about this nutty theory of yours on the drive out."

"Charlie, be patient. Please, finish your pasta. We have another course and then dessert. One doesn't rush a good meal. And this restaurant has some of the best homemade Limoncello in all of Rome. We eat, we digest, we enjoy a smoke, and then we go."

When Stefano left to use the toilet, our waiter sauntered over and slipped me a note—a small piece of paper folded neatly like a square envelope. I carefully opened it and saw a European phone number written in elegant cursive handwriting.

"Who sent this?" I asked.

Our cocky server kid nodded toward a table behind us in the far corner of the outdoor patio.

I turned around in my chair. The most gorgeous guy I'd ever seen, who was wearing the most form-fitting expensive silk suit I'd ever drooled over in a fashion magazine, lifted his globe-shaped glass of red wine and nodded with a wink. Light from the suspended pergola lamps illuminated the blue tones in his jet-black hair.

I raised my tumbler of cheap white wine in appreciation, my goofy smile quivering once or twice. I couldn't hold eye contact with him for more than a few seconds. Those steel blue eyes and that perfect dark whisper of a five-o'clock shadow. Fucking incredible dimples.

~

AND THAT'S WHEN I FIRST MET YVES.

Roman skeletons, an exotic dagger, and a sharply dressed gorgeous Frenchman: they all dropped into my life in less than a week during that smoldering July three years ago.

And that's when every-fucking-thing became intriguingly complicated.

End of Book 1

CAST OF CHARACTERS

Alphabetical list of the **major** and secondary characters in ***Dominus,*** Book 1.

The names inside the brackets are the commonly used names and/or nicknames for each character. An asterisk beside a character indicates a known historical figure; a link to that character's Wikipedia page is included when available. All other characters are original, fictional creations of JP Kenwood.

Note: There are more detailed "Profiles" of several of the main and secondary ancient characters over at my author blog. I will be adding more profiles. https://jpkenwood.com/character-profiles/

ANCIENT CHARACTERS

Achilles: Nicomedes' pet dormouse with the deformed foot

Allerix (Alle, *cățel,* Paulus, cub): Dacian prince, son of Thiamarkos, younger half-brother of Tarbus, pleasure slave of Gaius Fabius

Allethodokoles: Dacian peasant name

*Apollodorus of Damascus (Apollodorus, Appy): Syrian-Greek master architect and military engineer for Trajan, close friend of Gaius Fabius, husband of Helen

Atticus: Greek slave, steward of Gaius Fabius's villa in Campania

Aurelia: Roman noblewoman, wife of Lucius Petronius, mother of Petronia

Bulbus: Roman legionary veteran, temporary guard at the estate of Gnaeus Decius

Brasus: Dacian warrior

Bryaxis (Bry): male pleasure slave from Caledonia (ancient Scotland), birth name = Brendan, favorite concubine of Lucius Petronius Celsus

Callidora (Calli): Greek female household slave of Gaius Fabius, mother of Castor and Simon

Daphne: Greek female household slave of Lucius Petronius Celsus

Euphronia: Greek female household slave of Lucius Petronius Celsus, chief cook

Felix: Roman legionary veteran, military medic, blacksmith at Gaius Fabius's villa in Campania

Ferox: Thracian black stallion owned by Gaius Fabius

Gaius Fabius Rufus (Gaius, Dominus, Dom, Commander Fabius, Rufus, Fabius, Lion of the Lucky Fourth, Soldier): patrician Roman general and senator, Commander of the Lucky Fourth Legion, former ward of Marcus Ulpius Traianus (Trajan), ward brother of Publius Aelius Hadrianus (Hadrian), only son of Quintus Fabius and Julia Flaviana, husband of Marcia Servilia

Gnaeus Decius: Roman aristocrat, associate and client of Lucius Petronius Celsus

Gorgas: Dacian peasant, childhood friend of Allerix

Helen: Greek wife of Apollodorus

Livianus (Titus Claudius Livianus): Roman military officer, Praetorian Prefect

Lucius Petronius Celsus (Lucius, Luc, Counselor Petronius, Dominus): plebian Roman senator and lawyer, husband of Aurelia, father of Petronia, older brother of Titus Petronius and Tiberius Petronius Gallus

Macro (Flavius Macro): Roman legionary scout of the Second Legion

Manlius (Titus Manlius): client of Gaius Fabius

Marcia Servilia (Marcia, Domina): Roman noblewoman, wife of Gaius Fabius Rufus

***Marcus Ulpius Traianus (Marcus, Trajan, Esteemed Emperor, Dominus)**: emperor of Rome (AD 98-117), ward father of Gaius Fabius and Publius Aelius, husband of Plotina

Maximus (Max): Kushite (modern Sudan) male freedman of Gaius Fabius, birth name = Malqabar, former pleasure slave of Gaius

Melissa: Greek female pleasure slave of Marcia Servilia

Nicomedes (Nic, Lamb): Neapolitan (Italian Greek) male pleasure slave of Gaius Fabius

Petronia: Roman noble girl, daughter of Lucius Petronius Celsus and Aurelia

Plautus: Roman legionary veteran, cook at the stable house in Gaius Fabius's villa in Campania

*__Pliny the Younger__ (__Pliny__): Roman nobleman, lawyer, writer, magistrate, close friend of Gaius Fabius

*__Pompeia Plotina__ (__Plotina, Empress Plotina__): wife of Marcus Ulpius Traianus (Trajan)

*__Publius Aelius Hadrianus__ (__Hadrian, Legate Aelius, Princess Publius, Greekling__): ward brother of Gaius Fabius, emperor of Rome (AD 117-138)

Pyramus: African Serval cat and pet of Gaius Fabius

Quintus Fabius: Roman nobleman and magistrate, father of Gaius Fabius Rufus

Quintus Fabius Quietus: Roman nobleman and military officer, grandfather (paternal) of Gaius Fabius, husband of Memmia Cornelia

Septus: Egyptian slave dealer

Simon (**Pup**): Greek male pleasure slave of Gaius Fabius, son of Theodorus and Callidora, younger brother of Castor

*Sosius Seneco: Roman nobleman and consul

Tarbus: Dacian prince and warrior, older half-brother of Allerix

Theodorus (Theo): Greek male freedman, former pleasure slave of Quintus Fabius and Gaius Fabius, cobbler

Thiamarkos: Dacian king, father of Allerix and Tarbus

Tiberius Petronius Gallus (Gallus): Roman nobleman, youngest brother of Lucius Petronius Celsus

Titus Petronius (Titus): Roman nobleman, Roman military officer and commander, close associate and former tribune of Gaius Fabius, younger brother of Lucius Petronius Celsus, husband of Antonia, father of three children (Tiberius, Titus Minor, Petroniana)

Varius (**Claudius Varius**): Roman legionary veteran. Chief guard of Gaius Fabius's estates in Rome and Campania

*Vibia Sabina (Sabina): Roman noblewoman, grand-niece of Emperor Trajan, wife of Publius Aelius Hadrianus (Hadrian), former betrothed of Gaius Fabius

Zoe: Greek female pleasure slave of Gaius Fabius

MODERN CHARACTERS

Charlie Hughes (**John Charles Hughes**): American archaeologist, professor at an American college, co-director of the Via Tiburtina excavations

Maria: Italian archaeological assistant at Via Tiburtina excavations

Stefano Struzzo: Italian archaeologist, colleague of Charlie Hughes, co-director of the Via Tiburtina excavations

Yves Bouchard: French investment banker residing in London and Rome

ABOUT THE AUTHOR

When she doesn't have her nose stuck in a dusty old history book, JP Kenwood relishes writing erotic m/m fiction. JP prefers plot-packed, sexy, and romantic tales that explore loyalty, trust, betrayal, and sacrifice. She is currently busy penning the fourth and final book in this historical fantasy series, ***Dominus***. JP has a terrible habit of posting preliminary drafts of chapters and snippets of her latest work to her online blog prior to publication: https://jpkenwood.com

MORE BOOKS BY JP KENTWOOD

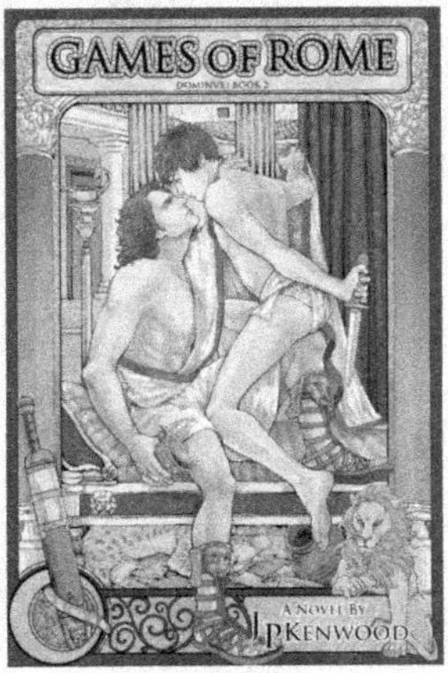

Games of Rome (Dominus Book 2)

Blood Before Wine (Dominus Book 3)

February and December (Dominus Calendar Series I)

Connect with JP Kenwood Online:

JP Kenwood's author blog: https://jpkenwood.com
Facebook: https://www.facebook.com/jp.kenwood
Twitter: @JPKenwood

Keep reading for a short preview of Book 2, ***Games of Rome***.

COMPLIMENTARY PREVIEW

A preview of Chapter 1 from ***Games of Rome***

AD 107
Lucius Petronius's house, the Quirinal Hill, Rome

Gaius stood outside the entrance, his fists clenched and his feet planted wide. Perched on the tiled roof of Lucius's home, a lone crow flapped its wings and squawked as if mocking his battle-ready posture. After retrieving a stone lying on the curb, he looked up, poised to hurl his missile at the pesky bird when he saw them.

Two torches in iron brackets hung high on the wall on either side of the grand door.

Both were unlit. Extinguished. Never again would their flames signal Lucius was alone and waiting, his gorgeous body free to defile. No more sneaking in for those risky but satiating afternoon fucks. No more sucking and kissing and rimming in the baths. No more forbidden games in the garden.

"Put an end to this dishonorable dalliance with Petronius Celsus!"

The emperor's command during that palace dinner was direct and unequivocal. Gaius had acquiesced like a dutiful auxiliary soldier following a centurion's orders. He'd ended the long-standing affair with his occasional lover and dearest friend.

Shit, the Lion of the Lucky Fourth was little more than a spineless coward. A mouse. Before he'd died, had Luc forgiven him for abandoning their bittersweet, illicit passions?

Gaius Fabius Rufus would never know.

And now the massive oak door through which Gaius had passed many times loomed in front of him, taunting him with its indifferent permanence. Heavy pine garlands drooped low, obscuring the white marble doorframe, their branches threaded with wilted red roses and the black ribbons of death. As he raised his fist to knock, heartache sliced through his chest. Gaius slowly lowered his arm and massaged his aching brow.

Before making the dreaded climb to the top of the Quirinal hill, he'd ascended the steep and sacred Capitoline slope. At the altar in front of Rome's greatest temple, he'd sworn an oath to almighty Jupiter. An oath of vengeance.

He would exact revenge, but now was not the time for war.

Now it was time to confront the awful, inescapable truth.

Time to say farewell.

"Commander? Are you all right, sir?"

"Announce our arrival, Maximus."

After he'd stepped back from the door, Gaius tossed the rock to the ground and gazed down the length of the curved, paved street. The painted plaster walls of the neighboring posh homes, with their colorful flowers cascading down from their high terraces, seemed less vibrant than they had in the past.

Lucius Petronius was dead, murdered in the prime of his life.

Who was to blame? Those nefarious spies from the palace, the envious bastards in the Senate? Of course, there was Luc's greedy widow, Aurelia, to add to the long list of suspects. And what if, gods forbid, his fellow ward—his little brother, his Greekling—was involved in this heinous crime?

Shit.

Gaius rubbed his whiskered chin and exhaled. "Varius, take two men to the back gate and make damn sure no one leaves this estate without my fucking permission."

"Yes, Commander."

After Max lifted and released the stout iron knocker three times, the door slowly opened, creaking on its metal hinges. A guard with a familiar face nodded and welcomed them into the vestibule.

"Greetings, Commander Fabius. We've been anticipating your arrival, sir."

Gaius patted the man on the shoulder before turning to address Maximus and his two guards. "Stay here—all of you."

Having left everyone behind in the entrance hall, he walked alone down the dimly lit corridor to the atrium. In that formal gathering hall, he would find Luc's corpse washed and dressed in a formal crimson-striped toga and laid upon an elevated funerary couch with his feet pointed toward the street. A golden crown of laurel would encircle Luc's dark hair, the coin to pay the ferryman of Hades already tucked in his mouth. Tall candelabra would stand at the corners of the couch, the air thick with the pungent smoke of fragrant herbs. Luc's once handsome face would be ghostly pale, his bright grey-blue eyes closed for eternity.

Lucius was dead.

Gaius paused to sniff the air. Where was the smell of burning herbs? Where was that unmistakable stench no amount of incense could mask?

He quickened his pace until he was jogging over the threshold to the stately atrium.

The hall was empty. No couch, no candelabra, no corpse.

"What is the meaning of this?" Every word was a struggle as if the wind had been knocked out of him. "Where—where is Lucius?"

"I'm afraid you're too late, Commander."

Draped in dark mourning robes, she stood off to the side with her arms crossed and her right hip cocked, a satisfied sneer twisting her severe features.

"What did you…?" His voice cracked. "Where is Lucius, Aurelia?"

"We burned his corpse in Mars' field yesterday. The omens were favorable and the kindling lit well. The gods seemed quite pleased."

Biting down hard on his lower lip, nearly drawing blood, Gaius collapsed against one of the massive columns that bordered the shallow pool in the center of the room. "He's gone?"

"Lucius has crossed the River Styx, and you failed to arrive in time to bid a proper farewell to your dearest friend."

Heartless bitch.

"We traveled from Campania as quickly as possible, but several roads were washed out and impassable. I hadn't anticipated you'd have the audacity to complete his rites before I returned to Rome."

"I postponed the funeral for as long as possible, Commander Fabius. My poor, dead husband's body laid here in the atrium for nine long days. The summer's heat and dampness took their toll. You should know I consulted with Empress Plotina on the matter of his funeral. The palace granted me permission."

With a grimace, Aurelia inhaled through her pointy nose. "I've had the slaves ventilate this room all morning, but the fetor of decay still lingers, doesn't it?"

Gaius dug his fingernails into the fabric of his tunic until they gouged his thighs. How easy would it be to wrap his hands around her bony neck and snap it like a twig?

Twirling the fringed edge of her robe, Aurelia sauntered across the atrium. "The funeral procession through the Forum was magnificent. Members of the Senate bore the gilded bier on their shoulders and our consul, Minicius, delivered a laudatory eulogy at the Rostra. I hired the most renowned undertaker in Rome to arrange the details: twenty-four professional mourners and a crew of talented trumpeters. We sacrificed a bull *and* a sheep in addition to the pig. I spared no expense, and the populace enjoyed a generous feast. The entire city will remember my devotion to my dear deceased husband for many summers to come."

The smugness on her face morphed to fear when Gaius took two steps toward her. "If you had anything to do with this…" After circling her, Gaius stopped and glared, his lips inches from Aurelia's terrified, rodent-like eyes. "If you were involved in Luc's murder, Aurelia, I will not stop until I see your callous corpse burned to a crisp on a pyre of rotted wood."

"I had no part whatsoever in Lucius's death! I loved my husband. Why would you believe otherwise?"

"What I believe isn't fucking relevant. Not legally. Tell me, have you also had the gall to unseal his will?"

"Commander, I'm fully aware the disclosure of my late husband's final testament requires all six witnesses to be present. Lucius's brother boarded a ship at Piraeus. Titus Petronius is sailing to the capital from Greece and, assuming the winds are favorable, he should arrive soon. My late husband's youngest brother, Gallus, attended the funeral and was most benevolent to me." Aurelia swallowed hard and continued, "And you are the executor of Lucius's testament. The magistrates would never unseal his will without your consent."

Gaius smiled although his eyes remained cold and hard. He stepped back and held out his hand. "Give me his ring. It's mine to safeguard until his final testament is read before the witnesses and the people of Rome. Perhaps, if the gods have any blasted sense, he will have left you nothing save the rags on your back."

"My husband was noble and generous. He would never..." Aurelia coughed softly into her fist before stammering, "Did—did Lucius reveal his bequests to you?"

He gritted his teeth at her stall tactic. "Surrender Luc's fucking ring. Now!"

Aurelia scurried over to the bronze chest in the far corner of the atrium and retrieved the sacred token of Lucius's identity and judicial rank—his unique gold signet ring decorated with an oak leaf.

"I pray this thing curses you as it did him." She pressed the ring into Gaius's open palm. As Gaius closed his fingers around the gold band, a boisterous commotion erupted in one of the corridors off the atrium. From the shadows, Varius hauled a man into the center of the hall. The fellow thrashed, pulling out of the veteran's grasp.

Gaius slipped Luc's large ring onto his middle finger. "Well, what do we have here?"

"We found this gentleman hiding by the back portal, Commander. It appears he was trying to leave the premises undetected."

"Sneaking about like a sewer rat?" Gaius grabbed the man's clean-shaven chin to get a better look at his pockmarked face. "Ah, it is you, Victorinus. I thought I recognized you. Why, for shit's sake, has a member of the emperor's guard sequestered his sorry arse by the back exit of the home of Lucius Petronius?"

"I..."

"Yes?"

"I'm—I'm on assignment. I was told to guard the grieving widow, Commander Fabius."

"Dressed in commoner's clothing?"

"I was ordered to be, well, furtive. Sir."

Gaius narrowed his eyes as he pointed at Aurelia. "You were instructed to leave the palace to protect this pitiless wretch?"

"Yes, sir."

Gaius scratched the dense, itchy golden-red bristles now blanketing his jaw and neck. As was customary, he hadn't had a shave since he'd first learned of Luc's murder. Fucking stubble was driving him mad. Even when he was on campaign, Gaius always preferred to keep his face clean-shaven, but he'd relented and allowed his aggravating beard to grow. Bloody tradition and all that.

"I'm not sure I believe our friend's far-fetched tale, my dear Varius. What do you think?"

"I've never known a praetorian to be charged with protecting a citizen, Commander. Discreetly or otherwise."

"Neither have I." Gaius crossed his arms and sneered. "May I assume our esteemed Emperor Trajan will corroborate your incredible claim, guard?"

"The Praetorian Prefect gave the order, not the emperor." Victorinus glanced at Aurelia and cleared his throat. "Sir."

"How lovely. I must remember to thank our most thoughtful Livianus when I next see him at the palace. Varius, escort our furtive guest to the front door for a proper departure. I wish you good health, Victorinus."

The guard nodded sheepishly. "Farewell, Commander Fabius."

While Varius shoved the smaller man towards the exit, Gaius shook his head. These recent praetorian recruits were fucking imbecilic, the whole lot of them. And the Prefect of the imperial bodyguard, Livianus, was a despicable, sycophantic boar. He'd never understood why Marcus had promoted the goon to such a prominent position.

"Commander?"

"Yes, Maximus?"

"Sir, my apologies for the interruption, but..." Max whispered into Gaius's left ear, "Bryaxis, sir. I can't find him anywhere."

"That's most curious," mumbled Gaius before thundering over to Aurelia and grabbing her by the folds of her dress. "Where is Lucius's Caledonian?"

"What?" she squeaked.

"Luc's concubine, Bryaxis. What have you done with his slave?"

"When that insolent slut dared speak its mind at my poor husband's deathbed, I had it beaten and locked in the library. That was quite a while past. It may be dead." She raised her eyebrows and shrugged. "I might have forgotten to feed it."

"That slut is under my guardianship now. You'd better pray he's not dead."

"Your guardianship?"

"Lucius and I signed documents, Aurelia—legal and binding. I'm now the guardian of his personal slaves until his will is read, and I had better find them all alive."

Turning to deliver instructions to his veterans, Gaius noticed Max staring at the floor, his strong arms hanging limply at his sides. Max and Bry had been close once.

Not lovers, though they knew every inch of each other's bodies.

They'd been more akin to brothers.

Friends brought together by the Fates.

"Maximus?"

Max looked up, and tears spilled over his cheekbones.

"Collect yourself and follow me to the library."

Max wiped his face. "Yes, sir."

Together they walked down the passageway, Max lingering two steps behind his patron.

"Maximus, I will see Bryaxis receives a proper burial."

After a moment of silence, Max answered, "When he was a child in the northern wilds of Caledonia, Bry survived far worse than a flogging and a few days without food, sir."

Gaius stopped and turned around, reaching up to brush the back of his hand along Max's jaw. "You two shared much over the years. I will take care of Luc's slave, whatever his condition."

"Bryaxis is alive, sir. He's strong."

Gaius flashed a weak smile. Max's loyalty to those he loved never wavered, did it?

"I do hope you're correct, but don't mistake my intentions. I will do what I must, whether he's alive or dead, but not because of any affection for Bryaxis. I've never cared much for that disrespectful, spoiled whore. But I will fulfill my duties because Lucius and I swore an oath many years ago to protect each other's families. The documents were designed to give each of us the necessary legal authority during those days before our respective testaments were unsealed. I will protect Bryaxis because it is my duty."

Gaius gnawed on the inside of his cheek and looked away.

"I confess I was the one who suggested the contract to Lucius since the odds were I'd perish on the battlefield long before he died. I needed to be sure my family—you and the boys and Zoe—that you would all be protected after my death. Lucius agreed, and we signed the papers."

Gaius inhaled hard to ease the ache in his chest. All this would have been much simpler if only he'd perished first. "Come, Max. Let's find Bryaxis."

The library was located off a grand corridor on the western side of the estate. It was a large square room with enormous windows and cupboards stuffed with correspondence, accounts, and legal records. The library had been Luc's pride and joy, his oasis from the political tempests of the courts. And it was the perfect private place for a quick fuck over a table. Gaius knew every piece of furniture in that damn room.

When they arrived, the doors were secured with a thick chain and a sturdy iron lock. The secured entrance looked more like a prison than a sanctuary for study or secret afternoon trysts.

Gaius gripped the chain with both hands and rattled the doors. "Bryaxis! Answer me, slave!"

No sound except his own pulse thumping in his ears and Max's labored breathing.

"There's no time to persuade our uncooperative bitch to hand over the key, assuming Aurelia even knows where the fuck it is. Find something to remove this chain, Maximus."

After Max had run off in the direction of the gardens, Gaius leaned on the door, his forehead pressed against his raised forearm. He slapped the wood panel with his palm and yelled, "Bryaxis!"

The muffled rumble of thunder shook the walls. Another violent summer storm was swooping down on the city.

"Bryaxis, fucking answer me!"

Soft, high-pitched cries drifted through the dark corridor to Gaius's right. A flash of lightning momentarily brightened the hallway, quickly followed a louder thunderous boom.

"Commander Fabius?" Euphronia trembled as she rocked back and forth, tears streaking her full face, her bright hair a mess, and her arms wrapped tightly beneath her sagging breasts. By the gods, the woman looked as though she might faint. "I knew—I knew you'd save us, sir. I prayed to the goddess every morning and night."

Gaius rushed over and embraced her; he buried his face in her disheveled curls and inhaled the savory scents of the kitchen.

"Euphronia, are you hurt?"

"I—I am alive." She nodded towards the library door. "That evil woman locked Bryaxis in there after Dominus died. I managed to smuggle in some water for him on the second day. She discovered my disobedience and had me caned."

"She did what?"

Euphronia paused to catch her breath. "I heard—we all heard a terrible scream yesterday before the funeral. Oh, Great Mother! Oh, Cybele! What has that woman done to Bryaxis? He's never hurt her. My poor boy would never injure anyone." She beat her pudgy hands against Gaius's chest in desperation.

"Hush, Euphronia." He grabbed her wrists, gently but firmly. "Maximus will be back any moment with something to break the chain. Be strong for me—for Lucius. Are you listening to me?"

Euphronia took a deep, cleansing breath as she pushed two damp strands of hair off of her face and stood a bit straighter. "Yes, Commander."

"You're under my protection now. Lucius and I made arrangements long ago. As soon as we get Bryaxis out of there, we're leaving."

"Dominus showed me the contract, sir. But..." Euphronia wiped her eyes. "How can I leave? I've lived here nearly all my life. This house is my home, where I watched our three young mischievous masters grow into honorable, fine men. So many memories..."

"Look at me." He gently lifted her face. "Lucius Petronius is gone. There's no master here to protect you. Your home—and Bryaxis' home—is with my family until Lucius's testament is unsealed."

Euphronia sucked in her plump, tear-drenched lips before nodding. "Yes, sir—but what about the child? What will happen to Dominus's daughter?"

Gaius blinked and swallowed.

"I don't know. As soon as Titus Petronius arrives from Greece, Lucius's testament will be read in the Julian basilica before the inheritance magistrates. The custody of Petronia and the ownership of this estate will be known then."

Their moment of solemn silence was broken by Max's holler.

"Commander!" Max charged down the corridor, huffing and puffing, a gardener's hatchet in his hand.

"Break the chain, Maximus."

After two blows, the chain crashed to the floor.

"Euphronia, fetch some broth from the kitchen."

"Sir?"

"Now, woman!"

After she'd hastened off, Max asked, "Do you believe he's alive, sir?"

"From what she just told me, Bryaxis was alive yesterday. He may no longer be and, if that's the case, I don't want her to see whatever we find in there. Remain here and make sure Euphronia doesn't enter until I give the word. Understood?"

"Yes, Commander."

Gaius pushed the door open and stepped inside the library. It was pitch black and, as a field following a battle, the air reeked of urine and blood.

"Bryaxis? Where are you?"

Feeling his way from a table to the cupboard to another table, Gaius padded over toward the windows when his left foot bumped against a lump on the floor.

"Shit."

He carefully stepped over it and opened the shutters wide. Menacing, grey-green clouds filled the sky, but the impending downpour hadn't yet begun to fall. Faint light crept into the library, enough for Gaius to see

Bryaxis curled up in a ball, naked and unconscious. A puddle of dark blood stained the floor near the slave's bent legs.

"Bryaxis," he whispered and crouched down, when another flash of lightning lit the space. The slave was breathing—shallow and faint, but he was alive. Gaius gently rolled him over onto his back. A bloody mess of bandages covered Bry's groin.

Gaius lowered his head and looked away. "Fucking unholy Furies."

Another crash of thunder followed by another blue flash of lightning.

"Commander?" Max's normally strong voice was barely audible.

"I told you to stand by the door, Maximus."

Gaius pushed the fringe away from Bry's face and brushed his hand across the lad's whiskered cheek. "Bryaxis is alive, but..." Gaius nodded towards the bloodied cloth dressing. "He's been castrated."

Max stumbled backward. "What?"

"He's lost quite a bit of blood. Dispatch one of my veterans to the home of my physician. Instruct him to transport Archigenes here immediately. Tell him to carry the old Greek coot on his damn back if need be. Then retrieve a clean cloak or sheet or whatever the fuck you can find and bring it to me quickly."

"He's..." Max choked on a sob. "Bry's been castrated?"

"By Hercules, Max. Move! And whatever you do, do not allow Euphronia to enter this room."

Gingerly, Gaius carried Bry over to the nearest couch and set him down. His long body was lighter than Gaius had expected.

Starved and dehydrated, no doubt.

Unprotected.

He'd been too late—too late to honor Lucius, too late to protect Luc's boy from harm.

He'd failed his best friend, again.

Gaius sat down on the edge of the couch and stroked Bry's unwashed hair as the heavy storm clouds rolled through the afternoon sky. From this high vantage point up on the Quirinal, the silhouette of Jupiter's enormous temple was visible in the distance, dominating the tempestuous horizon.

"I promise you, Luc—they will pay. All of them. As Jove on the Capitoline is my witness."

Follow JP Kenwood's author blog BY EMAIL for free stories and news about upcoming books and short tales: https://jpkenwood.com

CPSIA information can be obtained
at www.ICGtesting.com
Printed in the USA
LVHW090416250220
648082LV00001B/4

9 780998 154862